About the Author

Georgie Lee loves combi... storytelling through rom... professionally at a local ... Hollywood to work in the ... not writing, Georgie enjoys reading non-fiction history and watching any movie with a costume and an accent. Please visit www.georgie-lee.com for more information about Georgie and her books.

Regency Reputations

Regency Reputations:

The Cinderella Game

GEORGIE LEE

MILLS & BOON

First Published in Great Britain 2021
By Mills & Boon, an imprint of HarperCollins*Publishers*
1 London Bridge Street, London, SE1 9GF

www.harpercollins.co.uk

HarperCollins*Publishers*
1st Floor, Watermarque Building,
Ringsend Road, Dublin 4, Ireland

REGENCY REPUTATIONS: THE CINDERELLA GAME
© 2021 Harlequin Books S.A.

Engagement of Convenience © 2013 Georgie Reinstein
The Cinderella Governess © 2016 Harlequin Books S.A

Special thanks and acknowledgement are given to Georgie Lee for
her contribution to *The Governess Tales* series

ISBN 978-0-263-30261-5

MIX
Paper from
responsible sources
FSC® C007454

This book is produced from independently certified FSC™ paper
to ensure responsible forest management.

For more information visit: www.harpercollins.co.uk/green

Printed and bound in Spain
by CPI, Barcelona

ENGAGEMENT OF CONVENIENCE

A very special thank you to Natashya Wilson for seeing the potential in this story and for all her help. Thanks also to my editor Linda Fildew, my agent Ethan Ellenberg, and my friend Kristi for sharing her knowledge of horses.

Also, thanks to my dear husband Matt, who always believes in me, even if he wouldn't have believed it if someone told him years ago he'd someday be married to a romance writer.

Chapter One

$\mathcal{O}\!\!\mathcal{O}\!\!\mathcal{O}\!\!\mathcal{O}\!\!\mathcal{O}$

October 31, 1805

Julia heard the shot from the top of the hill. It split the early morning still, sending a shock through her body and silencing the birds in the surrounding trees. Pulling hard on Manfred's reins, she brought the large black horse to a halt and examined the woods below the riding path for signs of the shooter. Brilliant shades of orange, red and yellow dominated the trees and a gentle breeze sent many of the leaves cascading to the ground. A flock of birds rose from the forest, indicating the shot's origin, but she saw nothing of the gunman. Uncle George often hunted here, but he was not expected back from London until later today.

How dare they, she fumed, nudging Manfred down the sloping hill and into the thick cluster of trees growing along the small valley floor. Only a guest of their neighbours, the Wilkinses, possessed the audacity to hunt uninvited on Knollwood land.

Low branches tugged at her hair, freeing it from the loose bun fastened at the nape of her neck. Pushing it back out of her face, she knew her sister-in-law Emily would object to such a display, but Julia didn't care. She wasn't about to allow the Wilkinses' good-for-nothing friends to poach in her woods.

As she urged Manfred deeper into the thicket, it didn't occur to her to fetch the gamekeeper until the horse stepped into a small clearing as the culprit let off another shot in the opposite direction. Julia flinched at the thunderous noise, but Manfred, true to his warhorse breeding, stood rock still. Only his twitching ears acknowledged the explosion.

'What do you think you are doing?' Julia demanded.

The stranger whirled to face her and she drew in a sharp breath. Here was no fat wastrel, but the most handsome rogue she'd ever seen. The low sunlight cutting through the trees highlighted the deep-red tones in his dark hair and sharpened the bones of his cheeks. The shadow of a beard marked the square line of his jaw, emphasising his straight nose and strong chin. Her pulse raced with an emotion far different from fear. She could not name it, but it emanated from deep within her body.

'I'm hunting,' he answered plainly. Leaning his gun against a tree, he straightened into a stance reminiscent of the one her brother Paul assumed when a superior officer commanded him to relax.

'You are poaching in my woods. Now remove yourself at once before I call the gamekeeper. He's only a short distance away,' Julia lied, hoping he believed it. The knowing smile tugging at the corner of his lips told her otherwise.

'I'd like to see your gamekeeper try to remove me.'

Julia scrutinised him, hard pressed to imagine any of the servants, except perhaps the blacksmith, taking on such a sturdy man. He was tall and slender but solid, his wide shoulders and strong chest radiating a strength his loose-fitting hunting clothes could not hide. Following the line of his long arms to his hands, she imagined them around her waist, lifting her down from Manfred and pressing her against his body. She bit her bottom lip in anticipation of him claiming her mouth, the warmth of it driving away the morning chill.

Swallowing hard, the danger of the situation rushed back to her at the sight of the hunting knife dangling from his belt and she mustered her anger to counter the scandalous thoughts. His gun might be empty, but there was no way to know his skill with the blade. 'I demand you leave, at once.'

'I must say, I've never been addressed in this fashion before.' His blue eyes dipped down the length of her, then rose to her face. 'Especially not by such an attractive young lady.'

Julia grasped her riding crop tighter, ready to whip him if he threatened her, but he still did not approach. 'If I were trespassing on your land, I'd have the decency to be humble, but since you are trespassing on my land I may address you as I please.'

'You would have to travel a great distance to trespass on my land.' He laughed, much to Julia's chagrin.

'Then be off,' she ordered, 'for the sooner you leave, the sooner you may reach your land.' With all the grace of an accomplished horsewoman, she pulled Manfred around and cantered away.

James watched the woman disappear through the trees. Her horse, if one could call such a beast a horse, kicking up the soft earth, leaving behind clouds of dust to dance in the dappled sunlight. Nothing came to mind except pure awe, like the first time he'd been at sea with no sight of land. Neither the dark maidens of the

islands hardened by tavern life, nor the plantation own-
ers' daughters with their languid speech, ever struck
him as this woman had. No, she seemed too much of
the world, yet strangely innocent of it. What would he
give to slip her from her horse, lay her on the damp
leaves and make her more knowledgeable?

His body stiffened at the delightful fantasy before the
shifting sun piercing the trees nearly blinded him. Judging by its height, he knew it was time to go. Grabbing
the haversack from the ground with his left hand, he
felt pain tear through his shoulder and the bag fell from
his weakened hand, landing on the ground with a thud.

'Hell.' He snatched it up with his right hand and
flung it over his shoulder. The gun's recoil had irritated
his wound more than he'd realised. Despite the stinging
ache, he didn't intend to give up hunting. He'd already
lost too much to sacrifice more.

Picking up the gun, he hurried through the woods
along a small footpath leading up to the top of the hill.
Climbing out of the shallow valley, the pain and all the
emotions it brought with it taunted his every step.

Damn it, damn it all, James thought bitterly, striding
off down the opposite side of the hill and up the next
steeper one, scattering a small group of sheep grazing
in the wet grass.

Up ahead, Creedon Abbey rose before him, its grey
stone, small windows and numerous turrets and chimneys betraying its roots in the Middle Ages. James's old
friend Captain George Russell had done well for himself, investing some of the fortune he'd gained in the
Navy in this small estate. Only the broken and charred
roof timbers and smoke-blackened stone ruined the idyl-
lic scene. George had failed to extinguish an oil lamp
one night two weeks ago and the resulting fire had gut-

ted a large portion of the house. Scores of workmen now bustled about the front drive, unloading large blocks of stone from carts or carrying wood inside to begin the first day of repairs.

James shook his head at the damage, not sure whether to feel sorry for his friend or to laugh. Thirty years in the navy, fifteen as a captain and George had never once lost a ship. Within four years of resigning his commission, he'd nearly burned his house to the ground. For all George's bragging about how much he'd learned from his niece about running an estate, he'd failed to master the simple skill of not setting it on fire.

James's amusement faded as he walked. He'd seriously considered investing his money in an estate like this, but now he wasn't so sure. Whatever he decided to do, he needed to do it soon. With his wound sufficiently recovered, it was time to settle on something meaningful to occupy his days, instead of frittering them away.

He moved faster up the footpath following the drive, eager for activity, anything to shift the restless agitation dogging him this morning.

'What's the hurry?' a familiar voice called out from behind him. 'Run across a ghost in the woods?'

James turned to see George leading Percy, his large, cream-coloured stallion, up the drive. In his friend's wide, carefree smile, James caught traces of the bold captain he'd first met in the colonies ten years ago. At fifty, the lines of George's face were deeper now, while the quiet life of a country gentleman had lightened his once sun darkened skin and thickened his waist.

'I might have.' James fell in step with his friend. 'Describe your niece again.'

'Why?'

'Because I'm curious.'

George shrugged. 'Just what you'd expect from a girl of one and twenty. Clever, well formed, somewhat eccentric. Takes after me in that regard. Why?'

'I met her in the woods.' James remembered the striking young lady with her auburn hair falling in delicate waves about her face, her creamy skin flushed with excitement and a few headier emotions.

'Really?' A noticeable gleam danced in George's eyes. 'And?'

'Eccentric, well formed. Though from all your descriptions, I'd taken her for more of a dour governess and less of an Artemis.'

'When I described her she was still a girl.'

'She's no girl now.' James wondered if such a woman had ever truly been a girl or if she'd simply sprung from the foam of the sea.

'I'm glad to see you find her so interesting. Staying at Knollwood will give you a chance to get better acquainted. Who knows what you might discover?'

James shifted the haversack on his back, resisting the urge to run his fingers over the jagged scar on his left shoulder. 'Must we go to Knollwood?'

'Yes, it's all been arranged. Besides, by the end of the day it'll be more like a shipyard here than a house and, with the weather turning, you don't want the rain leaking on your head.'

'It wouldn't be the first time. I've lost track of the number of storms I've slept through at sea.'

'And my guess is you won't miss it. We wouldn't have stayed here last night if we hadn't dallied so long at Admiral Stuart's dinner, but I hated to disturb everyone at Knollwood so late at night.'

James laughed. 'I wasn't the one who insisted on opening another bottle of port.'

'It doesn't matter who caused the delay. I'll be happy to sleep in a comfortable room that doesn't smell like a cooking fire. And here I'd thought those bedrooms had escaped damage.'

'You've gone soft.'

George shrugged. 'You will, too, in time.'

James didn't respond, this revelation not improving his mood. He'd already lost too much since resigning his commission to contemplate losing something as simple as his hardiness. 'Why didn't you tell me before we left London that the house wasn't fit to live in?'

'I think I greatly underestimated the damage.' They stopped as two men carrying a large plank walked past them. 'Besides, the ladies are quite excited at the prospect of meeting a new gentleman.'

'You know I came here to escape such affairs.'

'Does any man ever truly escape them?'

'You seem to have avoided it.'

'And you wish to follow my lead?'

James scrutinised his old friend, suspecting more to all this than the extensive fire damage simply slipping his mind. 'What are you about, George?'

'Nothing.' George held up his hands innocently but only succeeded in looking guiltier. 'I want you to enjoy yourself while you're here. Now hurry and change. We're expected at Knollwood.'

George pulled Percy off to the stables and James headed around to the back of the house, his footsteps heavier than before. Reaching under the loose jacket, his fingers traced the raised scar on his left shoulder through the thin fabric of his hunting shirt. Unconsciously, he flexed his left hand, feeling the weakness and cursing it. He stomped on a large clump of mud, mashing it into the earth. This was exactly what he didn't want, the whole reason he'd allowed George to convince him to come to the country.

He cursed his luck and George's carelessness. If his friend had extinguished the lamp instead of leaving it to overheat, James could have spent the next two weeks here, not forced into Artemis's cave waiting to be ripped apart by her wild beasts. He'd experienced enough clawing and tearing in the ballrooms of London. He had no stomach for it here in the country. Give him a French fleet any day; it was preferable to a matron with a marriageable daughter.

A flash of movement on the opposite hill made him stop at the rear door. He watched the young woman ride at a full gallop over the green downs, the horse moving like a shadow, her amber hair a streak of sunlight through the dark clouds. The memory of the little Artemis astride the black beast, face flushed with anger, pert breasts rising and falling with each excited breath, filled his mind. His loins stirred with desire before he checked himself. It was one thing to idle away hours with the willing widowed sister of a provincial governor; it was quite another to dally with the niece of his best friend.

Besides, no spirited creature wants a broken man. He pushed away from the wall, angrily slapping the door jamb. The rough stone stung his palm, reminding him that any interest in Miss Howard could only be to learn from her estate management skills which, according to George, were considerable. If James decided to follow his friend into the life of a country gentleman, he'd need to know more about it than what little he'd learn from books.

Manfred reached the crest of the hill, breathing hard, his dark coat glistening with sweat. Julia eased him into a slow walk and they ambled down the bridle path tracing the top. A thin mist crept through the crevices of the valley while sheep grazed quietly in the green meadows. The three estates situated on the three high hills overlooking the rolling valley came into view. Creedon Abbey, the smallest, stood on the hill closest to Knollwood. Though some five miles off, the tips of the turrets were just visible above the surrounding trees. All the land here had once belonged to the old monastery before the Reformation and some debt-ridden descendant saw it sold off to create Knollwood and Cable Grange. There was little difference between Creedon land and Knollwood land, but drastic changes marked the boundary between Knollwood's lush, well-tended meadows and Cable Grange's weed-choked fields. Cable Grange stood on the third-highest hill in the area. Farther away than Creedon, she could just see it sitting on its hilltop perch, the distance obscuring its neglected state. Being so close to Knollwood, she knew Cable Grange could be one of the finest houses in the county.

If only it were mine. She didn't know who to curse more, her brother Charles for inheriting Knollwood or Mr Wilkins for ruining Cable Grange.

Adjusting her leg against the pommel, she wished she'd chosen her standard saddle instead of the sidesaddle. It was still early and the rest of the house had yet to rise, making it unlikely Emily would catch her riding astride. Soothed by Manfred's gentle gait, she settled into the seat, her mind wandering back to the woods and the handsome stranger.

He called me attractive, she mulled, remembering the heady way his blue eyes raked her body, their heat warming her skin. Four years ago, standing against the wall during London balls, she'd seen gentlemen examine other young ladies with similar hot eyes, nudging each other knowingly. For all her London finery, not one gentleman had cast a single amorous glance in her direction. How strange to garner a lustful stare while dressed in her old riding habit.

If only he weren't one of the Wilkinses' good-for-nothing friends. She sighed, wondering what it would be like to feel his lips tease her neck while he whispered forbidden things in her ear. A strange thrill coursed through her before she forced the wicked daydream from her head. He was a scoundrel and not worth a second thought.

Digging her heel into Manfred's flanks, she drove him hard across the open ground, guiding him towards a hedge separating the fields. Pulling back on his reins, she sat forwards as he leapt and they easily cleared the bushes before landing on the other side.

'Well done, Manfred!'

She slowed him to a walk and, coming to another path, looked longingly east. A smooth mound stood out against the flatter fields, the ruins on top silhouetted by the rising sun. At a full gallop, they could reach the old fortress in a few minutes and she might spend a quiet hour picking through the high grass searching for relics. Her heel itched to tap Manfred, but she resisted, reluctantly directing him back to Knollwood. Emily expected her at breakfast. Why, she couldn't imagine. Neither Simon nor Annette, her stepcousins, had risen before noon since their arrival and when they were awake, they only complained about the country.

What could Uncle Edward possibly hope to accomplish by sending them here? she wondered, wishing he'd hurry up and recall them to London.

They trotted into the paddock, greeted by the fresh scent of hay and the sharper smell of horses.

'I see you've had another fine ride, Miss Howard,' John, the head groom, remarked, helping her down from the saddle. 'I've always said the two of you were made for each another.'

'That's because I believed in him when no one else did. Didn't I, Manfred?' Julia rubbed the horse's nose and he shook his head as if in agreement. 'John, please speak to the gamekeeper. I saw a poacher in the forest this morning.'

'A poacher?' He held Manfred's reins, disbelief deepening the lines of his forehead. 'We've never had such trouble before.'

'Well, I believe the man is a poacher, though it may have only been one of Mr Wilkins's guests.'

'Mr Wilkins has no guests, Miss Howard.'

Then who could he be? Julia tapped her riding crop against her palm, then handed it to John. 'No matter. Please ask the gamekeeper to take care of it.'

'Yes, Miss Howard.'

'Oh, and please don't mention it to Mother or Emily. They'll only worry and then Emily will lecture me if she discovers I went riding without you.' Emily had been married to her brother Charles for less than a year, but she'd prove his equal when it came to chastising Julia about proper behaviour.

'I won't say a word.' John laid a knowing finger against the side of his ruddy nose before leading Manfred inside.

Thank goodness for his loyalty, she thought, fastening up the long hem of her riding habit. Without him, she and Manfred might never be allowed to enjoy their solitary rides.

Walking up the path from the stables, she passed through a small grove of trees and into the large, open lawn. Crossing the wide space, she kicked the head off a dandelion, sprinkling her skirt with bits of grass and dew.

I must speak to Bill about bringing the sheep here to trim the grass, she reminded herself before passing through a gate in the low stone wall surrounding the garden on the other side.

Wandering down the gravel path through the semi-formal plant beds, she saw the house rise up in front of her, its many windows reflecting the morning sun. She removed her right glove and grazed the top of a large rosemary bush with her fingers before snapping off a sprig and inhaling the tangy scent. All the troubles she'd forgotten during her ride came rushing back, especially Charles's letter.

'His estate.' Julia threw the rosemary sprig on the ground, crushing it beneath her half-boot. 'What does he know of running Knollwood?'

She'd burned the hateful parchment after reading it, watching with delight as the neat script crumpled and charred in the flames. However, all the burned letters couldn't stop her brother from claiming his inheritance.

Pausing at the small pond in the centre of the garden, she stared into the dark water. Goldfish flitted beneath the glass surface, failing to disturb the reflection of the thick clouds passing overhead.

Why should he have Knollwood? Tears of frustration stung her eyes. *He's never taken an interest in it the way I have.*

Nor did he appreciate all her hard work to keep it prosperous. Only Father and Paul had ever recognised it, but with Paul serving with Admiral Nelson's fleet and Father—

No, she commanded herself, refusing to cry. Tears would not help her deal with Charles.

Heading up the garden path, she passed her mother's cherished rose garden, then hurried up the stairs of the column-lined stone portico leading to the back sitting room.

'Good morning, Miss Howard,' Davies, the butler, greeted, pulling open the large French door.

'Good morning.' She handed him her gloves and he held out a small paper-covered parcel.

'This arrived from Mr Charles Howard.'

'My book.' She tore off the wrapper to reveal a leather-bound copy of *The Monk*. 'I can't believe Charles sent it. He's always so concerned about not disturbing my delicate female mind. It's fortunate he doesn't know the half of what Paul tells me.'

'Yes, very fortunate indeed,' Davies solemnly concurred. He'd been Paul's valet when Paul still lived at Knollwood, making him well acquainted with her brother's nature and most of his escapades.

'Has Uncle George returned from London yet?'

'Captain Russell arrived a short while ago to collect Percy and speak with Mrs Emily Howard. He's returned to Creedon Abbey to see to the repairs.'

'Uncle George was here and didn't wait for me?'

'No, miss, but it appears we are to expect another gentleman.'

'Who?'

'Mrs Howard did not say, but she instructed me to open Paul's room for him.'

Julia chafed at the news. 'When is he arriving?'

'This afternoon.'

'Thank you, Davies. Please tell Mrs Howard I won't be joining her for breakfast.'

'Yes, miss.'

Julia walked down the hall to the study, determined to avoid the breakfast room no matter how many lectures it might create. What right did Emily have to make decisions at Knollwood? The maids and footmen were stretched thin enough with Uncle George staying here and all her stepcousins' demands.

Crossing the study's large, woven rug, Julia sighed. Emily, as Charles's wife, had every right to invite whomever she pleased, even if it did mean additional work for Julia and the staff. For a moment she imagined herself mistress of her own home, free to make decisions and live without her brother's censure, then dismissed the thought. Once Charles took control, he'd soon realise the limitations of his estate management skills, or return to London for Parliament in the spring, leaving Knollwood in Julia's hands once again. Or so she hoped. Her brother had a habit of being very stubborn.

She sat down behind the large, mahogany desk situated at the far end of the study. High bookcases lined one wall while south-facing windows with a view of the garden dominated the other. A tall, wooden bookstand supporting a fine atlas stood guard near the window, flanked by two leather chairs. Her father had decorated the room, choosing every element down to each book. From here he conducted all family business, patiently bearing Charles's sermons about the proper education for Julia, dealing with one of Paul's many near scandals or teaching Julia to run Knollwood.

It'd happened by accident, after she'd fled here one day to avoid drawing lessons. Sitting with her father while he reviewed the figures, she'd asked questions and he'd answered them, noticing her interest. The next day, he'd invited her to join him again and it became their habit. In the afternoons, they'd ride the estate, speaking with the workers and learning their methods and the land. Then, one day, he told her to do the figures, allowed her to sit in the room while he met with the overseer and gave her correspondence to read and answer. No one in the family except Charles questioned her strange education and Father would laugh him off, saying he wasn't about to lose his best manager because she was a girl.

Julia smiled at the memory, then opened the large, leather-bound ledger. Settling herself over the accounts, she reviewed the figures, wrinkling her nose at the increased expenditures brought on by her stepcousins' visit. Closing the ledger, she gathered up the large bundle of letters resting on the corner of the desk. She read through the missives, the minute details of the dairy and reports from the tenant farmers helping her forget the excitement of the morning.

Chapter Two

The study door swung open, startling Julia, and her pencil slipped, leaving a dark mark across two rows of figures.

'Yes?' she answered testily as Davies entered the room.

'Captain Russell and his guest have arrived.'

Tossing down the pencil, she sat back in the chair, needing just a few more minutes to finish balancing the accounts. 'They're early.'

'I believe they are on time.'

She looked at the windows, finally noticing how the sun and shadows had shifted in the garden and the room. 'How long have I been working?'

'All morning, Miss Howard.'

'Then I'd better hurry and join them or I'll never know a moment's peace with Emily.' Closing the ledger, she stood and started for the door. 'Though I know Uncle George won't mind my being late. He isn't one for formality.'

'Excuse me, Miss Howard…' Davies coughed '…perhaps a change of dress is advisable.'

She stopped, inspecting the riding habit skirt, her loose hair falling over her face. Bits of leaves stuck to the honey-coloured fabric, making the damp hem noticeable and emphasising the creases along with the habit's older style. She hardly ever wore this habit, but she'd soiled her better one yesterday by taking Manfred over a fence and through the mud on the other side. Had she seen the puddle, she wouldn't have jumped him.

'I'll never hear the end of it if Emily catches me greeting guests in such a state. Where are they?'

'The morning room.'

'Do you think I can sneak upstairs and change before she sees me?'

'It is quite possible, Miss Howard.'

'We shall see.'

She hurried from the study and down the corridor. Approaching the entrance hall, she crept over the stone floor to the stairs, listening to Uncle George's robust laughter followed by the deep tones of the other gentleman in the morning room. The stranger's voice sounded oddly familiar, but she didn't dare peek inside for fear of being seen. Stealing past the open door, she turned the corner to slip upstairs, coming face to face with her sister-in-law.

'What are you doing in your riding habit?' Emily demanded in hushed tones, her delicate eyes darting nervously to the morning room. 'And your hair? You can't welcome your guests looking like a dairy maid.'

'My guests?'

'Never mind. We'll say you were out riding and then you can meet the captain now before Uncle George drags him off for who knows how long.' Emily pulled her in front of the gilded mirror beneath the stairs and out of sight of the door.

'Did you say Uncle George's guest is a captain?' Julia winced as Emily untangled a small twig from her hair.

'Yes, Captain Covington.'

'Uncle George's friend from Tortuga?' Julia twisted around to face Emily before her sister-in-law gently spun her back to the mirror, dividing her hair into three sections, then working them into a braid.

'Yes, I believe so.'

Julia forced down a frustrated sigh. Single gentlemen were a rarity at Knollwood and Julia could practically see Emily's matchmaking machinations. It was the only explanation for why she insisted on this hurried first meeting. Apparently, she didn't know as much about Uncle George's friend as Julia did or she wouldn't be so excited, or eager to make the introduction. 'Well, if Captain Covington is to stay with us, I'd better instruct Davies to lock up the brandy.'

'Captain Covington isn't that kind of gentleman.'

'Then I'd better lock up the maids.'

'Julia!' Emily stared at her in the mirror, her pale face alight with shock. 'Young ladies shouldn't know about such things.'

Thankfully Paul thinks I should. If Emily and Charles ever learned the full extent of what Paul had told her, they'd probably chaperon their every conversation.

Emily smoothed the sturdy wool of Julia's habit, picking off stray leaves, her hands fluttering while she worked.

'You received another letter from Charles, didn't you?' Julia asked. Emily's concern for propriety always increased after a letter from her husband.

Emily blushed, pink spreading from her cheeks to her light blonde hair. 'Am I so obvious?'

'I'm afraid so.'

'It's only because we want to see you well settled.'

'No, it's because Charles thinks I don't act like a

proper lady and such behaviour will cause a scandal and hurt his career in Parliament.'

Emily laid a motherly hand on Julia's shoulder. 'Your brother loves you and only wants to see you happy.'

Despite the well-meaning remark, Julia wasn't ready to concede defeat. 'I'm happy as I am.'

Emily moved behind Julia, fastening the braid into a small bun at the nape of her neck. 'I know, but time doesn't stand still. Some day you may want more.'

'What about Simon and Annette? They aren't greeting Uncle George. Why not censure them?'

'It's not my place to comment on their conduct.' Emily frowned and pulled her lips tight. 'They are both indisposed and will be down later.'

Julia bit back a sharp retort about the two of them always being indisposed when another idea came to mind. 'Perhaps I can speak to Captain Covington about Paul's promotion. Maybe he knows someone in the Admiralty who can arrange for Paul to get his own ship. I can't believe he didn't receive a command. If I ever find the man who wrote his bad recommendation—'

'I'm sure your brother is capable of managing his own affairs,' her mother interrupted, descending the stairs. Her grey eyes took in Julia, neither approving nor disapproving of her attire. Under her arm Charlemagne, her King Charles spaniel, panted, his pink tongue dangling from his mouth. Mother swept into the morning room, her plain dress whispering about her legs, her dark hair flecked with grey pulled neatly into a twist at the back of her head. Julia envied Mother's refined presence and decorum, wondering how many difficulties she could have avoided if fate had given her even a small portion of Mother's poise.

Emily, eager to fulfil her duties as hostess and, Julia

thought, to fling her in the captain's path, guided Julia to the morning room. 'Come along. We've kept our guest waiting long enough.'

Inside, Mother exchanged pleasantries with Uncle George and the captain, who stood with his back to Julia.

'Your lands are some of the best I've seen,' he complimented, the rich, familiar voice vibrating through Julia. She noticed the dark hair curling just above the collar of his uniform and the way the sunlight falling through the window highlighted the deep-red tones.

The stranger! A sudden rush of excitement mixed with fear jolted her and she froze just over the threshold.

'Are you all right?' Emily whispered and Julia shook her head, taking a large step back.

'No, I think I should change.' He'd seen her riding without a groom. If he mentioned it to Emily, there'd be no end to the reprimands.

'It's too late now.' Emily gripped her arm tight to keep her from fleeing as she motioned to Uncle George.

'And here is the party responsible for Knollwood's prosperity.' Uncle George ushered the captain to them. 'Captain Covington, Miss Julia Howard.'

If she had thought him handsome in plain hunting clothes, he took her breath away in uniform. The dark coat with the gold epaulettes emphasised his wide shoulders and the powerful presence she had felt in the forest. Without the advantage of Manfred's height, she had to look up at him. Though not overly tall, he stood a good head above her. The fantasy of being swept into his arms filled her mind once again and she swallowed hard.

'A pleasure.' He bowed.

Her eyes travelled the length of him as he straightened. Well-muscled calves stretched his hose tight while slightly looser breeches could not hide his strong thighs and other unmentionable areas. Feeling her cheeks burn, Julia focused on his face as she held out her hand. 'Captain Covington, welcome to Knollwood.'

He wrapped his fingers lightly around hers, then swept his lips across the bare knuckles. Julia drew in a ragged breath, trying not to tremble. The white-trimmed collar of the coat framed his now clean-shaven face and she curled her fingers slightly around his to stop herself from tracing the smooth line of his jaw.

'Good morning, Artemis.' His breath tickled the back of her hand and her body tightened in shock. 'I assume I am no longer trespassing on your land?'

She leaned closer, inhaling the earthy smell of his lavender shaving soap. 'That remains to be seen.'

He squeezed her hand, then let go. Julia stepped back, very aware of Emily shifting from foot to foot behind him.

'Have you two met before?' Emily asked in a high voice.

'I had the privilege of encountering Miss Howard while she was riding in the forest this morning,' Captain Covington explained, oblivious to the trouble he'd just caused.

Julia braced herself for the coming scolding, wishing the captain had held his tongue.

'You were riding without the groom again?' Emily asked, the nervous quaver in her voice more irritating than a bur in a boot.

'No, the groom was with her,' James lied before Julia could answer. 'But I'm afraid I failed to properly introduce myself and she mistook me for a poacher.'

Julia gaped at him, surprised he'd lie for her after the way she'd addressed him in the woods.

'George left no detail untold regarding your management,' he continued. 'You have quite an estate. I'm very impressed.'

'Thank you,' she faltered, the compliment catching her off guard. Usually gentlemen scoffed at her unusual accomplishment. 'I'm quite protective of it, as you may have gathered.'

'Indeed. I've never met such a fearsome protector of woodland creatures in all my life.'

'I'm sure many innocent creatures need protection from Navy men.'

Emily inhaled sharply and Uncle George snorted out a laugh while her mother continued to pet Charlemagne, barely noting the exchange.

The captain's lips tightened in an attempt to keep from laughing and suddenly Julia regretted her impudent tongue. With all she knew of him from Uncle George's stories, to fire off such forward remarks, no matter how innocent, might give him the wrong impression and it wasn't very gracious, especially after he'd lied to help her.

'Shall we sit down?' Emily interrupted, nervously studying Julia and the captain.

'Yes, thank you.' He allowed Emily to escort him to the sofa and chairs near the window, her mother following close behind.

Julia stayed by the door, hoping she could slip away without Emily noticing. Decorum dictated she stay and entertain the captain, but something about him unnerved her. It was one thing to speak so frankly to family, quite another with a stranger, no matter how well he knew Uncle George. Better to leave now than risk another slip.

'I see you hiding there.' Uncle George came up alongside her, thumbs hooked in his jacket lapel.

'I'm not hiding.'

'Then come and join us.'

Julia smiled half-heartedly, watching the captain as he answered one of Mother's questions, his smile steady as he spoke. Whatever the captain thought of her unconventional behaviour, he'd already forgotten it. Deep down, some part of her wanted him to notice her, the way he had in the woods. As if sensing her, he shifted in the chair, meeting her eyes, and she turned to Uncle George.

'No, I have business to attend to.'

'Leave it for later. I think you'll enjoy the captain. You two already have quite the rapport.' He tugged her ear playfully, the way he'd done since she was a child.

The friendly gesture usually made her smile. Today it increased the irritation chewing at her. 'My work can't wait.'

'If you insist. But you can't hide at Knollwood for ever. Eventually, you'll have to get out in the world and live.'

'I'm not hiding,' Julia protested.

'Of course not. Silly of me to say it.' He patted her arm. 'Go back to the study. I'll make your excuses.'

Julia left, pausing a moment to listen to the muffled voices, suddenly feeling very alone. Walking through the back sitting room, she took in the sturdy walls of Knollwood covered in hunting prints and old portraits of well-dressed ancestors. Here she felt safe and, when not entertaining guests, confident in herself. Anywhere else she felt awkward and unsettled. What would happen if Charles took this away from her?

She slipped out of the French doors and crossed the garden to the far corner where the tall boxwood hedges hid her from the house. At the centre of this private courtyard stood a fountain of a man and woman locked in a passionate kiss, a copy of some nameless Greek statue. It had been a gift to their father from Paul after his first visit to Greece. Having no use for the statue in the house, her father had it made into a fountain, scandalising Charles, who insisted on hiding it in this secluded corner.

Julia plunked down on the stone bench in front of the fountain, watching the water run over the naked marble bodies. The polished stone glistened in the noon sun, intensifying the urgency of the lovers' embrace. The man's fingers dug into the hard flesh of the woman's thigh, his hands entwined in her hair as she pressed her naked form against his. Her long, gracefully carved fingers rested against the taut muscles of the male's well-chiselled back. Studying the lovers' embrace, their bodies so close not even water could separate them, Julia felt her chest constrict. What would it be like to inspire such passion in a man?

Picking up a small stone, she flung it into the pool at the base of the fountain, sending a large splash up and over the side. Reaching down for another rock, she heard the pitter-patter of paws on gravel as Charlemagne barrelled down on her. The small dog threw his front paws up on her knees, his wagging tail shaking his whole body as Julia stroked his soft fur.

'I thought I'd find you here,' her mother said, scooping up Charlemagne and sitting down next to her.

'Did Emily send you here to chastise me for not being a perfect lady?'

'Emily is a sweet girl, good for Charles and I adore her,' her mother remarked, settling the wiggling dog on her lap. 'But I seldom listen to her advice or Charles's. I suggest you do the same.'

'I've tried, but it only makes them more persistent.'

'Yes, he takes after your grandfather in that regard.' Charlemagne refused to be still and Mother put him on the ground. 'You're worried about Charles taking over Knollwood, aren't you?'

Like Uncle George, Mother could be very direct and Julia found it both helpful and at times hindering. She watched Charlemagne sniff around the fountain, jumping back when an errant bead of water landed on his nose.

'When he does, what will I do?' Julia choked, digging the toe of her boot into the ground.

'I think you'll find something. You're much more resourceful than either Charles or Paul.'

'But what else could there possibly be for me?'

Her mother took Julia's face in her hands, pushing a strand of hair off of her cheek. 'That's up to you to discover.'

She kissed Julia's forehead, then rose, snapping her fingers at Charlemagne.

'Do I hide from the world here?' Julia asked before her mother could leave.

'Who put such an idea in your head?'

'Uncle George.'

The older woman laughed softly. 'Since when do you take my brother seriously?'

Julia shrugged. 'Emily and Charles are always saying it, in their own way.'

'I think only you know the answer.' She strolled out of the garden, Charlemagne close on her heels.

The quick click of a lady's perturbed step drew James to the morning-room door. Miss Howard strode into the entrance hall, moving like a tempest, oblivious to everything but her own energy. Fascinated, he wanted to draw her out, but hesitated. Better to let her go than risk the blunt blow of her dark mood. However, something in the troubled frown on her pretty face prompted him to speak.

'Miss Howard?'

The stomping girl vanished, replaced by an awkward young woman conscious of the world around her. 'Yes?'

She stood on the bottom stair, one small hand on the oak banister, poised like a doe to flee. He wondered what had happened to make such an exuberant creature so timid. 'I want to apologise for this morning. You took me quite by surprise.'

'Yes, I imagine I did.' She moved to leave, but he wasn't ready to let her go.

'I don't usually meet young ladies in the forest so early in the morning.'

'Why didn't you tell me who you were?' she demanded with startling directness.

'You didn't ask,' he laughed, his mirth evaporating under her stern glare. 'Allow me to apologise. I should have introduced myself.' He offered a humble bow, but it did not soften the small crease marring her smooth brow.

'I wish you had for it might have saved us both a great deal of trouble.'

'I shall endeavour to be more agreeable to you the next time we meet in a forest.' The image of them alone among the trees, her hair loose about her naked shoulders, their bodies entwined came to mind. His hand itched to reach up and trace the gentle curve of her cheek, slip his fingers behind her long neck and draw her close.

'There will be no next time,' she corrected, ending the pleasant fantasy.

'I think it quite possible,' he teased. 'Judging by this morning, I assume it is your habit to ride out alone in the mornings.'

'Shh.' She stepped closer, waving a silencing hand and filling the air between them with the faint scent of rosemary.

'Your mother doesn't approve of you riding alone?' he asked in a low voice.

'Mother doesn't care, but Emily does.' She stepped off the stair and stood in front of him, her face softening. 'Thank you for not telling her you saw me riding without a groom. You spared me a great deal of trouble.'

'It was my pleasure, and I'll gladly do it again if the need arises.'

'I hope it doesn't come to that.' She smiled, her face glowing with amusement.

'You're very pretty when you smile,' he offered without thinking, amazed at how much her pleasure delighted him.

Her smile disappeared and she raised one disbelieving eyebrow. Something of the confident Artemis he'd seen this morning flashed in her hazel eyes, rousing his blood.

'I know the country is lacking in diversions, but do not think to amuse yourself with me.'

James straightened, forgetting his desire. He should have been insulted, but he could hardly blame her for saying what he'd momentarily imagined. 'You misunderstood my meaning. I have never, would never behave as you intimate.'

She fixed him with the same scrutinising look he once used on seamen when they told him a tall tale to cover their misdeeds. 'I am not naïve, Captain. My brother and uncle tell me everything, so I know what Navy men are about.'

'Do you?' He struggled to keep the laughter out of his voice, still unable to believe a young woman with her hair pulled back like a dour nun could be so forward. He leaned against the wooden banister, bringing their faces much closer than intended. She did not step back. 'I may have to change your opinion of Navy men.'

'I'm afraid you have only worked to confirm it.'

Her saucy eyes teased him. Were this Tortuga, he would have covered her full mouth with his, allowed his fingers to free her hair from the bun as he pulled her close to kiss away the wry smile dancing about her lips. However, his good breeding, not to mention his status as George's guest, prevented such a blatant breach of etiquette.

'Julia!' Emily appeared at the morning-room door. Julia stepped back, her cheeks burning, awkwardness replacing her courage. Silently, she cursed her impetuous nature, wondering what it was about the captain that kept causing her to forget herself. A few minutes in the gentleman's presence and she was once again acting like a strumpet instead of a lady. How much had Emily heard? Hopefully nothing or she and Charles would feel vindicated in all their chastising.

Before anyone could say anything, baby Thomas's wail filled the upstairs hallway and the nurse appeared at the top of the stairs, carrying the infant. He was only two months old, but he'd been born early and Emily fretted over him like no other well-born mother in the county.

'Mrs Howard, it is time for his feeding,' the nurse called over the screaming baby.

Emily glanced from the captain to Julia to upstairs, weighing her desire to reprimand with the need to see to her child. Luckily, Thomas's cries grew louder, making the decision for her.

'If you'll excuse me, Captain, I must attend to my son.' Emily shot Julia a silent warning before hurrying up to escort the nurse to the nursery. For all of Charles's and Emily's priggishness, they were firm believers in Rousseau's ideas of breastfeeding. It was one of the few things Julia admired them for.

'Despite being born two months early, my nephew has a healthy appetite and powerful lungs,' Julia observed.

'His lungs will serve him well if he enters Parliament. Like his father, his opinions will always be heard,' Captain Covington teased.

Julia laughed, the captain's joke putting her at ease. She was about to respond when a small cough from the landing interrupted them.

'Good morning, Captain Covington.' Annette glided down the stairs, her blue eyes raking over him. Dressed in a fashionable walking dress of expensive yellow silk, she stepped in between Julia and the captain. Her haughty air irked Julia and she clasped her hands together to keep from smacking the chit on the back of her elegantly coiffed blonde head. Though they were the same age, they had nothing in common and had never been more than civil to each other since Annette's arrival.

'Miss Taylor, a pleasure to see you again.' The captain bowed over her extended hand, the relaxed Navy man from a moment before replaced by a proper gentleman.

Julia noted the change and her heart sank. Obviously, he respected the polished manners of a London lady to the questionable conduct of a country girl.

It doesn't matter, she told herself. *Neither of them will be here for ever.*

'How are your dear sister and mother?' Annette asked, her voice light and charming.

'My sister Charlotte is in Wiltshire with her husband. My mother is with them at the moment, though she returns to town next week. She prefers London to the country.'

'Who of us doesn't?' Simon yawned from the top of the stairs, his voice heavy with the Devonshire lisp so popular in town. Tall and lean, Simon wore a suit of the finest material cut tight to accentuate his slender body. He possessed the same sharp features as his sister, but the affected boredom of his dandified style softened them considerably.

Annette's face reddened at Simon's remark. 'You remember my brother?'

'Of course.' Both men nodded to one another, no affection lost on either side.

'We are going to the local town. Please join us for I'm eager for some society after such isolation.'

'Did I hear someone suggest a ride into Daringford?' Uncle George asked, coming up behind the captain.

'Yes. Care to join us?' Captain Covington invited.

While they made their plans, Julia started up the

stairs, sure no one would notice her absence. They had each other; they did not need her. She froze when the captain called out to her.

'Miss Howard, would you like to join us?'

Surveying the waiting group, Julia wondered how much more of his company she could endure without gaining a reputation as a hoyden. Until she could learn to control her tongue in his presence, it was probably better to avoid him. She moved to make her excuses when Annette's condescending sweep of Julia's riding habit changed her mind. 'Yes, but allow me to change. I'll only be a moment.'

'Your dress is passable. Come and let's be off,' Uncle George impatiently called.

Julia reluctantly stepped off the stairs. Emily would have a fit if she knew Julia wore her old riding habit into town. Oh, well, what was one more reprimand? Besides, it was worth the rebuke to annoy Annette.

'Come, Captain Covington.' Annette motioned for his arm and like a true gentleman he offered it, leading her outside to the waiting carriage. Julia watched the way her stepcousin moved, the rich material and fine cut of her dress emphasising her willowy figure. A slight twinge of jealousy took hold and Julia wondered if things would be different if she made an effort to dress so well every day or demonstrate proper, genteel manners.

'My lady.' Uncle George offered her his arm with an exaggerated flourish.

'Why, thank you, sir,' she answered with equally false formality.

'What do you think of the captain?' he asked in a low voice as they strolled out to the waiting carriage.

'He strikes me as quite the man about town. He's already caught Annette's attention.'

'Any man with a pocketbook catches her fancy,' George huffed. 'You shouldn't let her have him.'

'I have no interest in a Navy man, especially one with a thin London polish.'

'He's no Simon, if that's what you're worried about. He's rich, too. Thanks, I might say, in part to many of my lucrative schemes.'

Julia suppressed a laugh, knowing how proud Uncle George was of the numerous profitable ventures he'd embarked on during his time in the Navy. 'Why did the captain resign?'

'George, stop gossiping and get in,' Captain Covington interrupted from beside the open carriage door. 'No need to give away all my secrets on the first day.'

'Not possible, Jim. You've got too many.' Uncle George chuckled.

'May I?' Captain Covington held out his hand, a playful smile lighting up his face. Julia reached for his upturned palm, hesitating a moment before pushing against the strength of it to step up into the carriage.

'Thank you.' She didn't dare meet his eyes, but slid across the squabs and settled in next to the far window, her hand still tingling from his touch. Uncle George sat beside her in an attempt to place some distance between her, Annette and Simon and she was grateful. The captain took a seat across from them, next to Annette, much to the chit's visible delight.

Simon paused to adjust his cravat, then carefully climbed into the carriage, moving like an old lady to avoid wrinkling his morning coat. The door closed behind him, but Simon wasn't fully seated when Uncle

George rapped on the roof. The vehicle sprung into motion, throwing Simon into the seat next to his sister.

'I say,' Simon complained to George.

'Sorry about that.' George shrugged, unruffled by Simon's outburst.

'Men can be so silly, don't you agree, Captain Covington?' Annette laughed, reprimanding her brother with a look he pointedly ignored.

'Yes, they can be.' The captain allowed the conversation to drop, watching the countryside pass by outside the window, a strange melancholy clouding his face. Julia noted the way the afternoon sunlight spread over his features, highlighting a very small scar on his cheek and giving him a bit of mystery and depth she'd never seen in any London gentleman. Then his eyes darted to hers and she turned away, her heart fluttering, the heat in the carriage rising sharply.

What's wrong with me? she wondered, touching the warm skin of her neck. It wasn't like her to act so hen-witted in the company of a man, especially a Navy rake like the captain. Struggling to regain control, she concentrated on the river flowing in the gully below the road. No matter how much she focused on the clear water pouring over the rocks, the captain lingered on the edge of her vision. When she dared to look at him again, she found him still smiling at her.

'Captain Covington, were you at Lady Wellsingham's ball last month?' Annette asked.

'No, I'm afraid business kept me away,' he answered with a slight frown before covering it with a gracious smile.

Perhaps he's not so taken by London charms, Julia mused, sitting back to observe the conversation with a new interest.

'What a pity. You would have enjoyed it. All anyone could talk about was Lord Langston's comment on Napoleon. He said the Emperor's coat was too tight to suit a real gentleman, and if the Emperor had a better tailor, he might not be so fond of war.'

'I thought politics a taboo subject at balls?' Julia asked, more to annoy her stepcousin than out of any real interest.

'We were discussing Lord Langston's comment, not politics,' Annette arrogantly clarified. 'Surely you've heard of the earl, even here?'

Julia bit back a sharp retort, struggling through gritted teeth to remain cordial.

'Yes. Charles keeps me abreast of the latest London news, though I pay it no mind. I hardly feel the comments of a man who thinks only of clothes and dancing is worth the breath to spread it. Were he a man of actual accomplishments, such as Lord Nelson, I might take more interest in what he has to say.'

'Here, here, Julia.' George slapped his knee and Annette pursed her thin lips.

'Sounds like a rather American idea to me, Miss Howard,' Captain Covington asked.

'Have you been to America, Captain?' Julia asked.

'Yes, it's an interesting country.'

'I don't agree with the Americans. The French followed their example and all their patriotism and liberty turned out dreadful,' Annette interjected, but both Julia and Captain Covington ignored the remark.

'I'm a great admirer of Mr Jefferson. Are you familiar with his agricultural inventions?' Julia asked.

'Yes, I read one of his books while I was in London. I read quite a number of books while I was at home.' He paused, watching his left hand open and close before he looked up at her again. 'I don't recall the specific of Mr Jefferson's designs, but I remember them being quite innovative.'

'He devised a plough specifically for hills. It's proved most beneficial to Knollwood,' she volunteered, encouraged by his response. 'Like Mr Jefferson, I've discovered the best way to develop new techniques is to ask the workers. I regularly speak with mine to keep abreast of their progress and any potential problems.'

'How plebian to be so familiar with your servants,' Annette sneered.

Julia went silent, the conspicuous difference between her and her London cousin making her self-conscious.

'I agree, Miss Howard, servants are often aware of more than their employers realise,' the captain offered with a smile.

'Indeed, they know the land and conditions better than anyone else.'

Careful not to gloat over the obvious check to Annette's mocking remark, Julia continued her discussion of agriculture, encouraged by the captain's extensive knowledge. The bulk of it came from books, but he asked many questions about the practical application, eager to learn. While they spoke, Julia watched the way Annette hung on his every word, fluttering her eyelashes at him while praising his wit and intelligence. Each compliment brought a smile to his face and as much as Julia's opinion of him rose with their current discussion, his apparent infatuation with Annette lowered it. Perhaps the captain thought her cousin a better country amusement than Julia. After all, the way Annette fawned on him made her interest apparent. How typical of a man to fall prey to such a shallow woman.

* * *

The carriage rattled into town, coming to a stop near the centre of the High Street. James stepped out into the crisp autumn air and took a deep breath. Being confined for so long next to Miss Taylor reminded him of a tight gun deck on a humid day in the islands. Only Miss Howard's airy voice and sparkling eyes offered any respite from Miss Taylor's cloying company.

'What an exile,' Mr Taylor sighed, taking in Daringford's dusty streets lined with shops. 'I'll return shortly.'

'I thought you were going to stay with me?' Miss Taylor whined as James handed her out of the carriage.

Mr Taylor ignored her, strolling off towards the Sign of the Swan tavern, much to his sister's visible displeasure.

James turned back to the carriage to help Miss Howard out, only to see her alight from the other side before hurrying around to join them.

'I'm afraid I must leave you as well,' George announced. 'I have some business to attend to with my solicitor. Take good care of the ladies, Jim.' He went off in the opposite direction, leaving James alone with Miss Taylor and Miss Howard.

'Well, ladies, where shall we go?'

'The milliner's shop,' Miss Taylor decided. 'I must purchase some lace, though I doubt it will be of the same quality here as in London.'

'The milliner it is, unless Miss Howard has somewhere she wishes to go?'

Miss Howard shook her head. 'No, I'm simply here for the diversion.'

'One could hardly call this place a diversion.' Miss Taylor made for the row of shops lining the north side of the street, stepping gingerly around the dirt and mud.

'I suppose we must follow.' Miss Howard sighed.

'I suppose we must.'

Their progress across the square was slow, with Miss Howard stopping more than once to speak to some farmers' wives. He stood by while they conversed, noting how she addressed the women without arrogance or conceit. There were no signs of her former awkwardness and he thought it strange she should get along so well with these women, yet seem utterly out of place with people like the Taylors. It baffled him, but he enjoyed it, her friendly attitude a refreshing change from rigid London ways.

When they finally reached the milliner shop, James held open the door, then followed her inside. 'Do you come to the village often?'

'Yes, it seems I am always purchasing necessities for Knollwood.'

Miss Taylor ignored them in favour of the shopkeeper who hustled to help the London girl spend her blunt. Miss Howard did not shop, but loitered with him near the front window, as out of place here as Miss Taylor would be among estate labourers.

'You have no interest in lace?' James asked.

'I've come to town in my riding habit. I assure you, I have no interest in lace.'

He noted the older cut of the habit with its lower waist and fitted bodice. The style skimmed her flat stomach and accentuated her curved hips. He preferred the form-flattering shape to the high-waisted style dominating Rotten Row. 'I like your dress.'

'Do you?'

He heard disbelief in the question, but also a note of hope. 'I do.'

She played with a small piece of ribbon dangling off

the table next to her, then nodded at Miss Taylor, who stood at the counter negotiating with the shopkeeper over the price. 'She certainly drives a hard bargain. I'm amazed she bothers to be so economical.'

'Perhaps her situation is not what it seems.'

Miss Howard's puzzled face indicated her ignorance of the London rumours regarding the Taylors. However, before she could respond, a round matron followed by a blonde young lady with similar full features entered the store.

'Miss Howard,' the older woman called out, crossing to where they stood. 'What a pleasure to see you in here. I didn't think you one for the milliner's shop.'

Miss Howard's lips drew tight and James's ire rose at the belittling way the matron's eyes swept over Miss Howard, making her flush with embarrassment.

'Mrs Johnson, may I introduce Captain Covington.' Miss Howard motioned to him. 'He is a friend of my uncle and staying with us. Captain Covington, this is Mrs Johnson and her daughter, Miss Caroline Johnson.'

The two ladies curtsied to James, sizing up his value as a potential husband.

He bowed, unwilling to remain here or give this woman another chance to insult Miss Howard. 'If you'll excuse us, we were just about to step outside and leave you *lovely* women to your shopping.'

He offered Miss Howard his arm. She slipped her hand in the crook of his elbow and flashed the disbelieving Mrs and Miss Johnson a wide smile as he escorted her out of the shop.

'I see some mamas are as rude here as they are in London,' James fumed once they were outside. 'What did she hope to gain by being condescending to you?'

'I don't know, but please pay it no mind. I'm quite

used to it.' Miss Howard withdrew her hand and placed a respectable distance between them. He brushed his fingers over the spot where she'd held his arm, missing the soft weight of her touch.

'You should make a habit of responding to rude people,' James suggested.

'Why? Emily and Charles would only hear of it, then chastise me for being ill mannered. It seems I must be civil to everyone while everyone may speak to me as they please.'

'There are many ways to appear courteous, yet still strike a cutting blow.'

'Then you must teach me some for I'm tired of putting up with such nonsense.' She laughed, the charming sound carrying over the noisy rattle of equipage in the street.

'It would be my pleasure. What sort of remark would you like to learn first?'

'James Covington,' the long-forgotten but familiar female voice called out from behind them, slicing through him like a sword and shattering his jovial mood. 'I can hardly believe it.'

He turned, watching Melinda Knight saunter up the street, a wicked smile decorating her full lips. A low-cut gown showed off her ample white bosom, much to the appreciation of the passing village men. Many paused to admire her, elbowing one another as their lecherous eyes enjoyed the well-displayed assets. They obviously deemed her a beauty, but James, who'd known her in his youth, saw the toll London indulgence had taken. Her dark-brown eyes seemed tired and dull while her once slender form had grown more stout, filling out her face and keeping away, for a few more years at least, the lines forming about her eyes and the corners of her lips.

'Miss Knight,' he greeted through clenched teeth.

'I'm Mrs Wilkins now, or have you forgotten?'

James's lip curled in loathing. 'So you married him?'

'Is that any way to greet an old friend?' Her seductive voice had once heated his blood; now it left him icy with disgust.

'I would hardly call us friends.'

She wedged herself between him and Miss Howard, her bosom brushing his chest. 'At one time you called me a great deal more.'

'That was a long time ago.' He stepped back, fighting the urge to push her away. The reaction unnerved him. He thought he'd forgotten her treachery years ago. Taking control of his surging emotions, he turned to Miss Howard, noting her stunned expression. 'May I introduce Miss Howard of Knollwood.'

Melinda faced Julia, taking her in and dismissing her all at once. 'We already know one another. My husband owns Cable Grange. My, what a pretty riding habit. Did you ride here?'

'No,' Miss Howard retorted, her dislike of Melinda palpable.

'Must be the new fashion. I find it so hard to keep up. You country girls have such different tastes.'

Melinda laid a gloved hand on James's arm and he pulled away, leaving her fingers hanging like talons before she lowered them. Far from being embarrassed, she seemed to take pleasure in his revulsion. 'You should come and visit us, James. I know Rowan would love to see you. Now, if you'll excuse me, I must be going.'

She swept off down the street, collecting more appreciative stares as she went.

'You know her?' Miss Howard gasped.

'I knew her once, a long time ago. It's of no importance.' He wondered how best to correct whatever false impression his acquaintance with Melinda left. He refused to be judged by a past mistake, but no proper explanation came to mind.

'Here comes George.' James motioned over her shoulder, thankful for the distraction.

George rushed along the road, the light of delicious news in his eyes.

'I can tell by the way he's hurrying, he's heard gossip,' Julia observed. 'He enjoys a story more than any old matron in Daringford.'

James laughed at the candid and accurate description. 'It is good to know some things haven't changed.'

'Julia, you won't believe what my solicitor told me,' George blurted out between winded pants when he reached them. 'Cable Grange is to be sold at auction in ten days if Mr Wilkins can't pay his London creditors.'

Chapter Three

Julia jumped from the carriage the instant it halted in front of Knollwood. Flying up the front stairs, she ran down the hall, throwing open her mother's sitting-room door, not caring what anyone thought of her very unladylike entrance.

'Cable Grange is to be sold by the bailiff in ten days. You must write to Charles and tell him to arrange for my inheritance at once.'

'Julia, do not stomp about the house,' her mother instructed without missing a stitch in her embroidery. Charlemagne watched from a basket at her mother's feet, his tail wagging lazily.

'Mother, did you hear what I said?' she demanded, chafing in the face of her apathy.

'You know he won't approve.' Her mother pulled a long, red thread through the fabric. 'He hardly approves of you running Knollwood in his absence.'

'That's why I need you to write him. Demand my inheritance, but don't tell him why. I can't have him buying Cable Grange out from under me.'

'I have little influence with Charles, especially in this matter.'

'But he has to give me the money,' Julia cried, pacing the room. 'This could be my only chance to secure an estate of my own.'

Her mother paused mid-stitch. 'Without a husband? He'd never allow it. You must be married first.'

'To whom? One of the many young men throwing themselves at my feet?'

'My dear, don't sound so despondent. Some day you will find a gentleman who loves you.'

'Not in time to purchase Cable Grange.' Julia sat down hard in the window seat.

'Perhaps George can supply the necessary funds?'

'Creedon Abbey is profitable, but not enough to finance another estate, especially not with the repairs from the fire.' She knew because she often helped Uncle George with his accounting.

'Then I'm afraid Cable Grange will go to another.'

Julia bit her thumbnail in frustration, feeling like a rabbit caught in a snare. Though the money was hers, her father's will gave Charles control of it until she married or Charles died. At the moment, she wanted very much to kill her obstinate brother.

She picked at the gold thread on a pillow. 'Why did Father put Charles in charge of my inheritance? Why not Uncle George or even Paul? They wouldn't be so difficult.'

Her mother rose, sitting down next to Julia and taking her hands. 'It's what his solicitor advised. Your father intended to change it once George purchased Creedon Abbey, but his illness was so sudden—'

Silence heavy with grief settled between them. Outside, birds chirped in a nearby tree and Julia heard the distant bark of Uncle George's hunting dogs.

'It's not fair.'

'No, it isn't, but don't fret, my dear. Nothing is hopeless. Now, go and change for dinner.' Her mother kissed her gently on the forehead, then returned to her embroidery stand.

Julia wandered down the hall to her room, her mind working over the current dilemma. She had to have Cable Grange. She refused to be shoved aside at Knollwood by Charles or to let him control her life. Paul would never do such a thing if it were up to him.

Closing the door behind her, she wondered if Paul could arrange for the money. Knowing how freely he spent while in port, she doubted he possessed the means to buy an estate and his failure to gain command of his own ship hindered his ability to make his fortune. Even if he could help, there was no way to reach him before the auction.

Julia paced her room, her mind working to think of a solution. The only way to buy Cable Grange was to obtain her inheritance. The only way to get her inheritance was to marry. At present, she had no suitors. To be honest, she had never had suitors, not here or during her one Season in London.

Julia stopped pacing, her mind seizing on an idea. What if she was only engaged? If Charles thought she intended to marry, surely he'd give her the money in time to purchase Cable Grange. Even he could see the benefit of making Cable Grange part of the Howard lands. But what gentleman could she possibly convince to make her a false offer?

Through the window overlooking the garden, she spied Simon strolling among the roses. It wasn't like him to be awake at this time of day. Usually, he napped in the late afternoon in anticipation of an even later evening. How a man could spend all night gambling was beyond her comprehension.

The idea hit her like a bolt of lightning. Simon. As a gambler, he must need money. They could make a deal, pretend to be engaged and once she had her inheritance and Cable Grange, she'd give him a few hundred pounds to jilt her.

She rushed to the door, eager to strike the bargain, when a terrifying thought froze her hand on the doorknob. If he accepted the deal, could she buy his silence at the end of the engagement? If not, it would create a scandal, then who knew how Charles or even Mother would react. Charles might force her to go through with a ruinous marriage to avoid disgrace.

Julia resumed her pacing, desperate for a solution. Simon was no different from other London peacocks. How hard could it be to use her money, or the future possibility of money, to snare him? Instead of entangling herself in a potentially shocking agreement, she'd flaunt her wealth, then allow his greed to lead him to her. Once she had her inheritance and Cable Grange she could easily dismiss him. Simon would suffer no more heartbreak than the other London pinks who proposed to every unmarried rich woman who entered a ballroom. Even if breaking the engagement labelled her a jilt, it wouldn't matter. She'd have her inheritance and Cable Grange and everything else could go to the devil.

Standing at the wardrobe, Julia tore through the dresses, selecting one of her better frocks. Slipping off the habit, she put on the light-blue dress, then sat at her dressing table to do her hair. The sight of herself in the mirror dampened her enthusiasm. Though the cloth of her frock was fine enough, the cut was unflattering and her hair, which was still fastened in the simple braided bun at the nape of her neck, did nothing to improve her features.

'If only I were pretty enough to catch Simon without my money.' She sighed and then dismissed the ridiculous notion. 'I might as well wish for gold to fall from the sky.'

Pulling out the bun, she brushed out her hair. A man like Simon couldn't resist the allure of money and she'd parade herself in front of him like a fat cow at market. Dignity be damned. She had to have Cable Grange for if she ended her days as a spinster aunt, she'd do it on her terms in her own house.

'I never thought I'd see Melinda again.' James smacked the cue stick hard against the white ball, sending it skipping over the slate, off the table and across the library's wood floor.

George picked it up, laying it back on the table. 'You aren't still chewing on that, are you? Let it go. No good can come of it.'

'Except an estate. I wasn't planning it—I couldn't have planned it—yet here it is, in my lap. I only have to wait for the bailiff to act, then I'll watch them go and be done with it.' Revenge coiled inside him with unnerving force. Even in the days after Melinda betrayed him, he hadn't felt this much hate, but things were different then. His naval career had stretched out before him to blunt the disappointment and at sea he'd been too focused on succeeding and surviving to dwell on lost love. Now, with his career a shattered heap, his whole life crushed and bruised with it, there seemed nothing to distract him from old wounds. He flexed his left hand, cursing the dull pain. How he hated it and the way it made him hate everything.

George shook his head. 'That's not the Jim I remember.'

'A lot of things changed last year.'

'No, you just think they have. Look to the future. Don't concern yourself with some past offence that no longer matters.'

'You think it doesn't matter?'

'I think Rowan did you a favour, showed you who she really was before she leg-shackled you.' George leaned across the table and took a shot, scoring another point. 'Of course it's your decision and Cable Grange will suit you, but you'll need something more or you'll be bored in a fortnight.'

'You thinking running an estate won't be enough?' He reached for his glass of brandy sitting on the edge of the table.

'Not for a man like you. You need adventure and what better adventure than marriage?' George announced.

James stopped drinking mid-sip. 'Marriage?'

'Yes, marriage.' George hooked his thumbs in his coat, quite pleased with himself.

'What new scheme are you planning?' He didn't trust George's happy manner.

'Scheme? I never scheme.'

'Never scheme?' James laughed. 'What was all that business with the rum in Jamaica?'

'Merely an investment.'

'And the plantation owner's wife in Barbados?'

'One could hardly fault me for such an escapade.'

'Except the escapade's husband.'

George shrugged, unrepentant. 'You're a man of your own mind. I never forced you to participate in the rum venture or follow me to the plantation.'

'I followed you to save your hide and keep her husband from running you through.'

'Perhaps.' George fingered his cue stick, then levelled it at James. 'But you went along with the other ventures because you wanted to, making a handsome profit on more than one occasion if I remember correctly.'

'Yes, I have a great deal of my current fortune to thank you for.'

'So why distrust me now?'

It wasn't George he distrusted. It was himself. He hadn't seen Miss Howard since returning from Daringford, but following George through Knollwood, he kept searching for her in every room, hoping she might appear. Her presence touched a place deep inside him he thought destroyed with his career and the feeling left him wary and unsettled. One woman had already preyed on the weakness of his youth. He couldn't allow another to take advantage of his ruined life.

George fixed him with a stern, superior officer's stare. 'Seriously, Jim, you had a bad run last year, but you can't live in the past. You're young, full of possibility. You need a good woman by your side.'

'I suppose you have someone in mind? Your little Artemis, perhaps?'

George leaned towards James, the glint of mischief in his eyes. James knew this expression all too well. How many times had he followed it into a tavern, or the heat of battle? 'Now that you mention it, perhaps Julia is just the kind of woman you need. Sizeable inheritance. Brother in Parliament. Adept at running an estate. She's a good match.'

James shook his head as he readied his cue stick. Is this what his life had come to? Discussing marriage over a billiard table? Country life must be very dull to lead an old salt like George to such a pastime. 'Interesting suggestion—however, it has two flaws.'

'And they are?'

'One, I have no desire to marry, which you well know.'

'At the moment, yes, but there's always the future.'

'And two, your Artemis doesn't like me.'

'Of course she likes you. She's just an awkward girl. Spent too much time in the country, odd relatives and all that.'

'Odd indeed.' James hit the cue ball and it sailed past the red ball. 'I see a great deal of Paul in his sister.'

'There you are with the past again. Forget it. Paul was young. You were young and both of you stupid.'

'I'd hardly say stupid.'

'Stubborn, then, if you like. You'd be surprised to see him now.'

'"Surprised" is not the word. Does your Artemis know I wrote to the Admiralty against Paul's promotion?'

'I didn't see the need to inform her and I suggest you don't either if you wish to have a pleasant visit. You don't want to be on the wrong end of my niece's temper.'

As if I needed the warning. 'You don't think she'll find out?'

'He's off at sea and you're here, not likely to meet.'

James had to admire George's devil-may-care attitude. Here was a man who always believed everything would work out swimmingly and somehow for him it always did. What James wouldn't give for even a small measure of George's optimism, but the last year had left him anything but optimistic. The long days of his recovery followed by the even longer days of stalking the Admiralty, asking, then begging for another commission, had taken their toll.

During the year of his recovery, younger, fitter men with more prestigious connections had passed him by, and not even his loyal years of service were enough to secure him another ship. He could almost smell the oil on the wood panels of Admiral Stuart's office the day he told James there would be no more commissions and encouraged—insisted, one might say—James enjoy his fortune while he still could.

In the end, despite his disappointment, he'd secretly been relieved. It shamed him to admit it, but he couldn't lie to himself. Death had passed over him. Ten years ago he'd have shrugged it off and raced to face the devil once more. This time he couldn't. He wanted to live free of violence and risks, to take care of his family and see his sister's future children grow up, but without his command he saw nothing, no meaning or activity, just an endless set of days stretching out before him.

James refilled his drink from the small decanter of brandy on the table near the window. He hated this emptiness. It made him feel like a ship in a storm with a broken rudder at the mercy of driving winds and an unforgiving sea. He took a deep drink, careful not to enjoy too much the burning in the back of his throat. He'd seen other men come home and lose themselves in gin, women and cards, their energy wasted by a lack of duty and direction. He put the glass down, knowing his future wasn't at the bottom of a bottle, but was it really as close as Cable Grange? Perhaps an estate would give him a sense of purpose again, a chance to do something more than grieve for his past and the future he'd planned for himself.

James watched while George calculated his next shot. 'Why isn't your little Artemis already married?'

'Says she's not interested.'

'A woman not interested in marriage? Next you'll tell me you believe in mermaids.'

'I do. I saw one off the coast of Florida once. She's not interested in marriage. However, a man with an estate could change her mind. If you're determined to buy Cable Grange, she's the woman you need to run it.' George took his time lining up his shot, looking quite proud of himself for what he considered a brilliant idea.

James couldn't resist the opportunity to rib his old friend. 'So your niece is only interested in marrying a man for his estate?'

George whiffed the cue ball then straightened up, indignant. 'She's not that kind of young lady. She's clever, a real woman of substance, made running Knollwood her life, but the place isn't hers. Charles plans to assume control when he comes home at the end of the month. Where will she be then?'

'You could leave her Creedon Abbey.'

'I probably will…' George floundered. Clearly he hadn't thought of this and James enjoyed watching the older man work to recover himself. 'But I'm not at death's door yet. I plan to live at least another twenty years. Spend some time with her, get to know her, you'll see what I mean.'

James walked to the window, noticing the threatening clouds gathering overhead. Their darkness layered the hills with damp shadows, making the hour feel late. Somewhere across the hills and valleys sat Cable Grange. Watching the wind shake the tall hedges of the garden, he tried to picture himself as lord of the manor, spending his days in land management with all its hundreds of concerns, but he had trouble imagining it.

Reaching up under his jacket, he felt for the jagged, raised scar. Yes, he was lucky to be alive and sometimes it made him think he wanted a wife and a family. What would it be like to enjoy the kind of happiness he'd witnessed between his parents before his father died or the love he saw in his sister's eyes when she walked with her husband? He'd tried so many times while convalescing to imagine the future, but always it remained shrouded in a grey fog of uncertainty. The sudden end to his naval career made the years before him seem meaningless while old wounds and betrayals arose from the past to dominate his mind.

A bolt of lightning split the distant horizon and the image of Miss Howard atop that beast of a horse commanding him like a common seaman seared his mind. Tight desire coursed through him at the memory of her tongue tracing the line of her lips and the curious need illuminating her face. Her free spirit and courage reminded him of Caribbean ladies, bringing a smile to his face at the memory of warm afternoons and even warmer nights in the islands. Those days seemed like a lifetime ago yet today, in Miss Howard's presence, their carefree ease sparked deep inside him for the first time in over a year.

The feeling made him uneasy. He'd experienced something like it once before, allowing it to guide him, and he'd come to regret it.

He downed the last of the brandy, forcing back the encroaching sadness. He wasn't ready for another life-altering change and certainly had no intention of courting Miss Howard.

As James examined the cut-crystal glass, an idea

suddenly came to him, so simple yet brilliantly amusing. George was determined to meddle with yet another scheme. Why not catch him up in one of James's devising, give him a friendly taste of his own medicine?

'Perhaps you're right. I should give more thought to the idea of marriage,' James announced, strolling back to the table and scrutinising the position of the balls.

George's smile broadened. 'Indeed.'

'A man needs a woman to make a comfortable home for him.'

'One with a sense of how to run things properly.'

'The perfect mistress to complement him.'

'Exactly.'

'A woman like Miss Taylor.'

'Annette?' George sputtered. 'You must be joking.'

'I'm quite serious. She's well brought up and pleasing to view.' James leaned over the table to take a shot, pretending not to notice George's stunned expression.

'But there's nothing there, no substance.'

'Good. It makes life less complicated.' James hit the cue ball, sending it bouncing off the side to hit the red ball. Straightening up, he worked to contain his laughter as George stared slack jawed at him.

'Annette?'

James smiled to himself, realising just how much fun this harmless revenge would be.

Chapter Four

The clock in the hallway chimed six times as Julia rushed across the marble floor, late for dinner again. Stopping outside the dining-room door, she ran her hands over her hair, tucking a loose tendril into her *coiffure*. Mary, her lady's maid, had been too busy with Annette to arrange Julia's hair so she'd done it herself, pulling it back into a more flattering bun and allowing a few curls to hang about her face. The *coiffure* was far from stylish, but it framed her features much better than Emily's plain creation. Pulling the bodice of the light-blue muslin dress lower, she hitched up the pink sash in an effort to make it appear more fashionable. The ribbon refused to co-operate, slipping back down to her waist. With a sigh of frustration, she gave up, knowing she'd dressed as well as could be expected for dinner at Knollwood, which was never a formal affair.

Until tonight. The instant Julia stepped into the dining room she remembered Emily's instructions to dress for their new guest. She'd been so distracted by planning her tactics with Simon, she'd completely forgotten.

'I'm so glad you could join us. I was afraid Knollwood business would keep you away.' Emily's high, nervous voice pulled Julia out of her momentary shock and she took in everyone's attire. Mother's deep-maroon mantua, though of an older style, suited her matronly frame while Emily and Annette's dresses were the height of London fashion. Simon wore a coat of the finest material and Uncle George and Captain Covington looked dashing in their uniforms. Plain muslin in the face of so much silk only emphasised her lack of fashion. For a moment, Julia contemplated making her excuses, feigning a headache or some other feminine nonsense, then changed her mind.

I've already made a fool of myself. No sense starving now. Throwing back her shoulders, she strode into the room.

'Yes, Knollwood business can be quite exacting, but I wouldn't dream of missing dinner.' She took her place next to Simon, across from Annette and Captain Covington.

'You look very lovely this evening,' the captain offered across the table.

'Thank you.' Was he teasing her? It was difficult to tell. His beguiling smile reminded her of the one Paul always used to flatter pretty ladies at the assembly hall.

'The affairs of Knollwood must be very demanding to make you lose track of time,' Annette mocked.

'No, I was quite aware of the time,' Julia replied coolly, annoyed by her stepcousin's condescending tone.

'Perhaps you could learn a thing or two about managing your affairs, Annette,' Simon suggested, dabbing the corners of his mouth with his napkin.

'Now you prefer bluestockings?' Annette frowned. 'I thought you felt education was wasted on women?'

'I do. It leads a woman to interfere too much in a

man's business.' He fixed an icy stare on his sister, who coloured under the remark, but said nothing.

Julia sensed more to this conversation than a simple debate of female education, but having no interest in the intricacies of the Taylors' personal business, she concentrated on enjoying her meal.

'Julia, Jim was telling us the latest news from London regarding Napoleon,' Uncle George announced. 'It appears Admiral Nelson will face him before the month is out?'

The food turned to dirt in her mouth. 'Do you think so?'

'It's a very real possibility,' the captain answered with measured words, fingering the spoon next to his plate.

'Paul's ship, *HMS Pickle*, is with Admiral Nelson's fleet. He could be injured, or worse.' Her voice quavered with worry and she didn't care who heard it or what they thought.

'Even if there is a battle, *HMS Pickle* is a small ship used to send messages or fetch supplies. She won't see much action.'

'But there's still a chance Paul will be involved in the fighting?'

'There is, but let's hope if Admiral Nelson and your brother face him, the battle is quick and decisive in Britain's favour.'

His sympathetic eyes touched her and she wished they were alone so she could pour out all her worries to him. He would understand, perhaps even take her in his sturdy arms and, with tender, reassuring words, drive away all her fears for Paul.

'Admiral Nelson will lose more than a battle if he continues his indiscretion with Mrs Hamilton,' Annette added, indifferent to Julia's concerns. 'Don't you agree, Captain Covington?'

'I'm afraid I don't follow town gossip,' he answered, but Annette refused to relinquish his attention or the table's.

'Don't you find his indiscretion scandalous?'

Julia noticed the way his fingers tightened on the stem of his wine glass. 'Great men are always granted some leeway.'

'If society shunned him, then who would lead the Navy against France?' Julia demanded, irritated by Annette's prattle. 'Or would you prefer the French on our shores? Perhaps they would be more delightful in the drawing room.'

'How droll to discuss politics at dinner,' Annette sniffed. 'Captain Covington, you must tell me all about your sister's wedding.'

With a twinge of regret, Julia left the captain to Annette and focused on the dandy beside her. How could she possibly capture his interest? She couldn't simply announce the size of her inheritance and hope he took the bait. Conversation seemed the key, but since his arrival they'd barely exchanged ten words. Now she had to captivate him with witty repartee? It seemed a Herculean feat, but one she had to accomplish.

'Simon, do you ride?' she asked in her most pleasing voice. The young man turned his pointed chin over his starched cravat, staring at her as though she possessed three heads.

'Of course,' he sneered.

Julia clamped her hands together in her lap, screwing the smile on her face. 'I suppose no country ride could compare to the fashionable hour in Rotten Row?'

'On at least that point you are correct,' he lisped, returning to his meal.

Her cheeks burned with the strain of holding her smile. For a moment, the game felt like more trouble than it was worth, but the thought of having her own estate urged her on. 'You must be an excellent horseman.'

Simon's knife and fork clanked against the plate. 'I prefer the elegance of a phaeton—surely you've heard of them, even here in the country.'

She resisted the urge to empty her plate in his lap, continuing to remain charming as though nothing was amiss. 'Oh, yes. When I receive my inheritance I plan to purchase one. Perhaps you can help me select the best?'

'Your inheritance?' His bored eyes almost sparkled at the mention of money. She leaned towards him, dropping her voice.

'Yes, I receive it as soon as I'm married. Tell me about your phaeton. I imagine it is one of the finest in London.'

Just as she suspected, flattery worked. Simon puffed up at the opportunity to discuss himself. 'It's second only to the prince's.'

Despite the loss of her appetite, Julia soldiered on. 'Oh, you know the prince? How wonderful.'

'He complimented me on my rig.' Simon's voice dripped with pride.

'Please, tell me all about it.'

What followed was the most boring and tortuous hour of Julia's life as Simon described, in minute detail, his phaeton. From the corner of her eye she noticed Uncle George and Emily exchanging baffled looks. Even Captain Covington threw her a sideways glance and for a brief moment she felt ashamed of her plan. Only her mother seemed indifferent, slipping bits of food to Charlemagne, who sat on the floor next to her chair.

'The squabs are far more comfortable than the average phaeton. I had the leather dyed dark green,' Simon continued and Julia gazed up at him through her lashes, mimicking the way Annette flattered the captain. If only her dress were cut as deeply as Annette's. However, such a ploy might make her scheme too obvious.

After what felt like an eternity, Emily rose, ending dinner. 'Shall the ladies retire to the drawing room?'

Julia forced herself not to jump up and run into the adjoining room. Instead she smiled coyly at Simon as she rose. 'Perhaps we can discuss it more later?'

'Perhaps.' He didn't seem enthusiastic at the prospect.

Massaging her aching cheeks, Julia followed the other women into the drawing room. Taking *The Monk* out of her dress pocket, she situated herself on the sofa to read, hoping the others would leave her in peace. Her hope was short lived when Emily walked over to the card table near the window and shuffled the deck. 'Ladies, would you care for a game of piquet?'

'I'd love to play,' Annette announced, choosing her place at the table and taking the deck from Emily. 'I'll deal.'

Julia buried her nose in her book, pretending not to hear the invitation, even when Emily cleared her throat to gain her attention.

'Come play, Julia,' her mother gently ordered.

With a sigh, Julia put down her book and joined the others at the table.

'We're always playing in London and the stakes are

often very high. Sometimes gentlemen lose a great deal at the tables,' Annette explained, dealing the cards.

'Perhaps the men of London are not very sensible, for it takes only a tiny amount of sense to know one should not bet what one cannot afford to lose.' Julia laid down a card, then chose another.

'No gentleman worth his salt would dare refuse a wager.'

'Then there must be many poor fools about the London ballrooms.'

'Do you consider Captain Covington a fool?'

Julia shrugged, trying to imagine the captain dancing, but she could only picture him gambling in some tropical den of iniquity. She fought back a laugh, struggling to keep her face a bland mask of uninterest. 'I haven't known the captain long enough to comment on the merits of his wit—however, if he lives in London, the odds are against him not being a fool.'

'I assure you, Captain Covington is no fool,' her mother interjected. 'He has proven himself a hero on more than one occasion.'

Julia didn't respond, wondering what her mother would think if she knew about the captain's involvement with the Governor of Bermuda's widowed sister. She'd overheard Uncle George telling Paul about it once. It was quite shocking.

'How long has George known Captain Covington?' Annette asked.

'Ten years,' Mother answered. 'Captain Covington was a lieutenant on George's ship in the war against France during the First Coalition. His service was so distinguished he was given command of his own ship. He's very well travelled, Julia.'

'Is he now?' Julia barely heard her. She was too busy

concentrating on which card to play next so she could lose and end the game.

'George tells me Captain Covington is a very sensible man when it comes to money, much like you, Julia,' her mother remarked, attempting to draw Julia into the conversation.

'Interesting,' Julia mumbled, disappointed by her excellent hand for it made losing very difficult.

'Captain Covington and I spoke a great deal this afternoon and it was as if we've known each other for years. We have a great deal in common for we both adore cheese,' Annette continued.

Julia selected another card and scowled for it was a good one. 'Most men in London adore food. That's why there's so much gout in town.'

Emily coughed disapprovingly.

'London is a gourmand's paradise,' Annette insisted. 'I advised Captain Covington to hire a French chef. All the best houses have them. He's a very affable man. I'm surprised he's not married for he'd do well with a wife.'

'A man of thirty with a sensible head is a rarity these days,' Emily said more to Julia than to Annette.

'He's very handsome,' Annette added.

'Yes, he is, don't you agree, Julia?' Mother entreated.

Julia took another card and smiled to find it a bad one before she noticed the three women waiting for her response. 'Pardon me?'

Emily scowled at Julia's inability to follow the conversation. 'Captain Covington is very handsome, don't you agree?'

Yes, she did, but she was not about to admit it. 'I hadn't thought on the matter.' She rearranged her cards, needing only another bad one to lose.

'I'm told he's a very accomplished horseman,' Emily

added. 'Perhaps, Julia, you could accompany Captain Covington on a ride tomorrow?'

Julia watched the rain hit the window, streaking down the panes. Without his afternoon ride, Manfred would need a good gallop. She did not relish the idea of trying to control him in a gentle trot alongside Captain Covington's mount. Hopefully the weather would clear by morning and she could take Manfred out before duty intruded on the day.

'I'm sure Uncle George will escort him if he wishes to ride.' Julia continued to study her cards, avoiding Emily's chastising scowl. 'He's better company for the captain than I am.'

'Of course nothing can compare to Rotten Row at the fashionable hour. Captain Covington promised to join me there when we return to London,' Annette said, drawing another card. Julia judged from the smile on her narrow face that Annette had a good hand. It was only a matter of moments before Julia could lose the game and put an end to this tiring conversation.

'I won. I won,' Annette announced much to Julia's great relief, though she pretended, like Emily and Mother, to be disappointed. They slid their sovereigns across the table and Annette swept the coins into her palm, making Julia wonder how someone from London with a carriage and four could covet a few crowns.

'Shall we play again?' Annette shuffled the deck and the entrance of the men saved Julia the trouble of declining.

'Ladies, we're here to amuse you,' Uncle George announced, making his way to the card table. Simon didn't come in with the men and Julia wasn't the only one who noticed his absence.

'Where's Simon?' Annette asked, dealing the cards.

'It appears he had some pressing business in Daringford,' Uncle George explained with obvious disdain, taking Julia's place at the table.

Julia stood behind Uncle George, drumming her fingers on the back of the wooden chair, watching him arrange his hand. She felt disappointed, but also relieved at being spared another hour of Simon's pompous chatter. Unable to charm a missing man, she decided to learn more about gambling, thinking it might be the only real way to capture her stepcousin's very small heart.

James stepped into the room, his eyes seeking out Miss Howard. She didn't acknowledge him, but stood over George's shoulder watching the play. He resisted the urge to join her and initiate the intelligent conversation he now craved after a dinner spent listening to Miss Taylor's vapid gossip. However, showing Miss Howard too much attention would only make George more determined in his matchmaking efforts. Instead he walked to the sofa and picked up the small book lying open on the cushions.

James examined the cover of *The Monk*, then held it up. 'Miss Taylor, I believe you left your novel here.'

'That is mine.' Miss Howard crossed the room, gesturing for the book.

'I wouldn't have guessed you one for Gothic novels,' he quipped. He expected her to read dry tracts on crops, not notorious novels. What other passions lay hidden beneath her quiet exterior?

'You think a woman who manages an estate can't enjoy novels?'

She took the offered tome and her fingers brushed his, sending a shock through him. She must have felt it, too, for he noticed the slight hint of a blush under the scattering of freckles across the bridge of her nose.

'Not at all. What other books have you enjoyed?'

She sat down on the sofa, looking as though she wasn't sure if she should tell him. A single ringlet teased the soft sweep of her jaw and the flickering candlelight caressed the fine line of her cheeks. 'I recently finished Edward Ive's *A Voyage from England to India*.'

He sat on the sofa across from her, leaning against the padded back. 'An excellent book.'

Her face brightened. 'You've read it?'

'You think a man in the Navy can't enjoy books about travel?' he teased, delighted by the easy smile it brought to her lips.

'Not at all.'

He sat forwards, his elbows on his knees. 'I read a great deal last year. Have you travelled?'

'Only as far as Portsmouth. But with the way Mr Ives describes India, I know one day I will have to see it.'

Her face lit up at the prospect of visiting India, the passionate response striking his core. She might dress like a stern governess, but he'd seen too much of the woodland nymph to be fooled. What would it be like to make her blaze with more sensuous emotions, his fingers stoking the heat simmering beneath her compliant exterior? He shifted on the sofa to cover the sudden fullness in his loins. What a powerful effect this curious young woman had on him. 'Then why not set out for Bombay?'

She laid the book on her lap with a sigh. 'A woman does not have the freedom of a man to travel.'

'Perhaps you need an adventurous husband.'

She raised one disbelieving eyebrow. 'No such creature exists.'

'Then you'll have to go alone.' He couldn't resist teasing her, delighting in the honest reaction it provoked. 'Someone of your pluck would prove quite the explorer.'

She glanced at the card table and, satisfied the others were too busy playing to notice, leaned forwards, bringing them much closer than decency allowed. He smelled the crisp scent of rosewater, noticed the slight curl of her long lashes. He chanced a brief peek at her breasts. Though well hidden by the dress's high bodice, they pressed against the blue fabric, offering a hint of the creamy skin beneath. The heaviness in his manhood increased and he dug his fingers into his thigh to keep from leaning forwards to claim her full, teasing lips.

'Do you assume because my accomplishments are unusual that I have a flagrant disregard for convention?' Her mischievous eyes dared him to respond.

He leaned closer, dropping his voice, eager to meet her challenge. 'I very much admire your accomplishments. And your disregard for convention.'

'You like unconventional women?'

'Indeed. It gives them a certain mystery.'

'Really?' She leaned closer, her heady voice and smouldering eyes tightening the desire coursing through him. 'I suppose you've met many mysterious women.'

'I've known a few.'

'Yes, your time in the Navy must have acquainted you with many ladies in many ports.'

'Julia!' Emily exclaimed.

They both turned to see everyone staring at them. He'd forgotten about the others and obviously she had, too. He expected the rebuke to make her retreat back into a compliant, self-conscious miss. Instead, she rose with all the composure of a lady of the first water.

'It was a pleasure debating with you, Captain.' Ignoring her sister-in-law's stunned face, she dipped a slow, graceful curtsy, then strode from the room. He watched her leave, captivated and impressed. Here was no Artemis, but Venus waiting for the right man to draw her out.

'She's a real spitfire, Jim.' George laughed.

'A bit too forward, if you ask me,' Miss Taylor remarked and George snorted.

'No one did, Annette.'

Julia closed her bedroom door, leaning against the smooth wood to catch her breath. Her fingers felt beneath the doorknob for the brass key and, turning it in the lock, a sense of relief accompanied the click.

What had just transpired? She didn't know, but it thrilled her as much as riding Manfred at a full gallop across the hills. What had she seen in the captain's eyes? Desire, excitement and a few more dangerous emotions she felt along the back of her spine.

She hurried to the window seat, her hands shaking as if she'd almost been caught rifling through Charles's private papers. Leaning her forehead against the cool glass, she watched the rain falling in sheets, running down the window and blurring the view of the garden. If Paul were home, she could tell him about the captain and the taunting riot of emotions tightening her stomach. He'd put a name to them, help her understand why the captain ignited her senses.

Fingering the books strewn about the upholstered window seat, she pushed aside a pamphlet on crop rotation to reveal a large book on India. Flipping through it, she examined the coloured plates of Indian gods and goddesses and the dark ladies with their almond eyes, veils and jewels. Pictures of the Mughal emperors riding their elephants, accompanied by exotic animals and splendidly dressed courtiers, decorated the pages.

The women in the paintings of the palace stretched their arms out towards the men, their breasts taut against crimson saris, their round hips hugged by the delicate fabric. The image of Captain Covington's sharp eyes, the rich tones of his voice and the heat of his fingertips brushing against hers filled her mind. There'd been a moment during their discussion when she thought he meant to kiss her.

No, I must have imagined it. The captain couldn't possibly possess an interest in her and if he did it was an entirely dishonourable one. The idea should have scandalised her, but deep down she felt flattered.

As she turned the pages, thoughts of the captain continued to dominate her mind. She imagined him sitting atop an elephant, inspecting the fields of an exotic plantation as the monsoons overtook the land, the heat and spices all coming together in his skin, hair and eyes. She pictured herself beside him, standing on a veranda overlooking the jungle. With steam rising from the hot earth, she'd run her hands up over his chest, push the jacket off his shoulders, then follow the line of his back to his waist and hips. She'd tug the white shirt from his breeches, trace the hard flesh and muscles of his stomach with her fingers, then dip lower to more sinful places.

Abandoning the book, she hurried to the wardrobe and pulled the doors open. Dropping to her knees, she felt around the bottom, behind shoes and old quilts, to a plain box near the back. She took off the lid and removed a shimmering red-and-gold silk sari, a present from Paul many years ago after his first trip to

India. Slipping off her frock and the cotton chemise, she wrapped the shiny silk around her naked body. It felt glorious next to her skin and she could almost smell the curry in its deep-red sheen. She imagined the cool feel of the silk to be the monsoons washing over her, rinsing away the dust and heat of Bombay.

A flash of lightning caught her eye. She turned to see her reflection in the window as the thunder rolled overhead. She pulled her hair out of its bun and it fell over her shoulders, their creamy white colour further whitened by the dazzling sari. The way the fabric traced the curve of her thighs, hugging her breasts and hips like the alluring women in the pictures, delighted her.

Is this what the captain meant by mysterious? Her skin tingled to discover his meaning and she wondered if the weight of him on top of her would feel as heavenly as the silk? Perhaps he'd run his hands over the firm, round line of her hips? Cup her breast like the men in another, more wicked book she'd once seen.

Suddenly the other book came to mind, the one she'd found a few years ago hidden in Paul's wardrobe. Those pages held the same almond eyes, voluptuous women and robust men, only the pictures were more intimate, sensual and forbidden. What would it be like to delight in some of those illicit poses with the captain?

She shuddered, simultaneously excited and embarrassed. What would Charles or Emily think if they knew she had such wicked thoughts or acted like a Cyprian in private?

Unwinding the sari from her body, she folded the fabric, then returned it to the box and the back of the wardrobe. She slipped on her shift, blew out the candle and settled into bed. Staring up at the dark ceiling, she wondered if she should have set her cap at the captain instead of Simon. Lightning flashed, branding the twisted shadow of the oak tree outside across the ceiling before the room went black. Like the shadow, the idea of pursuing the captain gave her a small shock of fear. He acted on her nerves like no man had ever done before, the effect both thrilling and terrifying. If she played her game with him, could she jilt him? Would he let her?

Sitting up, she bunched the flatness out of her pillow. Of course he'd let her jilt him. Hadn't he spent the entire meal entranced with Annette, making his preference for her stepcousin clear? He'd only showed an interest in her when she'd acted like a strumpet. In the future, she must behave like a perfect lady in his presence.

She rolled over, pulling the blanket up under her chin and nestling into the warm mattress. Another bolt of lightning illuminated the room, followed by a deep roll of thunder. The steady plunk of rain hitting the window lulled her to sleep, weaving into her dream about monsoons falling on thick jungles, swelling the river roaring past the grassy bank where she stood, Captain Covington at her side.

Chapter Five

'Thoughts of a certain someone keep you up last night?' George nudged James as they made their way down to the stables. The clouds had cleared overnight and though everything was wet, there was no hint of rain in the brisk morning air.

James laughed, pulling on his riding gloves. 'I never thought you for a romantic.'

'We all have our secrets.'

'What secrets are you hiding?'

'Never mind.' George adjusted his white cravat. 'What exactly were you two so intently discussing?'

'Travel.'

'Who knew it was such an engrossing subject.'

'Very.' James didn't elaborate, for once not wanting to discuss a lady with George. His tête-à-tête with Miss Howard had disturbed him far more than he wanted to admit. He'd seen her surprise when she realised she wasn't properly dressed for dinner and had expected her to flee the room. When she'd determinedly crossed the threshold, he'd silently applauded her decision to stay. Then, during their exchange, the low cadence of her voice and her irrepressible enthusiasm made him feel again like a carefree young naval officer.

James slapped the riding crop against his tall boot. What was he now? A crippled man fit only to languish in the country, the past hounding the unfilled hours, the future torturing him with its emptiness. He'd come so far since his first days in the Navy, the prospect of advancing to commodore discussed more than once with the Admiralty. Not until the bullet struck him had he realised how fast fate could crush a man.

Near the stables they came upon Mr Taylor. Dark circles hung under his red eyes and his clothes, normally as fine as five pence, were ruffled as if he had spent the night in them.

'Simon, fancy a morning ride?' George asked, much to James's surprise. He planned to inspect the Cable Grange land and didn't want any additional company. But sensing George's eagerness to give his stepnephew a difficult time, James didn't object to the invitation.

'I have no interest in a ride,' Simon sneered, trying to slink past them, but George refused to be put off.

'Come, some fresh air will do you good.' He threw his large arm around Simon's slight shoulders, directing him back to the stables, much to Simon's visible displeasure.

The stables occupied a flat parcel of land hidden from view of the house by a small grove of trees. Crossing the paddock, George led them inside where the groom sat polishing a saddle.

'John, please help Simon find a suitable mount,' George instructed, pushing Simon at the man.

'Yes, Captain Russell,' John answered. 'If you'll follow me, Mr. Taylor, I have just the animal for you.'

'Happy to see me, Percy?' George stood at the first stall, running a hand over his horse's chestnut mane. 'Choose any you like, Jim. They're all some of the finest horseflesh in the county. Another of Julia's accomplishments.'

'Yes, an impressive collection.' James walked down the line of horses, trying to decide which to ride. All the stallions impressed him, but none so much as the black one in the last stall. Here was the darkest, largest, most sinister horse he'd ever seen. He recognised it as the animal Miss Howard had ridden when she'd surprised him in the woods.

'That's Manfred. Miss Howard's horse,' John offered with pride. 'She jumps him when she has a mind, too.'

James moved to rub the horse's massive neck, but it backed up, its eyes wide and wild. 'If I hadn't seen her riding him myself, I'd say he's too much animal for such a young lady.'

'If he's truly too much animal, Captain Covington,' a soft female voice sang from behind him, 'I'm sure we can find an even-tempered gelding for you.'

James turned to see Miss Howard watching him, a challenging smile decorating the corners of her full lips. She wore a stylish dark-blue riding habit, well tailored to her petite figure. The same saucy air she'd captivated him with last night made her cheeks glow, igniting his blood. The image of her beneath him on a fresh mound of hay, the golden morning sun illuminating the pink tones of her flesh while his fingers undid the long row of buttons on the back of her habit, teased his already aching body.

'I'm sorry if I've given offence, Miss Howard. It's not my intention,' he apologised, letting the image of the soft velvet sliding from her shoulders linger for just a moment longer before forcing it away. 'I'm merely surprised such a beast is suitable for a lady.'

She walked past him, rubbing the horse lovingly on the nose, taming the fire in the creature's eyes.

'Or do you think the lady is unsuitable for the horse?' she challenged with a sly grin, the playful curve of her lips exciting him more than he cared to admit. 'Would you like to ride him?'

James examined the beast, hesitant. One throw might undo the last year of recovery. However, something in the way the little Artemis challenged him made the risk irresistible.

'May I?'

'If you think you can handle him. He'll need a firm rider since he didn't have his afternoon exercise yesterday.'

James flexed his left hand, feeling the loss of strength more keenly than ever before. He shouldn't ride. He should admit he couldn't handle the beast and decline like a reasonable man, but this morning he didn't feel like being reasonable. 'I've handled a ship in a storm. I can handle a horse.'

'If you like.' She stepped back, motioning for John to take control of Manfred.

'Good luck to you, sir. Thrown off everyone who's tried to ride him, 'cept Miss Julia and Mr Paul Howard,' John remarked, leading Manfred out of the stall. The horse strained against the harness with pent-up energy and James balled his left hand.

'Shall we?' James waved towards the paddock.

Following Miss Howard outside, he admired the gentle sway of her hips as she strode into the sunlight, realising there was more to her than exuberant youth.

She possessed a firm determination he admired, even if others in society did not.

John led an agitated and now saddled Manfred into the yard, ending all of James's pleasant thoughts. George, sitting astride Percy, shot him a questioning look, but James brushed it aside, his attention firmly focused on the beast. He'd never shrunk from a challenge, but if the horse proved too difficult to manage, the idea of being thrown in front of such an audience held no appeal. Unconsciously, he touched his shoulder.

'You aren't afraid, Captain? Are you?' Miss Howard teased, her capricious smile steeling James's resolve.

'What's to fear? He's only a horse and I've certainly faced worse.' James took the reins and Manfred shook his head, pawing at the packed dirt. 'Easy, boy.'

He stroked the horse's neck, cautious of the animal's dark, wild eyes. Manfred settled down long enough for James to step into the saddle. Ignoring the throbbing in his left shoulder, he gripped the reins with both hands in an effort to hide his weakness. Once comfortably astride, James shot Julia a surefire grin.

'I told you I could handle him.'

No sooner were the words out of his mouth than Manfred, contemptuous of a foreign rider, bucked. James clamped his thighs tight against the animal, determined to stay in the saddle. Manfred landed hard on all fours, then bolted, shooting out of the paddock. The countryside flew by, the wind more cutting than the pebbles and mud kicked up by Manfred's hooves. James sat back in the saddle, choked up on the reins and pulled hard, but the beast fought him. Gritting his teeth at the searing pain tearing through his shoulder, James seesawed the reins until Manfred, tired from his exertion, had no choice but to relent. Slowing down,

Manfred trotted in a circle, breathing fast and snorting before finally coming to a halt.

James bent over in the saddle and closed his eyes, the pain in his shoulder making him dizzy. His right hand shook from fatigue and his thighs burned when he eased his hold on the beast's flanks. With a deep breath, he straightened and allowed his body to relax. The throbbing in his shoulder subsided to a dull ache and he opened his eyes, amazed by how much ground they'd covered.

'Well done, Manfred!' James shouted, his excitement echoing off the nearby hills. He laughed hard for a long time, the thrill of the ride charging him like St Elmo's fire. He'd experienced the same feeling once before during a hurricane off Barbados when he'd manned the helm after the rigging broke loose and knocked out the helmsman.

'Now I see why your mistress enjoys riding you. Perhaps there is some excitement in the country after all.' Still laughing, he slapped Manfred on the neck. 'Come, let's return to your lady. I think she'll be surprised.'

The horse's ears twitched and the animal settled into a challenging but manageable trot. They returned to the paddock, greeted by the cheers and shouts of the gathered crowd. Word of his daring ride must have spread among the servants for there were double the number of grooms and stable hands than before and James noticed a fair bit of blunt changing hands. Even George caught a coin flipped up from John. It wasn't the first time James had found himself the subject of a wager, but today it held a certain triumph intensified by Miss Howard's impressed eyes.

She stood away from the others in the shade of the stable, clapping her gloved hands in congratulations.

He manoeuvred Manfred next to her, clucking him to a stop. 'An enjoyable beast, Artemis. No trouble at all.'

With an impish smile, she tapped his right hand with her riding crop. 'Then perhaps you should loosen your grip.'

Releasing his tight hold, he knew she'd caught him out, but he didn't mind. Having controlled the horse and proven his mettle made the experience worth the agony he'd surly endure tonight.

Manfred snorted, stepping back and forth. 'Whoa,' James soothed, calming him with a quick tug of the reins.

'Jim, if you're done playing with Manfred, then let's be off,' George joked, guiding Percy towards the bridle path. Simon's gelding fell into step behind Percy, much to its rider's visible displeasure.

James nodded at Miss Howard, who curtsied in return, her upturned face and playful smile calling to him. He wanted to pull her up behind him, dash off across the countryside with her clinging to his back, the two of them alone together. Unfortunately, such daydreams were better left to poetry and he kicked Manfred into a walk, directing him next to Percy.

'Never thought I'd see the day when anyone but Julia or Paul took Manfred's reins,' George said, impressed.

'I still can't believe the woman rides this beast.' Manfred tensed as if intending to rear, forcing James to concentrate on the animal beneath him. This would be no leisure ride for the horse would throw him if James ever let his control wane. No, he had to keep working Manfred to make him behave.

'I'm surprised to see you taking such a risk.'

'So am I,' James admitted, feeling something more than pain, bitterness and anger for the first time in months. He was careful not to revel too much in the feeling, knowing it might not last.

George led them along a path circling the woods, past newly planted fields and pastures full of grazing sheep. A wide valley stretched out around them. Beyond it, woods surrounded by neat rows of well-ploughed fields extended up into the hills. Labourers worked while the overseers stood nearby giving directions.

'They rotate the four fields to get a better crop. Julia introduced the idea after reading about it.' George turned in his saddle to face Simon, who'd fallen behind. 'You could learn a lot from Julia, Simon.'

'I doubt it.' Simon hunched over in the saddle, shielding his eyes from the morning sun. 'I have no interest in riding further.' He turned his horse around and cantered off to the stables.

George moved to recall him, but James stopped him. 'Let him go. Looks like he's been in his cups all night.'

'You don't know the half of it.'

'Why not put a stop to it, or speak to your brother about ending it?'

'If Simon wants to ruin himself, so be it.'

'What about Miss Taylor? Shame to let him drag her down.'

'She has a small inheritance from her mother and will probably catch some poor fool with a sizeable income.'

'I hardly call myself a fool.' James puffed up with mock indignation.

'You aren't for her.' George scowled.

They rode for some time, George relaying London gossip as they crossed meadows, streams and fields. James listened to George's tales with half an ear, enjoying the crisp air and the steady gait of the horse. A few wispy clouds hung in the sky, which shone a rich shade of blue like many he'd seen during still days at sea. The chill of autumn filled the air, but it wasn't sharp or biting, and James hoped the winter cold would come late this year. After spending so much time in the dirty air of London, he craved more days like this.

'We're on Cable Grange land now,' George announced after they'd ridden a good distance.

James took in the sudden change in the landscape. The topography was the same, but the meadows showed the lack of the prosperity so evident at Knollwood. Thin, ragged sheep grazed in the meadows while the fields, many of which should have been well ploughed, stood fallow and full of weeds.

They moved from the small path to a wide country lane. The road split, one branch winding down the hill, the other sloping up to the iron gates of Cable Grange. Stopping at the fork afforded them a view of the rutted and muddy drive leading up to the main house. Even from this distance the neglect was evident in the dingy grey capstones, dirty windows and ivy-choked walls.

'Quite a difference,' James remarked.

'No revenge you could have exacted would have done what they've done to themselves.'

James didn't answer. He'd expected to find satisfaction in seeing Melinda's ruined estate. Instead he felt a certain pity for her, the emotion taking him by surprise. Maybe George was right. Perhaps the past didn't matter now.

'Let's go before someone sees us.' George turned Percy around and James followed. They had started down the road when a curricle came over the hill, slowing as it approached. James's stomach tightened at the sight of the driver and his female companion.

'Well, well, well, now of all times James Covington gets on his high horse to pay me a visit,' Wilkins sneered from his seat, taking in James and Manfred. Rowan still possessed the greasy features of a scoundrel and his dark hair, cut short, failed to enhance his thin face or hide the hard lines under his red eyes. As with his wife, London living had taken its toll. 'Here to kick me while I'm down?'

'You brought this on yourself, Wilkins.'

'Still the moralist. You'd think killing all those foreign soldiers might have taken it out of you. But I suppose you didn't come to see me.'

'No, he's not so hard-hearted, Rowan, though he's not above bragging,' Melinda answered with a sweet smile that turned James's stomach. 'He's come to flash his blunt at the auction, show me what I missed out on all those years ago.'

'Shut up, you. We're not going anywhere,' Rowan spat.

'Of course we aren't.' Melinda laughed, then blew James a kiss. 'Have a lovely ride.'

Rowan flicked the reins, setting the curricle into motion. It tore down the drive, pitching when the wheel caught a rut before righting itself.

'Now you've seen it, do you still want it?' George asked.

'Yes.' Memories of a summer in Portsmouth twelve years ago when he'd loved a woman and she'd thrown him over for lack of a fortune taunted him. He'd been a fool to lose his heart to someone like her. Studying the crumbling stone walls and overgrown fields, he knew her decaying life should vindicate him, but he wasn't cruel enough to delight in her misery, only his own.

'It won't suit you,' George said.

'What won't?'

'The peace of the country. It'll do for a time, but eventually you'll need more adventure than just what crops to plant and when.'

'I'm done with adventure.'

'Says the man riding Manfred.' George laughed, turning Percy around.

The desire to return to sea hit him with the force of a hurricane. He craved the peace of the ocean, the gentle roll and pitch of the ship, his only concerns their position and the strength of the wind. Feeling under his jacket for the scar, bitter bile rose up in his throat, choking out everything except the throbbing in his shoulder before he forced it down. He would not let anger and longing torment him. No, he would command his feelings like he'd commanded his crew, setting a course and not allowing the fickle winds of emotion to drive him about. The sea was no longer his life and there was no use pining for it.

The small china clock on the mantel chimed the noon hour. Julia sat at her dressing table, knowing there was no way to avoid nuncheon today. Mary stood behind her, arranging her hair into a simple style. Out of the bedroom window, Julia watched Uncle George and Captain Covington ride across the meadow towards the stables.

'Are you all right, miss?' Mary asked, hearing Julia sigh.

'Yes, thank you.' *I'm having my hair done while the*

captain is riding Manfred. This would be her perma-
nent lot if Charles and Emily had their way.

Mary hummed a soft tune while she worked and Julia's mind drifted back to the stables and Captain Covington. She hated to admit it, but he was dashing atop
Manfred. She'd almost taken John's wager that the captain would be thrown, but the captain's tenacious eyes
matched with the steady, fluid way he pulled himself
into the saddle made her hold on to her coin. His daring reminded her of Paul, but he possessed a seriousness and maturity her brother lacked. Unlike Charles's
self-imposed austerity, the captain's seemed more con-
templative, as if something weighed on him. It only appeared in small flashes when he thought no one was
looking, but she'd seen it more than once. Whatever it
was, it failed to dampen his deep humour. She enjoyed
his wit, even if she was jealous of his ability to act and
display his talents without fear of rebuke. How often
was she able to display hers?

'What do you think, miss?' Mary asked.

Julia examined herself in the mirror. The hairstyle
was simple, but not fashionable, and the white muslin
dress with the pink check obscured all hint of her figure. Even with the promise of money, dressing like a
frump would not help Simon imagine her decorating
his arm at a London ball. She might not want to marry
him, but she had to make him believe her suitable for
society or he'd never make an offer.

'Mary, please bring down my London dresses from
the attic,' Julia instructed. The gowns were no longer
the height of fashion, but they'd suit her better than her
current attire.

Mary's stunned eyes met Julia's in the mirror before the older servant caught herself and dipped a quick curtsy. 'Yes, Miss Howard.'

James watched Miss Howard enter the dining room, Miss Taylor's idle chatter fading away into the background. She glowed like a white sand beach on a sunny island, the sight of her as welcome as land after a long voyage. She took in the room, briefly meeting his eyes. Her face lit up, making the breath catch in his chest. He leaned forwards in his chair, ready to rise, cross the room and feel her hand on his arm while he led her to her seat. He didn't care who saw them or what they said. Let George rib him; it would be worth the teasing to enjoy the sound of her light voice.

The image shattered when her eager eyes went to Mr Taylor and she took her place next to him. James picked up his ale glass and took a long sip to cover his near move, all the while watching Miss Howard over the rim.

'Simon, did you enjoy your morning ride?' she asked.

'It was far from pleasant.' He picked at the food on his plate, his lips turned up in exaggerated disgust.

Her smile faltered before she bolstered it, but her irritated eyes betrayed her true feelings. James wondered what she was about and why she worked so hard to appeal to the dandy. Perhaps Mrs Howard desired their better acquaintance, though from everything he'd witnessed Miss Howard rarely complied with her sister-in-law's requests.

'Captain Covington,' Miss Taylor interrupted his thoughts. 'I would be happy to paint your portrait.'

'Thank you.' He continued to watch Miss Howard, feeling Miss Taylor's irritation. He tossed her a charming smile, exhausted by the constant effort involved in foiling George's matchmaking plans.

Miss Taylor started to say something and James put down his glass, leaning towards Miss Howard. 'Thank you for allowing me to ride Manfred.'

Miss Howard paused in a comment to Mr Taylor. 'You're welcome.'

'I'd like to ride him again if you don't mind.'

'Of course,' she replied off-handedly, turning back to the fop.

'Tomorrow, perhaps?'

Her perturbed eyes snapped to his. 'Any time you wish.' She returned to Mr Taylor, but James refused to let her go.

'Tell me, how did you come by such a beast?'

'Ah, now there's a story.' George laughed from the end of the table.

Miss Howard forgot her irritation, flashing what James sensed was her first genuine smile of the meal, Mr Taylor forgotten. 'It's Uncle George's fault. He bought Manfred in London.'

'I had a mind to breed warhorses when I first left the Navy,' George added between bits of meat. 'He's a Friesland and who knows what else, but steady as a rock around gunshot.'

'Certainly explains his colour and height,' James remarked. 'But how did you end up with him, Miss Howard?'

'Manfred may be steady as a rock, but he has a temper.'

'Horse dealer failed to mention it,' George admitted.

'The price alone should have made you wary,' she chided.

'Horse dealer did seem awfully eager to be rid of him, but it's my own fault. What do I know about horses? I'm a Navy man.'

'And not one to think through any scheme.' James laughed.

'Perhaps there's some truth to it.' George clapped his hands together. 'Well, none of my men could control him, and after a fortnight I had a mind to put him out to pasture.'

'But this time, he asked my opinion first. I observed Manfred with the grooms and something about him just called to me. Uncle George's men were trying to make him behave, but they were going about it all wrong. Manfred needed a patient hand and a gentle but strong voice.'

'And you possessed both,' James complimented.

'I suppose I did, but I prefer to think it was because I believed in him when no one else did and he thanked me for it.'

'You may be right.'

Miss Howard smiled and he delighted in the dimples at the corner of her lips. For a moment, there was only the two of them in the room. Her amber eyes met his and he felt their heat deep in his body, but the moment was short lived.

'How wonderful you're such an amazing horsewoman,' Miss Taylor interrupted. 'Are you also a skilled painter?'

'I'm adept at no art except running an estate,' Miss Howard admitted with confidence and James silently cheered her for standing up to the ridiculous criticism.

'Yes, I forgot. I plan to draw in the garden this afternoon. I've asked the captain to accompany me. He even volunteered to carry my easel for it can be such a cumbersome thing.' She smiled at James, who shifted in his seat, having forgotten about his offer and wondering how he could extricate himself from it without being rude.

'I think some time outside would do us all a world of good,' Emily announced, trapping James in this bland game.

Half an hour later found everyone in the garden enjoying the unusually warm autumn weather. Even Mr Taylor deigned to drag himself outside, much to Miss Howard's visible delight.

James listened in disbelief when she complimented Mr Taylor on his excellent description of his last evening at White's.

What is she after? he wondered. Was she playing him for his money? Surely she knew he had nothing more than the ready extended by his London creditors. James shifted restlessly, hating the way she nodded, enraptured by the pretentious pink's description of a card game. He refused to admit his anger was jealousy, but there it sat, gnawing at him.

Swallowing it back, he watched Miss Taylor arrange Emily and George into a formal pose on the opposite side of the fish pond. Was this really his life now? Garden parties and flattering London chits? He kept glancing at Miss Howard. Here was a woman who would keep life interesting—if only he could tear her away from the damned coxcomb.

'Should I pull my arm in my sleeve?' George joked once Miss Taylor returned to her canvas. 'I may not be as handsome or slender, but I think I might make a good Nelson.'

Everyone laughed except Miss Taylor, who sketched with her charcoal, and Mr Taylor, who took a pinch of snuff from his silver snuffbox with an affected flourish.

'Rather shameful, the Admiral continuing in such a ruined state,' Mr Taylor lisped. 'Hardly speaks well of Britain to have such a specimen leading our Navy.'

James almost leaned over and punched the idiot in his pursed mouth. If they'd been at White's he'd have called him out, but for the ladies' sake he allowed the comment to drop.

Miss Howard, despite her newfound infatuation, refused to let it stand. 'I think it very fitting he continue. It shows weakness in a man not to carry on after an injury, if he can.'

The remark hit James like a cudgel to the chest. 'Do you extend that opinion to all Navy men, or just Admiral Nelson?'

'All Navy men. If every sailor with a cut or scrape retired we'd have no hope of winning any war.' There was no malice in the statement, just a simple declaration. He wondered if George had told her about his wound.

'What of duty to one's family? Is an only son to die at sea for no other reason than to prove he's not a coward, leaving the future of his family to the cruel whims of fate?'

'A man who chooses the Navy knows the dangers. If his family truly faces ruin then perhaps he should apprentice himself and enter a safe trade, such as tailor.'

'What if he comes home wounded to find responsibility for his mother and sister upon his shoulders?' James flexed his left hand, the memory increasing the pain in his shoulder.

'I cannot speak for every man's situation, but if Admiral Nelson soldiers on then so can other brave men.'

'I think you speak a great deal about something you know nothing about,' he chastised, but she refused to back down. He had to admire the girl's courage, despite her infuriating views.

'And I think you, like most men, dislike opinionated women.' She didn't wait for his response, but turned on her heel and strode off.

'Julia, where are you going?' George said, but she didn't stop.

'I have some urgent business to attend to,' she answered over her shoulder, then disappeared inside.

Mr Taylor coughed as he took another pinch of snuff. 'As I said before, bluestockings always get in a man's business.'

James turned a hard eye on the dandy, who wilted under the harsh gaze. He had a mind to thrash the man, but even with his weak arm it wouldn't be a fair fight. Instead, he decided to enjoy the fine afternoon and have his portrait done as a Christmas present for his sister. He leaned over Miss Taylor's shoulder to admire her sketch, but, unable to keep still, he began pacing, chewing over Miss Howard's remark.

Had she just called him a coward? Did she even know about his injury? Maybe George hadn't told her. Despite George's love of gossip, he had an annoying habit of conveying worthless stories while forgetting to relay critical information, such as Melinda living next door or just how close Miss Howard was to Paul. It was a wonder George had thought to tell him about Cable Grange before the actual sale took place.

'What do you think, Captain?' Miss Taylor asked.

He paused long enough to watch her apply the first colour to the sketch. 'Excellent portrait.'

Why did he care so much about Miss Howard's opinion? It was only the assumption of an ignorant country girl with no real understanding of the world. Let her think him a coward. Once he returned to London, he'd never be troubled with her again.

'Jim, what's wrong? You're acting like a nervous hen,' George called and James finally noticed everyone's curious eyes.

'I just remembered a matter I must attend to.'

'But your portrait,' Miss Taylor protested.

'Another time, perhaps. Please, excuse me.' He bowed, then headed into the house.

Julia scratched out the last line of figures, marring the ledger page with yet another mistake. Outside, Uncle George laughed and her temper flared. Throwing down her pencil, she leaned back in the chair, watching the others laugh and pose for Annette and noticing Captain Covington wasn't with them. After this morning, she'd thought him a different type of man. Just now, he'd proven himself exactly like all other men, dismissing her opinion, then getting angry when she refused to defer to his better judgement. Of all people, he should have supported the logic of the argument, not defended a London fool.

Outside, Simon sat on the garden bench swatting at a fly.

To think my future lies in the hands of such a pathetic specimen. Reluctantly, she closed the ledger and rose. She'd allowed Captain Covington to interfere with capturing the dandy's affection. If she wanted Cable Grange, she had to continue her pursuit and secure a proposal before the auction.

The door clicked open and Captain Covington stepped into the room.

'If you mean to bait me further, please refrain. I'm

in no mood for arguments,' she snapped, tense at the idea of facing him so soon after their disagreement.

'I have no intention of baiting you. I thought I might read. George said you have an excellent book on crop rotation.'

'Crop rotation?' She eyed him suspiciously, doubting his interest in the subject.

'Yes.' He fingered a small wooden figurine on the table near the door.

'It's there, on top.' She pointed to a stack of books on the table next to a large leather chair, then sat back down. Opening the ledger, she expected the captain to thank her and leave, but instead he lingered.

'Do you mind if I browse your other books?'

Julia waved her hand at the bookshelves without looking up from the ledger. 'You're more than welcome to anything in my collection.'

'Thank you.'

He walked along the row of bookshelves, examining the spines, his tension evident by the way he kept tapping the crop book against his hand. Julia tried to ignore him, shaking her head at a miscalculated line of figures. He stopped at the large, coloured atlas on the bookstand, flipping through the pages before marching to stand in front of the desk.

'Do you really think a man is a coward for retiring after being wounded?' He stood before her the way a superior officer stands in front of a line of sailors.

She fixed him with a hard stare, refusing to be cowed. 'I told you I won't be baited.'

'Surely you don't believe it applies to all men?' He walked back and forth across the carpet as though on the deck of a ship, hands behind his back, every inch the Navy officer. 'What if your brother was wounded and forced to resign his commission. Would you call him a coward?'

Julia opened her mouth to answer, but the captain raised his hand, stopping her. Irritation flared, but she forced it back. Shouting at a guest, no matter how rude he might be, was definitely a breach of etiquette.

'What if the man's father died a few years ago and the investments he left to support his wife and daughter failed, leaving his son responsible for his sister's dowry and his widowed mother's affairs?'

The strange conviction in his eyes warned her off meeting the challenge. 'I respectfully decline to answer. We obviously have a difference of opinion so I see no reason to continue the debate.'

'Then you'd insist he return?'

Julia stayed silent, the lingering sadness in his piercing eyes hinting at the truth. Had he been wounded? Is that why he'd resigned? No, it wasn't possible. Running her eyes up the length of him, admiring his trim waist, flat stomach and wide chest, he was too strong to be injured. Surely if he were, Uncle George would have said something. Perhaps he'd lost friends or maybe his father had died in debt? Whatever drove him, it emanated from somewhere deep inside and she knew to tread carefully.

'Each man must decide what is best for him,' she answered in an even voice. 'It's not up to me to make such decisions.'

The tightness in the captain's jaw eased while the feverish hunger to debate faded from his eyes. 'This is quite a room for a young lady,' he remarked, his voice softer, but no less strained than before.

'A great many people have said so,' she agreed, relieved at the fading tension. 'It was my father's. He did his business here. I saw no reason to change it.'

'Do you think your father would approve of you hiding yourself away from the world in here?'

The anger rushed back and she jumped to her feet. 'And where do you hide, Captain?'

'I don't hide.'

'Then why are you here in the country?'

He turned to the window, staring past the garden with a sense of loss she could feel. 'London wearies me.'

'Ghosts have a way of haunting a person to exhaustion,' she observed, more to herself than to Captain Covington. Why else was she so desperate to stay at Knollwood if not to hide? Who outside its walls had ever accepted her or her talents? If she lost Knollwood, she lost her life's meaning for she could see no other. Unless she secured Cable Grange.

'You think I'm haunted?'

'I can't pretend to know the full measure of your mind. I only know everyone has fears.'

'We must face our fears to overcome them.'

'Then neither of us is hiding, are we?' No longer interested in his company or conversation, she made for the door. There was work to do outside, the prospect of which suddenly tired her.

James watched her leave, stunned, the full impact of her accusation striking him. He walked to the large atlas near the window and turned the coloured pages until he came upon the familiar maps of the Atlantic and the Caribbean. With his finger he traced the shipping routes, the miles of ocean once so familiar to him. England to Africa, Africa to Jamaica, Jamaica to America, America to the coast of Spain.

He slammed the book shut. He'd faced pirates, angry colonists, hostile natives and the French. He did not hide from his problems.

'There's one.' James pointed at a duck flying up out of the tall grass along the edge of the lake.

George took aim and fired, but the bird continued its ascent and flew off. 'Missed another one. I think I'd do better with a cannon and grapeshot today.'

'Perhaps,' James concurred, finding little humour in the joke. He'd joined George in the hopes the fine afternoon would take his mind off his shoulder and his irritation. After more than an hour of walking through tall grass or watching the sun reflect off the lake, he still felt tense and plagued by pain.

George handed the empty gun to a waiting footman and took a new one. 'Are you sure you won't shoot?'

'Not after this morning's exertion.' He rolled his shoulder, trying to ease the ache, but it didn't help. No doubt he'd strained it by showing off this morning and it nagged at him as much as Miss Howard's comments in the study.

They picked through the mud and damp of the marshy bank before George aimed at another bird rising from the reeds and fired. The duck crumpled in mid-air, falling with a splash into the lake. A dog bounded past them, flinging itself into the water and swimming excitedly towards the carcass.

'Excellent shot,' James muttered, unable to rouse much enthusiasm.

'What's got you so glum?'

'Nothing.' James stomped off, his boots sinking in the soft dirt, George close on his heels.

'If you say so.'

'Did you tell Julia about my injuries?'

'No.'

'Why not?'

'It's not my place to choose who to tell. That's your decision.'

So she didn't know. It explained her strong opinion, but not her remark about him hiding. 'Would you say I hide from problems?'

'I've never known you to back down from a challenge.'

'But do I hide from them?'

George thought for a moment. 'Other people's or your own?'

'My own, of course.' He didn't like the sound of this last question. 'Miss Howard is under the impression I hide from problems.'

'Do you?'

'Of course not.' George's inability to directly answer led him to believe Miss Howard might be right. 'Though I suppose it depends on the problem.'

George laid his gun over his shoulder and stared at the ground, thinking while he walked. 'Jim, a man goes to sea for a number of reasons. I was a second son, I had to make my way and the Navy appealed to me. You joined to avoid a career in law.'

'You know I had no interest in it.'

'But your mother did.'

'She thought I'd make an excellent barrister. There was quite a row the night I informed her I'd purchased a commission. Mother is very formidable once she sets her mind to something.'

'Yes, I know.' George chuckled.

'How do you know?'

'From everything you've told me, of course,' George

stammered, tugging on the sleeves of his coat. 'So you escaped the law.'

'You could say that.'

'And you accepted my invitation to the country to escape London.'

'I wouldn't say "escape".' James ran his hand over the back of his neck, seeing George's point all too clearly. 'But two instances hardly make me a coward.'

'You're no coward. I've seen you in enough battles to know. But what man doesn't sidestep a problem now and then? I've been known to turn tail a few times myself. Why do you think I never married? But seriously, there's a lot of unpleasant business in life. We deal with it as we can. You and I have seen enough of it in all corners of the world. Julia, she's seen her share here and in London. A brave man faces what he can, but no one has the strength to face it all. You're no coward, but, like all men, you have your weaknesses.'

James flexed his hand, admiring the peaceful green hills of Knollwood rising in the distance. 'Is my weakness so obvious?'

'I wouldn't call it a weakness and I'm amazed Julia mentioned it, though of all people she'd be the first to recognise it.' A suggestive twinkle replaced the pondering thoughtfulness in George's eyes. 'Why do you care what my niece thinks? I thought you had no interest in her?'

The urge to escape suddenly gripped James. 'I don't. I only wondered at what she said, nothing more.'

'Then it's settled. You're no coward and you have no interest in my niece. Now, let's head back. I have business to take care of before dinner.'

James followed George through the high grass to where the horses stood tethered to an old post, his mind far from clear. Why did he care so much about Miss Howard's opinion if he wasn't interested in her? He couldn't lie to himself. She intrigued him with her disregard for convention and her bold, adventurous spirit. However, her interest in Mr Taylor, combined with her disdain for wounded naval officers, infuriated him.

Would she change her opinion if she knew about his shoulder? He flexed his left hand. It was useless to ponder. She had no interest in him and there was no point pursuing such a woman. Besides, Miss Taylor now expected his attention and, despite her annoying simpering, he couldn't be rude.

He mounted Hector, the stallion he'd chosen to ride, and gritted his teeth with the effort of pulling himself into the saddle. Once astride the brown horse, he settled into the seat, his grip light on the reins. The animal was so well trained, it took little but a tap of his foot or pressure from his legs to control it. With such an easy horse beneath him, he couldn't resist the solitude and freedom of wide open fields.

'You go back to the house. I'm going for a ride.'

'I think a storm is coming in.' George pointed at the dark clouds hovering on the horizon.

'It doesn't matter.' James dug his heels into the stallion's sides and the animal tore off over the grassy field.

Julia hurried across the paddock, the wind playing with the bottom of her habit and scattering leaves across the path. She'd made absolutely no progress with Simon. The minute she'd returned to the garden, he'd pleaded a headache and went to his room to lie down. Emily then cornered her with an impromptu drawing lesson from Annette. It resulted in nothing but a mangled green blob meant to resemble a tree and the urge to dump the paints in her sister-in-law's lap.

Thankfully, baby Thomas's nurse appeared with the crying infant, freeing Julia from Emily's attempts at female education. Pleading the same headache as Simon, Julia fled to the quiet of her room to read. However, with the weather holding and the daylight fading, she knew this would be her only chance for a ride before dinner.

'Good afternoon, Miss Howard,' John greeted, brushing down one of the horses.

'Saddle Manfred,' Julia called out, hurrying past him down the line of stalls. 'Use the standard one.'

'Yes, Miss Howard.'

While John went to work, Julia slipped into the small closet at the back of the stable. Pushing the lid off the large chest on the floor, she pulled out the horse blankets to reveal an oilcloth-wrapped bundle. Untying it, she lifted out the special riding habit crafted of dark-blue wool. Removing her regular habit, she donned the other garment. When walking it hung like a skirt, but the excess fabric hid the trouser-like design sewn into the dress. Julia had paid John's wife to sew it and for a tidy profit she also kept it laundered and mended.

Once dressed, she grabbed *The Monk* from the regular habit's pocket and hurried to where John stood holding Manfred.

'Watch the clouds,' John advised, helping her up into the saddle. 'You don't want to be caught out in a storm.'

'I'll be careful.' Julia kicked Manfred into a steady gallop, directing him east.

They followed the valley down to a small brook and across a crude wooden bridge constructed to herd sheep back from pasture. The land on the other side flattened out, leading to another higher hill visible in the distance. Julia pointed Manfred at it and horse and rider moved seamlessly past a large lake, another small forest, and through a herd of sheep scurrying to make way for them.

During afternoon rides, Julia and Manfred usually ambled so she could take in the condition of the sheep, the walls, the fences, the height of the river, all the things so important to running the estate. Today she had no interest in business, only the desire to be alone.

They approached the next hill and she slowed Manfred to a walk, guiding him up the rocky path to the stone keep commanding the top. It was a Norman relic, abandoned ages ago by men who no longer mattered. She loved coming here for its lichen-covered stone walls offered a solitude she sometimes failed to find at Knollwood. Guiding Manfred alongside a large stone wedged into the ground, she slid off his back, her boots gripping the coarse surface. Pulling *The Monk* from her pocket, she tossed the reins up over his back, leaving him free to graze on the sweet grass covering the ancient site. He never wandered far and she was safe to steal an hour alone among the ruins.

Inside the old tower, she picked her way up the narrow stone staircase, her left hand clutching the book, her right hand tracing the wall as it rose up towards the battlements. At the top, she stepped out on to the last of the rampart, taking in the view of Knollwood and some of Creedon Abbey. Thick, menacing clouds covered the horizon while birds criss-crossed her view, arching and rolling as they chased each other.

A small alcove in the stones sheltered her from the wind and she settled in with her book, tucking the length of the riding habit about her legs for warmth.

She opened *The Monk* and began to read, the sound of Manfred's whinny mingling with the warble of birds and the whistles of the wind through the grass. She devoured the descriptions of far-off places she'd probably never see, and frustration plagued her, subtly at first, but growing stronger with each new line. She snapped the book shut and tilted her head back to look at the sky, breathing in the heavy smell of rain and noting the dark clouds floating overhead. Today, her future seemed dim and bleak, the chances of obtaining her inheritance in time to purchase Cable Grange an impossible feat. What future could she hope for without her own estate? Perhaps she could live with Paul and keep house for him? Even then she wouldn't be free, but tethered to the whims and demands of Navy life and open to the gossip of vicious people who would wonder why she wasn't married.

Why is everyone so concerned with what I do? she thought, picking a piece of moss off the wall. She'd never crossed the lines of propriety and in public she always acted like a proper young lady, even if she did occasionally wear her riding habit to town. Yes, she preferred riding to the pianoforte, but Father had always encouraged the exercise and besides, every unconventional thing she did was always done among family who understood her. Or did they? Obviously Charles and Emily didn't. No, in their minds she was a veritable Jezebel for riding without a groom or preferring the business of an estate to the latest fashions. They were more concerned with the opinion of the few local families who laughed at Julia's strange habits, but dismissed them as nothing more than eccentricities. After all, her father and mother were, in their own ways, eccentric. Why should Julia be any different?

A hawk screeched and she watched the bird float on the up draught, searching the field for prey. If only she could be more conventional and refined like the other young ladies in the county. How many times had she tried and failed? After all, she couldn't spend days painting screens when the entire fortune of an estate rested on her shoulders.

The hoofbeats of an approaching horse echoed through the keep.

Am I never to have a moment's peace? she fumed, peering over the battlement and spying Captain Covington approaching. Ducking down behind the stone, she cursed her luck. Of all the people to happen upon her, did it have to be him?

'Manfred? Where's Miss Howard?' he asked in an anxious voice.

She thought of staying hidden, but she didn't want him to worry. Gripping the rough wall, she pulled herself into view. 'I'm here.'

He looked up at her, his dark hair falling back off of his forehead. Her heart skipped a beat at the sight of him atop the chestnut stallion. Dressed in the same hunting clothes he'd worn in the forest, their brown tones warmed his face and softened the line of his jaw. For a brief moment she wished she could draw so she could capture the way the greying light caressed his features.

'What a relief. When I saw him alone, I thought something had happened.' He rose up in the saddle to dismount.

'Stop there,' Julia demanded. 'If you're as contentious as you were at nuncheon, then leave now. I've had enough of irritable people for one day.'

Instead of sitting, he swung his leg over the horse and dropped to the ground. 'You're a very direct young lady.'

'And quite serious.' She crossed her arms over her chest.

'I promise to be pleasant and cheerful.' He placed his hand on his heart, bowing deferentially, then snapping up into a formal military stance. 'Permission to come aboard.'

The stories she'd heard about him demanded a refusal, but they also fuelled her curiosity. If nothing else, here was her chance to discover the truth behind Uncle George's tales. Emily would faint if she discovered them alone, but if the captain kept this meeting a secret, then what was the harm in conversing? 'Granted. Tie Hector to the post.' She pointed at the ruins of an old fence near the keep's entrance.

He wrapped the horse's reins around the mouldering wood, then made his way inside, taking the stairs two at a time before stepping out on to the rampart. Julia admired the steady, sure way he crossed the ledge.

'I'm surprised to find you here,' he remarked.

'I often come here to be alone.'

'Then I apologise for intruding on your solitude.'

'It does not matter.' Julia leaned against the short wall, admiring the view and struggling to appear indifferent despite the strange nervousness creeping through her. The captain leaned next to her, resting his elbows on the stones, the nearness of him making her jittery excitement worse.

'This is an impressive place.' His eyes scanned the landscape and for the first time she noticed the small lines about his mouth.

'Indeed.' She moved closer into his circle of warmth

and for a brief moment considered slipping into the crook of his body, out of the wind and damp air.

'Are all Uncle George's stories true?' she asked, eager to break the awkward silence and distract herself from Captain Covington's warm body.

'What do you know?'

'I know about his liaison with the plantation owner's wife, the rum running and your dalliance with the governor's sister.'

Captain Covington threw back his head and laughed. 'Yes, it's all true and then some, for I doubt he told you everything.'

'He told me enough. You have quite a reputation, Captain.'

'Me? No, I take no responsibility. It was all George's doing.'

'Including the governor's sister?'

The corners of his lips pulled up. 'I assure you, the story was exaggerated.'

'Why didn't you marry her?'

He sobered, but not enough to remove the wicked smile. 'We were not suited for marriage. Nor was the lady inclined. It seemed she'd had enough of husbands and very much liked her freedom.'

For a moment Julia envied the woman, especially her intimacy with the captain. What she wouldn't give to have such control over her life and enjoy someone like him without censure. 'What of your other adventures with Uncle George?' she asked, trying to distract her wandering mind.

'Some were true. I leave it to you to discover which ones.'

'Then you admit you went along.'

'Only to keep a very good friend out of trouble.'

'And to make a bit of profit.'

'In that regard I am guilty.'

'I envy your grand adventures.'

'Do not envy them. They weren't all grand.' He straightened, rubbing his left shoulder, a scowl darkening his features.

A gust of wind hit the keep, pulling a strand of Julia's hair loose. Tucking it behind her ear, she noticed the thickening clouds moving faster across the sky. It was time to ride back, but she wasn't ready to leave. Emily would scold her if they got caught in the rain, but she no longer cared. What did any of it matter—propriety, etiquette—if one were always confined to this small corner of the world? Julia sighed and the captain turned a curious eye on her.

'Something troubles you?'

She shook her head, wondering how much to confide in him. In many ways he reminded her of Uncle George or Paul, of someone who would listen without judgement. But for all his resemblances, he was still a stranger. 'I wish I could be more like Annette,' she admitted, throwing convention to the wind.

'Do not envy her. She has nothing you don't possess.'

'Except perfect manners.'

'Your manners are not so very imperfect.'

'But they're not polished enough for my brother or Emily or most of the countryside.' She picked a small stone off the ledge and hurled it over the edge. It arched in the air before dropping to the grass with a soft thud. 'I don't shun propriety, Captain. I do my best to follow Emily's suggestions, only—'

'—they're always at odds with your nature.'

Yes, he was very much like Paul and Uncle George. 'It was different when Father was alive. He didn't mind if I wore the wrong dress or went riding alone in the mornings.'

'And your mother?'

'She's quite content with her roses and Charlemagne. She loves me, but doesn't fret like Charles and Emily. They don't realise how much I try to behave. They think I'm like Paul and being contrary for the sake of being contrary. Charles believes because it's so easy for him to be proper that it's easy for everyone. He's turned into a dreadful, puritan bore.'

'I wouldn't call Charles a puritan,' the captain snorted.

'What do you mean?' What did he know about Charles that she didn't?

'Nothing. I was only thinking of your brother Paul. I'm sorry if I confused the two.'

'Oh, yes, well, Paul certainly doesn't follow convention. But he's a man and allowed to do as he pleases.' She turned back to the view, her world suddenly feeling small. 'Paul is out there having adventures and Charles is in London, making great speeches and deciding my future.'

'No one decides your future unless you let them.'

'Those are the words of a man who can make his own choices and live as he pleases.' She reached back, tucking the waving strand of hair into the loose bun.

'Men don't always live as they please. Sometimes they live as they must,' he responded with some resignation.

'Even then you have choices,' she encouraged, willing him to be strong. If a man like him gave in to fate, what chance did she have?

He moved to object before his lips spread into a

smile. 'You don't strike me as a young lady resigned to someone else deciding her future.'

She picked at the stone wall. 'Perhaps, but for the moment, here I am.'

James watched her work loose a pebble, her face bereft of a smile. No, she was not a woman to give up, no matter what she might say. She would continue to strive, to struggle, to fight for what she wanted. 'Where would you be if you could be somewhere else?'

'India. Paul gave me a book about it once. It seems so magical. Have you been to India?'

'Once, a long time ago.'

'Was it magical?'

He turned to her, admiring the excitement of youth and innocence reflected in her eyes. While he pined for what he'd lost, she waited to hear about what she might never experience. Suddenly his sadness seemed self-indulgent, giving him a new appreciation for his past. 'Yes, it was. Blazing white palaces crowded with men and women in dazzling colours. The air so thick with curry and moisture, you feel as though you could slice it with a sword.'

'Paul brought me curry powder once. I gave it to cook and she didn't know what to do with it. She put it in the chicken and the house reeked of it for days. It's like nothing I've smelled or tasted before. Would you go there again?'

He watched a pair of deer race through the high grass before disappearing into a thick clump of trees. Would he go back? There was nothing to stop him. He could go there and a hundred other places he longed to see. He thought of Paris, Vienna and Venice and for a moment pictured himself walking through the ancient city, Miss

Howard by his side. The image startled him though it wasn't an entirely unpleasant idea. 'Yes, I would.'

'I wish I could go.' The wind pulled a small curl across her cheek.

'Perhaps some day you will.' He tucked the strand of hair behind her ear, allowing his fingers to linger at the nape of her neck. She didn't pull away. Instead her eyes held his with nervous anticipation. He stepped closer and her head tilted up invitingly. He felt her rapid pulse through the warm skin beneath his fingertips and was close to claiming her soft, parted lips when a loud clap of thunder broke overhead.

A sudden gust of wind pungent with rain swept past them, ruffling the skirt of her habit.

She stepped away from him, an awkward blush colouring her cheeks. 'We'd better get back before it rains.'

He didn't want to leave, but he couldn't object. Staying alone together here was dangerous and he possessed no desire to expose her to vicious gossip or her sister-in-law's criticism. To compromise her in such a way would only confirm Julia's previous suspicions about him and he very much wanted her good opinion.

Julia followed the captain down the stone steps, watching his broad shoulders lead the way through the tower's deep shadows. He'd almost kissed her. She'd almost allowed him to kiss her. She stopped in the middle of the staircase, fear gripping her. How could she have been so weak? It was unlike her to lose her head over a gentleman, especially one with questionable intentions.

At the bottom he hopped off the last step, turning to help her down. 'Is something wrong?'

'No, not at all.' She hurried down the stairs, taking his offered hand and allowing him to help her. She delighted once again in the feel of it, the strength and warmth. Their eyes met as a bolt of lightning cracked overhead followed by a deep roll of thunder.

'We'd better hurry.' He pulled her towards the horses.

Julia grabbed Manfred's reins and led him next to the large stone. She saw the captain's surprise when she threw her leg over Manfred's back, revealing the trousers in the riding habit.

'Very clever.'

'Please don't tell Emily.'

'Your secret is safe with me.' He winked, then swung into the saddle, pain flashing across his face before he settled his feet in the stirrups.

She was about to ask if he felt well when another heavy blast of wind hit them, flattening the tall grass and scattering bits of earth and leaves.

'Do you think we can outrun the storm?' he called over the gust.

'I think we should try.' Digging her heels into Manfred's flanks, she shot off down the hill. In seconds the captain was next to her, leaning over Hector's neck, spurring him on. Remembering the way he'd ridden this morning, she pushed them hard, guiding them around trees and boulders and over the crest of hills. She avoided the hedges, not knowing the captain's capacity for jumping, but she couldn't resist leaping the small gully. Though Hector was no match for Manfred, the captain never let up or veered off course. He urged the stallion up and over the rushing water, meeting her on the other side, his wide smile revealing his excitement. Her heart skipped a beat at the sight of his exuberant face and she kicked Manfred back into a gallop. The captain followed, his body matching Hector's gait with satyr-like fluidity.

The horses were fast, but the storm moved faster. She could have ridden for ever with the captain, but the icy rain fell hard, pouring down her hair and soaking her back. With visibility declining, she guided them on to a wide country lane. Racing around a bend in the road, the horse's hooves kicked up mud from the deep puddles, the rain matting their manes against their necks. The captain's speed did not waver as he kept pace with her. Water dripped from his chin and his keen eyes watched the road, at intervals meeting hers with an intensity as highly charged as the lightning.

The glowing windows of Knollwood came into view through the deluge and the captain followed Julia down away from the house to the stables. She pulled Manfred to a halt in the yard, the captain drawing Hector up alongside them. She breathed hard, every inch of her wet, her fingers aching with cold, but she didn't care. The exhilarating ride warmed her, as did the captain's blazing eyes. Large drops of water dripped off the wet hair matted against his forehead, sliding down his cheeks, tracing the fine sinew of his neck before disappearing beneath his collar. His charging pulse beat against the exposed skin, echoing the steady rhythm in her chest. She wrapped the reins around her fingers as he leaned hard on one hand, tilting towards her and she leaned closer, noticing the small beads of water sticking to his eyelashes. He was exactly as she'd imagined him in her dream about the monsoon, his chest rising and falling with each deep breath.

The wind cut a sharp line through them and Julia shivered.

'We'd better get inside,' the captain yelled over the pounding rain. Julia nodded, water running into her eyes as she walked Manfred into the warmth of the stable.

'I'm glad to see you back. I was getting worried.' John rushed to take Manfred's reins and help her down.

'I'll only be a moment,' she called to the captain, then slipped into the small room. Stripping off her soaked riding habit, she hung it on a hook, knowing John's wife would see to its cleaning like she always did. She wrung out the bottom of her chemise then pulled the dry habit over her damp stays and hurried out of the room to where Captain Covington waited by the open stable door. Water dripped from his coat, pooling on the hard-packed dirt.

'Should we wait it out?' he asked, pushing the wet hair off his face. The rain fell in thick sheets on the paddock with no sign of letting up.

'No. Wet or dry, I'm sure to receive a tongue lashing for this.'

'Then we'd better hurry. The sooner it begins the sooner it may end. After you.'

She ran past him into the downpour and in two large strides he was next to her. They rushed up the small hill, but she stumbled, her boot sticking in the mud. He grabbed her by the elbow, pulling her free and into the grove of trees. Lightning split the sky and the air crackled with electricity, the deep roll of thunder vibrating in Julia's chest.

'Perhaps we should go back to the stable until it passes,' the captain suggested, pulling her closer, his hand protectively on her arm.

Julia gauged the distance between the house and the stable, seeing no safe, clear path in either direction. 'No, we're halfway there. We might as well keep going.'

'Come along, then. I have no desire to be struck by

lightning.' He slipped his hand in hers and pulled her out of the trees. She hung on tight, his strength soothing some of her fear during their mad dash over the gravel path and up the back portico.

Another lightning bolt cracked overhead as the captain closed the French door behind them. He followed Julia laughing and dripping into the hall at the front of the house, wet footprints trailing them across the stone floor.

'Maybe we should have stayed in the stable.' Julia smiled, shaking the water off her skirt.

'No. I enjoyed our adventure, even if I won't dry out for a week,' he laughed, wiping his hands on his soaked trousers.

'Julia, Captain Covington.' Emily's voice echoed off the walls. Julia whirled around to see her standing at the top of the stairs, her delicate face red and her pale eyes dark. 'What is the meaning of this?'

'We were caught in the rain.' Julia shifted from foot to foot, her stockings squishing in her half-boots.

'Forgive me, Mrs Howard. It was my fault. I allowed Miss Howard to dally on our ride and the storm came upon us faster than we anticipated.'

'And was the groom with you? No, he wasn't because John came to the house looking for Julia after it started to rain,' Emily answered before he could. 'He was worried about her—we all were.'

Emily flew down the stairs, her stern face fixed on the captain. 'Such behaviour from Julia does not surprise me. She is young and not well versed in the ways of the world, but not from you, Captain. If you wish to remain in my house, I insist you behave like a gentleman.'

'My apologies, Mrs Howard. It was not my intention to offend you or place your sister-in-law's reputation at risk.'

'I certainly hope not. Now come along, Julia.'

Julia resisted the urge to unleash a torrent of words as Emily hustled her up the stairs and into her room. Inside, her mother sat on the small sofa by the window, petting Charlemagne, a slight smile raising the corners of her mouth.

'How dare you speak to the captain like that, or me? How dare you make such accusations?' Julia said sharply.

'Don't you see how compromising such behaviour is? To be out alone with a man who knows where doing who knows what.'

'Out riding and doing nothing. Why do you and Charles always believe the worst of me? What have I done to make you think I might do anything compromising?'

Emily twisted her hands in front of her, some of her anger fading. 'Even a young woman of solid character may slip and cause herself a great deal of grief.' From the adjoining dressing room, baby Thomas let out a wail, nearly drowning out the nurse's soothing coos. 'Besides, your mother was worried about you.'

Her mother stopped petting Charlemagne, shocked to find herself pulled into the conversation. 'No, my dear, I was not worried for this is not the first time you've been caught out in the rain.'

Emily stared at her mother-in-law in frustration. 'She was alone with a gentleman.'

Mother rose, tucking Charlemagne under her arm. 'As I said, I was not concerned.' She left, closing the door behind her.

'See, it is only your own fear playing on you.'

Emily placed her hands on Julia's shoulders, her face softer than before. 'I am only trying to help. Others will speak badly of you if they witness such behaviour.'

'You're the only one talking now.'

'But think of the Taylors. What would they say?'

'I don't care what they think and I'm tired of enduring Annette's foolishness.'

'Please try to be more cordial to her. There are things concerning the Taylors of which you are not aware and they may have a direct impact on Annette's current mood. She can be a very sweet young lady.'

Julia crossed her arms with a disbelieving huff. 'Annette constantly derides me, points out my faults to all and yet you describe her as sweet. I do nothing and you treat me like the whore of Daringford.'

Emily pinched the bridge of her nose, the dark circles under her eyes made deeper by the candlelight. Julia knew Emily was tired from nursing Thomas through the night in keeping with Rousseau's ideals and Charles's instructions, but at the moment she had no sympathy for her sister-in-law. 'You must learn to get along with people. Life is not all deferential servants and friendly tenant farmers.'

'Of this you and the Taylors have made me very aware,' Julia fumed through clenched teeth, barely able to stand still with the anger coursing through her.

'Forgive me. I was not clear.'

'No, I understand perfectly,' she seethed, balling her fists at her sides. 'Despite everything I've done and can do, you two are ashamed of me. I'll have no peace until I become a simpering wet goose or marry and leave. Why not simply send me to Paul, then you might never be bothered with such an embarrassing sister?'

'Julia, please…'

'No, I've heard quite enough for one day.' She left, afraid of what she might say if she stayed longer.

Once in her room, her hands shook so hard with anger she could not undo the buttons on her habit without Mary's help.

'You are soaked through, miss,' the maid giggled, dropping the soggy garment in a large china bowl along with her wet hose and gloves.

'I'm quite aware of my current state of wetness.' Julia bristled, then instantly regretted it. 'I'm sorry, Mary. I don't mean to be cross.'

'It's all right, miss.' Mary smiled, lacing the dry stays, then helping Julia into an afternoon dress. 'An exciting run with a man like the captain would be enough to send any woman into a state.'

'I wish it was the captain who'd put me in such a state,' she let slip, then caught herself as Mary shot her a knowing glance. Snatching the towel from the washstand, Julia rubbed her soaking hair, eager to do anything to relieve her agitation. 'That will be all, Mary.'

Mary curtsied, then left. Julia threw down the towel and braided her hair, fastening it with a ribbon at the base of her neck.

How could Emily say such a thing to me and the captain? She flipped the braid over her shoulder and, determined to put the incident from her mind, headed for the study, craving the solace.

Once inside, she took a deep breath, hoping to gain some measure of calm from the familiar surroundings, but for once not even this comfortable place made her feel better. The fire had been allowed to burn out, taking with it all remaining warmth and leaving only the ashen tones of the rain-drenched light from outside. It made the room cold, the books heartless, the large mahogany desk uncaring. Despite the chill, she loved it all, but it wasn't hers, as Emily had made abundantly clear.

'Her house,' Julia snorted. Emily might be Charles's wife, but since her arrival she'd never lifted a finger to do more than arrange dinners or fuss over Thomas. The urge to march upstairs and hand the accounts to Emily was overwhelming. Let her manage the estate if she was so quick to call it her own. Instead Julia sat down at the desk and took the pencil in her shaking fingers. If nothing else, she still loved Knollwood and owed it to Father to keep it prosperous.

Lightning lit the room and a hard wind drove the rain against the window. Julia watched the heavy drops bounce off the stone patio. Her thoughts wandered back to the captain and their mad dash across the garden. Was this the kind of life he offered? Turning a rainstorm into an adventure, a ride into an energetic race? Chewing the end of the pencil, she remembered his face when he'd leaned close to her at the keep, the way his fingers brushed her neck sending chills of excitement racing along her skin. She'd wanted him to kiss her, to taste him, to give in to the urges swirling inside her. It might be worth compromising herself to live in such a daring way.

No, a man like the captain might make her forget herself, but he'd also make her regret it.

Tapping the pencil against the desk, she debated calling a footman to relight the fire, then decided against it. She didn't feel like being alone. On rainy days when he was with them, Uncle George usually played billiards in the library with a warm fire and a glass of port. She hesitated, knowing Captain Covington would be with him. The thought of his company appealed to her as did the desire to spite Emily, though it would hardly be spite with Uncle George playing the chaperon.

'I wondered when you'd join us,' Uncle George greeted when she stepped into the library, the crackling fire and friendly faces a welcome contrast to the lonely study. 'Will you play?'

She caught the captain's eye. He offered an apologetic smile before disappearing into a glass of port.

Julia shook her head. 'No, finish your game. I'll join the next one.'

'She's quite the player, Jim. Takes after me.' George leaned over the table, taking aim at the red ball and striking it with the cue ball.

'She also has your spirit of adventure.' The captain strolled to the scoreboard standing near the fireplace behind her. 'I'm sorry to have caused you trouble,' he whispered, sliding a tally along the line.

She ran her fingers over the smooth-wooded side of the billiard table. 'It's not your fault. Emily has a great concern for propriety.'

'Which is surprising considering,' Uncle George commented, sipping his port as James took his shot.

'Considering what?' Julia asked.

George turned a strange shade of pink, then pulled on the sleeves of his jacket. 'Nothing.'

'Tell me. You know you can't keep a secret.'

'Of course I can keep a secret.'

'No, you can't.'

'Name one secret I've failed to keep.' Uncle George leaned over the table, practising before he took his turn.

'Only one?'

'One will do, thank you.'

Julia thought a moment, studying the wood-beam

ceiling, debating whether to reveal a certain scandal-ous and unladylike bit of knowledge. With Emily's re-buke still ringing in her ears, she decided to be bold. 'The woman you visit in London.'

Uncle George whiffed the cue ball and jerked up straight. 'You know better than to distract a man when he's taking a shot. You'll ruin his game. Besides, how do you know about her?'

'Paul, of course.'

'Did he tell you who she is?'

Julia sighed in frustration. 'No.'

'You see—' he pointed his cue stick at her '—I can keep a secret.'

'I'm sure it's the only one.'

'Who is she, George?' the captain joined in. 'Miss Howard is right, you know. You can't keep a secret.'

'Don't think the two of you will get me to reveal it.' He was about to say more when Davies stepped into the room.

'Captain Russell, the foreman from Creedon Abbey is here to discuss the progress of the repairs.'

'Excellent.' George straightened, his smile wider than Julia would have liked. 'If you'll both excuse me.'

'You can bring him in here if you'd like,' Julia of-fered, uneasy about being left with the captain.

'No, I'll return shortly and tell you all the details. In the meantime, please continue my game.' Uncle George handed her his cue stick, then left, the proud way he carried himself making her suspect there was no fore-man for him to meet.

She gripped the cue tightly, worry creeping through her. Despite her previous desire to spite her sister-in-law, the very real threat of Emily catching her alone in a room with a gentleman worried her.

'So, who is this woman George is seeing in London?' the captain asked, the mischief in his eyes dissolving some of her concerns.

'I don't know. I wasn't even sure she existed until just now.'

'Clever.'

Julia swelled her chest with mock pride. 'Paul taught me well.'

The captain leaned far over the table to execute a difficult stroke and Julia admired the way his breeches pulled over his backside. She wanted to run her hands from his hair, over the length of his back to the snug breeches, feeling every contour of his body.

A small medallion slid out from beneath his shirt, glinting in the candlelight and stopping her mind from wandering too far.

'What's that?'

'A reminder.' He fingered the pendant, his voice more measured than before. Distant thunder rolled outside, the storm moving off deeper into the countryside. 'I had it on the last time I was aboard ship. We were off the coast of Spain when we came across a French frigate and it opened fire.'

He unclasped the chain from around his neck and handed it to her. She examined the bronze surface, running her thumb over the dent with its worn and nearly illegible letters.

'It stopped the bullet?'

'Yes, but there were two.' He took the medal back, fastening the chain around his neck and tucking it into his shirt.

'And the other?'

He hit the cue ball with such force it rolled around

the table, bouncing off the sides and missing the red ball. 'It struck me in the left shoulder.'

Their eyes met and she realised why he'd reacted so vehemently to her comments about Admiral Nelson. No wonder he'd been so intent on challenging her reasoning. What must he think of her? Would she never learn to control her tongue? Embarrassment overwhelmed her accompanied by the urge to make her excuses and flee. 'Is that why you resigned?'

'Mostly.' He picked at the end of his cue stick. 'But I had other responsibilities. My father died four years ago, while I was at sea. He left a large share in a shipping company to maintain my mother and sister, but the company faltered after losing a number of ships to storms. My mother tried to manage as best she could, but neither she nor my sister possess your business acumen. I discovered the troubles a few weeks into my recuperation when a bailiff appeared to collect the debts. I instructed my solicitor to pay them and once I was sufficiently recovered, took over Mother's affairs and saw to my sister's dowry.'

'Once everything was settled and you were well, couldn't you have gone back to sea?'

'I wanted to, but it seems the Navy is quick to forget a man once he's away from active service.'

'Didn't they know you were recuperating?'

'They did, but there are always younger, eager men craving ships and, unlike me, those men have not been badly wounded.'

'But Admiral Nelson was wounded and he commands the fleet.'

'As Admiral Stuart was kind enough to point out, I am no Nelson.'

She gasped. 'How could he be so cruel?'

'He wasn't cruel. He was honest. Admiral Stuart and I have known each other a long time and, despite a mutual respect, we both know the way of things. I just needed someone to state it plain enough for me to acknowledge it.' He laid the cue stick on the table and traced the polished wood with one finger. 'The Navy isn't an easy life. George is one of my oldest friends, but I've lost too many others to sickness or French bullets. Most men pursuing commands need to face those hardships to make a living. I'd made a handsome fortune and the Admiralty knew it. Thanks to Admiral Stuart's honesty, I have the chance to enjoy my rewards instead of suffering who knows what fate.' He touched his shoulder, a far-off sadness filling his eyes before he jerked his hand to his side and turned to face her. 'It wasn't easy resigning my commission and it still troubles me, as much as my shoulder.'

Julia stepped back, rolling the cue ball, wishing lightning had struck her on their run, allowing her to avoid this embarrassment. 'I'm sorry for what I said about wounded men. I shouldn't have been so callous or spoken so freely.'

He slid his hand along the table's edge, allowing it to rest very close to hers. 'Don't berate yourself for your views. It's a brave person who does not bend under pressure to others' opinions.'

His fingers brushed the tops of hers, sending a shiver through her body. All of this was inappropriate, his touch, the seclusion but she couldn't bring herself to leave. He stepped closer, his expression more tender than she deserved. She met his soft eyes, anxious, wanting, eager to follow him down whatever road he led her.

The clock on the mantel chimed, the tinkling bells bringing her back to reality.

Cursed interruptions. It was almost time for dinner. If she wished to avoid her *faux pas* from the night before, she needed time to prepare. 'Please excuse me. I must dress for dinner.' Sliding her hand out from beneath his, she noticed his fleeting disappointment as she hurried from the room.

Chapter Six

'Are these all of them?' Julia stared at the dresses draped over every surface, her room resembling the inside of a milliner's shop.

'No, miss. I left the three formal dresses in their trunks.' Mary laid an assortment of gloves on the writing desk. 'Should I bring those down, too?'

'Yes, for heaven knows I may have use for them yet.' Julia fingered the hem of a pink-silk pelisse.

'Which dress would you like to wear tonight?' Mary asked, arranging a few fans on the bedside table.

Julia circled the room, examining each one, trying to remember which one had looked the best on her. She barely remembered the ensembles, having banished them to the attic the instant they'd returned from her horrible Season in London. She'd have gladly given it all to Mary, but her mother had stopped her, insisting she might one day need it. Tonight, Mother would discover how right she'd been. 'Which do you suggest?'

'The green one, it was so pretty on you in town.'

Julia nodded, allowing Mary to help her out of the simple afternoon frock and into the fancy, green-silk creation. The dress highlighted her amber eyes and showed off her curves to their best advantage. However, the low-cut bodice made her feel exposed and very self-conscious. Examining herself in the mirror, she felt all of her London awkwardness come rushing back.

Her embarrassment increased when, half an hour later, after patiently bearing Mary's many attempts at a fashionable *coiffure*, Julia curtly dismissed her. As she stared at the lopsided style in the mirror, tears of frustration stung her eyes. How could she possibly hope to capture Captain Covington's interest with dishevelled hair?

Not his interest. Simon's, she corrected herself, furiously combing out the style, then tossing the brush down on the table where it rattled against a small vase with a lone rose. *Obviously my money isn't enough to attract him. The stupid peacock.*

Despair crept along the edges of her irritation, but she shook it from her head with the last of the hairpins. She couldn't afford to lose hope now.

I will catch Simon's eye. I have to. With renewed determination, she twisted her hair up the way Mother did, fastening it with a tortoiseshell comb while leaving the front curls, Mary's sole accomplishment, to fall about her face.

James trailed his fingers on the marble mantel, wincing at another of Miss Howard's hollow laughs. Twice today he'd nearly kissed her. Twice he'd allowed the wanting in her eyes to overcome his better sense, yet there she sat on the sofa next to Mr Taylor, seemingly enthralled by the twit. What game was she playing in her London finery, her white, round breasts well displayed by the curving neckline of the green dress? What hold did Mr Taylor have over her? He wondered if she knew about his affair with the dowager baroness or the wager at White's as to whether or not they would elope to Gretna Green? Surely she must know, having previously claimed a broad knowledge of London gossip.

Flexing his left hand, he leaned his elbow on the mantel, pretending to study a small horse figurine. He'd watched her throughout dinner, noticing the way her eyes lost their sparkle whenever Mr Taylor turned away. This was not the same woman who'd dared him to keep up with her on the downs or challenged him in the library.

He thought of asking George what his niece was about, but it would only make his feelings obvious. What where his feelings? He'd struggled against them ever since they'd met, yet this afternoon at the keep he could no longer lie to himself. She enchanted him, amused him. She was an original in every way, fresh and free spirited, tethered by a prudish brother and an indifferent mother. How she'd blossom if she ever cut herself loose from Knollwood. Yet she clung to it like a man clings to a sinking ship, praying against all odds it might still save him.

Miss Taylor's voice accompanied by the tinkling notes of the pianoforte drifted to him from the far corner of the room. She flirted with him from across the instrument's polished surface, dropping her head coquettishly, her eyes betraying her true intention. James knew he could not go back to such women. However, it was a fool's errand to chase after a young lady who held no real interest in him. Melinda had taught him that lesson years ago. He must find some way to draw Miss Howard out and drive thoughts of Mr Taylor from her mind.

* * *

While Simon spoke of his London house at length, Julia stole a number of glances at the captain. He stood by the fire, watching the flames consume the log with a sense of distant wondering. He wore his blue uniform, the high collar framing his strong chin. The firelight danced in his dark hair and blue eyes. For a moment she pictured him on the deck of a ship as it sailed into Bombay, watching the far-off coconut trees on the rolling hills sway in the warm breeze, just as Mr Ivers described in his book. Only the strange sadness surrounding him interrupted the lovely dream. Seeing the way it darkened his eyes, she wanted to take him in her arms and caress it away, but with so many people around them, she couldn't even entreat him to tell her what troubled him.

'It is such a bother to turn one's own music,' Annette remarked from her place at the pianoforte. 'Captain, will you turn the pages for me?'

'Simon can turn the pages for you,' George responded.

Simon stopped his chattering long enough to heave a small sigh. 'She knows the tune by heart and can play without the sheet music.'

Annette's face went pale before she fixed a charming smile back on her lips. 'How silly you are, Simon, to make such a joke. You know very well I do not know this piece.'

Julia caught Uncle George's eye. He glanced from her to Simon, scrunching his brow with a silent question. Julia flicked her hand in his direction, waving the question away, but she could tell he wasn't deterred. Panic stole through her. Uncle George didn't believe her sudden interest in Simon and suspected something.

Had he guessed her scheme? She hoped not. She didn't need any more obstacles.

'Mr Johnson told me Mr Wilkins is hosting a game at the Sign of the Swan tonight,' Uncle George announced with a sly grin.

Drat, Julia thought, wishing they were still at dinner so she could kick him under the table. She didn't need him working against her, but she also wasn't ready to let him in on her plan.

'A game, you say?' Simon asked, taking his gold chronometer out of his pocket and checking the time.

'Quite a large one from the sound of it. A man could make a lot of money. It seems Mr Wilkins is very keen to win back some of the blunt he lost last night. Though I doubt he'll succeed. He's a terrible player.'

'Simon, tell me more about your horses,' Julia implored in a feeble attempt to outmanoeuvre Uncle George, but it failed. Simon rose and sauntered over to the card table, quite forgetting their conversation.

'You've played the man?' he asked.

'Once or twice. He has no face for the game. Reveals his hand—hardly a challenge.' George laid a card on the table and drew another.

'Where's the fun in an opponent who gives away the game? A real gentleman wants a challenge, a chance to truly flaunt his talent,' Annette chided Simon, who, for the first time since their arrival, didn't respond to his sister's rebuke. Instead he stood, fingering the button on his coat, appearing to weigh Uncle George's announcement with Annette's comment before the gambler in him won the debate.

'If you'll excuse me, I believe I'll retire for the evening.'

'But it's only nine. Stay,' Annette pleaded. 'I'm sure George can make room for you at the table.'

'The country has tired me. Goodnight, ladies.' He bowed to Mother and Emily, then made his way out of the room. He didn't fool anyone with his excuse and Julia knew it would only be a matter of minutes before they heard him sneak out of the front door.

Annette's hands lingered over the keys and she looked torn between following him and returning to her pursuit of Captain Covington. It took only a moment for her to reach a decision and she resumed her pretty playing.

Julia sat on the sofa, clutching her hands in her lap in frustration. Beyond a few dinner conversations, she hadn't made any progress with the dandy.

'Captain Covington, would you mind turning the music for me?' Annette sang to him.

'Would you care to accompany me across the room?' The captain stood in front of Julia, his hands behind his back. She had no desire to watch Annette fawn over him, but with no Simon or interest in cards, annoying her stepcousin seemed the only thing left to do.

'It would be my pleasure.'

'Perhaps Miss Howard and I may play a duet,' Annette suggested with false gaiety when they approached.

'You are quite aware I don't play.' She was in no mood for another discussion of her accomplishments.

'You don't play. And you don't draw.' Annette's fingers paused, giving her astonishment the most effect before she resumed her piece. 'How do you expect to find a husband without such accomplishments?'

Julia restrained her urge to slam the keyboard cover on Annette's pale fingers and wipe the pompous look off her face.

'I think many gentlemen would be pleased to have a wife skilled in running an estate for he would never have to agonise over his purse or hers,' Captain Covington offered, coming to her defence against Annette again.

'Even without a gentleman, it's a comfort to handle one's own affairs instead of trusting them to men who only gamble them away,' Julia added, staring down her nose at Annette.

Annette struck a sour note, then stood, turning hard eyes on Julia. 'Do not be so proud. A lady's fortune is always in the hands of her male relations, no matter what her accomplishments.'

Her words rang more of sad bitterness than malice and Julia's spirits fell, the realisation striking deeper than any other comment Annette had ever made about her. For the first time, Julia felt sorry for her stepcousin, thinking they had more in common than she knew.

'If you will excuse me.' Annette pushed past them towards the door, disappearing upstairs.

'If I had an estate, I would wish for a wife like you to run it,' Captain Covington offered and Julia responded with a weak smile, unwilling to accept his pity.

'But you have no estate. And neither do I.'

'Perhaps in time that will change for both of us.'

'Yes, you will buy an estate and I—well, I'll wait for my brother to return and then I can be the spinster aunt.' She meant the comment to sound like a joke, but it fell flat. Desperate for something to occupy her hands, she sat down at the despised instrument and began picking out the tune in front of her. She tried to concentrate on the black notes in their cosy lines and not the captain standing close behind her.

'No, you will not be a spinster. Do not listen to the

likes of Miss Taylor. There are many gentlemen who
want a lady with a head for business.'

'Then they must all be married for I've never met
such a gentleman.'

She came to the end of the stanza and he reached
over her shoulder to change the page, his cheek tantalisingly close to hers. She closed her eyes, listening to the
sheet music rustle, hearing his heavy breath in her ear.
She only had to turn her head to sweep her lips across
his skin, bury her face in the warm crease of his neck
while reaching up to lace her fingers in his dark hair.

'I am not married,' he whispered, his breath teasing her neck.

Her hands dropped to the keyboard, the clanging
notes snapping her out of her daydream. Going back
over the stanza, she tried to make her awkward fingers behave, but they kept tripping over the keys. She
glanced at the card table, noting the way Emily watched
them before Uncle George distracted her with some
comment. She also felt the captain's eyes lingering
on her. Why did he insist on staring? Julia hit another
wrong note, increasing her agitation until she could no
longer bear it.

'If you'll excuse me, Captain, I'm tired.' She stood,
closed the keyboard, then fled for the door.

George leaned back in his chair. 'Retiring so early,
Julia?'

'Yes, goodnight.'

She hurried from the room before Uncle George
could compel her to stay. Reaching the top of the dimly
lit stairs, she heard a faint noise, like someone crying.
She followed the sound, tiptoeing over the carpet, expecting to see a maid in one of the small chairs situated
near the window. Moving past the cushioned retreat

with a view of the garden, she found it empty. Down the hall, light slipped out from beneath Annette's door. Cautiously approaching it, Julia heard her stepcousin's muffled sobs. She felt sorry for the girl and raised a hand to knock, then thought better of it. If Annette was rude downstairs, Julia could only imagine her fury if she interrupted her now.

Once in her own room, Julia sat in the window seat, snatching up the agricultural report in an attempt to lose herself in the dry pages. She read the first two lines, then tossed it aside, too frustrated to concentrate. Leaning her forehead against the cool glass, she watched a few stars peep out through a break in the moving clouds.

What did the captain mean by suggesting gentlemen wanted women with a head for business? Did he mean he wanted such a lady? No, he was not interested in a sensible wife, only a country fling, no matter how much tender sincerity filled his eyes. Paul had warned her about a man's ability to charm a woman for purely dishonourable reasons. She could not let herself fall into the captain's trap, no matter how easily her body reacted when he stood so close.

The idea that she might be too weak to resist him scared her as deeply now as it had at the keep and in the library. Pulling her knees up under her chin, she wrapped her arms around them in an effort to ward off the sudden cold. Everything felt so uncertain, as if the captain's arrival had changed more than just the place settings for dinner. Not even Knollwood or her own conviction to buy Cable Grange seemed steady any more.

If only Paul was here. He'd know what to do about the captain, the Taylors and Cable Grange. However, he was at sea and about to face unimaginable dangers. Even if she could get a letter to him, it wasn't right to burden him with her concerns at a time like this. She would have to solve these problems herself.

James lay in bed, staring at the white plaster ceiling, his aching shoulder preventing any chance of sleep. He'd gritted his teeth more than once during the ride back to Knollwood, but the pain seemed a worthy price to pay for the excitement he experienced racing Miss Howard. Outside, the wind rattled the window, knocking a tree branch against the house. Thoughts of Miss Howard continued to torment him despite all attempts to drive them from his mind. He could not care for her. He would not. What did he have to offer her but a weak body and a meaningless life?

As he pulled the medallion back and forth across its chain, those old familiar protests sounded hollow tonight. Over the last few days, he'd felt freer than he had since being wounded and dreams of the future crept into the long hours of the night. Perhaps he'd travel to Rome, inspect the ruins, then carry on to Greece or Constantinople. He might even return to India and explore more than the port cities. Miss Howard's eyes would flash at the sight of the palaces and market places.

James twisted the chain tight around his finger until the metal bit into his flesh. How many times had he lain here, distracting himself from his painful shoulder with dreams of her young, supple body? He'd almost groaned when she'd appeared in the dining room tonight, her low-cut gown displaying the delicate curves of her body. He wanted nothing more than to slip his hands beneath the green silk, to feel the soft flesh of her thighs, taste the sweet hollow of her neck while his hands caressed her stomach. Did she know how she teased him and made him ache with need? She wanted him as much as he wanted her. He'd seen it in her eyes at the keep, felt it in the way she'd held his hand when they'd run through the rain. Yet still she went back to the dandy.

Smacking his fist against the sheets, he tried to ignore the subtle throbbing in his member as it overcame the sting of his shoulder. He'd placed his happiness in the hands of a woman once before, only to be cruelly disappointed. What did Melinda matter now? George was right; she was in the past where she belonged. Thinking about her did nothing but weaken his spirit. No, there were other, more pleasant things to consider, such as the taste of Miss Howard's lips. He'd been tantalisingly close so many times today, yet she continued to elude him.

Shifting on the bed, he searched for a more comfortable position. Guilt filled his mind. He couldn't ruin George's niece, not for simple need, nor could he ask for her hand. Or could he? A woman with her talents would be an asset and he could well imagine her accompanying him to India or on any other whim. But were these reasons good enough to tie him to a woman for life? Miss Howard would certainly keep things interesting, assuming she'd have him. He remembered George's suggestion that a man with an estate could capture her heart. He'd wanted Cable Grange for revenge; now he had another, sweeter reason. For once the idea of marriage didn't seem distasteful, but was he ready to spring the parson's mousetrap? If so, he'd need a tempting bit of cheese to catch this mouse.

Chapter Seven

Julia ambled back from the stables, the cold, early morning air chafing her cheeks. Stifling a yawn with the back of her hand, she tried to blame last night's restlessness on Annette or the problem of Simon, but it was Captain Covington who'd kept her up until almost sunrise. With the auction date drawing closer, it was time to put such foolishness aside and be serious about her pursuit. She calculated again the ready locked in the desk drawer, wondering how much it would take to buy Simon and his silence. Father had always kept the money at hand, mostly to send to Paul when one of his frequent letters arrived asking for more. She'd left it there out of habit; now she could use it to her advantage. She'd corner Simon once he finally awoke and came down to eat, assuming he'd even returned from his rousing night at the Sign of the Swan.

A flash of pink caught Julia's eye and she noticed her mother, parasol in hand, inspecting her roses. Charlemagne trotted beside her, his tail wagging in happy excitement. The rose garden was her mother's domain, the one area of Knollwood off limits to both Father's and Julia's management, and she coaxed from it flowers of amazing beauty. Watching her with her precious bushes, her hem wet, feet encased in sturdy shoes instead of slippers, she knew her mother played a small part in her own love of the land.

In no mood to risk a serious discussion, Julia slunk past the garden, hoping her mother wouldn't turn around. She was nearly to the house when Charlemagne let out an excited yip.

'Come here, dear,' her mother called in a voice Julia could not ignore.

She wondered if Emily had told her about their conversation yesterday. It wasn't in her mother's nature to scold, but she was not above the occasional reprimand. 'Yes, Mother?'

'Do you have feelings for Simon?' She turned over a leaf, searching for signs of disease.

Julia hesitated, hating the blunt questions. It made evading it difficult. 'He's an affable gentleman.'

Her mother stared hard at her. 'The truth, please.'

'No, certainly not,' Julia admitted, knowing it was better to level with her mother than continue the charade.

'Then why show him so much preference?'

'I thought if I could make him ask for my hand, then an engagement would be enough for Charles to give me my inheritance in time to purchase Cable Grange.'

'I suspected as much.' Her mother plucked off a wilted bloom and tossed it over the wall. 'Even if he did propose, Charles wouldn't allow it. Simon has too much of a reputation in town.'

'Must my entire life be governed by what Charles does and does not like?'

'I thought you didn't care for Simon?'

'I don't, but I hate Charles's high-handed meddling.'

'Be kind, dear. He does love you and only wants your happiness.'

Julia didn't agree, but held her tongue. Arguing with her mother would get her nowhere and with the plan to entice Simon unravelling, she needed her help. 'What am I going to do?'

'Have you considered Captain Covington?'

Julia fingered a stem, snapping off a thorn with her thumb. During the long hours without sleep she'd considered the captain many times, in many different ways, none of which was suitable to discuss with her mother. 'I chose Simon because I thought the promise of a fortune would be enough to attract him. I won't have the same influence with the captain. Besides, he's infatuated with Annette.'

'I don't believe he is. I've watched him and I think he tolerates her simply to be courteous.'

Julia knew she was right. At certain unguarded moments, the captain did appear bored or annoyed with Annette.

'I'd have to tell him directly of my scheme and what if he told others?' She knew he wouldn't, but she felt the need to make some kind of protest. If she agreed too speedily to the idea, her mother might suspect something more, something Julia didn't even want to admit to herself.

'I don't think he'll reveal your secret. He's honourable, possesses a good reputation and George can vouch for him. Charles is more likely to accept him. And think of Paul. A friendship with the captain may help his career. He must know people in the Admiralty and he might be in a position to bend their ears.'

Despite her mother's reasoning, Julia hesitated. Such a game with the captain would prove far more dangerous than with Simon. Could she trust herself to spend enough time with him to give the appearance of genuine affection without compromising herself? Of course she could. Couldn't she? 'I'll think about it.'

'If nothing else, imagine how it will annoy Annette,' her mother suggested with a wry smile.

Julia gasped. 'I never knew you were so wicked.'

'I'm your uncle's sister, am I not?'

'Indeed.'

'Now come along, for I believe George has a surprise for us about nuncheon.'

Uncle George's nuncheon plans did come as a surprise. Somehow, without Julia discovering it, he'd arranged for an outdoor picnic on a grassy hill near Knollwood. He'd ordered a number of oilcloths spread on the still-wet grass and brought over from Creedon Abbey a large canopy acquired during a visit to India. From their high vantage point, they could see Cable Grange perched on a distant hill and one turret of Creedon Abbey peeking above a far-off line of trees.

Julia sipped her tea, studying the captain and Annette over the rim of her cup. Annette served him a slice of cake while leaning over to reveal the tops of her breasts pushed up by her low-cut bodice. Uncle George had advised them to wear clothing appropriate for the cool autumn weather but she'd ignored his advice, dressing instead for husband hunting.

'Annette will catch her death of cold pursuing the captain,' Julia whispered to Emily, noticing the chit's goose bumps from across the oilcloth.

'You shouldn't laugh at people,' Emily chided, popping a small sandwich into her mouth to cover an agreeing smile.

Julia focused on the captain, noting how often he turned away from Annette's charms to take in the view. After a moment, his eyes met hers and she concentrated on her tea cup, sipping the tepid liquid with as much ease of manner as she could muster. The idea of revealing her scheme to him and asking for his help terrified, yet intrigued her. Would he go along? If she kept the mood light, made him understand it was all a game, why wouldn't he? After all, he'd participated in many of Uncle George's schemes.

If it all seemed so simple, then why was she afraid of asking him? She'd almost risked her reputation on a dandy. Why did a man like Captain Covington frighten her?

Deep in her heart she knew the reason. His dashing features and the easy way they laughed together would make it difficult to jilt him and jilt him she must. As a single woman, Cable Grange would be hers completely. Married, the property would belong to him, leaving her in a position no better than her current one with Charles. Though she doubted Captain Covington would act like her brother, it was still risky to gamble her future on a man she barely knew.

She turned towards Cable Grange, watching the sunlight dance off the dirty sandstone, trying to imagine it clean, the sheep well fed and bred, the fields high with wheat and barley. The thought of such a beautiful estate left to moulder broke her heart. No matter what her fears, she had to face them and get Cable Grange.

Julia put down her tea cup and stood, smoothing her dress with her gloved hands. 'I think I'll go for a walk.'

Catching the captain's eyes, she nodded in the direction of the woods. He met it with a questioning frown before comprehension dawned on his face, bringing with it a roguish smile. Julia, confident he understood, turned and walked off down the hill. What exactly he understood she wasn't sure. He certainly wouldn't expect her proposal, but he couldn't anticipate a sordid rendezvous, not with everyone sitting only a few hundred feet away.

'More tea, Captain Covington?' Miss Taylor asked, forcing James to stifle a smile. He'd seen the signal, the same one George used to use when they needed to escape a room and discuss their next move. What did Miss Howard wish to tell him that the others could not hear?

'Annette, leave the captain alone. He'll float away if you ply him with much more tea,' George chided.

'I'm sure Captain Covington is quite capable of knowing when he has and has not had enough tea,' she snapped and James seized the chance to leave.

'I think I'll join Miss Howard.' He hurried after her before Miss Taylor or anyone else could offer to join him.

The hill quickened his pace and his feet fell hard on the firm dirt. Miss Howard watched him approach from where she sat on the twisted trunk of a fallen tree, standing once he reached her. A strange sort of nervous anticipation decorated her face and he wondered what serious secret made her so eager to speak with him in private.

'You've set their tongues wagging by following me.' She walked deeper into the woods and he followed, leaves crackling beneath his boots.

'George's tongue is already wagging.'

'What do you mean?'

'He's playing the matchmaker and would like very much to see us married.'

She stopped and her fingers flew to her lips in fearful surprise. 'Really?'

'You didn't know?'

'No.' She resumed her languid pace, her face more tightly drawn than before.

'As much as I enjoy teasing him, if I have to spend one more minute eating out of Miss Taylor's hands just to see the stunned expression on his face, I may expire from fatigue,' James admitted with a smile.

'Thank heavens,' she breathed, sounding more nervous than amused. 'I was afraid you'd succumbed to her fake charm.'

'I might say the same of you and your present infatuation with Mr Taylor,' he countered, eager to get at the truth of her relationship with the dandy.

'You can't believe I'm interested in him.' She picked up a stick and smacked a brown leaf off an overhanging branch. 'He's weak and useless and no woman wants such a man. Like you, I was merely pretending.'

James flexed his left hand, resisting the urge to feel under his shirt. 'Why would you feign interest in a man? You aren't after a husband, are you?'

She stopped abruptly and turned to him. 'No, I'm in search of a fiancé, or, more correctly, someone like you who can pretend.' The words came out in such a winded rush he almost missed their meaning. He stared at her, waiting for a laugh, smile or some other indication of a joke, but she only watched him with the same nervous fear as before.

'You're serious?'

'It's my intention to purchase Cable Grange with my inheritance, but I don't receive it until I'm married. However, if Charles believes I'm engaged—'

'—he'll give you the money.'

'Yes. Once I've purchased the estate, I'll cry off the engagement and you'll be a free man.' She broke the stick in half and tossed it aside.

James stepped back, unsure how to respond. An engagement for Cable Grange? It seemed impossible, yet exactly like something a girl of her pluck would suggest.

'I'd hoped to entice Simon into an engagement,' she continued when he didn't answer, 'but the gentleman is thicker than mud and, according to Mother, quite unsuitable. Charles isn't likely to approve of the match. But as an old friend of Uncle George's you're—'

'—perfect.'

'Well, I wouldn't say "perfect", but you'll do.'

'Will I now?'

'You have a fondness for schemes.'

'So it seems.' James leaned back against a large oak, crossing his arms over his chest in amusement. The woman was unbelievable.

'Please. It's the only way. I have to have Cable Grange.' The desperation in her voice and the dejected way she drew the pelisse's satin ribbon through her fingers touched him. He wanted to take her sad face in his hands and kiss away the small line between her brows. The idea was doomed to fail. He knew something of Charles. Her brother was exacting and wouldn't simply give her the money on a promise. If James agreed to the scheme, it could only end in either their marriage or her ruin. He might have contemplated marriage in the middle of the night, but in the light of the day, under such dubious circumstance, it was quite a different prospect.

She bit her bottom lip in anticipation of his answer. Did she care for him? Sometimes, when he caught her observing him, he suspected some interest. However, she was a determined girl and she'd set her mind on

Cable Grange. She'd never admit any feelings for him if they interfered with her plans.

'What will you tell your brother when you end the engagement?'

'I don't think Charles likes Navy men, so I doubt he'll be too put off by the idea.'

'Or he might insist.'

'You're a free man—refuse him.'

'It's that important to you?'

'It's the only future I have.'

If this were any other woman, he'd think she was trying to trap him, but the way she admitted her situation with such raw agony told him she had no designs. Like him, the realities of life frustrated her and she did her best to overcome them. It took courage to reveal her situation and propose the plan and he respected her bravery. An engagement would force them together, giving him a chance to know her better, perhaps convince her not to jilt him if his feelings and hers proved true. If he was wrong and there was no interest, they'd break the engagement. It all seemed so uncomplicated, but he knew it wasn't. Was he ready to agree to her arrangement and risk the very real possibility of marriage?

'You have George's talent for schemes,' he said.

'So it seems,' she agreed.

'You know about most of the plots I was entangled in?'

She nodded.

'Then I'll have to tell you the rest during our engagement.'

'You'll do it?'

'I followed George. It seems only fitting I follow his niece.'

'Thank you, Captain, thank you.' She threw her arms

around his neck, hugging him close. He breathed in the clean scent of her soft hair, felt the warmth of her neck so close to his lips. He moved to wrap his arms around her, put his hand on the small of her back and draw her deeper into the arc of his body. His member eagerly responded to the sudden rush of desire, but knowing his breeches wouldn't hide it and in no mood to embarrass himself, he removed her arms from around his neck. Her eager eyes met his and he saw more in her happy expression than a scheme. He released her wrists, afraid of what might happen if he held her for too long.

'We must play the role of courting couple,' she explained matter of factly, covering the lingering tension. 'Give ourselves time to develop an attachment and for the others to see it. Charles must believe it is real. When would you like to begin?'

'Now, my little Artemis, before we change our minds.' He offered her his arm and she took it, allowing him to walk her back through the woods.

Was it his pulse or hers she felt racing beneath her fingers? Pausing for him to hold back a branch, she moved forwards, barely able to keep her body from trembling. Up ahead, the trees began to thin, the green hill just visible beyond the forest's deep shadows. Once they stepped out together, the game was on and would not end until she either had Cable Grange or—or what?

She stopped, nervousness making her whole body vibrate. 'You could turn back now,' she offered, more to herself than the captain.

'I wouldn't dream of it.' He took a step forwards, but she didn't move. 'You aren't afraid, are you?'

'Of course not.' *I'm terrified*, she thought, but didn't

say it. Having her scheme turn real in so short a time was overwhelming.

'Good.'

He pulled her forwards, out of the trees and she blinked against the sunlight. He kept a tight grip on her arm, escorting her up the hill. Julia could almost feel the shock rippling through the group at the sight of them in such an intimate attitude. Annette's jaw dropped, Uncle George choked on a biscuit, Simon inspected them through his quizzing glass and Emily's eyes went large. Only her mother appeared not to notice, doting on Charlemagne in an attempt to hide a knowing smile.

'I think we've made an impression,' Julia whispered, her fear fading in the face of this small triumph.

'I believe we have.'

They sat down together on the oilcloth, a short distance from the others who continued to watch them in silence. Not even Uncle George had recovered enough to ask questions or do anything more than stare. Julia acted like nothing was amiss and for the first time in days felt hope for her future. Neither Annette's sour face nor Emily's dumbfounded expression could ruin the feeling.

'Tea?' Captain Covington offered, holding up the small teapot.

'Yes, please.' She held out her cup. When it was full she exchanged it for a small plate of tarts. 'Would you like one?'

'Thank you.' He reached for a delicacy, but Julia pulled it away, then held it out for him to taste.

'Subtlety,' he whispered, taking the treat from her fingers and breaking off a small bite.

'Why?' Julia whispered back. 'If I'm going to do this, I'm going to do it well.'

* * *

'George, you've outdone yourself with surprises today,' James congratulated when they returned from the picnic to find a game of battledore and shuttlecock arranged on the lawn.

'I'm not the only one,' George remarked as James took two battledores from the footman and handed Miss Howard one with all the tender flourish of a smitten suitor.

'What do you mean?'

George scowled in answer, then turned to Miss Taylor. 'Annette, you should play.'

Miss Taylor's pinched eyebrows drew closer together. 'I have no intention of remaining outside. My shoes are already soaked through.'

Holding up the wet hem of her thin gown, she marched inside.

'I believe I'll join her,' Mr Taylor added and no one tried to stop him.

James and Miss Howard began their game while the others fell into furious whispering. He noticed the volley of looks thrown their way, but the ping of the shuttlecock hitting Miss Howard's battledore forced him to focus on the game.

He ran for the wispy target, smacking it back to her and sending her running. She whacked it inches from the ground and it sailed through the air towards him. Lunging for it, he ignored his stinging shoulder, enjoying the lively play. With a quick swing, he shot the shuttlecock over her head and into the tall grass.

'You're an excellent player, Miss Howard.'

'You're trying to flatter me.' She laughed, retrieving the shuttlecock and preparing to serve.

'I never offer a compliment I don't mean.'

Their vigorous game continued, Miss Howard chasing the shuttlecock, her face flushed with excitement, hair slightly dishevelled and eyes vivid from the exertion. It reminded him of the moment they'd first met in the forest. What would it be like to drive her to such a state by the play of his fingers along her skin? Hopefully, he'd get the chance to discover it, but for now vigorous exercise must suffice.

James played with equal enthusiasm, chasing the shuttlecock all over the field. Then, in the middle of one challenging set, something over Miss Howard's shoulder made him pause. He let the shuttlecock drop to the ground, watching the stable boy run up the lawn towards them.

'What's wrong?' She turned and at the sight of the boy, threw down her battledore and rushed to meet him. 'Samuel, what is it? What's happened?'

'There's been trouble, Miss Howard.'

James hurried to her side and the flustered stable boy, breathing hard from his run, warily took them in.

'What? Tell me,' she demanded.

He hesitated, visibly torn between telling his mistress and getting in trouble.

James knew whatever he'd come to report had happened under suspicious circumstances.

'Tell her what happened,' James commanded, ignoring the disapproving glance Miss Howard tossed his way.

'There was a fight in the clearing near the lower pasture,' he explained, James's order loosening his tongue. 'Mr Wilkins's man was knocked out and Bill's bleeding badly.'

'I must put a stop to this at once. Come along, Samuel.'

'Can I stay here, miss?' the boy stuttered.

'Whatever for?'

'I believe the lad is afraid of losing face,' James offered, sensing the boy's predicament. He'd seen it many times aboard ship. 'Whatever's going on is a secret and the others might hold it against him if they learn he told you.'

'All right, Samuel, you may stay. But when I return I'd better find you working, not dallying or daydreaming.'

'Yes, miss.' He dashed off in the direction of the stables.

Miss Howard turned to the others, who watched from their place along the edge of the court. 'Mother, send John to fetch the medicine chest. Emily, have Davies send two men and a stretcher to the clearing near the pasture.'

'Where are you going?' Emily asked in a heavy, warning tone.

'To deal with this incident.' Miss Howard turned, striding off.

'I insist you let the farm manager deal with it,' Emily called after her to no effect. Miss Howard kept walking, pretending not to hear her sister-in-law.

'I'll go with her.' James knew the hot tempers of fighting men. He couldn't imagine the diminutive Miss Howard facing them alone.

'Me, too,' George offered.

Despite her quick clip, James easily caught up to her, his long legs giving him an advantage. Behind them, George huffed and puffed, struggling to keep pace with their steady strides. 'What will you do when you find them?'

Miss Howard didn't slow, but kept on down the rutted path. 'I don't know.'

'Do you think this is wise?'

'Is it wise to allow workers to neglect their duties?'

'Perhaps there is a better way to handle the situation.'

'How? By letting you command them? Perhaps you would like to oversee their wages as well or direct them where to plough?'

'The boy talked, didn't he?'

'That's not the point.'

'Then what is?'

'I have no wish to discuss it at this time.'

They walked a fair distance from the house, across one large field and down a rolling slope to where the land flattened again. Sheep watched them march by until they reached another clearing.

'What's going on here?' Miss Howard took the lead, her voice carrying across the grass to the circle of men. They turned, guilt washing over their faces. James stifled a laugh as the gruff field hands dropped their heads like a bunch of schoolboys caught cheating. He recognised a number of men from Julia's staff. The others appeared to be Mr Wilkins's men for they leered at Miss Howard, making James very glad he'd decided to come.

An unconscious man lay on the ground. Another, larger man sat next to him, holding his bloody arm. The two fighters were naked from the waist up, but Miss Howard seemed not to notice as she strode into the thick of things.

'I said, what's going on here?' she demanded again upon reaching the circle, her hands balled against her hips. All the men had strapping builds from years of labour and towered over their employer. James might fear for her safety, but he had to admire her spirit. She reminded him of a certain well-known tavern owner in Tortuga who didn't tolerate fighting in her establishment.

When no one answered, she turned to the bleeding man on the ground. 'Bill, tell me what happened.'

He blinked against the sun, his face long with shame. 'It was a friendly wager, Miss Howard. Tim said I could beat Mr Wilkins's man, and you know I can. But he had a knife. Cut me before I laid him out.'

'You lie,' one of the greasier men challenged, his lascivious eyes raking Miss Howard, making James's blood boil.

'It's the truth,' Bill challenged, sparking a round of heated accusations.

'Bloody liar—'

'He cheated—'

'Can't trust a Wilkins servant—'

'That's enough!' Miss Howard shouted, her voice lost in a swirl of angry shouts and jabbing fingers. The jabbing rapidly escalated to shoving with Miss Howard caught in the middle. James pulled her from the centre as the first punch swung close to her head. Pushing her towards George, he summoned all his years as a commander and addressed the tangled rabble.

'Attention!' The men with military experience straightened up while the others stopped arguing long enough for him to take control of the situation. 'I want silence this instance. You men there, get back to Cable Grange.'

'And who are you to be ordering us around?' the greasy one sneered.

James stepped toe to toe with the man. 'What's your name?'

'Mark.' He spat on the ground at James's feet.

James fixed him with an insolent-wilting glare.

'Then get back to Cable Grange, Mark, and take your companion with you.'

The men slowly crept across the pasture towards Cable Grange. Mark and another man pulled up their groggy friend and with his arms over their shoulders dragged him off through the high grass.

'The rest of you listen to Miss Howard or you'll have me to answer to.' He stepped aside, waving his hand at the workers. 'Your men are ready.'

Her angry eyes flashed at him before she stepped forwards to face her servants.

'You know I don't condone fighting. I should dismiss every one of you for what you've done.' Alarm swept through the men, but they did not answer back. Watching her walk up and down the line of servants, she reminded him of a petite captain. It was strange to see a lady in such a position, but it boded well for a woman who, depending on how their scheme played out, might accompany him throughout the world under who knew what circumstances.

'I know you men all have families and you're all good, hard workers, so I'll forgive you today,' she continued. 'But if I ever catch any of you doing something like this again, you'll be instantly dismissed. Now, return to your duties at once, except you, Bill. We must see to your arm.'

The men filed past, thanking her profusely. She nodded sternly at each and when they were gone, turned to Bill. Behind her, John and two other servants appeared with the stretcher and a small wooden medicine chest.

'Well, Bill?' Miss Howard asked, standing over the injured man.

'Am I to be dismissed?' he asked, shamefaced.

'No, I think you've been punished enough for today.' She knelt down beside him. 'I want to see your arm.'

She motioned for it, but he held it fast, drops of blood seeping out from between his fingers.

'It's no sight for a lady.'

'Let me see it,' she insisted.

He removed his hand, revealing a gaping cut. It was small but deep and bleeding heavily. She didn't blanch, but examined it with care, then motioned for the chest.

'You need the surgeon.' She pulled off one glove and removed a bandage roll from the medical box, winding it tightly around Bill's wound. 'John, please fetch the surgeon. You two, help Bill back to the stable. Uncle George, can you accompany them?'

'Yes, but I want James to escort you back to the house.'

'I can find my own way.' She started to rise and George took her by the elbow, helping her to her feet.

'I insist he see you back.'

'Very well.'

George joined the servants making their way back to the house, leaving James alone with Miss Howard.

'That was very brave of you. I don't know another lady with such command of her staff and quite the strong stomach.' He kicked loose dirt over the small puddle of blood on the ground. 'I think you'd be very good in any crisis. You have a way with authority.'

'And you, Captain, have a way of interfering when you shouldn't. Kindly remember you are a guest at Knollwood, not its owner.'

Julia pushed past him, making for the path to the house. She heard the heavy fall of his boots on the ground as he caught up to her and she quickened her pace, nearly breaking into a run.

'Julia, wait.'

She whirled to face him, closing the short distance between them. 'How dare you address me in such an intimate manner?'

'I think it only fitting since we're engaged.' There it was again, his knowing smile, the one she found so infuriating. What was it about this man who annoyed her with such charm?

'Yes, engaged, and not even that, yet you already act like a husband.'

The comment wiped the smile from his face. 'Is this my thanks for helping you?'

'You weren't helping. You were undermining my authority, giving orders and interfering with my management of Knollwood.'

'If I hadn't undermined your authority, some servant would have pummelled you.'

'I do not wish to discuss it.' She continued on up the path, too worked up by the fight, the wound and the captain to stand still. A small pang of guilt needled her for being so cross. Yes, if he hadn't stepped in she might well have been injured, or worse. But she couldn't bring herself to thank him. She suddenly wished she were at Cable Grange with all of this ridiculous business behind her.

'Julia, please stop.'

The tender request held more power than any of his commands, bringing her to a halt. He walked around to stand in front of her, but she refused to meet his face. She kept her head down, studying his boots, noting the mud stuck to the sides and a small scuff on the toe.

'Whatever you think of my interfering, I only meant to help and whether our engagement is real or fake doesn't matter. I had no desire to see you hurt.'

She pulled on her glove, fumbling to fasten the small button at her wrist, unsure how to continue. He was right. She shouldn't be angry and she had insulted him again without good reason. Would she never learn? 'Perhaps we shouldn't play this game.'

He took her hand, his fingers slipping the ivory button through its hole.

'I very much enjoy this game, my little Artemis.' His thumb stroked the inside of her palm, firm and warm through her glove. Her heart raced and she worked to breathe evenly.

'Don't call me that.'

'But it suits you.'

Her anger, the fighting men and all her troubles faded away and she was aware of nothing but his hand on hers. 'I'm sorry if I seem ungrateful. I shouldn't be, especially after everything you've agreed to do for me. I do thank you for your help.'

'We all need help sometimes.'

'I'm not accustomed to asking for it.'

'You didn't ask. I offered.' He swept her into his arms, covering her lips with his. All the stories Paul had told her about Navy men urged her to pull away, but she didn't. Instead she went soft in his arms, falling into him as he pulled her close. His warm, firm lips drove everything from her mind: Cable Grange, the fighting servants, Charles. A thrill coursed through her, like riding Manfred over the hills on a sunny day. Her heart raced, her mind spun and then suddenly it was over. He stepped back, and she smiled as she stared at him, resisting the urge to throw herself into his arms and demand he continue.

'I think we should return to the house,' she stam-

mered. What else did one say after allowing a gentleman to take liberties?

'Indeed.' He offered her his arm and she took it.

She hadn't been able to command one coherent
thought on the walk back. So much had happened so fast
she couldn't make sense out of any of it. Only when they
entered the garden to find her mother and Emily waiting
on the stone patio did her head finally clear. Emily's lips
were drawn tight with worry, but her mother only raised
a curious eyebrow at the sight of them walking so close
together. Julia's grip on the captain's arm tightened.

'What's wrong?'

'I'm going to hear a great deal from Emily about
being so rash. I don't suppose you wish to help me
again?'

'If only I could.' The captain laughed. 'But I'm afraid
you must handle this matter alone.'

Chapter Eight

Emily's clipped steps carried her across the morning-room rug, crossing back and forth in front of Julia, who stood by the fireplace, tapping her foot in irritation. Every day Emily sounded more and more like Charles and the constant lectures were proving quite tiresome. Cable Grange could not be hers soon enough.

'First you go out riding with the captain, alone,' Emily said.

'We didn't go out riding. He happened upon me at the keep.'

'Then you put yourself in danger by involving your-self with the servants in front of him.'

'You'd rather they fight instead of work?' Julia silently pleaded with her mother, wishing for once she'd intervene, but she did nothing except adjust Charlemagne's collar.

'Come, Emily, don't be so hard on Julia.' Uncle George stepped in, refilling his glass of port from the decanter near the window. 'Girl has responsibilities.'

'Don't you understand the way this behaviour appears? Whether innocent or not, it is compromising.'

'In James's eyes, never.' Uncle George laughed. 'He

isn't such an old biddy to get fired up over a ride or an incident with the field hands.'

'I believe you are both failing to see the point.'

'Excuse me, Mrs Howard.' Captain Covington entered the room, respectfully deferential. 'I believe I have some information to put your mind at ease.'

'Information?' Emily asked.

Julia shook her head, but he ignored her, reserving his gracious smile for Emily.

'This afternoon in the forest I asked Miss Howard to marry me and she accepted.'

The room went silent.

'Is it true?' Emily demanded.

Julia wasn't sure how to answer. She hadn't expected him to announce their engagement so soon, but now it was done and she had to play along. 'Of course it's true.'

'But—you hardly know one another.'

'In the short amount of time we've spent together we've discovered a great deal in common. It's as though we've known each other for years.' Captain Covington took Julia's hand and gazed lovingly into her eyes. Her heart fluttered with excitement before she reined in her runaway emotions. Reminding herself it was all a ruse, she returned the loving smile with one of her own, careful not to exaggerate it too much.

Emily twisted her hands in front of her. 'What will Charles say?'

'I have already spoken to Mother and Uncle George,' Julia lied, hoping they would play along, too.

'She did?' Emily asked her mother-in-law, who nodded.

'We discussed it this morning.'

'And you?' Emily turned to Uncle George.

'Jim mentioned it during our ride,' he mumbled, tossing back the last of his port.

Julia let out her breath. Uncle George would demand an explanation, but he could always be counted on to go along.

'Please excuse us, Captain.' Emily grabbed Julia by the arm, pulling her into the hall and closing the morning-room door behind them. 'What's going on?'

'I thought you'd be pleased. You and Charles are always telling me to marry.'

'Yes, but—?'

'But what? Isn't Captain Covington a respectable man?'

'To be sure, but—'

'But what? Uncle George has known him for years, he has a sizeable fortune, and he's amiable and well spoken of. What objection could you possibly have?'

'Marriage isn't something to be entered into lightly.'

'Why shouldn't I be as happy with him as any other gentleman?'

Emily took her by the shoulders, examining her with an older sister's overprotective concern. 'Is there something else to this I should know? You haven't engaged in any compromising behaviour?'

The captain's kiss suddenly came to mind, but her rising anger pushed the memory away. 'Beyond the list you've accused me of?'

'Please, be serious.'

Julia threw up her hands in exasperation. 'Of course not—how could you even make such a suggestion?'

'Because this is all so sudden. Do you love him?'

Julia looked out one of the tall windows flanking the front door where two turtle doves walked in the shade of the portico. Watching them coo to each other, Julia wondered at the question. Love. How would it feel to truly be in love? The fountain in the garden came to mind. Could she find such passion with the captain? No, he'd only prove as meddlesome as he had with the labourers.

'Well?' Emily demanded, breaking the long silence.

'Of course,' Julia lied. She was pretending to be engaged; why not pretend to be in love, too? 'He's the most interesting, well-travelled man I've ever met and quite handsome. You remarked on those exact qualities yourself the other night at cards.'

'Yes, but you seemed so uninterested.'

'I did not know him well then.'

Emily tapped her fingers on her chin, examining Julia, struggling to comprehend the strange turn of events. 'Do you think you'll be happy with him?'

'Yes. I'll have my own home to run. How could I not be happy?' This certainly wasn't a lie and it helped put Emily's mind at ease.

'Then I am glad for you.' She hugged Julia with all the affection of a sister before her smile tensed at the corners. 'Of course, Captain Covington should have asked Charles's permission first—he is your guardian—but I don't think he'll object. I'll write to him about it at once.'

Julia didn't share Emily's worry. No doubt she'd already written to him about Julia's behaviour. If so, she knew Charles would jump to give his consent, if only to see her settled and out of Knollwood. For once, the idea didn't trouble her. 'I'll write him, too. I want him to know of my good fortune.'

They walked back to the morning room, a slight smile tugging at the edges of her lips. Cable Grange and freedom were in her grasp.

Inside, Uncle George pumped Captain Covington's hand, the port in his glass sloshing high along the rim. 'Congratulations, Jim. You don't know how glad I am to hear it. Julia, you couldn't have asked for a better man.'

Julia felt a slight twinge of guilt. If he was this excited by their engagement, how disappointed would he be when it all came to an end?

'Now I have some news to add to yours,' Uncle George announced. 'I've secured invitations to the Johnsons' ball Wednesday night. You two can announce the engagement to everyone.'

'I can't go. I have no dress and I can't have one made in such a short time.' She hadn't planned on making a public announcement. If no one outside the family knew, she could easily break it off with very few consequences.

'One of your London gowns will do,' her mother said and Julia blanched. Her mother knew the engagement wasn't real. Why would she encourage the ball? It must only be to convince Charles of its validity. What other reason could she have? She was almost afraid to imagine it. 'We'll choose a dress today, in case it needs any alterations.'

'Yes, of course.' Julia tried to sound excited, but with no desire to attend the ball it was difficult.

'Do you mind if I have a private word with your groom-to-be?' Uncle George asked and Julia had a good idea what he wished to discuss. At least it meant another person on her side against Charles, one who would speak up for her far more than her mother.

'Not at all. I must write to Charles and I believe Mother wishes to discuss dresses.'

* * *

Once the ladies were gone, George turned a suspicious eye on James. 'Out with it. What are you two up to?'

'You don't believe in true love?'

'Until today you've done nothing but tickle Annette's fancy—now suddenly you and Julia are engaged? Did something happen out on your ride?'

'I assure you, it's nothing like that.'

'Then what?'

'Cable Grange.'

George frowned. 'I thought you were over all that.'

'I am—apparently your niece is not. She thinks an engagement might force her brother's hand.'

'It may just force yours. Charles isn't like Paul and Julia. He may make you go through with it.'

James walked to the window, watching the shadow of clouds pass over the gravel drive. 'Perhaps by the end of it I may not mind.'

'You want to marry her?' George stammered.

'I suppose by the auction, we'll see.' He'd taken a chance announcing the engagement and wasn't sure what would happen by the time Cable Grange came up for sale.

'James...' George joined him at the window, dropping his voice, one eye on the morning-room door '...I've known you a long time and we've been through a lot together, but where Julia is concerned I'll side with her if things go badly. I hope it doesn't come to that, but if it does, you'll find me and Charles standing against you.'

James flexed his left hand, keeping his eyes fixed on a tree in the distance. 'I have no intention of allowing things to go badly. I will do the honourable thing where your niece is concerned, but she may not have me in the end.'

'What do you mean?'

James explained her plan to George, who nodded gravely, taking it all in with a large sip of port.

'I see what you mean.' George rubbed his chin with his hand. 'I knew she wanted the place, but I didn't think she'd go this far to get it.'

'I will do all I can to protect her and her reputation. But as you yourself said, she's spirited.'

'Yes, but better you than the fop.' He slapped James on the back, then headed for the port. 'If nothing else, it will be interesting.'

James laughed, joining his friend in a drink. Yes, it would be interesting.

'Well done,' her mother congratulated when Julia entered the sitting room after giving Davies the letter to Charles to post. She'd written it a few days ago in an effort to phrase her case without distraction or emotion, then simply rewritten it, replacing Simon's name with the captain's.

'Emily did not react well.' Emily had yet to join them and Julia knew she was busy writing her own letter. She could only imagine its contents and hoped Charles's business in London kept him from coming home to see the situation for himself. 'I thought she would be pleased.'

'She'll be less pleased if you jilt the captain.'

'When I jilt the captain,' Julia corrected, sitting at the small table across from her. 'You won't tell her, will you?'

'No, though at some point you'll have to tell Charles.

That alone may stop you from breaking the engagement.'

'Surely you don't want me to marry the captain?'

Mother offered Charlemagne a titbit from the plate next to her. Julia picked at the lace tablecloth, the silence punctuated by the dog's chewing. It wasn't unusual for Mother not to answer, but this time something about it made Julia uneasy.

'I must also find a way to avoid the ball,' Julia added. 'I can't have the whole countryside knowing of my engagement. It will create a scandal when I break it.'

'You'll have a stronger case if it's public knowledge.'

At least Julia had been correct about her mother's motives. 'Yes, but if everyone knows, I'll be the talk of every country party this winter. I'd rather not subject myself to such gossip.'

'My dear, you must learn not to care so much about what people think.'

If only it were so easy, Julia thought, Emily's entrance ending their private conversation.

What followed was a boring hour of flipping through pattern books and discussing trimmings. They invited Annette to join them, but she declined, stating she had no need to rework a dress as those she had brought from London were adequate for a country ball. Very soon Emily and Mrs Howard were debating the merits of their different dresses and doing their best to engage Julia.

'See the way they've used the ribbon here. Wouldn't that be lovely on my white-silk gown?' Emily asked.

'Yes, lovely.' Julia listlessly flipped through a pattern book, eager to be free of all this idle chatter and return to plans for Cable Grange. She still couldn't believe Captain Covington had agreed to go along with her scheme and wondered why.

Julia touched her lips, the memory of his kiss searing the flesh. With all the excitement of the engagement, she hadn't had time to think about it. Now it came rushing back, followed by an unsettling feeling deep in her stomach. Why had he kissed her? Could he have feelings for her? Had she finally turned a man's head? No, of course not. He had no interest in her beyond their amusing game and she only wanted him in order to secure Cable Grange. As for the kiss, what did she expect? She'd acted like a strumpet more than once, so of course he treated her like one. She would have to be more careful in the future.

'I think your blue-silk dress will do very well,' her mother said.

'What blue dress?'

'The one you wore at Almack's.'

Julia shuddered at the memory.

'Oh, yes.' Emily clapped. 'It was so beautiful on you. Fetch it and we'll see if it needs any alterations.'

Julia reluctantly rose and went to her room. Cable Grange couldn't be hers soon enough for she was tired of all this ordering about.

Inside her room, she stood before her wardrobe, wondering which gown Emily meant. She remembered many things about her dreadful night at Almack's, but what she'd worn was not one of them. Too distracted to care, she snatched the first blue dress she saw. Walking back to her mother's room, a ribbon fell off, fluttering to the floor. Julia stooped to pick it up, then stopped at the sound of heated voices from Annette's room.

The door stood slightly ajar and Julia slowly approached, peering through the small crack. It wasn't her habit to stare in keyholes, but the angry tones made her more curious than cautious.

Inside, Annette sat crying on the small padded bench. Simon stood over her, his face red with anger.

'What I do is none of your concern.' For the first time there was emotion in his voice and no hint of his affected dandy lisp.

'Of course it's my concern. You'll ruin us both with your foolery.' Her tears came faster, but they did not soften Simon's hard expression.

'I'm not entirely to blame, dear sister. I've seen your milliner's bill.'

'What choice do I have? I must find a husband before you gamble away my dowry.'

'If you're pursuing Captain Covington, you're wasting your time. I heard him announce to Emily his engagement to Julia. You might as well set your cap at George for all the good it'll do you.'

'I'd rather marry a rich oaf than be sent to the workhouse by you.'

'Don't be so theatrical. You'll always have Mama and Edward to live with.'

'As a spinster if you spend everything. What man wants a penniless woman?'

Julia waited for Simon's response, but all she heard was the muffled sound of Annette's crying.

'If you're finished,' Simon sneered, 'I've hired a coach to take me back to London tomorrow.'

'But Mama and Edward said we must stay until he sorts out your debts with the creditors.'

'I don't care what Edward or Mama say. Stay if you wish, but I'm leaving.'

Simon headed for the door and Julia hurried down the hallway and around a corner. She watched from her hiding place as he emerged stiff-rumped and made his way down the stairs.

In his haste to be rid of his sister, he'd left the door wide open. There was no way to return to her mother's room without walking past Annette's. Releasing her tight hold on the dress, Julia crept down the runner, hoping to sneak by without being seen. Annette still sat on the bench, her face buried in a handkerchief, her shoulders racked with sobs. Despite everything Annette had done and said, Julia felt for the girl. Though she called Charles a great many things in private, he was not quite so hard-hearted as Simon.

Julia took a step and the floor squeaked. Annette's head jerked up in alarm. Caught, Julia hesitated, debating whether or not to comfort the broken-hearted girl. Embarrassment and shame marred Annette's features and Julia knew now was no time for reassuring words. She fled down the hall, hearing the door slam shut behind her.

'What's wrong?' Emily asked when Julia hurried into the room.

'I've just learned the most horrible thing.'

'Is it news from Paul?' Her mother clutched Charlemagne to her chest.

'Heavens, no. It's about Annette and Simon.'

'Oh.' Emily exchanged a knowing look with her mother-in-law. 'So you've found out?'

'Is this what you meant by her situation?'

'Yes, it's the reason they're here.'

'Our brother,' her mother interrupted, for she always referred to her elder brother Edward as 'our brother'. When Edward had married the much younger widow Mrs Taylor, it had sent Uncle George and her mother into fits. 'Thought it wise to remove them from London for a while in the hopes of curbing Simon's expenses.'

'You mean his gambling.'

The older woman nodded.

'Why doesn't his mother stop him? Or Uncle Edward?'

'The inheritance is entailed to Simon. Though he does pay Annette's bills, his debts have taken the vast majority of the money. If he does not stop gambling, he will be bankrupt by year's end.'

'Poor Annette. It certainly explains her peevish behaviour.' Julia sat on the sofa next to her mother.

'She does have a small inheritance of her own, but she regularly spends beyond her income. Our brother hoped you might make friends with her, teach her economy. He failed to take into account her difficult nature.'

'I'd be happy to help if only she weren't so disagreeable.'

She expected Emily to chastise her for the remark, but instead Emily leaned forwards, placing a hand on her arm. 'You must not speak of this to anyone outside the family.'

'Why would I?'

'No, I don't suppose you would, despite how nasty Annette has been to you.'

At least she has a high opinion of me in this regard, Julia thought, but held her tongue.

Chapter Nine

'What a beautiful day for riding, Artemis,' Captain Covington sang out from behind her. At first his nickname had irked her, but the more he used it, the more she liked it.

'I'd ride every day if only the weather would allow it.'

'So you should for that beast should never be cooped up.'

Manfred's ears twitched and Julia laughed, petting his strong neck. 'Ignore him, Manfred. You are no beast.'

Captain Covington laughed. 'Just a poor misunderstood creature.'

'I think we are all misunderstood in our own way, wouldn't you say, Captain?' Julia caught Annette's eyes over the captain's shoulder, but Annette turned away, fiddling with her gelding's reins.

The good weather had held strong overnight and Julia, Captain Covington and Uncle George decided on a ride after nuncheon. Emily encouraged Annette to join them and, for the first time since arriving at Knollwood, she did. Julia suspected it had something to do with what Julia had discovered yesterday afternoon.

Throughout the ride, Annette regarded her with caution, as if waiting for Julia to use her new knowledge in retaliation for everything she'd done. Julia might harmlessly annoy the chit from time to time, but it wasn't in her nature to be deliberately mean or spiteful and she had no intention of taunting Annette about her unfortunate circumstances.

They crested the hill along the boundary between Knollwood and Cable Grange, happening on a bit of excitement in a field on the other side. Two men raced questionable mounts across the field, turning around a moss-covered tree stump at the far end before galloping back to the starting point. The drunken group cheered, their own horses grazing in the grass and waiting for the chance to race. Julia recognised a few riders as the less savoury men of Daringford, more apt to be outside the Sign of the Swan and worse for their experiences inside, than bent over an honest day's labour. The rest of the men were strangers, probably travellers on their way north from London with more hope than brains.

Mr Wilkins sat atop his prize racehorse, Chester, watching the proceedings with a cool eye. Mark stood next to him managing the wagers and collecting a fair amount of blunt at the end of the race. A short distance away, a large barrel balanced on an old stump. Next to it, another of Mr Wilkins's servants dispensed generous tankards of ale to the gathered riff-raff who cheered Wilkins's health with each gulp.

Captain Covington stopped Hector next to Manfred. 'Is this a regular hobby of his?'

'Only when he's lost too much money. How no one has discovered his scam and warned those silly fools, I don't know.'

'Scam?'

'Mr Wilkins doesn't ride Chester into Daringford. Instead he rides Chester's father, Darby, a spry but older horse with markings almost identical to Chester's, but he's not nearly as fast. Inside the tavern, he befriends a few gullible travellers from London then convinces them to race. Once the men agree, Mr Wilkins rides home and exchanges Darby for Chester. These men, sodden with drink, don't realise they're racing one of the finest bits of blood in the county.'

'Don't the country men warn the town men?'

'No, they bet against them and win a few shillings, only to lose them again at the tavern.'

'How do you know so much about it?'

'I heard rumours from the servants after Tom, one of the new ones, lost some money to Wilkins. I wanted to know what he was up to, so I sent Tom back with a few coins and a horse.'

'You spy on your neighbour?'

'Of course. Doesn't everyone? I think it ungentlemanly of Mr Wilkins to wager against unsuspecting travellers. I know they're just as much to blame for trying to win money instead of earning it, but he's sorely mistaken if he thinks he can save Cable Grange off these poor souls.'

'I wouldn't be so sure. A small amount of blunt may be enough to stave off the bailiff.'

'No, he can't.' She watched another set of horses and riders take off across the meadow, noticing the money changing hands with Mark. She'd come too far to let Cable Grange slip from her fingers now. 'We must stop this, if for no other reason than to save those silly men from themselves.'

'For no other reason.' The captain winked. 'What do you propose?'

'It would be wonderful to give Mr Wilkins a taste of his own medicine.'

'So we shall,' Captain Covington replied, mischief igniting his eyes. 'Manfred against Chester—it's a fitting match.'

'I'd love to race Manfred and reveal Mr Wilkins for the scoundrel he really is.'

'It is unladylike for a woman to race, especially against men.' Annette manoeuvred her horse next to Manfred, the warning in her voice clear. 'Even here in the country.'

Julia wondered at the advice, unsure if it was meant to be friendly or yet another insult. Either way, she couldn't ignore the truth of it. Then the idea came to her.

'Captain Covington, we can change saddles and you can ride Manfred.'

'Won't Mr Wilkins recognise the beast?'

'Tell him he's a different horse. He can't risk challenging you and having his secret revealed. Offer him an appealing amount. I'm sure his greed will overcome any hesitation.'

'You don't fear for my safety?'

'Manfred will take care of you just as he's always taken care of me.'

Uncle George leaned forwards in his saddle to peer around Annette at Captain Covington. 'Has a lot of me in her, wouldn't you say?'

'Yes. Sounds very much like something you would have concocted.'

'Then you'll do it?' Julia asked.

'Of course.' The captain threw his leg over the saddle and slid off Hector. He walked around to Manfred and reached up to help Julia down. 'Lean against my right shoulder so I don't drop you.'

'You won't drop me.'

Julia slid from the saddle into the captain's waiting arms, careful to place her weight on his right shoulder. She wound her arm around his neck, allowing her fingertips to brush the smooth skin between the collar and his hair. He lowered her to the ground, the tart smell of his warm skin filling her senses. Their eyes met and for a moment the sound of the cheering men and snorting horses faded into the distance and there was nothing but his body so close to hers.

'I knew you wouldn't drop me.'

'Thank you.' He raised her gloved hand to his lips.

'James, I believe you have a race to attend to.' Uncle George coughed behind them, clearly enjoying what he saw.

She withdrew her hand, her face warm with a blush before she recovered herself. 'Uncle George is right. We must hurry.'

They set to work unbuckling the saddles on their respective horses. When they were free, James placed his saddle on Manfred while George worked to fasten Julia's side-saddle on Hector. When they were done, James helped her mount, then swung atop Manfred. The horse took a couple of agitated steps at the extra weight, but seemed to recognise him and relaxed and James knew Julia's faith in the beast was well placed.

Out of the corner of his eye, James saw Julia start Hector down the hill and he reached out, taking hold of the stallion's bridle.

'What are you doing?' she protested.

'I'm no stickler for convention, but Miss Taylor is right. It isn't proper for a young lady to be seen in such company. Watch from up here.'

She scowled, but didn't argue. 'If I'm to stay here, then you'd better give me a show worth watching.'

'Don't worry. I'll exact your revenge just as you instructed. Come, George, we have work to do.'

George guided Percy into step beside Manfred and the horses picked their way down the small hill. James kept the reins light, surprised by Manfred's docile turn. The horse, unlike before, didn't fight him, but responded fast and quick to the smallest tap of James's foot or the pressure of his legs, answering to these subtle commands as though the two of them had been riding together for years. James smiled, thinking Julia's acceptance of him had in some way secured Manfred's acceptance, too.

They approached the gathering as a race ended and the men exchanged money while enjoying more ale.

'Good morning, Rowan,' George called out. Rowan nodded coolly at George, his sly eyes fixed on James.

'What do you want?' Rowan sneered.

'To race, of course.'

Rowan's lips curled at the sight of the ladies watching from the top of the hill. 'This is a private race.'

'Nonsense,' George insisted. 'It wouldn't be November if you weren't racing and the captain has a mind to wager some blunt.'

'My poor old Darby is no match for Manfred.' Rowan shrugged apologetically, but James was not about to be put off, especially with everyone now listening intently to their conversation.

'This isn't Manfred—this is Whizzer.' James patted Manfred's flank, trying not to laugh.

'He looks exactly like Manfred.'

'Manfred was a bit lame this morning. Didn't see fit to bring him out. Whizzer here is an older horse and I

think a suitable match for Darby.' With a look, James
dared Rowan to challenge him and reveal the truth,
making it clear he knew Rowan's game.

Rowan hesitated. Julia was right; he would not risk
exposing James for fear of exposing himself, but James
could tell he was forming another excuse and knew it
was time to make his move. 'I'll wager five hundred
pounds Whizzer can best Darby.'

Interest replaced the distrust on Rowan's face. 'You
seem very confident in Whizzer.'

'He's the fastest old horse in the county. What do
you say?'

Greed flickered in Rowan's eyes and James knew
he had him.

'I accept your wager,' he answered loudly so the others could hear. 'Five hundred pounds says Darby can
beat Whizzer.'

Sharp whistles and drunken shouts went up from
the crowd and they rushed at Mark to place their bets.

'Shall we?' Rowan gestured to the starting line and
James brought Manfred into place.

A horse whinnied from behind them and Julia turned
to see Mrs Wilkins ride up next to her. She wore a tight-
fitting habit of deep red. It highlighted her pale skin
and emphasised her painted lips. 'Miss Howard, I see
you're enjoying the races.'

Julia stuck her chin in the air, determined not to let
this strumpet act like her better. 'Any excitement is always welcome in the country.'

Mrs Wilkins squinted at the riders. 'Is James about
to race Rowan?'

'Yes, and he will win.'

'How sweet of you to root for him. One would almost think you cared for him.'

'She and the captain are engaged,' Annette volunteered.

Julia went stiff in the saddle, not sure how to react.

'Engaged?' Mrs Wilkins exclaimed in mock amazement, her wicked smile growing wider. 'Oh, you poor dear. I was engaged to Captain Covington once, a long time ago, in Portsmouth. Marry him fast, Miss Howard. He isn't the type of man to follow through on a promise.' She clicked her horse into motion, guiding it down the hill to join the spectators.

Julia watched Mrs Wilkins go, her head spinning, her stomach tight. The captain and Mrs Wilkins? It couldn't be true, could it?

'Why did you tell her?' She turned on Annette. 'I had no intention of sharing such personal information with that woman.'

'Better to tell someone like her yourself than let her hear it from others,' Annette answered, the advice almost friendly. Was she trying to help her? It didn't seem possible.

'You know her?'

Annette shook her head. 'I know of her. She has a terrible reputation in London. According to the *on dit*, a French count paid her bills when her husband couldn't. No one in good society will have anything to do with her.'

Surely a woman with such a scandalous reputation was capable of lying about the past. The hostile meeting in Daringford came to mind, adding a sickening validity to Mrs Wilkins's revelation. He had said he'd known her a long time ago. Could they have been set to marry? It scared her to think he might not honour the engagement, though she didn't know why since she had no intention of marrying either. She thought of his kiss and the way he'd helped her down from Manfred. Had he held Mrs Wilkins like that once?

No, it doesn't matter, she told herself, stamping down the jealousy. With the race about to begin, there were more important things to think about.

James held Manfred at the starting line, the beast tense and ready to run. He noticed Melinda on her horse making her way down from where Julia and Miss Taylor watched. Anger filled him and he took a deep breath, forcing himself to calm down and focus on winning. He would not lose in front of Melinda.

'I can't wait to give you a beating and knock down some of that chit's pride,' Rowan spat, his horse pawing at the ground.

James tightened his grip on the reins. 'I hope you have the five hundred pounds to make good on your wager.'

'Gentlemen, are ya ready?' Mark stood between the horses, arms raised.

'Don't fail me, Manfred. Your mistress is counting on us both,' he whispered and the horse's ears twitched in response.

Mark dropped his arms and James dug his heels into Manfred's sides. They shot out over the meadow, James crouched low over Manfred's neck, the wind stinging his eyes. He didn't try to control Manfred, but concentrated on moving with the horse, letting the animal guide them to a win. In a flash of brown, Rowan and Chester raced up beside them, the horses' heavy breaths and pounding hooves drowning out the cheering men. Rowan nearly slammed Chester against Manfred, trying to drive them off course, but Manfred proved the more dominant animal. He bumped Chester's flank, knocking James's legs into Rowan's with a thud.

'Hell,' Rowan cursed as Chester relented, falling behind enough for James to manoeuvre Manfred around the stump first and place a bit of distance between the racers. Under the crook of his arm, James watched Rowan slap Chester's flanks with his crop, urging him faster and faster, but the gap was too wide and Manfred dashed across the finish line.

'Well done!' Julia shouted, her kidskin gloves muffling her exuberant claps.

The captain rose up in his saddle, saluting her before the men crowded around, cheering as money changed hands.

'That'll show the Wilkinses,' Julia laughed, her excitement fading at the sight of Mrs Wilkins riding up next to the captain. They exchanged a few words, then James pulled Manfred's reins to the right, trotting over to where Uncle George and Percy stood.

Watching them, Mrs Wilkins's revelation sat like a dark shadow over Julia, dampening her enthusiasm. How could he have ever been involved with such a woman or had she once been respectable?

'Do you know anything about Mrs Wilkins's past?' Julia asked and Annette shook her head.

'No. I only know the rumours.'

Had Mrs Wilkins fallen from good society because of her involvement with the captain? Did the same fate await her?

'We shouldn't be here. It isn't proper.' Julia ignored the way Annette's eyebrows rose in disbelief. Without waiting for an answer, Julia turned Hector around and galloped back to Knollwood. She wanted to be alone, to think and settle the trouble gripping her heart. Surely there was another explanation. The captain didn't seem like the sort of man who ruined women and Uncle George would never have such a friend. Whatever the truth, she must make certain they played at nothing more than the pretend engagement. Her reputation would suffer enough when she jilted him. She did not need the additional scandal of being a fallen woman.

James walked with George back from the stables, a sense of unease nagging at him. Melinda's sudden appearance combined with her happy salutations for their engagement made him suspicious. He knew from her malicious smile she'd told Julia of their engagement, probably portraying their relationship in the worst possible light. Who knew what lies she'd attached to it? He had to find Julia and undo any damage the vile woman had done.

Davies met them at the back door with a letter. 'This arrived for you, Captain Covington.'

James took the note, not recognising the hand until he broke the seal and scanned the contents. Crumpling the letter, he stuffed it inside his coat pocket.

'What's wrong?' George asked.

'She wants to see me.'

'Julia?'

'Melinda. She wishes to discuss Rowan's debt and the sale of Cable Grange.'

'So you do still want it. Julia won't take kindly to you purchasing it out from under her.'

James laced his fingers behind his back. 'With Rowan in my debt, perhaps I can convince him to sell it to her. It's more reliable than an auction. Please tell everyone I had business to attend to in Daringford. I'll return as soon as I can.'

'Let me come with you. I don't trust Melinda or you with her.'

'You think I'm so weak?'

'I think you're too angry. I thought you'd let go of the past, but I can see by your reaction to that letter that you haven't. My guess is, neither has she.'

The past still stung, but it no longer dominated his mind. Nor did the future seem so vague or purposeless thanks to Julia. Her spirited laugh, hopeful eyes and honest manner helped him imagine a life filled with travel, family and friends, all of it with her by his side. He loved her and he wanted to capture her heart, make it burn for him as powerfully as it did for her beloved Knollwood. He could no longer deny it was the real reason he'd agreed to the engagement.

Fear tinged the revelation. He'd been deceived by a woman once before, but he couldn't imagine Julia ever betraying him. She loved as strongly as she lived and would give herself completely to the man who captured her heart. He hoped by the end of next week he could make her his. If securing Cable Grange meant winning her, then he would buy it. 'The past is done. It's time to see to my future.'

James knocked on the heavy oak door of Cable Grange and waited, drawing his coat tight around his face to ward off the frosty night air. The sun had slipped below the horizon and although light still filled the western sky, the night's first stars sparkled overhead. The scrape of wood across stone and the squeak of rusty hinges split the silence as Mark pulled open the door.

The single candle in his brass holder flickered in the draught, shadowing his bloodshot eyes.

'She's waiting for you upstairs,' he snarled.

James stepped inside, the dingy entrance hall no warmer than outside. Larger and more spacious than Knollwood's, it echoed like an old cavern, the chandelier overhead thick with cobwebs. 'Then lead the way.'

Without ceremony, Mark started up the staircase, the smoking tallow candle not doing much more than threatening to burn out. James peered down through the wavering shadows, trying to get a sense of the place. Dust covers sagged over the few scattered pieces of furniture and glaring clean spots on the dirty walls betrayed the paintings long since sold to pay bills.

At the top Mark turned, leading James down the dank hallway. The carpets were missing here, too, along with the furniture.

'She's in here.' Mark stopped at the last door at the end of the hall. 'You can find your own way out when she's through with ya.'

'I trust I can.'

Mark walked off, taking the light with him.

Without knocking, James pushed open the door, blinking against the sudden light. The house might be decaying around them, but no expense was spared to make Melinda comfortable. The room resembled a Cyprian's palace with gilded chandeliers filled with candles. A grand four-poster bed hung with sumptuous draperies sat in the far corner of the room. At the other end a large fireplace blazed with a well-laid fire. Melinda reclined on a chaise before its heat, dressed in a mantua of red silk. A bottle of wine sat on the table in front of her, along with a small box of sweets.

James could see half the contents of both had already been consumed.

'I didn't think you'd come.' She ran her fingers across the back of a velvet pillow.

'I almost didn't. What do you want?'

'Please sit down.' She motioned to the sofa across from her. In the low light there was something of the woman he'd once loved, the faint echo of her girlish beauty, the tempting smile and inviting eyes that had captivated him in his youth. Back then he hadn't recognised the worldliness in their shallow gleam, but it stood out now, repulsing him.

'You said you had news.' He sat on the edge of the cushion, eyeing the minx with caution. The elaborate scene felt like a gilded wire waiting to ensnare him.

'I do. Wine?'

He shook his head. 'Let's have it out. I can't stay here all night.'

'Why?' She leaned over the table to refill her glass, her mantua gaping open to reveal her breasts almost to the nipples. 'You have no wife to go home to.'

'But you have a husband.'

Disgust crossed her face before she hid it behind the wine glass, taking a long sip. 'He's in town trying to win enough money from your friend Mr Taylor to ward off the bailiff and you. I suspect Mr Taylor is as destitute as we are.' She chuckled callously, lying back on the *chaise* like an Egyptian queen. 'So you're to be married to the Howard girl? She's not woman enough for a man like you.'

'What do you know of me?' he demanded and she rose, sauntering forwards, the firelight silhouetting her round hips and curving body.

She sat down next to him, her eyes heavy, the sickeningly sweet smell of her perfume mixing with wine in the air between them. 'You loved me once.'

'I was too young to know the difference between love and lust.' He leaned back against the arm of the sofa. 'And if I remember correctly, I didn't have enough money to suit your tastes.'

She shrugged off the accusation. 'But you're here now.'

'Only to discuss the sale of Cable Grange.'

She smiled out of the corner of her hard eyes. 'You plan to give it to your fiancée.'

'How do you know?'

'Everyone knows she wants it. Her father offered to buy it before he died. He hoped to leave it to her. I convinced Rowan not to do it. As much as I hate this tomb, I'd rather see the bailiff sell it than let that bitch have it.'

He was on his feet in an instant, staring down at her with a rage he fought hard to control. 'We have nothing further to discuss.' He stormed to the door, determined to leave her in the past once and for all.

'I have an offer to make,' Melinda called after him.

He stopped, his hand on the doorknob, but didn't turn around. 'I'm listening.'

She slid up to him, wrapping her hands around his shoulders and laying her head on his back. Her fingers played with the skin of his neck, working their way under his collar and down to his chest. He resisted the urge to flinch. 'I'll talk Rowan into selling you this crumbling pile of bricks if you spend the night with me.'

He whirled around, grabbing her wrists and pulling them from around his neck. 'You overvalue any feelings I ever had for you.'

Her wine-heavy eyes flared and she snatched her

arms from his grasp. 'When did you ever care for me? You indulged your whim, then abandoned me?'

The accusation struck his sense of honour, increasing his anger. 'You gave yourself with wild enthusiasm, then trampled over me to get to Rowan and his money.'

'If you'd truly loved me, you'd have won me back, not left me to that drunkard. My life is a shambles, ruined, and it's your fault.'

'You have no one to blame but yourself.' He reached for the doorknob, but she threw herself between him and the door.

'If you go, I'll tell the trollop you were here tonight.'

He leaned in close, waving a menacing finger inches from her nose. 'You say anything and I'll tell your husband you tried to seduce me.'

Fear flashed in her eyes. 'He wouldn't believe you.'

'I have your letter. If he finds out I was here, he'll toss you in the gutter where you belong.'

'You wouldn't dare,' she whimpered like a spoiled child.

'Not as long as you keep your mouth shut.'

He pushed her aside and strode into the hallway, his eyes struggling to adjust to the darkness. At the top of the stairs, his hand found the banister and followed the dusty wood down into the empty hall. He pulled open the front door, wincing at the sharp scrape of wood on stone.

Not until he was free of the house and galloping back to Knollwood did he dare reflect on what had happened. Why had he answered her letter? He should have known it was all a ruse, but once again he'd allowed himself to be fooled by her. Now there was a new fear. She might twist tonight's events to her own advantage and throw them in Julia's face. What would

Julia think of him then? Only the worst and all hope with her would be lost. No, there was little chance she and Melinda would meet and even if they did, Melinda had no proof of their meeting.

James brought Hector to a stop at the turn to Knollwood. If he continued straight, he'd reach the road to London and it was little over two hours' steady riding to town. Melinda might hate Cable Grange, but Rowan had proved obstinate about selling it. Now, with his debt to James hanging over him, Rowan might be more desperate and willing to part with the estate. James could instruct his solicitor to make enquiries and to keep his identity secret since he doubted the Wilkinses would sell to him, no matter what their circumstances. It might all come to nothing. For all he knew, Rowan's luck had changed and he'd won enough to halt the auctions. However, if the deed to Cable Grange meant securing Miss Howard's affection, he was willing to try.

Julia lay in bed, turning over on her back for what seemed like the hundredth time since she'd blown out the candle. Captain Covington hadn't come to dinner. Uncle George said he'd gone to town, but by nine o'clock he still hadn't returned. She'd waited up for him in the study, hoping to discuss Mrs Wilkins and put some of her fears to rest, but by eleven o'clock she could no longer endure the silent waiting so she went to bed.

She rolled on her side, pulling her cool pillow close. The moon had set at least an hour ago, casting the room into darkness. Closing her eyes, she tried to sleep, but the memory of his lips, warm and tender, parting hers, kept her awake. She bit her lip, trying to banish the strange yearning coursing through her. Tracing a crease in the sheets, she remembered the feel of his neck beneath her fingers when he'd helped her off Manfred, his hands around her waist, his eyes riveted on hers. She imagined him laying her down in the soft grass, his body covering hers, his mouth doing things to her she could almost feel.

Julia sat up, smacking her pillow in frustration. She's never given a fig for any gentleman, yet the captain filled her with all sorts of sinful thoughts. They brought to mind another curiosity: Paul's book, the secret one she'd discovered hidden in the back of his wardrobe a few years ago. She wondered if it was still there and if she could get it without being seen. Everyone else was in bed and she had not heard anything to indicate the captain was back from Daringford. She could sneak in and out of his room without anyone ever knowing.

Rising, she threw on her wrapper, then cracked open the door and peered down the hallway. Small candles flickered in the sconces and a sliver of light showed under the door of Emily's room, but her mother's room was dark. Thankfully, she was a sound sleeper and Julia didn't expect her to rise. She listened for evidence of servants walking about, but only baby Thomas's muffled cries broke the sleeping silence. She sighed with relief, knowing his wails would cover any sound and keep Emily from leaving her room.

The hardwood floors alternating with the soft plush of the rugs teased her bare feet as she stole down the hallway. Stopping at the captain's room, she peeked through the keyhole to make sure he hadn't returned unnoticed. Orange coals glowed in the grate, throwing some light on the flat bed with its unwrinkled coverlet. Twisting the doorknob, she froze when it squeaked, her heart pounding against her chest while she listened for any evidence of discovery. The only sound was the continued cry of baby Thomas.

She pushed open the door and slipped inside, swiftly closing it behind her. The faint light from the fireplace barely illuminated the room, but Julia knew it well. It was just as Paul had left it with a large wardrobe on the right, a four-poster bed between the two windows and a washstand and chair against the far wall.

Julia hurried to the wardrobe, pulled open the double doors and began feeling for the book. Her hands ran over the scratchy wool of Paul's old uniforms, slid under the folded trousers and bumped a pair of worn Hessians. She caught them before they hit the floor and, with a relieved breath, put them back. Reaching in deeper, she thought maybe he'd moved the book but then her fingers brushed against the leather tome.

She eased it out, careful not to disturb the folded garments or boots. Once it was free, she stood, clutching it to her breast. She traced the gold-edged pages, eager to open them and explore the forbidden content. The possibility of being discovered in a single gentleman's room added a certain thrill to the anticipation, but having no wish to be discovered in such a compromising situation, she moved to close the wardrobe doors. Only then did she hear the heavy fall of a man's boots in the hallway. She froze, her heart almost drowning out the sound. The footsteps drew closer, followed by the flickering light of a candle visible beneath the door. Julia searched for an escape, but there was no way out. As the doorknob turned, splitting the silence with its metallic squeak, she stepped inside the wardrobe and pulled the door closed behind her.

The wardrobe door hadn't fully closed, allowing Julia to see through the slight opening. Crouching low, her knees on the scratchy wool uniform, she watched the captain enter and place his candle on the washstand before closing the door. He removed his blue-wool coat and she clutched the book tight, afraid he might hang it in the wardrobe. She let out a long, silent breath when he threw it over the chair next to the bed. He poured some water from the pitcher into the basin, then splashed it on his face. Large drops dripped from his chin while he examined his face in the mirror, a dark scowl marring his features. Whatever he'd done that evening must not have been pleasant.

He walked around the bed, sitting down hard, facing the wardrobe. Julia rocked back away from the crack, her legs crying out from the impossible position. She hoped he went to bed quickly for she had no desire to stay in such a cramped situation all night. He removed his boots, tossing them off to the side, then reached over his head and pulled off his shirt. Julia's breath caught, but this time it was for quite a different reason. Through the crack, she examined his solid chest, the tight muscles of his stomach and his slim waist. In the candlelight his smooth skin glowed, soft and strong at the same time. She noticed at the base of his left collar-bone the puckered skin of a scar. He stood and turned away from her, revealing a similar scar on his back. If only she could slip up behind him, run her fingers over his wide shoulders, trace the line of his spine to where it tapered down to his trousers and explore what lay covered by the fabric. He walked back to the washstand and she gripped the book, leaning further forwards to take him in. As he examined his scar in the mirror, his hands flew to his neck and he jerked up straight.

'Damn.' He tore through the fabric of his discarded shirt and jacket, then tossed them back on the chair in frustration. He dropped to his hands and knees, feeling under the bed. Whatever he searched for remained missing for he sat back on his heels, balling his fists on the edge of the bed, his anger changing to sad resignation.

He must have lost his medal. He said he always wore it, but she hadn't seen it when he'd taken off his shirt. She felt for him, knowing it must hurt to lose something so personal.

Her sympathy vanished when he stood, his fingers working the buttons of his trousers. She moved closer to the crack, a delicious sort of anticipation filling her. He hooked his thumbs in the waistband of his trousers and she leaned forwards, placing her hands on the wardrobe door, waiting, eager, hungry to see all he was about to reveal. Suddenly the door swung open and she tumbled out, her knee hitting the floor hard, the book landing with a thud in front of her.

'Artemis?' The captain buttoned his trousers with one hand while the other took her by the arm and pulled her to her feet. 'What are you doing in the wardrobe?'

What she wouldn't give for a good answer, but she had none. Instead she continued to stare at him, too embarrassed, shocked and bruised to answer.

'Well?' he demanded, his face inches from hers, his voice low and gruff.

'You weren't here and I wanted one of my brother's books.'

'From the wardrobe?'

'It's special.' Her eyes darted to where the book had fallen, relieved to see it lay closed. Then the captain reached for it.

'No, I'll get it.' She lunged for it, but he was faster, snatching it up and away from her.

'I know this book.' He turned it over in his hands,

then to her horror flipped it open. He thumbed through the pages, his eyes widening, then his mouth settled into an amused grin. 'Special indeed.'

She wished the floor would open up and swallow her. It was bad enough to be caught in his room, but worse with him half-naked and with that kind of book. She followed the small line of dark hair leading down from his bare stomach into his trousers. His chest rose and fell much quicker than before while he examined the illustrations.

'May I have my book back?' She put out her hand, determined to reclaim as much of her dignity as possible.

He closed the book, then held it out, struggling to remain serious.

She took it, clutching it to her chest like a plate of armour. Her mind kept telling her to turn and leave before she compromised herself even further, but she found her feet rooted to the floor, her eyes riveted to his.

'I should be going,' she whispered.

He nodded, stepping closer. 'Yes, you should.'

She didn't move, but continued to stare until he bent his face down to hers. She closed her eyes, feeling his soft lips envelop hers. The heat of it spread through her body and her mouth responded, parting to accept his tongue. It caressed the line of her lips, sending a shiver through her body.

The book fell, landing with a thud on the carpet as he pulled her close, pressing every inch of him against her, his deep kisses making her forget about the noise and consequences. Only the captain mattered. As she leaned into his chest, her shift and wrapper did little to separate their bodies or hide his hard anticipation pressing against her stomach.

She slid her arms around his waist and ran her hands up his back, her fingers brushing his scar before curling over the roll of his shoulders. She'd imagined being this close to him, but never realised how delicious it would feel or the way it made her whole being come alive. Suddenly, she understood something about those pictures in Paul's book, but none of them captured the desire she felt in the captain's arms.

She inhaled the faint scent of smoke and wine in his hair as he traced the line of her jaw with his lips. Where had he been? She didn't know or care as his teeth grazed her earlobe, his breath hot on her neck. Julia closed her eyes, his touch increasing the need coiling within her.

'Captain?' she whispered, unable to tell him what she wanted, but eager to follow him wherever his caresses led.

'Artemis.' His husky voice tickled her ear before his lips found hers again.

He guided her to the bed and pressed her down on the thick coverlet. His body covered hers, firm and strong, as his hands caressed her arms, then trailed the side of her stomach. A shock went through her when he cupped her breast and his thumb stroked the nipple, bringing it to a tender point. Closing her eyes, she realised now how a man could make a woman forget herself.

He slipped the shift from her shoulder, exposing her breast, and the cool air tickled her heated skin. She gasped, her fingers digging into his arm when he took her nipple in his mouth, flicking it with his tongue. Pleasure curled deep in her body and she moaned, wanting everything the captain offered. His deft hand traced the line of her leg, skimming the smooth flesh of her hip and sliding the shift up around her waist. While his tongue circled her breast his fingers brushed the top of her thigh until they found her aching centre.

Clinging to him, she thought she would die when he caressed the delicate skin. No pictures in any book could have prepared her for this. She moved against him, her body tightening, craving, hungry, and soon she was without reason, her breath fast, her body bending towards something she couldn't name, but it was there, in his fingers, his mouth, the smell of him. She arched her back, his mouth covering hers to muffle the cries as waves of pleasure tore through her body.

He withdrew his fingers and she lay against the pillows, weak and trembling like a newborn foal, but at the same time eager and anxious.

'Again,' she whispered, kissing his neck, his need evident against her leg. She ran her hand over the firm muscles of his chest, following the ripples of his stomach down to his breeches, knowing there was more and wanting to experience it all.

He took her hand and she opened her eyes, studying his face in the dim light. It burned with passion and wanting and something very much like guilt.

'We can't do this.' He pulled her shift down over her legs, then stood.

She sat up, confused and in some way wounded. 'Why?'

'Because it's not right. And there might be consequences.'

What she wouldn't risk to feel such pleasure again, but his sober face drained away her passion, replacing it with shame. 'You don't want me?'

'I want you very much.' He traced her jaw with his finger, brushing the hair back off her shoulder. 'But I can't dishonour you like this.'

'No, of course not.' He didn't want her. No man did and the hurt cut deep. She pulled her shift tighter, her embarrassment more powerful than her sense of caution as she fled the room, struggling to hold back tears.

In her haste, Julia failed to notice Emily standing in her darkened room, her door ajar. Baby Thomas had finally settled to sleep and she'd heard a loud thump. She never expected to see her sister-in-law emerging from Captain Covington's room.

Chapter Ten

Julia pulled back the bow, aiming for the centre of the target. Opening her fingers, the arrow flew, hitting the large white area outside the target. She nocked her next arrow with a huff, convinced nothing was meant to go her way this week. Even riding Manfred this morning hadn't cleared her mind. Luckily the captain had accompanied Uncle George to Creedon to help make some decisions concerning the repairs, sparing her the embarrassment of sitting across from him at breakfast.

Memories of last night tortured her. She let another arrow fly, watching it sail over the target to land in the grassy field. He was right—what they'd done was wrong—but the lingering sensation in the deepest parts of her and the delicious way he'd brought her to pleasure replaced the shame and increased her yearning. Only the thought of his quick dismissal made her blush with embarrassment.

She pulled back the bowstring, struggling against her shaking hands to aim. How did one face a gentleman after such an encounter? How would he react to her? He would be discreet and she'd never tell anyone, but she feared when they were together with other people, the pleasure of their brief encounter would be written all over her face for everyone to see.

She released the arrow and this time it hit closer to the centre.

'Excellent shot, Artemis,' Captain Covington congratulated from behind her.

She whirled to face him, her chest tight with fear. A meeting was inevitable, but she hadn't expected it so soon.

A smile graced his features, but it fell when Julia pinned him with a hard glare. He stood near the equipment table arranging the arrows, his tousled hair falling over his forehead. She longed to run her fingers through the dark strands, then caress the smooth skin of his face. Plucking the bowstring, she willed the urge away and forced herself to remain calm. This constant craving for him made her feel like a runaway carriage no one could stop and she hated it.

'There is a slight wind, otherwise I would have hit the mark.' She tried to sound nonchalant, but it came out more irritable than intended.

'I see.' He held up the fletched end of the arrow, but not one feather moved. 'I think the wind has died down. Perhaps you should try again.'

She snatched it from his outstretched hand, then stormed back to her mark. Knocking the bow, she aimed and fired. The arrow missed the bullseye again but stuck in one of the centre rings.

'Yes, I see the wind has increased,' the captain observed dryly, his meaning all too clear. She realised this probably wasn't his first awkward morning encounter with a lady. If only she were as well schooled in afterpleasure etiquette.

Julia stepped aside, sweeping her arm in the direction of the range. 'Please, take a shot. Being a sailor, you must know a great deal about how the wind blows.'

'I do, though I'm not always correct.' He nocked his arrow, pulled back the bow and let it fly. The arrow stuck in the outer ring of the target. Lowering the bow, he grimaced in pain before recovering himself. Despite her anger, she moved to comfort him before catching herself, feeling a little guilty at goading him once again into straining his wounded shoulder.

'It appears you judged wrong this time.' Julia clapped, the sound hollow in the quiet between them. Selecting an arrow, she stepped forwards, aimed and hit the target dead centre.

'You seem to have a much better grasp of how it blows—perhaps you can advise me?'

'A gentleman of your experience hardly needs my advice.'

'My experience is not quite as developed as you believe.'

Julia moved to choose another arrow but Captain Covington stepped in front of her, his eyes pointed. She smiled up at him, refusing to betray the fluttering in the pit of her stomach at his commanding presence. Despite her anger and embarrassment, having him so close only made her think of his hands on her bare skin, the strength and weight of his chest, the hot feel of his lips and tongue playing with hers. She turned away, laying the bow on the table and fingering the leather strap of her armguard. She did not want to have feelings for a man who only feigned interest in her or who might abandon her as he had another.

'Let us be frank with one another. I apologise for my inappropriate behaviour. It will not happen again. Can you forgive me?'

Something in the sincerity colouring his blue eyes while he searched her face for a response made her want to forgive him, to throw herself in his arms and reveal—reveal what? How could she express feelings she barely understood herself? If she told him, he would laugh and she couldn't face more humiliation.

'Perhaps we should end our sham engagement now.' She worked the leather knot of her armguard, refusing to meet his face. If they ended the game, they wouldn't be forced into each other's presence and she could collect her thoughts and return everything back to normal. There was still time to find another way to get Cable Grange.

'If that's what you wish.' He took her elbow and untied the leather strap. His eyes told her the truth but the way he held her arm said more and it scared her. If she asked him to end this, he would. She only needed to speak, but she didn't possess the words or strength to end the pleading in his eyes.

'Please know this is no longer a game for me. I am quite serious and I believe you are, too.' He moved nearer and she closed her eyes, his breath warm on her cheek before he kissed her. In his lips she felt a need and hope echoed in her own heart. She added her silent questions to his, unsure of the answers. No, this was no longer a game. It was something much deeper.

Someone cleared his throat and they jumped apart. Davies stood a short distance away, his calm demeanour betraying nothing. 'Miss Howard, your presence and the captain's is requested in the study.'

'Requested? By who?'

'Captain Russell.'

Julia almost reprimanded Davies for interrupting them, then realised she should thank him. Once again she'd been weak in the captain's presence. Davies might be the most discreet of servants, but what if someone less reliable had seen them?

'Shall we?' Captain Covington offered Julia his arm and she took it.

The tangle of emotions continued to plague her until she wanted to scream with frustration. What did he mean it was no longer a game? She knew, though she refused to admit it. Why couldn't people leave her alone so she could think? Instead here was yet another demand and from Uncle George of all people. Usually, he was the one person at Knollwood who didn't order her about. Perhaps there was news from London or of Paul? A new fear filled her and her hand tightened on the captain's arm.

'Is something wrong?' the captain asked, squeezing her hand.

She shook her head. 'Davies, is it news of Paul?'

'No, Miss Howard.'

Her grip relaxed and they followed Davies up the stone steps and through the back sitting room. The instant they entered the study, everything became clear.

'What are you doing here?' Julia demanded.

Charles turned around, his grey eyes growing darker at the sight of her hand on the captain's arm. Her mother sat quietly in the window seat, her lips drawn tight, and Julia knew she'd been forced to endure another of his long-winded tirades.

'I received Emily's letter.' He held up the wrinkled paper as though Julia needed reminding. How typical of Charles to be so dramatic.

'I was told Uncle George wanted to see me,' Julia answered.

'I'm the one who summoned you. I knew you wouldn't come if Davies said it was me.'

'I thought as much.' Julia crossed her arms, already tired of Charles. 'Did you bring my inheritance?'

He stepped closer, but she did not step back. Try as he might, he didn't scare her for she knew he was more bluster than any real threat. To his credit and her relief, the captain remained by her side. 'I'm here to find out what you're up to and save you from who knows what scandal.'

'What scandal?' *If only he knew.* Julia dug her nails into her palm to keep from laughing. For once Charles was correct, but she'd deny it to the grave before she let him know.

'Riding alone with a gentleman, confronting a mob of angry men…' Charles ticked off on his fingers '…visiting a gentleman in the middle of the night.'

He knows! Someone must have seen her leaving the captain's room. It didn't matter for she had no intention of admitting anything. 'I don't know what you're talking about.'

'Don't dare deny it. Emily saw you last night.'

Over Charles's shoulder, Emily sat, shamefaced, the tips of her pale ears red. Julia's heart pounded in her chest and she tried to think of some explanation or way to redeem herself. No, despite his proof, she would give him nothing. If she let him bully her now, she'd never be free of his heavy hand. She drew herself up to face him, but the captain spoke first.

'Mr Howard, I assure you nothing inappropriate took place. She was retrieving one of your brother's books while I was gone. Unfortunately, I came back early.'

'Thank you, sir, for your explanation, but you have a great deal to answer to in regards to my sister's honour.'

'Charles,' her mother chided, 'you of all people should not give such lectures.'

Charles's face went red and his mouth fell open, his stunned expression matched by Emily's. Julia threw her mother a silent question, but received no response before Charles recovered himself.

'Captain Covington, please excuse us for a moment. I wish to have a private word with my sister before you and I speak.'

'Of course.'

James closed the door behind him, taking a deep breath in the cool dark of the hallway. Through the heavy oak he heard Julia and Charles arguing at the top of their voices.

'I don't know what you're up to with this rash engagement, but after last night you will marry him,' Charles insisted.

'I will do no such thing.'

'Be reasonable.'

'Reasonable, from the man who is the most unreasonable.'

'It's only a matter of time before the story is known.'

'Why? Do you and Emily intend to spread it?'

James had not confessed his feelings to her. He'd been on the verge when they were interrupted. Now everything stood in the balance. Charles knew about their encounter last night, but Julia's stubborn nature worried him more than Charles's. Despite her true feelings, of which he had a good sense, she would never marry him if her brother insisted.

The door opened and Mrs Howard marched up to him.

'Captain Covington, if you have any interest in my

daughter, now is the time to make it known, especially to her.' She walked off down the hall, her spaniel trotting behind her.

Inside the study, the sibling argument rose three octaves.

'If you had no intention of marrying him, why did you become engaged?' Charles demanded.

'You wouldn't understand.'

'Then Emily's suspicions were right.'

'You'd like nothing better than for all your suspicions to be right. Perhaps if you suspected good in me, you'd be less disappointed.'

'Please lower your voice.'

'Stop ordering me about.'

'Julia, be reasonable.'

If he didn't intervene now, he might lose all chance with her. The more her brother insisted, the more she'd resist, no matter what was in her heart. And what was in her heart? He'd seen it in her eyes outside: passion, longing and the faint traces of love. But there was trepidation there, too, of loving without return, broken trust and betrayal. He knew the power of those emotions, but, striding into the study, he refused to succumb to either her fears or his own.

Charles sat at the desk, his head in his hands. Julia stood on the other side, her back to James, her palms flat on the smooth wood surface. Did she know how formidable she was? He doubted it, for with men like Charles always underestimating her, she greatly underestimated herself.

'Excuse me.' James cleared his throat.

Brother and sister looked at him.

'Tell him nothing happened for he obviously doesn't

trust me,' Julia insisted, her eyes pleading with him to help.

'If I may,' James addressed Charles. 'I believe I have a solution to the current dilemma. But I must speak to Miss Howard, alone.'

Charles studied the two of them, his frustration reflected in his nervous, wide-eyed wife, who sat by the window. 'As you like. But I only wish to entertain one resolution.'

'On this we are both in agreement.'

Charles nodded. 'Come, Emily. Let's leave them alone.'

Emily took Charles's hand and together they left, closing the door behind them. Once they were alone, Julia turned fiery eyes on James.

'There is nothing you can say to solve the situation. I suggest you return to London at once so we may avoid any more of these awkward situations.'

'I have another, more practical solution.'

'Which is?'

'For us to marry.'

'Marry?' Her eyes widened with surprise and, unless he was mistaken, flattered hope, before narrowing in suspicion. 'Whatever for?'

'Mutual enjoyment and benefit.' At this moment with her temper high, he doubted she'd believe him if he told her the truth behind his very sincere proposal. Once he had her, there would be time to reveal his heart. 'I know you don't relish the idea of marriage, but do you really wish to stay here at Knollwood with your brother, for the rest of your life?'

'Of course not. I want Cable Grange.'

'What if I offered you more than Cable Grange?'

'More?'

He cocked one suggestive eyebrow. 'Much more.'

She crossed her arms over her chest. 'And when the thrill of much more fades?'

'There is a great deal more than that.' He drew her to the atlas, the delicious scent of rosewater filling his senses. He longed to touch her face, caress her cheek with his hand, but he had to proceed slowly or she would spook and all would be lost. 'The Caribbean, perhaps, or Venice, even India.'

His fingers traced the illustrated countries and seas and her eyes followed the routes with interest. 'But what about Cable Grange?'

'You may still have it, and this—' he tapped the gilded pages '—but unmarried, you'll have neither.'

She shook her head. 'And when there is a parcel of children dragging at my heels, will I really have this?'

He leaned in with a wicked smile. 'I'm a Navy man. I know a great deal about a great many things, including avoiding a parcel of children.'

'You didn't last night.'

'I was unprepared by your sudden appearance. In the future I'll be more ready for such situations.'

Her eyes widened in shock. 'Really?'

'Yes, my little Artemis. Though I may insist on one or two children.'

'Well, that's not unreasonable.' She turned back to the atlas, eyebrows knitted while she pondered his suggestion. 'Why me? Why not Annette or some other woman?'

'Because you have a courageous nature well suited to adventure.'

'And the rest?' The word lingered between them.

'In time, it will come.' He brushed her lips with his own, feeling her excitement and anticipation.

Gently, his mind cautioned. He stepped back, her sultry eyes stealing the wind from his chest, yet he found the breath to whisper, 'Marry me?'

Chapter Eleven

With a single word, Julia found herself at the centre of a frenzy of activity. For two days she was tugged in a hundred directions while Emily and her mother rushed to plan the wedding. The captain was spared the madness. Shortly after his proposal, he received word from his solicitor in London and departed to take care of business. He also planned to buy their wedding rings and make arrangements for a short honeymoon while in town. He was set to return this evening, in time for the ball, and there they would make their engagement public.

She shivered at the thought.

'Are you all right, miss?' The seamstress looked up at Julia from where she knelt, pinning the hem of the London dress they'd chosen for the wedding.

'Yes, thank you.'

'You'll need a proper shift, perhaps more than one,' Emily said from the sofa, reviewing the ever-growing trousseau list.

'Whatever you think is best,' Julia agreed, her mind still whirling. What had she done?

'I don't believe you'll need linens,' Emily mused and her mother nodded.

'She can have my mother's set.'

Julia did her best not to roll her eyes in frustration at this inane conversation. Here she was, prepared to lash herself to a man she barely knew, and all Emily could think about was linens and lace. Though the captain's long friendship with Uncle George gave her some measure of confidence in her current and what would very soon be her future situation, she still worried. A gentleman was apt to act differently with other gentlemen than he was with ladies, especially a wife.

The seamstress motioned for her to turn and she complied, her mind lingering on the memory of the captain when he'd asked—no, bargained with her to marry him. His eyes had held a pleasant mix of hope and—dare she believe it—love? No, it wasn't possible. But if it wasn't, then why would he insist she marry him? He had nothing to gain by the union. And what had he meant at the archery range by the game meaning more?

'My man of affairs secured the special licence and I spoke to the vicar. The ceremony is set for tomorrow at three,' Charles announced, stepping into the room. A wave of dread hit Julia, but she couldn't move for fear of being stuck by one of the many pins in her dress. Besides, she wasn't about to let Charles know she harboured any doubts about her decision.

'I can't possibly arrange everything by then,' Emily complained, tapping her list. 'And what about Captain Covington's family? He isn't expected back from London until this evening and with his mother and sister in Wiltshire, how can he possibly arrange for them to be here by tomorrow?'

'I'm sorry they'll miss it, but if Julia wants her inheritance and Cable Grange, she will marry tomorrow.'

'Or, instead of being so high handed, you could simply allow me to purchase the estate. Then the captain and I can marry at our leisure,' Julia suggested, her brother more irritating than the pins in her dress.

'No, I don't want any reason for you to decline. I've sent instructions for my solicitor to arrange the money for Saturday's auction. Once you and Captain Covington are married, I will bid for Cable Grange on your behalf, then establish it in trust for you.'

Baby Thomas let out a small cry. Charles picked him up from where he lay in the rocker at the nurse's feet. He held the baby in his arms, his hard expression softening as he carried the infant to the window, laying a kiss on his little head. Emily rose and joined them, moving aside the blanket so they could see more of the baby's smiling face. For the first time in her life, Julia envied Charles and Emily. They both annoyed her, but they loved each other and always did what they thought best for everyone in the family.

Julia's stomach tightened. What if she never found such love and happiness with the captain?

'Enough wool-gathering,' her mother interrupted, picking up Emily's list and examining it. 'There is still much to do.'

Julia slipped out into the garden, eager to escape all the talk of both her wedding and the ball and be alone so she could think. She pulled the neck of her pelisse close, trying to warm her cheeks in the high collar. The fine weather had turned and, though the sky was clear, the air was sharp and cold. As she ambled over the gravel, the confidence she'd felt a few days ago while sitting here with her mother felt like a distant memory. Her future at Cable Grange had seemed so secure then; now she could see nothing but the unknown dotted with the chance of adventure and travel. What would life hold for Mrs James Covington? Would it really be like he promised or did she run the risk of becoming Mrs Wilkins? Wandering into the hedged garden, she sat down in front of the fountain, listening to the gentle plunk of water dripping into the pool from the clinging bodies.

Captain Covington offered many things in his proposal, but not love. He said it would come in time, but there was no guarantee. If he never grew to love her did it matter? Cable Grange would be hers and she could live the way she'd always dreamed of, but with the freedom of a married woman. The thought should have comforted her, but it didn't. Instead it only added to her loneliness and confusion. Turning back to the fountain, she felt her heart catch. Love was not part of their deal. It never had been.

The sound of someone walking on the gravel caught her attention and a moment later, Annette came around the corner, her heavy dress and pelisse more appropriate for the chilly day.

'Good afternoon, Julia,' she greeted with a light voice.

'Good afternoon,' Julia mumbled, in no mood for her stepcousin.

To Julia's surprise, Annette sat down next to her, drawing her pelisse tight. Julia watched her with caution, wondering what she wanted. It wasn't like her to be so cordial and her sudden nearness felt awkward. In no mood to entertain the chit and knowing she did not possess the patience to be polite, Julia moved to make her excuses and leave, but Annette stood first. 'Would you please take a turn with me around the garden?'

Julia almost declined, but something in Annette's manner, less arrogant than before, made her curious. She didn't like the idea of spending time alone with Annette, but with nervous fretting over the wedding being the only thing waiting for her inside, walking seemed very appealing. 'Of course.'

She rose and led Annette away from the hedges and down the main garden path. Small birds, searching the stones for food, hopped out of their way, then flew up into the surrounding bushes, chirping in protest at being disturbed.

Annette further surprised Julia by taking her arm in a casual, sociable manner. Julia didn't pull away but braced herself for an insult, knowing all this friendliness had something to do with Julia discovering the girl's secret.

'You are aware of the situation concerning my brother and myself?' Annette asked, confirming Julia's suspicion.

'I inadvertently learned of it.' There was no reason to lie since they both knew what Julia had seen.

'I realise our relationship has not been the best these past few weeks.'

It has never been good, Julia thought, but remained silent, wondering where all this was leading.

'I know I have no right to ask for your confidences or your discretion, but I implore you to keep what you know a secret.'

'I have no intention or reason to tell anyone.' And she didn't. Besides, Julia guessed from previous comments by both the captain and Emily that everyone already knew their situation.

'Why wouldn't you tell?' Annette demanded. 'It would be perfect revenge for my less-than-courteous behaviour.'

'Yes, but I'm not interested in revenge.' Julia sympathised with Annette, knowing she lived in a world where people tore each other to pieces without hesitation or remorse. The same pity she'd felt for her a few days ago came back along with Uncle Edward's hope that Julia could advise Annette on her finances. Helping Annette would prove a welcome distraction from Cable Grange, Charles, Emily, Captain Covington and everything else determined to plague her this week. 'I might be able to help you, if you wish.'

She snatched her hand from Julia's arm. 'I don't need your charity.'

'I don't mean charity,' Julia continued in an even tone, 'but advice on how to arrange your finances. Emily told me about your small inheritance. Perhaps we can devise a budget to relieve some of your debts and your worries.'

Annette's eyes softened, then narrowed as if contemplating many things at once, all of which seemed somewhat incomprehensible. 'I didn't think, especially after how mean I've been, that you'd be so generous. Why?'

'Because I know what it's like to have one's future influenced by a less-than-understanding brother.'

'At least Charles genuinely cares for your happiness.'

'Does he?'

'He's gone to a great deal of trouble to maintain your reputation and assure himself of the captain's suitability. Simon would never do the same for me.'

Julia resumed her languid pace, Annette staying by her side. She didn't want to admit it, but Charles did have her best interest at heart. If he wasn't so domineering, she might appreciate it more.

'I'll have to examine your finances to decide the best course of action,' Julia hazarded, the opportunity to review figures irresistible. 'You'll need to make a list of everything you owe, your expenses and your income.'

Annette fingered the lace of her pelisse, contemplating Julia's offer. 'Why do you want to help me?'

'Because it's the proper thing to do.'

'You're right—London is ridiculous,' Annette admitted with a laugh. They'd spent the last two hours reviewing her debts and income. She owed a great deal to a milliner and other London merchants, but her situation was not beyond hope.

'I never thought I'd hear you say it.' *Or be so friendly*, Julia thought, enjoying the new warmth between them.

'I don't think I'd admit it to anyone else. The silly things I have to do to try to secure my future.' She waved her hand over the scraps of paper littered with figures. 'And still nothing is settled.'

'Since you live with Uncle Edward and your mother, you can save a great deal, but you'll have to economise. No more lace and no more dresses.'

Annette sat back with a sigh. 'It won't be easy, but I suppose I must.'

'Just until you find a rich husband,' Julia teased, putting the finishing touches on Annette's plan to pay her debts and invest her inheritance, then passing it to her for inspection. 'I think this will do very well.'

'Yes, it will.' She laid the paper aside. 'I'm truly sorry for being nasty to you, only I've been so worried lately, what with Simon's gambling and Mama no help. I thought Captain Covington might be an answer.

I never thought of taking matters into my own hands. You're lucky to have a man like the captain. He'll make a good husband and you two will be quite the talk of the ball tonight.'

Julia twisted the pencil in her hands, apprehension replacing her former calm. 'I don't particularly care for balls.'

'Why? You can dance, can't you?'

'Yes, it's one of the few social graces I mastered while in London.' Charles had hired a dancing instructor for that purpose and Julia had proven a quick study. If only everything else about London society had come so easily.

'And you can converse with people.'

'Of course.'

'Then why are you afraid?'

'Because everyone sneers at me for running Knollwood instead of painting screens. They seem to have nothing else to occupy their simple minds except how I choose to spend my time.'

'Well, I can't stop them from thinking that running an estate is strange, but I can teach you not to care.'

Julia shook her head. 'It's not possible?'

'Of course it is. All London women do it. Do you know how many girls would cry in the halls of Almack's if they didn't pretend not to care?'

'No, I've seen the women in London. They possess more confidence in society than I could ever master.'

Annette stared her straight in the eye. 'Come now, Julia. I've seen you stand up to Mrs Wilkins and your brother. I know you aren't lacking in courage. You helped me—now allow me to help you.'

'How?'

Annette stood, taking Julia's hand and pulling her

to her feet. She spun Julia around, studying her with a practised eye. 'First, to play the part, you must dress the part.'

An hour later, Julia stood before the mirror, admiring her transformation into a diamond of the first water. She wore her finest London gown of white silk with thin, shimmering gold stripes running through the fabric and a gold ribbon around the waist. At the gentle swell of her bosom, Annette fixed one of Emily's diamond brooches and loaned her a pair of teardrop-pearl earrings. Annette then instructed Mary on how to style Julia's hair in the Roman fashion with a gold ribbon threaded through the *coiffure*.

'Anyone who saw you would instantly think you're a member of the *ton*.' Annette stepped back, inspecting her handiwork.

Julia gazed at her reflection, turning from one side to the other to view her dress and hair. For the first time in a long while, she felt beautiful, but there was more to commanding a ballroom than a pretty gown. 'I may dress the part, but I don't feel it.'

'It's an easy one to play. Come, I'll show you.' Annette led Julia to the far side of the room. 'When you walk, keep your head up, your shoulders back. Meet everyone with confidence and don't forget to smile.'

Annette demonstrated the walk, then motioned for Julia to try it. Julia felt silly, but she'd come too far to stop now. Pulling back her shoulders, she put her chin in the air and crossed the room.

'Very good, but this time smile, acknowledge everyone and remember to hold their gaze a moment before moving on.'

Julia repeated the walk with more purpose, smiling and nodding to the imaginary guests.

Annette clapped at the performance. 'If the captain wasn't already in love with you, then he'd lose his heart tonight.'

Julia stopped, stunned by Annette's announcement. 'The captain doesn't love me.'

'Of course he does. It is as plain as the sun.'

Julia opened and closed the ivory fan dangling from her wrist. 'Now you're teasing me.'

'Do not think so little of yourself, Julia. He loves you as much as you love him.'

Julia opened the fan, studying the painted roses twining together along a vine. Yes, she loved him. She'd spent days denying it, but hearing Annette state it so plainly she could no longer pretend it wasn't true.

But did he love her?

She examined herself in the mirror and for the first time saw not Julia, the awkward girl of Knollwood, but a sophisticated lady engaged to the handsome captain. It seemed too unbelievable to be real. Deep down, she feared everything would come crashing down and she'd wake tomorrow to find it was all just a dream. Unless, as Annette thought, he really loved her. If not, the humiliation would be more than she could bear. It seemed there was only one thing to do. Tonight she would have to find out.

Chapter Twelve

Julia stepped out of the carriage, the biting night air cutting through the delicate material of her gown. Young people, accompanied by matrons and older men, wound through the crush of carriages to the Johnsons' wide front door. Julia followed her mother and Annette, admiring the tall, white columns lining the façade, thinking similar details would make Cable Grange stately. She tried to take in more of the house's architecture, but the crowd pressing into the entrance hall made it difficult. They were supposed to arrive earlier, but baby Thomas had taken ill, causing a delay when Emily and Charles decided to stay behind. She'd noticed Uncle George's carriage outside and knew he and the captain were already here. The captain had returned from London in the early evening, but Annette refused to let him see her and insisted he and Uncle George ride on ahead to the ball. She wanted Julia to make an entrance and surprise the captain.

Once inside, Julia looked for him, eager for him to see her. However, nothing except the tall ostrich feather in the hair of the lady in front of her was visible in the crush.

They stepped into the receiving line, moving forwards to where Mr and Mrs Johnson and the eldest Miss Johnson stood and Julia's stomach tightened. Despite Annette's lessons, she didn't relish the idea of facing the scrutiny of the other country families. Picking up the short train of her dress, she knew she had no choice but to carry on.

'Mrs Howard, how lovely to see you,' Mrs Johnson addressed Julia's mother, who curtsied with her usual grace. She turned to Julia, her beady eyes wide with astonishment. 'And, Miss Howard, your gown is beautiful.'

'The colour makes you glow,' the eldest Miss Johnson offered. Taller and less buxom than her younger sisters, she'd always been kinder than either they or their mama.

'Thank you.' Julia curtsied, enjoying Miss Johnson's compliment and taking pride in showing Mrs Johnson she could dress as fine as any other lady.

Her mother led her off to the left and through the hall leading to the ballroom. Numerous gentlemen and ladies filled the space, chatting and enjoying aperitifs and ices. Julia paused at the threshold, taking in the crowd before Annette linked her arm in hers.

'Remember what I told you. Everyone will be watching us for I am new and you are unexpected. There'll be lots of stares and whispers, but walk like you know, but don't care.'

They stepped together into the thick of the revellers and a hundred glances and whispers were thrown their way. The mothers and young ladies who'd always ignored Julia now stared, taking in the fine style of Julia's dress and the graceful figure she cut. She did her best to emulate Annette, smiling at Miss Diana Johnson, who sat surrounded by her usual set of admirers. Miss Diana spied Julia, her jaw dropping before she fell to whispers with the young bucks, but Julia never let her smile falter. For once Julia enjoyed being the subject of so many conversations.

The soft strains of Handel greeted them at the entrance to the ballroom. Sweeping the room, her eyes immediately set upon the captain. His blue uniform highlighted by a crisp white shirt, brass buttons and gold epaulettes made him stand out in the sea of men in sober black evening attire. The unmarried young ladies and their mothers covetously examined the captain while Miss Caroline Johnson claimed the envious position of chatting with him. Her fan fluttered in front of her face while they spoke, but Julia could tell he wasn't listening for his eyes roamed everywhere but over the silly goose's round, exuberant face.

He's looking for me. Her heart jumped with excitement and she started forwards, eager to join him, but Annette held her elbow tight.

'Wait. Make him come to you.'

She could barely stand still, waiting for him to notice her. As if sensing her presence, he turned, starting at the sight of her. His blue eyes swept her before an impressed smile spread over his face. Making his excuses to Miss Johnson, he started across the room. Many ladies dipped behind their fans to comment on the handsome stranger striding towards Julia. She didn't care what they said or thought—only the captain mattered. She hadn't seen him since the proposal and until this moment didn't realise how much she'd missed him.

'You're gorgeous, Artemis,' he breathed, standing over her and taking in the transformation.

Julia arched one saucy eyebrow, enjoying the confidence created by his admiration. 'Are you trying to flatter me?'

'No flattery of mine could do you justice.' The musicians began an allemande and the captain offered her his elbow. 'May I have this dance?'

She hesitated. It had been a long time since she'd danced and, with her confidence soaring, she didn't want to trip over her feet and bring herself crashing back down to the ground.

'Come now. A woman who faces fighting men isn't afraid of a dance?' he teased.

Julia laid her hand on his arm. 'I'm not afraid.'

'Good. I'm glad to hear it.'

The captain swept her through the steps of the dance, the heat of his body radiating between them during the turns and acting like wine on her senses. The image of him shirtless above her filled her mind and she nearly stumbled, but his strong presence kept her steady and with even steps they moved in time with the others over the polished floor.

Whispers swirled around them from all those who knew her and her family and for the first time Julia didn't care. Instead of wanting to escape, to run back to Knollwood and the comfort of the study, she grasped the captain's hand tighter and raised her head higher. She enjoyed exceeding these people's expectations, for most of them believed spinsterhood to be her fate. It felt wonderful to prove them wrong and be more than they, and perhaps even Charles, ever thought she'd be.

All too soon the dance ended and the captain escorted her to where Annette stood.

'Well done, Julia,' she congratulated. 'You've set the room ablaze and are to be commended.'

'Do you really think so?'

'Most definitely.' Annette strolled off to rejoin Mrs Howard as Miss Diana Johnson hurried up to them, her eyes raking over the captain.

'Miss Howard, we did not expect to see you here tonight. I didn't think you liked balls,' Diana said, her voice innocuous, but the cutting remark clear.

'Whatever gave you such an idea?' Julia asked.

Diana's smile faltered, leaving her at a loss for an answer. Not wishing to prolong the awkward moment, Julia turned to the captain. 'Allow me to introduce my fiancé, Captain James Covington.'

'Fiancé?' Diana dipped a wobbly curtsy, her small eyes wide with surprise.

'Yes, I asked Miss Howard to be my wife and she accepted me.' The captain patted Julia's hand proudly.

'Best wishes to you both. If you'll excuse me.' She hurried off across the room to rejoin a group of young ladies Julia recognised, but didn't know well. They bowed together in a furious mingling of waving fans and gasps while Diana conveyed the news.

'The whole room will know in a matter of minutes,' Julia remarked.

'Good.' Behind them the musicians started the next dance. 'Shall we?'

'Of course.'

The hour slipped by in a blur of music and the captain's touch. She revelled in the feel of him next to her while they moved through two more dances, oblivious to everything but each other. She could dance with him for ever if only one fear didn't continue to plague her. She was no closer to knowing the truth of his heart, but she was reluctant to break the ball's beautiful spell with an awkward discussion or some horrible revelation. Tomorrow she'd discover the truth. Tonight she'd enjoy herself.

At the end of the Scottish reel, he led her to the edge of the room. She waved her fan, the heat of the crowd and the rousing dance making her flush.

'Would you like some punch?' the captain asked, his hair damp at the temples from the exhilaration of the reel.

'Yes, thank you.'

He made his way to the refreshment room, leaving Julia near a large painting of some Johnson ancestor. She wrinkled her nose at the round face staring out from the canvas, thinking it very unfortunate such a feature should be so dominant in the family.

'Good evening, Miss Howard.'

Startled, she turned to see Mrs Wilkins standing behind her. She wore a deep-green dress of velvet cut too low, her modesty saved only by a wide gold necklace.

'Mrs Wilkins,' Julia greeted icily, making it clear she had no wish to speak to the woman, but Mrs Wilkins seemed indifferent to the rebuke.

'Had I not seen it for myself, I never would have believed it. You strike me as too dour for a man like James.'

'The captain likes his women refined.' Julia's heart pounded in her ears. She'd never been confronted like this and she wasn't about to let the woman get the better of her.

'You needn't be so high and mighty with me, Miss Howard,' Mrs Wilkins snapped. 'Do you really think he'll marry you?'

'I believe you're bitter because he didn't marry you.'

'I could have had him if I'd wanted him, but I'm not

one to pine for the past. Perhaps this time he'll actually go through with the marriage.'

'Come to the church tomorrow at three o'clock and you'll see for yourself.'

'I think not. Please give him this. He left it in my room when he came to see me the other night.'

Mrs Wilkins held out James's dented medal and it dangled between them, glittering tauntingly in the candlelight. Julia held out her hand, struggling to control the shaking while Mrs Wilkins coiled the gold chain in her upturned palm. 'Oh, and please tell him we sold Cable Grange yesterday.'

'You sold it,' Julia choked.

'Yes. A solicitor in London purchased it for his employer. Rowan and I just returned from London this afternoon to see to our things as the new owner wishes to take possession at once. Frankly, I'm glad to be rid of the place. I never did enjoy the country. I always found the society a bit too small.' Mrs Wilkins sauntered off across the room.

Anger, hurt, betrayal, disappointment and sorrow all slammed together, making it impossible to think or make any sense of the emotions crushing her. Julia gripped the medal tight, her heart shattering along with her dreams. After everything she'd done, Cable Grange was gone and with it Captain Covington. She forced herself to remain composed, refusing to fall apart in front of everyone who'd seen her so happy only a moment before. She needed somewhere to go, a place to hide, but the crowded room offered no sanctuary.

Before Julia had a chance to think or clear her mind, the captain appeared at her side. 'What did she want?'

'To offer her congratulations,' Julia replied through clenched teeth.

'What's wrong?'

She laid open her palm, revealing the medallion. He turned to where Mrs Wilkins disappeared in the crowd, his eyes narrow with seething hate. 'That miserable woman. Whatever she told you, it is a lie.'

'Were you with her the other night?'

'Yes, but allow me to explain.'

She shook her head, the room around her threatening to whirl. If Mrs Wilkins had the audacity to confront her tonight, it wouldn't be long before she told everyone the story of James's indiscretion. Moments ago she'd been the belle of the ball; now she'd end the evening the subject of vicious gossip. They'd laugh and say she wasn't ladylike enough to keep her intended. They'd watch her with a mixture of pity and condescension all because she'd trusted him and allowed herself to believe he loved her. How could she have been so foolish? He'd dallied with Annette in jest, then turned to her when it suited his lust only she'd been too blind to see the truth.

'Please, let's go outside and discuss this?' the captain said, taking her elbow.

'Why?' she retorted. 'So you may tarnish my reputation further?'

Before he could answer, a loud gong reverberated through the room. Everyone turned to watch Mr Johnson, accompanied by a servant carrying the gong, step up on the dais in front of the musicians.

'Everyone, please may I have your attention?' The music trailed off, bringing the dancers to a halt. Whispers swept the room, everyone speculating on what announcement was important enough to interrupt a ball. 'News has just reached us from London. The British Navy met Napoleon's fleet at Trafalgar and won a stunning victory.'

The room erupted in cheers, applause and whistles, but Mr Johnson rang the gong three more times, cutting the excitement short. 'Britain has also suffered a great loss. Though we won the battle, Admiral Nelson was killed.'

Men gasped and women burst into tears, the hero's death touching everyone.

Uncle George appeared next to Julia. 'There is other news from London.'

Fear turned her cold. 'Paul?'

'Yes, we must return to Knollwood at once. Your mother and Annette have already left. We'll take my carriage.'

Uncle George led them through the sober crowd and out of the large front doors to the waiting carriage. Inside, James sat next to her as Uncle George climbed into the seat across from them. He rapped on the roof, setting the carriage in motion.

'Do you know anything?' Julia asked, barely able to get the words out, her throat dry with dread.

'Only that Charles received a letter concerning Paul. I don't know the contents. Jim, did you hear anything in town about the battle?'

He shook his head. 'No, I was too busy this morning and I didn't see any of the papers before I left London.'

They fell into worried silence, the jangling equipage grating on her strained nerves. Anticipating the awful news waiting for her at Knollwood made her body shake. Was Paul dead or just badly wounded? What would she do without him, especially now?

The captain slipped his hand in hers and squeezed it, but she snatched it away, in no mood for his sympathy. She felt him watching her, the weight of his concern adding unwanted tension to her already tormented mind. She scanned the darkness outside the carriage for any landmark indicating their distance from home, but only the vague silhouettes of trees stood out in the dim light of the rising moon. The carriage drove for what felt like an eternity before the bright windows of Knollwood came into view. The moment the carriage stopped, she threw open the door and rushed inside, James and Uncle George close on her heels.

She hurried into the morning room, taking in Mother, who sat next to Emily, her face a white mask of controlled pain. Annette stood behind them, sombre.

'Is Paul all right?' Julia asked.

Mother held out her arms and Julia rushed into them, doing her best to hold back tears of worry.

'He's alive, but wounded and missing,' Mother answered and Julia sat back.

'What do you mean?'

'Lieutenant Lapenotiere, his commander, sent us a letter. *HMS Pickle* arrived in Falmouth on Monday. They came home because Lieutenant Lapenotiere was charged with telling the Admiralty about the battle and Admiral Nelson. Paul, because of his wound, rode with Lieutenant Lapenotiere to London to see Dr Childers.'

'Excellent fellow,' Charles muttered.

Mother scowled at Charles, then continued her story. 'They arrived very early this morning and Lieutenant Lapenotiere, after finishing his duties at the Admiralty, paid a call to Dr Childers to make sure Paul was all right. According to Dr Childers, Paul never arrived and now no one knows where he is.'

'Perhaps the wound is worse than he realised and Paul's in some hospital, alone,' Julia said worriedly.

'Lieutenant. Lapenotiere doesn't know and, because of his official duties, he can't search for Paul. It's why he sent us an urgent letter suggesting someone from the family come to London at once to find Paul.'

Julia turned to Charles. 'When are you leaving?'

Charles looked aghast. 'I'm not leaving. I've written a few letters and will send them tomorrow.'

'Letters? You're sending letters?'

'What else would you have me do?'

'Go to London and search every hospital until you find him.'

'Search the hells and coffee houses, you mean,' Charles scoffed from his place by the fire, tapping the mantel. 'No doubt instead of going straight to Dr Childers, Paul decided to visit his mistress, or some hell to run up more debts.'

'How can you say such a thing?' Julia demanded, her voice high and tight. Only the firm squeeze of her mother's hand prevented her from hurling more words at Charles.

'I can say it because I've spent more time than I care to admit dealing with our brother's creditors. Now, through his foolishness, he's gone and got himself in another mess.'

'He's wounded. He may be ill and in need of our help. Now is no time to preach about his responsibilities.'

'Why not? He's a grown man and it's time he took them seriously.' Charles snatched up the poker and jabbed at the logs. 'Besides, Paul has a talent for surviving and for trouble. He's sure to turn up soon.'

Julia stood, balling her fists at her sides to keep from pounding them against Charles's unfeeling chest. 'London and all your airs have made you hard.'

'You don't understand the ways of the world,' he replied with marked condescension, returning the poker to the stand.

'I quite agree with Julia.' Her mother rose, pinning Charles with angry eyes. 'You have become too hard for my liking.'

'Mother, please, you misunderstood my meaning,' Charles began, but his mother raised a silencing hand, then swept out of the room.

Charles chased after her, his weak protests trailing them both down the hall.

Julia dropped into a chair, biting her thumb. Across the room, Uncle George and Captain Covington stood by the fireplace, each contemplating the evening's news. Her eyes briefly met the captain's, their blue depths filled with a need she would not answer.

Paul wasn't dead, but wounded, and Charles had no intention of helping him. She knew the condition of hospitals and how a healthy man could easily succumb to illness while a wounded one stood almost no chance of recovering. Paul must be found and brought back to Knollwood to be cared for properly, not left to die in who knew what squalor.

'Charles will find him. Everything will be all right— you'll see,' Emily offered, patting Julia's shoulder. Reaching into her dressing-gown pocket, she produced a letter and handed it to Julia.

'What's this?' She recognised Paul's large handwriting.

'It arrived after you left for the ball. He must have sent it some time ago.'

Julia sat on the edge of her seat, fingering the letter, afraid to open it for fear it might be the last she ever received from him.

Emily made her way out of the room, followed by Annette, who offered a comforting smile.

Julia tore open the letter.

Dear Julia,

Forgive my brevity. We are in port taking on supplies for the fleet and I wanted to send word since it may be my last opportunity to write for some time. I hope everyone at Knollwood is doing well. Uncle George wrote to inform me of his plan to bring Captain Covington to stay at Creedon Abbey in November, and to meet you all. I was shocked by his announcement, given our history, of which Uncle George has surely informed you. Perhaps it means the captain has finally forgiven me and will rescind his poor recommendation and I shall have my ship after all. If he hasn't forgiven me, I depend upon you to do nothing but speak of my great character and change his mind for you can be quite persuasive when you want something.

I must go now, but I'll write more when I can. Give my love to Mother.
Your devoted brother,
Paul

Without thinking, she marched up to the captain, the paper fluttering in her shaking hands. 'It was all about revenge, wasn't it?'

He stared at her, stunned. 'I don't understand.'

'You wrote Paul's poor recommendation. You stopped him from getting his own ship.'

'I did.'

'Why?'

The captain ran his hand through his hair. 'Your brother served with me many years ago in Portsmouth. During that time he failed to demonstrate qualities necessary to command a ship. There were questions about whether or not he could be trusted to follow orders or do the honourable thing.'

'It was more complicated than that,' Uncle George added.

'You knew about this and didn't tell me?' She gaped at Uncle George, who tugged on the sleeves of his jacket. She felt lied to and betrayed by both of them and, combined with her worry for Paul, it was more than she could bear.

'Julia, please.' Captain Covington moved forwards, but she stepped away.

'How dare you speak of honour when you have none. For years you've had a grudge against Paul and when you couldn't strike at him you decided to take advantage of me.'

'That's not it at all. Please allow me to explain.' He took her by the arms, but she shook off his grasp.

'Explain what? How instead of receiving his own ship and perhaps being hundreds of miles from danger, he's now missing? How you went to Mrs Wilkins, exposing me to the humiliation of the entire countryside because you made me think you cared?'

'I do care. Don't you see?'

'No, I won't have any more of your lies.' She ran from the room and up the stairs, not daring to breathe until she crumpled to her knees in the privacy of her room, large tears rolling down her face.

'I was a fool to go or at the least I should have taken you along,' James lamented, remembering his brief time in Melinda's room. He should have known she'd strike at him like this. Once again he'd underestimated her. He thought of her letter in the drawer upstairs. He could make good on his promise and send it to Rowan, but what difference would it make now?

'What I don't understand is how she got your medal.' George paced back and forth across the room with slow, heavy steps.

'I remember Melinda putting her arms around my neck. She must have taken it then.'

'Sounds more like a cutpurse than a lady.'

'From everything I heard of her while in London, I wouldn't be surprised if she's turned to thievery to keep herself from ruin.'

George paused near the card table, fingering the deck, his face long. 'I should have been honest with Julia, told her about you and Paul. I hate to think I've hurt her.'

'She loves you too much not to forgive you and once everything is settled, she'll understand why you did it. She might even thank you for it,' James offered, trying to bolster his friend's spirits. He'd only seen George this upset once before when a young officer they both admired was killed in a skirmish off Martinique. Despite winning the skirmish and taking a grand prize, the entire crew had been affected by the officer's death, much like tonight's news had touched everyone at Knollwood.

'I hope you're right. She means the world to me.' George took a deep breath, flipping over a card and laying it face up on the table. 'I only kept it a secret because I wanted her to give you a chance.'

'Then why did you write Paul about it?'

'Because I didn't think he'd write to her about it. Apparently, I was wrong.' He flipped over another card and laid it beside the other. 'But enough about my troubles. What'll you do?'

James shook his head. 'Tonight, nothing. In the morning I'll make her listen to me—whatever it takes to get her to the altar.'

Julia leaned against her bedroom wall, wrung out and tired. The evening had started out so glorious, and now it was gone, all of it: the captain, Cable Grange, her future. Fresh tears rolled down her face at the thought of enduring the wagging tongues of the countryside and Charles's endless sermons. She scowled, hating her brother very much at this moment.

Across the room, she noticed her books and agricultural tracts stacked in a neat pile on a table next to the window. On top sat the book Paul had given her on India. Where was he? Why wouldn't Charles search for him? She would if she could.

She sat up, drying her cheeks with the back of her hand as the plan began to form in her mind. Paul. She could find him, nurse him back to health if need be and live with him, away from Charles, Knollwood and the captain.

It was dangerous and if she went through with it, there would be no going back, not that it mattered now. Even if Julia told Charles the truth about Captain Covington, he would still insist on a wedding. No, she wouldn't be bound to a man who didn't love her or who wouldn't be faithful. Life with Paul was the only option, if she could find him, if he was still alive.

Rising, Julia cracked open the door and peered into the empty hallway, listening to the muffled voices of the captain and Uncle George from downstairs. Hurrying along the hall, she slipped inside Paul's room, careful to lock the door behind her. Pulling open the wardrobe, she grabbed one of Paul's old uniform jackets, a shirt, a pair of breeches, the Hessians, a hat and haversack. Stuffing the clothes in the haversack, she felt around, hoping to find a pistol or even a sword, but there was nothing else except a few old blankets. Closing the wardrobe, she carefully opened the bedroom door. Charles's whining tone carried from their mother's room, his pleas fading down the empty hallway.

A few candles flickered in their holders, the flames dancing as Julia stole by. At the bottom of the stairs she stopped, listening for the captain and Uncle George. The clink of a crystal stopper followed by a slight cough punctuated the low cadence of their voices. The bottom stair creaked and she froze. The men's muffled conversation didn't falter and she slipped unnoticed past the door and to the study.

Inside, she didn't dare light a candle. Pulling the key from its hiding place in the ink blotter's handle, she unlocked the top desk drawer and drew out the money pouch. It jingled loudly and she clutched it tight, silencing the coins. Slipping it into the haversack, she locked the drawer, returned the key to its hiding place, then fled the room, making her way out of the house through the back.

Her feet flew over the gravel walkway as she ran down the hill to the stables, gripping the haversack with one hand while her other one held up the hem of her dress. The frosty night air bit at her exposed skin while the satin slippers failed to protect her feet from every stone embedded in the path.

Pushing open the stable door, the horses whinnied, then shifted back and forth in their stalls. They watched her run to the small room at the back where she stripped off the white-and-gold dress and hung it on a peg. It sagged there like an old skin, taunting her with what might have been. Why had she tried to be anything other than who she was? And who was she? Not Mrs James Covington, nor a polished London lady, only the fallen, spinster sister of a lieutenant in his Majesty's Navy. She forced the bitter sadness from her mind, knowing she'd never accomplish anything tonight with such heartache weighing on her. Paul needed her and he was all that mattered.

She slipped on the jacket, the rough wool scratching through the simple linen shirt, but giving welcome relief from the cold stable. She pulled on the trousers and then the Hessians, which fit surprisingly well for being two sizes too large. Walking in a tight circle, she admired the easy way the outfit allowed her to move. Removing the pins and ribbon from her hair, she arranged her locks into a ponytail, securing it with the ribbon and tucking it up under the hat. It was a poor disguise, but with luck it would be enough to keep anyone with a mind for trouble from picking her out. Tossing the haversack over her shoulder, she pulled open the door, letting out a yelp when she came face to face with John.

'Miss Howard,' he gasped, holding a pitchfork tight. 'I thought you were a thief. What are you doing here at this time of night and dressed like that?'

She pushed past him, grabbing Manfred's saddle. 'I'm going to London, to find Paul. He's been wounded and he's missing.'

'You can't.' John took hold of the heavy saddle, but she didn't let go. 'Not without Mr Howard or Captain Russell. If anyone found out, you'd be ruined.'

'I have to find him.'

'But think of your mother and brother.'

'Charles doesn't care about anything but his propriety.' Julia tugged on the saddle, but John held it tight.

'Miss Howard, I can't let you do this.'

The concern in his face touched her. He'd kept so many secrets for her in the past. Now she needed him to keep one more.

'Please, I must. Paul needs me. He's wounded and might die if I don't find him.' She hated sounding so desperate, but she couldn't keep the fear out of her words.

John shook his head, relaxing his grip on the leather. 'You know I can't refuse you.' He took the saddle into Manfred's stall and threw it over the horse's back.

Julia joined him, helping with the buckles. 'Thank you, John.'

When they were done, John led Manfred out to the paddock, then helped her up.

'Please be careful. Your family needs you. Knollwood needs you.'

Regret hit her with surprising strength and for a moment she considered returning to the house and finding some other way to help Paul. No, there was no other way and no life except the one she could create with him in some distant port. For all his silly faults, at least he would understand and not judge her. He was her future now, not Knollwood, Cable Grange or Captain Covington.

'I'll be careful.' She kicked Manfred and horse and rider cantered out into the night.

James leaned against the mantel, watching a smouldering log collapse. Admiral Nelson was dead. He'd been wounded so many times, survived so many battles and now, on the brink of perhaps his greatest victory, he'd been killed. A shiver ran through James—he might have shared the same fate a year ago, or perhaps even today if he hadn't resigned his commission. He'd wasted so much time lamenting the past, mourning everything he'd lost instead of living. And what had he lost? He wouldn't know until morning when he could speak to Julia, explain what had happened at Cable Grange and confess his love. He berated himself for not telling her sooner.

'Excuse me, sir.' John stood in the doorway, his hair dishevelled and his lined face stricken.

'What's wrong?' George asked.

'Miss Howard—she's taken Manfred and left for London.'

'What?' James couldn't believe it.

'She's gone to find Mr Paul Howard. Found one of his old uniforms and rode off dressed like a sailor.'

'Why did you let her go? Don't you know how dangerous it is for a woman to travel the roads alone at night?'

The groom shrunk back. 'I couldn't stop her.'

It seemed too far-fetched to be real, but knowing Julia's impetuous nature it sounded exactly like something she would do. 'Saddle up Hector. I'm going after her.'

'Thank you, sir.' John left to prepare the horse.

'I'll go with you,' George said.

'No, I need you to stay and tell Julia's mother what's happened, but not until morning and not unless we haven't returned.'

'What about Charles?'

'Wait as long as you can to tell him. I don't want him following us. He'll only make things worse. I'm sure I can catch up to her and convince her to come back.'

'And if you can't?'

James opened and closed his left hand. 'Then on to London to find Paul. I'll send word when I can.'

George clapped him on the back. 'I hate to miss this adventure. Good luck, Jim.'

James ran upstairs to change into his older uniform, buckling his sabre to his waist before he left the room. Outside, he hurried down the hill to the stable where John waited in the paddock with Hector. The lanterns from the stable shone off the stallion's dark coat but did little to pierce the darkness beyond the building.

'When did she leave?' he asked, pulling himself into the saddle, ignoring the sting to his shoulder.

'Right before I came to get you. She's sure to take the main road, but if you go through the woods, there's a path that leads west. It's not hard to find and comes out further down the road. If you hurry, you can cut her off. She's not likely to run Manfred in the dark and risk injuring him.'

'Thank you.' James turned the horse for the woods, riding as fast as he could without risking Hector. Despite the high half-moon, heavy clouds kept passing in front of it, plunging the countryside into periods of darkness.

He rode a good distance without finding a break in the trees or anywhere where the bald path diverged. He thought of doubling back, fearing he'd missed the fork when the trail split, veering off into the dense copse. He slowed the stallion, nudging him to the right and the trees closed in around them, blocking out all but the faintest slivers of moonlight. James's eyes strained against the darkness to see the hard-packed earth in the dim light.

A low, sharp branch caught his neck and he reached up, feeling warm blood. Wiping it away, he laughed, remembering the last time he'd ridden hell-bent towards a town in the middle of the night. It was in Bermuda and he never thought he'd be doing it in England or chasing after a headstrong girl to aid a man he disliked. Life would never be this exciting without her and, if helping her find Paul meant winning her, he'd ride the length and breadth of the country.

An owl screeched, dipping down over the road in front of Julia and Manfred before flying off over the trees. Julia sat up straight, startled, her skin crawling with goose bumps. She might be dressed like a man, but any thieves in search of easy prey would discover the truth the moment they pounced. Then what would she do? She didn't have so much as a riding crop to defend herself with.

Somewhere in the distance a dog barked and Julia hunched over in the saddle, pulling the coat closer around her face. The ball, Mrs Wilkins and the captain's betrayal all mingled with the night to press down on her and dampen her spirit and resolve. What seemed a rational idea in the midst of a disappointing evening now felt like a mistake. Even if she made it to London, she had not the first idea where to begin her search. She should go home. It would be easy to slip into the house without anyone being the wiser, but then what would she do? Charles was too stubborn to help and even Uncle George had sided with the captain against Paul. If only the captain hadn't been such a scoundrel. He would have helped her.

Fresh tears threatened to fall and she bit her lip to keep from crying. She'd been so forward with her silly engagement scheme. No wonder he took advantage of her and thought nothing of exposing her to the censure and ridicule of the entire countryside. Though if he only sought to amuse himself with her innocence, why had he stopped the night he found her in his room and why had he suggested they marry? She smacked the saddle as she remembered the momentary weakness and the easy way he'd cast her aside. It must have all been a cruel joke because he obviously preferred the charms of a Cyprian like Mrs Wilkins to a silly girl like her. Wiping her eyes, she wondered if she'd ever be able to love again and her heart tightened with loss.

Rustling in the bushes up ahead put her on edge. Manfred's dark ears, tipped with moonlight, turned towards the noise and he raised his head higher, sensing something in the trees lining the road. She squinted, trying to see the source of the sound, but a heavy cloud passed over the moon and everything darkened. Branches cracked and her body tensed, her feet ready to kick Manfred into a gallop.

She heard the unmistakable thud of hooves on packed earth before the horse and rider sprang from the trees. The strange rider positioned himself in the middle of the road in an attempt to block her, but she moved fast, digging her heels into Manfred's side.

'Yah!' Manfred bolted past the rider, his hooves pounding the road. The stranger launched into pursuit, his horse matching Manfred's steady gait, but not his speed. Fear gripped Julia. She couldn't take Manfred into the forest without risking a broken leg. All she could do was rely on him to outrun the danger.

'Come on, Manfred,' she urged before the faint strain of a familiar voice reached her ears.

'Julia, wait.'

The stranger called out twice more before she recognised the captain's voice. Pulling Manfred to a halt, she watched the captain bring Hector to a stop a few feet away.

'What are you doing here?' she demanded, hoping the horses' heavy breathing covered the sound of her thundering heart.

'I've come to stop you from making a mistake.'

'I've already made many mistakes.' The sky briefly cleared and the moon's soft light caressed his face. Sadness hit her more powerfully than the fear she'd experienced only a moment before. They'd never be together with the same love and desire as before. She turned Manfred around and started him down the road and Captain Covington brought his stallion alongside hers.

'Why are you doing this?'

Julia didn't answer, unwilling to tell him the truth and be vulnerable to him again.

'Julia, please?' He manoeuvred Hector in front of Manfred, bringing them both to a stop. 'Tell me what's wrong and how I can help.'

'Why? You don't care. Go back to Knollwood and Mrs Wilkins. Leave me be.'

'Whatever she told you was a lie.'

'She said you were at Cable Grange. Is that a lie?'

He drew in a ragged breath. 'I was. But not for the reasons you think. I received a note from her regarding Rowan's debt. I'd hoped to use the money he owed me from the race as leverage to purchase Cable Grange. When I arrived she was alone and threw herself at me. I refused her, which is why she did what she did at the ball.'

'You wanted to buy Cable Grange? Why?'

'For you.'

Hope flared in Julia's heart, but she stamped it down. 'I don't believe you.'

'Would I be here on a lonely road in the middle of

the night following a woman dressed as a naval officer if I was lying?'

Was it possible? Did he really want her with all of her silly habits and unconventional traits? Her heart wanted to believe him, but her mind couldn't. The image of Mrs Wilkins smiling in victory crushed her hope. No, she could not trust the captain in matters of love.

'Go back to Knollwood.' She manoeuvred Manfred around him, but he refused to be put off.

'I'm coming with you to London.'

'You needn't bother. I don't need your help.'

'I'm still coming.'

'Why?'

'Because you must have an accomplice in this adventure, especially someone who knows his way around town and can help you.'

'Adventure?' Until this moment she hadn't thought of it in such terms, but now the idea, despite her hurt and anger, appealed to her.

'What else would you call it?'

He was right, though she didn't want him to be right. She didn't want him to be anything but a distant memory. However, now that he was here and determined to stay, he could prove useful.

'Do as you like. But as soon as we find Paul, I never want to see you again.'

'Let's get to London first. We'll worry about the rest later.'

He started Hector down the road and Julia followed, the darkness not as frightening or lonely as before. Despite her decision to remain wary and angry with him, she felt a genuine thrill to be on an adventure like all the ones Paul and Uncle George had described. Her excitement was tempered by the heartache spurring her on. Despite his betrayal, deep down she knew he was honourable enough to protect her if they met any unsavoury characters. This offered some measure of comfort and she settled into the saddle for the long journey.

The time passed slowly, the moon falling towards the horizon before disappearing behind dark clouds. Early on he tried to talk to her, but she cut him short, unwilling to hear any more of his lies or to speak for fear her voice would reveal too much of her true emotions. Eventually, he gave up and they rode for miles in silence. Fatigue crept into her muscles and soon the gentle bob of Manfred's gait made her sleepy. She nodded off before a sturdy hand roused her.

'Don't fall asleep.'

Her head jerked up. 'I wasn't sleeping.'

A distant flash of lightning streaked across the horizon. 'The storm will be upon us soon. Is there an inn near here or a house, anywhere we can take shelter until it passes?'

Julia examined their surroundings, trying to get her bearings. Another distant lightning flash silhouetted a large, twisted oak tree near a bend in the road, a familiar marker she knew well.

'There's a coaching inn not far from here, but it isn't the most reputable establishment.'

The captain laughed. 'Two lone travellers, one a single woman dressed like a man. Sounds like a perfect place for us.'

The first heavy drops started to fall when they reached the inn and the quiet stable next to it.

'Stay here while I see to the horses,' James ordered. Julia didn't argue, but waited near the stable entrance while James spoke to the groom. The weather kept the rest of the patrons indoors, leaving only the groom and one stable boy who ignored them while he mucked out a stall. James paid the groom well to see to the horses then, taking Julia by the arm, led her across the muddy yard to the inn's front door.

'What are you doing?' she demanded, stepping through a large puddle.

'Shhh.' He pulled her under the eaves where two large drops slipped off the wood overhang and dripped down his neck. 'Once inside, say nothing. Your voice will give you away.'

'Do not order me about.'

He held up a warning finger. 'You have no experience in these matters. As we are both dressed in our uniforms...' he shook his head at the absurdity of the situation '...take direction from me as any junior officer would.'

'But—'

'No disobedience. Follow me or I'll throw you over Manfred and drag you back to Knollwood.'

'Yes, sir.' Julia saluted.

'That's more like it.' He pulled open the door. 'Come along, Julius.'

'Julius?'

'A suitable name for a boy of your temperament.'

They stepped inside, the overpowering stench of dirty travellers, tobacco and meat assaulting them. He expected Julia to blanch, but she stared through the smoky room, fascinated by the men hiding in dark corners and the barmaids plying their trade.

'What do you think?' he asked, enjoying her reaction.

'It's exactly like Paul described.' Her eyes followed

a voluptuous blonde who walked by with two tankards and a surprising amount of uncovered flesh. 'Is she a—?'

'Yes. Come along, Columbus. Let's get something to eat.' He took her arm and pulled her through the benches of drinking, carousing men to a small, isolated table near the stairs. From a shadowed corner across the room, a man leaned against the wall, chewing on the end of a pipe. James noticed the way he watched them from under a dirty tricorn hat pulled low over his face. Something about him seemed familiar, but the stranger tilted down his head, obscuring his features.

'Wait here. I'll see to our room.' He pushed her into a chair with her back to the wall and a good view of the patrons.

'Shouldn't we stay here, in public?' she whispered with unmistakable worry.

Being alone with him seemed to frighten her more than a lonely road or a common room full of thieves, drunks and whores. He cursed himself for allowing the distance between them to widen, determined by the end of today to fill her eyes with wanting and love, not suspicion and worry.

'Privacy is safer in a place like this.' He was about to walk away when a woman with wild red hair and large breasts teetering precariously along the top edge of her dirty dress perched herself on the table.

'Fancy something special, Captain?'

'No, nothing, thank you.' James smiled, eager to send the woman on her way without any trouble.

The trollop's hooded eyes swept Julia. 'Then perhaps something for the lad?'

'He's fine, I assure you.'

'Seems kind of green to me. Perhaps he needs just

a taste.' She leaned across the table and slid her hand between Julia's legs. The woman's eyes met hers in stunned shock, but before either of them could say anything James took the harlot's hand, slipping two sovereigns into her palm and placing it against his chest.

'I know you can understand such a delicate situation and as a true lady will maintain your discretion.'

Her fingers closed on the coins, a sly smile spreading over her pocked features. 'Whatever you like, love, makes no difference to me.'

'I knew you'd understand. And I know you'll do anything to help us.' He held up two more sovereigns in front of her face. 'We need a room, the best you have, and your continued discretion regarding the lad.'

'Anything you say, Captain.' She took the coins, then walked off, her large hips swaying.

He sat down next to Julia, noticing the wary mistrust in her eyes. 'You seem quite practised in the art of charming women.'

'Better a woman is your friend than your enemy.'

'What am I?'

'Much more than a friend.' He reached for her hand under the table, but she pulled it away.

'Don't.' She leaned back in the chair, watching the room from under her hat. James missed her easy trust and wondered how he could regain it. He wanted to reveal his true feelings, but this was no place for such an intimate conversation.

Very soon the harlot hustled back to them. 'Your room is ready, milord.' She dangled a key in one dirty hand while the other held a candle in a pewter holder.

'Not milord, just Captain.'

'Is that what she calls you?' She threw back her large head of red hair and laughed, the gravelly sound barely carrying over the din. James nodded for Julia to rise and they followed the wench up the stairs and down a pokey hallway to the back of the inn. The stench of unwashed bodies and stale beer increased, as did the heat, laughter and other assorted sounds from all the people packed into the small space under the eaves.

'Here ya are. The best we have.' The harlot threw open the door and James held up another coin.

'Your help is very much appreciated.'

'My pleasure,' she purred, taking the coin from his hand and sliding it over the flesh of her breasts and down the front of her dress. 'Ya wouldn't be needin' me to help you and the lad, would ya?'

From beside the harlot, James saw Julia's jaw fall open. 'Thank you, but we couldn't possibly intrude on your hospitality any longer.'

'Well, ya know where to find me if you change your mind.' She handed James the candle, then sauntered off down the hall.

'Did she just ask if...?' Julia gasped.

'Yes, she did.' James nudged her into the room, not wanting to linger in the hallway or explain any more about the proposal than Julia had already grasped.

He closed the door, placing the candle and key next to the chipped china bowl on the battered washstand near the door. Julia approached the narrow bed situated against the wall and pulled back the thin blanket with her thumb and forefinger to inspect the sheets.

'Does it meet with your approval?'

She jumped back, almost knocking over the rickety chair under the window. The room was tight, with little space for two people to walk around. He stood over her, keenly aware of her warm body so close to his.

'Yes, I suppose it will do.'

'What do you think of your adventure now?' The tightness in his voice caught him off guard and he realised he'd only been alone with her like this once before. The memory of it made his body ache with need and he busied himself removing his gloves.

'It keeps getting stranger.' She took in the small, dingy space, her hat shadowing her nervous eyes. 'Where are you going to sleep?'

'The floor.'

'The floor?'

'It's only appropriate.' Disappointment flashed across her face before she sat down to pull off her boots. 'Leave your clothes on and keep your coat and boots nearby in case we need to make a hasty retreat.'

Her eyes lit up. 'Really?'

'Yes, now get some sleep.' James slid the coat off his shoulders and a bolt of pain shot through him. He sucked in a quick breath, waiting for it to pass.

'What's wrong?'

'Nothing. I overworked the arm perhaps.' He grimaced, working to slide off the coat without making the pain worse.

'Let me help you.' She reached up to assist him, but he pulled away.

'I can manage.'

'Please, I insist.' She took the coat by the collar and gently pulled it down his arms. Once it was off, she draped it over the back of the chair. The tender move touched him and he knew, despite everything that had happened tonight, she still cared for him.

'Thank you.' He started to rub his sore shoulder, but she pushed his hand away, massaging his aching flesh with her slender fingers. The nearness of her teased his senses and clouded his mind.

'If it bothers you too much, I can sleep on the floor and you can have the bed,' she offered.

'I'm not weak enough to kick a lady out of her bed.' He laughed, but it came out choked. He stood, removing her hands from his shoulder to keep from losing all self-control. Did she know how she affected him? He wasn't sure, but he couldn't take advantage of her innocence, no matter how much hesitant yearning filled her eyes. He'd never win her back if he gave in to the desire raging through him. 'I can leave if you prefer and try to find another room.'

Her hand clasped his tighter. 'No, I don't want to stay here without you.'

He glanced at her chest, the linen shirt barely hiding the gentle curve of her full breasts rising and falling with each fast breath. He stepped closer, a desire deeper than lust driving him forwards. He wanted to smash all the obstacles between them and feel her in his soul. Did she want the same thing? 'Are you sure?'

'Yes.'

Pulling her to him, he covered her lips with his.

Julia slipped her hands around the captain's neck, heady with the heat of his body so close to hers. She knew she should stop, but she couldn't. She'd already abandoned good society tonight. Now she wanted to give in to her desire and curiosity and experience everything she'd been denied the night he'd first touched her in Paul's room. In the morning she could regret again.

His free hand slid up under the shirt, cupping her breast and she moaned softly as his thumb made her nipple hard. With his other hand, he pushed the linen from her shoulders and she pressed against him, dizzy with need. He kissed her neck, then lowered to take one pert nipple in his mouth. Her legs went weak when his tongue traced wet circles around the tender point, his breath on her damp skin making her sigh. Scooping her up, he laid her on the bed, then stood over her, removing his breeches and revealing his desire. A twinge of fear filled her for she knew something of what came next, but wanting drove all other thoughts from her mind.

He pulled his shirt off over his head, dropping it on the floor before settling down next to her in bed. Perched on one elbow, he admired her body, the hot desire in his eyes making her shiver. She reached for the sheet to cover her nakedness, but he stopped her.

'Don't.' His hand traced the curve of her stomach, heightening the need coiling within her. She grasped his arm when his fingers slid into her moist depths, his gentle caress bringing her closer and closer to her passion. Then he stopped, withdrawing his touch.

'No,' she pleaded, wanting him to fill the emptiness and lead her to the same ecstasy she'd experienced the other night.

'We shouldn't,' he whispered, but she was beyond reason or caring about anything except being close to him.

'Yes. Please.'

His knees nudged open her legs and he settled his hips between them. The heat of his manhood touched her thigh and she trembled in anticipation. He covered her mouth with his, his member probing her depths, sliding, stretching her until she opened to take him in. She gasped at the pain, but it quickly disappeared, replaced by a sensation of fullness as he rocked within her.

His thrusts were slow at first, caressing, teasing, but grew more frenzied as she tightened around him.

Clinging to his back, she moved her hips to match his pace, thrilling at the sound of his heavy breath in her ear while he continued to push into her, deeper, harder until the spasms of her pleasure exploded through her. Inside she felt his body quiver before he collapsed on top of her, panting with his own release.

Julia stroked his back, their heavy breathing subsiding as they clung to one another. The thump of someone stumbling down the hallway accompanied by a wench's throaty laugh reminded Julia of where she was and why.

'James?' she ventured, wanting to know what this all meant to him and them. Did he love her? Did he care for her or did he think her no better than the harlot who'd showed them to their room?

He withdrew, kissing her forehead, then cradling her against him. 'Tomorrow, everything will be clear,' he whispered as if sensing her questions. 'Tonight we need sleep.'

Julia closed her eyes, his damp skin on her cheek, his beating heart soothing her worried mind. Yes, tomorrow they'd deal with everything and one way or another it would seem right. Or would it? She didn't know. Snuggling into the crook of his arm, she closed her eyes, fatigue pulling her into a deep sleep.

Julia awoke with a start, struggling through thick sleep to recognise her surroundings. The dirty walls and rough sheets on her bare body brought the events of the night before rushing back. Emotions collided: betrayal, love, pleasure, heartache—all plagued her as powerfully as the exhaustion pulling at her muscles. Wrapping the sheet tighter around her neck, she sank back into the bed, snuggling close to James, eager for more sleep, but it eluded her. His steady breathing reminded her just how far she was from Knollwood and good society, and she had no idea what would happen when he awoke. For a brief moment he'd made her forget his unfaithfulness and the reason she'd first set out for London. Paul.

Her eyes flew open. Outside the window, the orange glow of the inn's lantern mixed with the grey morning light. Muffled snoring punctuated the silence, the other patrons deep in either their travel-weary or ale-laden sleep. She gazed at James and the way the dim light outlined his features. Reaching up to stroke his cheek, she stopped, afraid to wake him. She'd trusted him with her body, savouring the pleasure and hope in his touch, but she couldn't trust him with her heart. Under different circumstances, perhaps they could be happy together, but not with his infidelity hanging over them. There was no use continuing the journey with him or torturing her mind with what could never be. If she left now, she'd have the beautiful memory of their lovemaking instead of the awkward scene of facing him and listening to his lies and explanations. He'd surely follow her, but with a head start, he'd never be able to find her in the crowds of London.

She slid from the bed, careful not to disturb him. Gathering up her clothes from the pile on the floor, she dressed, anxious he might awake, but his breathing remained steady. Tying back her hair, she tucked it up under her hat. She grabbed the boots, unlocked the door and slipped into the hallway, closing it behind her. She didn't pull on her boots until she reached the top of the stairs, then she descended into the common room, noting the few people asleep at the tables or stretched out on the wooden benches. One man remained awake. He sat in the corner, a tricorn hat pulled down low over his eyes. She sensed something familiar in the cut of his jaw, but she could not see his features clearly through the heavy shadow covering his face. Having no desire to be recognised dressed as a man in a coaching inn during the early hours of dawn, she didn't linger, but hurried across the room and out of the door.

A few stars still twinkled in the grey sky, but the horizon glowed lighter with the approaching sunrise. The stable was empty except for the horses and, walking along the stalls, she found Manfred, who greeted her with a nervous toss of his head.

'Steady, boy. It's only me.' She reached up to caress his nose, but he pulled back, his dark eyes wide. Only then did she hear the sound of boots crunching the hay on the floor behind her. Turning around, she expected to see the groom or James and let out a scream when the man with the tricorn hat flew at her.

He grabbed her by the throat, pinning her up against the wall, his hands cutting off her scream. His hat toppled off and she recognised Wilkins's man, the one who'd challenged her about the fight.

'I thought it 'twas you. How lucky for us to meet when I'm on me way back from London,' he sneered, pressing his body against hers. 'Not so high and mighty now, are ya?'

'Get away from me,' she choked, scratching at his hand, but his grip on her neck remained tight.

'Oh, no, me minx, now you've shown yer true colours, old Mark's going to have a reward. I sees you and I thinks to myself, what would a proper lady like yourself pay to keep me from spreading this around the whole county?'

'You'll get nothing from me,' she spat, her throat burning with the effort to breathe.

'Oh, I think I shall have something.' He leaned closer, his ale-laden breath stinging her face.

A large shadow rose up behind him, pulling him back. The fingers around her throat released and she dropped to the ground, gasping for air. James slammed Mark against the opposite wall, his sword pointed at the scoundrel's throat.

'Please, governor, I meant no harm,' he pleaded, his eyes wide with terror. 'I only wanted to help the lady, her being a good neighbour and all.'

'You have a strange way of helping,' James growled.

'Please, sir, I was helping. I can prove it. I know about her brother, the one in London.'

Julia was next to James in an instant. 'What do you know?'

'I know where he is.'

'How? Where?' Julia's heart leapt with hope.

Mark hesitated and James brought the edge of his sword up against Mark's neck.

'Answer her.'

The servant started to shake. 'Giltspur Street Compter.'

'Debtors' prison?' Julia cried.

'You're lying.' James pressed the sword deeper against Mark's flesh. A small drop of blood slipped out from beneath the blade and Mark's eyes widened, his fingers clawing at James's hand.

'No, I helped put him there. Mrs Wilkins told me to do it. She saw him when we was in London. Mrs Wilkins knows one of his creditors, so she sent me to fetch the man and he had me fetch the bailiff. It's why I'm back from London so late.'

'Why would she have Paul arrested?' Julia asked, trying to make sense of it all.

'To spite you both for wanting Cable Grange and for putting Mr Wilkins in debt to Captain Covington at the race.'

'But Paul had nothing to do with it.'

'The loathsome woman doesn't care. If she can strike a blow, she'll do it, no matter who it hurts.' James released Mark, who slumped to the ground, clutching his bruised neck. 'Mrs Wilkins paid you well for this?'

'Yes, sir.'

'I'll pay you better for your silence.' James tossed a few sovereigns at Mark's feet. Forgetting his sore throat, Mark snatched up the coins. He stretched to reach the last one, but James stopped him with his sword, resting the shiny blade against his cheek. 'I hear one whisper of either Paul's story or Miss Howard's and you'll regret it. I know a press-gang boss who'd gladly take a man like you for a ship. Do I make myself clear?'

'Yes, sir.' He cowered back, clutching the money to his chest.

James hauled Mark to his feet, shoving him at the stable door. 'Now get out of my sight.'

The servant stumbled before running off into the morning.

James sheathed his sword, fixing Julia with hard eyes. 'Why did you run off?'

She turned away from him, her shaking hands fumbling with Manfred's saddle. 'I don't owe you any explanations.'

He stepped up behind her, his body vibrating with anger. 'Do you know what could have happened if I hadn't found you?'

She knew exactly what she'd have suffered if he hadn't followed her. Having come so close to danger, she wanted to cry from fear, throw herself into his arms and let him comfort her, but she didn't have the courage to face him.

'Don't ever scare me like that again.' He walked to his own horse, throwing the saddle over its back in a noisy clank of stirrups and buckles. Tears burned at the corners of her eyes, but she refused to let them fall, determined not to cry in front of him.

Chapter Thirteen

The sun crested the horizon, glinting off the tightly packed roofs and wet streets of London. Smoke rose from the thousands of chimneys, joining the voices of ballad singers, fishwives and hawkers beginning their day. Despite the growing tightness in her stomach, Julia followed James into the sprawl of farmers, dyers and the like crouched outside the city proper and spreading into the surrounding countryside. The stench of rot and filth grew stronger the closer they got to town, the smell instantly taking her back to her Season in London and conjuring up the feelings of loneliness and inadequacy she'd suffered then. She wondered at the odd circumstances bringing her back here today. Was this her future, the rank air of London instead of the clean air of Cable Grange?

James sat rigid atop his horse. They'd barely spoken since leaving the inn and if he didn't want her before, she felt sure he couldn't wait to be rid of her now. How tired he must be of chasing after a hoyden with a knack for getting in trouble. He'd probably leave her the moment they found Paul.

She buried her nose in the wool sleeve of her jacket,

noting how James seemed impervious to the odours. 'How can you stand the smell?' she asked, unnerved by his continued silence and eager to reclaim the easy familiarity between them.

'Compared to a few months at sea with filthy men, bilge water and dead rats, this smells positively charming.' He sounded almost jovial and her shoulders relaxed, glad to see he'd lost some of his irritation. The feeling disappeared when his eyes went stern. 'Here, just as in the inn, do as I say.'

Julia nodded, rubbing her sore throat.

They manoeuvred their horses down the wide streets, dodging carriages, carts and various workers going about their morning business.

'How do you know where it is?' she asked.

'This isn't the first time I've had to bail a fellow officer out of debtors' prison. Though I never thought I'd be doing it for Paul Howard.'

'I find it hard to believe you dislike one another. You're so much alike.'

'No need to insult me,' James laughed.

'I meant it as a compliment,' she teased, happy to see the light return to his eyes.

They approached the old stone prison, the morning sun just beginning to rise over the tops of buildings. Giltspur Street Compter seemed strangely situated next to shops, its uninspiring façade dotted with rows of windows. A parade of women and children wandered in and out of the iron gates. The more fashionable ladies buried their faces in white handkerchiefs, crying over the loss of a dowry or their only source of income while the common women carried large baskets of food or dragged crying children into the prison.

James signalled for them to dismount, then handed her his reins. 'Stay here while I speak with the guards.'

'I want to come with you.'

'No. We can't leave the horses unattended or some desperate person might steal them. Don't worry. It isn't as bad as you think.' He cuffed her under the chin, then hurried across the street to talk to the guards lounging on either side of the main door. She watched them perk up when he slipped them a few coins before they ushered him inside.

She stood with the horses, cautious of the people walking the streets. Shady characters eyed the horses with appraising interest and she wondered how many of them would gladly slit her throat to steal the animals. Clutching the reins, she worried as she waited, imagining Paul lying in some dank cell, his wounds uncared for and at risk of infection. Once James had freed him, she'd take him straight to the London town house and call for Dr Childers. Hopefully, she was not too late. She didn't know what she would do if she lost him to gaol fever or gangrene.

Finally, James emerged from the jail and if it weren't for the horses, she'd have rushed across the street to meet him. Instead she waited, her fears receding some when he came to stand next to her.

'I spoke with the warden. He'll summon your brother's creditors, then I'll settle the debt.'

'I brought money.'

He held up his hand to silence her. 'Allow me, please. I've dealt with these matters before and will not be cheated.'

She nodded, embarrassed once again at how unprepared she was for London. At Knollwood she was master of her realm; here she found herself at the mercy of others. 'Can I see Paul? I want to make sure he's all right.'

'Yes, I've made arrangements.'

He paid a guard to attend to the horses, then escorted Julia inside. The stench of unwashed bodies and damp stone rivalled the smell outside and Julia covered her nose with her hand.

He led her into a small office off the main entrance. Inside a large man wearing a dirty wig sat behind an old desk, poring over paperwork. Julia took a deep breath, the dusty smell of the office preferable to the noxious odours outside.

The gruff man ignored Julia in favour of James and what he knew to be a large and generous purse. 'You want to see him?'

'The lad wishes to see him, older brother and all. Mother wants to make sure he's being treated right.'

'A visitation will cost ya,' the warden finally acknowledged her, his wig slipping off to one side of his bald head.

'Cost?' Julia's voice came out high and she covered it with a cough. 'Cost?' she repeated, trying to deepen her voice.

'You'll have to excuse him—he's young.' James fixed her with a reprimanding glare, then slid two coins across the desk. 'He doesn't understand things the way we do.'

'Young officer needs to learn this is a business. A man has to make a living.' The warden stuck two fat fingers on the coins and drew them to him. He dropped them in his dirty pocket, then nodded to the man standing behind Julia. 'Harvey there will take you back. Captain stays here to discuss the financial arrangements.'

'But—' Julia started, but James waved her off.

'Not to worry, Julius. The warden here is a sensible man. He knows the value in making sure no harm comes to you.'

The warden raised a greedy eyebrow, grasping James's meaning. 'Of course. Harvey will see nothing happens to the lad.'

'Yes, sir.' Harvey opened the door, hustling Julia into the hallway. 'This way.'

Julia followed him deeper into the prison, worry helping her ignore the eye-watering smell. At every cell they passed, a man's hand jutted out between the bars, his hoarse voice begging for money to buy food, his own cell or freedom. They reached the day rooms where children of various ages ran circles around men and their wives, who sat nursing babies.

'There are families here?' she asked, astonished.

Harvey grunted at her ignorance. 'Them that can afford it lives in the Rules of the Compter.'

'Rules?'

'Three miles 'round the Compter. Them that can't stay here.'

Taking in the wretched conditions, Julia fell silent, afraid of what she'd find when they reached Paul. He might already be sick, lying in squalor at death's door with no one to even bring him water.

Finally they reached a small row of cells near the back of the jail. The accommodations here weren't nearly so dirty, but Julia wouldn't call them 'clean'. A rat scurried across their path and she jumped back with a high squeal.

Harvey laughed, the key ring in his hand jingling. 'You wouldn't make it long on a ship.'

'How is my brother?' Julia adjusted her coat, following him to the last wood-and-iron door.

'Doing as well as ya can imagine. Here ya are.' He slid a large, black-iron key into the lock. The grating sound of metal against metal filled the hall before he threw open the door. ''ave a visitor for ya, Lieutenant.'

Julia stepped forwards, steeling herself for the worst and caught off guard by what she saw inside. The room, by no means palatial, was tidy and better appointed than the one she'd slept in last night. A wooden bed with white linens took up one wall while a well-built writing desk occupied the other. In the centre of the room, in a cushioned chair, Paul sat with a book in his lap, reminding her very much of a pirate captain surrounded in a cave by his sumptuous loot. Only the angry red cut on his forehead kept her from laughing.

He started at the strange sight in front of him, then rose, taking in the uniform with a lopsided grin.

'Well, fancy this. I didn't expect you of all people to rescue me, especially not like this.'

'Rescue you—' Julia balked, looking around at the cell '—I should have known you'd arrange the best accommodations, even in gaol.'

'Right crafty, this one,' Harvey mumbled. 'Wouldn't mind if we had more like him.'

Despite the humour, the emotions of the last day combined with the exhaustion of the night and her relief to find Paul overcame her. She threw herself into his arms, hugging him tight, quite forgetting herself and her disguise.

'Now then, lad, I know the ship has missed me, but really.' Paul patted her back, attempting to maintain the charade.

A deep, raspy laugh rolled out of Harvey. 'No point pretending. She ain't the first to come here dressed like that.'

'She's my sister,' Paul protested and Harvey laughed harder.

'Ain't the first to say that, too.'

Paul hugged Julia close while she cried into his dirty coat. It smelled of smoke and gunpowder and the scratchy wool reminded her of James. 'Now then, what's all this? You've never been this excited to see me.'

'I was so worried. They said you were injured.' She reached up to touch his head and he caught her hand. 'What happened?'

Julia and Paul sat down on the bed and Harvey stepped out of the cell and closed the door, giving them a little privacy.

'After the battle, we were rescuing French seamen. We should have left the scoundrels to drown. They were so thankful, they tried to take over *HMS Pickle*. We beat them back, but not before one of the French dogs got hold of a sword and rushed at Lieutenant Lapenotiere. I stepped between them, running him through just as he brought down his sword. He caught me here.' He touched his wound and winced. 'I was out for a while and bled like a stuck pig. Lieutenant Lapenotiere thought I might die, but the surgeon patched me up. Said all I needed was rest and I'd be back to fighting form in no time, though I'll have a scar to show for it. Lieutenant Lapenotiere was so grateful, he invited me to accompany him back to London.'

'Thank heavens.' She hugged him again, but he leaned back.

'Now, what are you doing here and dressed like that?'

'You have no idea what's happened this last week.'

'Then tell me all about it.'

She described at length the events of the last week, telling him everything except her very intimate encounter with the captain last night. Paul might listen without judgement, but she knew even he had limits where her honour was concerned. A few moments after she finished her story, Harvey pulled open the door.

'Come on. It's time for you two to go.'

They followed Harvey out of the cell and back down the halls.

'Paul, Dr Childers said you never arrived at his office. What happened?'

Paul rubbed his neck, a shamefaced smile spreading across his face. 'I'm afraid I didn't go straight to Dr Childers, though I wish I had.'

'Yes, it would have saved us all a great deal of trouble and worry,' Julia chided. 'Where did you go?'

'I was on my way to Dr Childers when I ran into an old friend and he invited me to a card party.'

'Paul, how could you?' She wasn't sure who she was more angry with: Paul for being so silly or Charles for being right. 'You were supposed to rest.'

'I spent the last two weeks of our voyage back to England resting. I needed a little fun. I saw the Wilkinses there. Mr Wilkins was bragging about selling Cable Grange for more than it's worth. I'm sorry you weren't able to get it. You'd have really made something out of it.'

She offered him a half-hearted smile, not wanting to think about it.

Harvey stopped at a small sitting room across from the main office. 'You can wait here while the captain finishes settlin' your accounts. It's the warden's private room.'

'Thank you, good man. We'll have cake with our tea,' Paul ribbed.

'I've changed my mind. I'm glad to be done with ya,' Harvey grumbled, closing the door.

Paul walked leisurely about the shabby room, fingering the chipped porcelain knick-knacks probably left behind by some long-ago tenant. 'Now that Cable Grange is gone, what will you do?'

'I'll stay with you.'

He leaned against the thick windowsill, crossing his arms over his chest. 'You can't stay with me.'

'What other options do I have? I can't go back to Knollwood, not under these circumstances.'

'You could marry Captain Covington.'

'Haven't you heard anything I've told you?' Julia threw up her hands, for the first time in her life frustrated with Paul.

'I heard it all, which is why I think you should simply admit you're in love with him and put all this business behind you.'

'I don't love him.' Julia threw herself into a nearby chair, a puff of dust escaping from the threadbare fabric. New tears fell down her cheeks, leaving small watermarks on the dingy chintz. 'I did love him, but not any more.'

Paul sat on the chair's matching ottoman, taking Julia's hands in his. 'I think you still love him very much. Do you know how I know?'

She shook her head, wiping her eyes with the back of her hand.

'Because I've never seen you cry.'

'Of course I cry.'

'Not like this.' He pulled a stained handkerchief from his pocket and handed it to her.

'Well, what do you expect? I'm not a statue.' She wondered if she shouldn't have taken Charles's advice and left Paul in London.

'Come now. Why the tears?'

'Because he doesn't love me.'

'What makes you think he doesn't love you?'

'Mrs Wilkins.'

'He explained why he was there.'

'He was lying, like all Navy men.'

'Captain Covington may be a Navy man, but he's no liar. He's also not a man of whims. If he didn't love you, he wouldn't have come to London to help you, especially not to help me. I think he loves you just as much as you love him. He just needs to get around to telling you so you'll finally believe him.'

Julia twisted the handkerchief, unable to deny his logic. The captain had followed her to London, saved her from Wilkins's servant and helped her find Paul, but she'd continued to doubt him because of her own fears and because he hadn't said the words. Could the answer be so simple? Her head ached from trying to figure it all out. 'What about your recommendation?'

'I understand why he wrote it. At the end of my first year, we were in Portsmouth waiting for our orders. It was rather dull there and I got into some trouble with a parson's daughter.'

'Paul, you didn't.'

'Unlike your captain, I am a typical Navy man. But I wasn't the first officer she'd taken long walks with in the woods. I just had more money than the last bloke. The next thing I know she tells her father I ruined her and the parson complains to my superior officer.'

'Captain Covington.'

'Of course. Well, it's his first ship so he's a real stickler for rules and orders me to marry her.'

'But you refused.'

'I wasn't about to introduce a girl like her to Mother, or Charles for that matter. Luckily, before Captain Covington could bring me up on charges, her fiancé comes in to port. His ship took a frigate off the coast of Africa, so now he has money and they run off to Gretna Green.'

Julia clapped her hand over her mouth to cover a laugh. This was just the kind of trouble and escape Paul always managed to find. 'Once the truth came out didn't Captain Covington understand?'

'He did, but I'd still disobeyed a direct order. Caused him quite a bit of embarrassment.'

'So now, all these years later, he writes a poor recommendation. Seems rather petty.'

'I don't blame him. Besides, he's more than made up for it now.'

He patted her hands, then the door opened and James entered the room.

James took in brother and sister. She clutched an old handkerchief, watching him with large, red eyes glistening with tears. He could only imagine what she'd told her brother and wondered how his old crewmate would react. He didn't relish the idea of a duel.

To his amazement, Paul crossed the room, holding out his hand in greeting. 'Captain Covington, thank you for getting me out of this pinch.'

'You have Miss Howard to thank.' James hesitantly took his outstretched hand and Paul pumped it heartily.

'Don't be so modest. I know you played a part in it. My sister told me all about your exciting journey last night.'

'Did she?' James tightened his grip and Paul matched the hold with a smile. *The man is as arrogant as ever*, James thought, determined to make Paul relent first, despite the numbness in his fingers.

'Come now, Jim.' Paul leaned forwards, dropping his voice. 'We both love the little lady, so why not put the past behind us?'

James released Paul's hand, flexing his fingers to bring the blood back. What had she told him?

'Now, if you'll both excuse me.' Paul moved towards the door. 'I have some private business with the warden and you two have a great deal to discuss.'

'Paul, wait.' Julia jumped to her feet, but Paul didn't stop, winking at her before slipping out of the door.

A small porcelain clock on the mantel ticked off the long seconds of silence. James stood unmoving, his eyes watching her with honest longing. Could Paul be right? Did he really love her? She searched for the words to ask, the right phrase to confirm everything in her heart and cross the chasm of uncertainty dividing them, but words were unnecessary. He marched across the room, swept her into his arms and kissed her.

All the worry about her actions and future disappeared. Pressing close, she surrendered more now than she had in the late hours of the night, giving him her heart, soul and life, knowing he would guard them as faithfully as he'd guarded her through this entire journey, binding their hearts together so nothing could ever separate them again.

Their lips finally parted and she felt the rough stubble of his cheek against hers. 'I love you,' he whispered.

'I love you, too.' She buried her face in his jacket, revelling in the peace and comfort of his beating heart.

She'd never felt this happy or content and it filled her with a new energy and the eager anticipation to begin their life together.

'There's plenty of time to make it to Gretna Green,' she suggested, tracing a brass button with her finger.

'Nonsense. If I know George, he's convinced your brother not to cancel the wedding.'

'I'm surprised Charles hasn't hurried after us with a vicar already.'

'Then I know the wedding will still take place. We just have to get there on time.'

The clock chimed eight o'clock.

'Then we'd better hurry or we'll never make it.'

Outside the jail, Paul waited with the horses, winking at a young woman sauntering past.

'I'm glad to see you've resolved your differences.' He laughed as Julia and James approached.

'I suppose it's my turn to thank you,' James said.

'You'll have plenty of time to thank me once you're married. But first, we need to eat. I know a place not far from here where we can get some food and a horse.'

'You mean I'll have to hire a horse for you since you have no blunt,' Julia corrected.

'How kind of you to offer, sister, though I have plenty of blunt, just not here in London—'

'If you don't mind,' James interrupted, 'I have a much better suggestion.'

Chapter Fourteen

'I thought you said your suggestion was better?' Julia hissed, taking in the dark-wood entrance hall of the well-appointed town house, her stomach tight with worry.

The captain put his arm around her shoulders and offered an encouraging squeeze. 'Have faith, Artemis.'

Her worried eyes met Paul's, not sure what to expect. The butler had left them to fetch the mistress of the house, which belonged to none other than James's mother.

'Perhaps we should go to Charles's town house,' Julia pleaded, stepping back towards the door.

'No, I want to introduce you to my mother.'

'Like this?' She waved her hand over the uniform, not wanting to meet her future mother-in-law in such scandalous attire.

'She'll understand.'

A stout woman in her early fifties appeared at the top of the stairs, her plump frame draped in a silk morning wrapper. A linen cap covered her dark hair and she had the pinched groggy expression of someone who'd just been roused from bed. 'What are you doing here?'

'Good morning, Mother.' He met her at the bottom of the stairs with a respectful hug. 'I see you're safely returned from Charlotte's.'

'And very, very late last night thanks to the miserable roads, which is why you'd better have a good reason for disturbing me so early this morning.'

'Who's in a spot of trouble now?' Paul chuckled in Julia's ear and she elbowed him silent.

Mrs Covington stepped back from her son, taking in the motley, unwashed group dressed in dirty uniforms, her forehead wrinkled in confusion. 'I thought you were in the country?'

'I was but I had business in town, some of which might interest you.'

'I doubt it, but get on with it so I can return to bed.'

He took Julia's hand and pulled her forwards. 'I want to introduce you to my fiancée.'

'What kind of joke is this?' she sputtered, grasping her robe tight around her neck. 'I will not stand for this kind of tomfoolery so early in the day.'

'I assure you, this is no joke. I'd like you to meet Miss Julia Howard.'

He pulled off her hat and Julia's long braid tumbled down her back. She squared her shoulders, put her chin in the air and stepped forwards with as much grace as she could muster in a pair of men's Hessians.

'Mrs Covington, I'm delighted to meet you.' Julia curtsied, using everything Annette had taught her about behaving in society to stay poised, but Mrs Covington's eyes remained stony.

'And the gentleman?' she asked, nodding at Paul.

'My brother, Lieutenant Paul Howard.'

'A pleasure, madam.' He swept into a low bow, more to cover his smile than to show his respect.

'Am I to assume the three of you have stopped here on your way to Gretna Green?'

'Of course not,' James said. 'We have an appointment at the church near Miss Howard's estate today at three. Miss Howard is George Russell's niece.'

Mrs Covington's stony eyes warmed. 'The one who runs the estate?'

'The very young lady.'

'Well, why didn't you say so sooner?' She rushed at Julia with arms outstretched, enveloping her in a big hug. 'My dear, I'm so pleased to have you here.'

'Thank you.' The sudden change in emotion caught her off guard, but she preferred it to the rebuke she'd imagined.

Mrs Covington stepped back, clasping her hands together in excitement, the lace at her sleeves fluttering. 'Your uncle told me a great deal about you, but of course my son doesn't write to tell me he's getting married and to George's niece of all people.'

'It all happened very fast and you were travelling. The letter wouldn't have reached you.'

'That's no excuse for showing up like a vagabond and announcing it.' She wagged a reprimanding finger at Paul. 'I hope you have more respect for your mother.'

'Of course.' Paul nodded solemnly but Julia noticed the laughter in his eyes.

'Mother, we must borrow the chaise if we're to make it back to Knollwood in time,' James informed her, attempting to regain control of the situation, but Julia could tell Mrs Covington had no intention of relinquishing it.

'Borrow—oh, no, I'm going with you. But first, we must get Miss Howard some suitable travelling attire.'

'There isn't time.'

'Then we'll be quick because if you think I'm going to have my future daughter-in-law traipsing about the countryside dressed like a man, you're quite mistaken.' She examined Julia's dust-covered uniform, tutting under her breath. 'You're about Charlotte's size. My daughter always leaves a couple of dresses here. One is sure to fit. Come along and we'll find one. And, James, arrange to have breakfast sent up to your sister's room. You probably haven't even fed the poor girl. You two can have breakfast in the morning room.' Mrs Covington took Julia's arm and escorted her up the stairs.

Julia wasn't sure which moved faster, their chaise or Mrs Covington's conversation. The woman talked without breathing or pausing, jumping from one topic to the next as they sped past the mile posts. Paul had left town shortly after breakfast, riding ahead on James's London stallion to inform Knollwood of their impending arrival and to arrange their meeting at the church. Manfred and Hector were stabled in James's mews, enjoying a well-deserved rest.

James, Julia and his mother had not started for Knollwood until nearly eleven. Business had delayed them in London, something to do with the Admiralty, though James never said what. Now, if they hoped to make it to Knollwood by three, they had to hurry. Mrs Covington's post-boy was an excellent driver and they made good time, despite one stop to change the horses.

They'd maintained a sensible pace until the turn to Daringford, then Mrs Covington insisted on speed. Despite the post-boy's skill, Julia found the fast pace unsettling. She might have developed her brother's taste for adventure, but an overturned carriage did not figure into any of her plans.

'Perhaps we should slow down? If the vicar was convinced to hold the ceremony today, he'll be just as easily persuaded to hold it tomorrow,' Julia suggested while Mrs Covington paused to take a breath. The woman shook her head, grasping the windowsill when the carriage took a sharp corner, forcing James to hold the strap to keep from leaning into Julia.

'Heavens, no, my dear. You two have a date at the altar and I intend for you to keep it. Do you know how many years I've waited for James to marry? I have no intention of putting it off any longer. Besides…' she leaned forwards, patting Julia's hand and smiling '…I like you and I have no intention of letting you get away from him.'

'Or perhaps you have no intention of letting George get away from you,' James suggested.

'I have no idea what you mean.' Mrs Covington flapped her handkerchief in front of her face.

The captain offered Julia a conspiratorial wink. 'Perhaps we can make it a double wedding.'

'Oh heavens, who said anything about marriage?' Mrs Covington hid a wicked smile behind the coloured silk.

Julia's mouth fell open. 'You mean she and Uncle George?'

'Exactly.'

'How long have you known?' Julia asked, still trying to take it in.

'I've suspected it for a while, but she only just confirmed it.'

'Oh, you think you are so clever,' Mrs Covington huffed.

'I don't know if I approve of my mother conducting

herself in such a fashion,' James playfully chastised and Mrs Covington pointed one stern finger at her son.

'In your present circumstances, you have no right to criticise.'

Julia didn't know what to say after the stunning revelation, but then Daringford appeared in the distance, ending the discussion.

Hesitant anticipation filled her at the sight of the familiar rolling hills and river-etched valley. Though very eager to reach the altar, she had no idea what waited for them at the church. Mother and Uncle George would take the events of the last day with their usual detached demeanour. It was what Charles might say which worried her. Would he object to the marriage, afraid to entrust his sister and her inheritance to a man he might now view as a scoundrel? Or would he drag her up the aisle as fast as possible in an attempt to keep her and the family's reputation intact? Either way, he was sure to cause a scene she had no stomach for.

'What's wrong?' James asked. 'Not having second thoughts, are you?'

'I'm dreading another of Charles's lectures.'

'He has no cause to lecture anyone.'

'What do you mean?'

'Haven't you guessed about your nephew?'

The truth she'd somehow missed before hit her like a ton of stones. 'Thomas wasn't early. Charles and Emily, they—I mean, well, you know, it must have happened before they were married.'

'According to George it did,' James confirmed.

'It explains why they were so quick to marry last February. I can't believe I never realised it before.' Julia sat back, shaking her head in indignant disbelief. 'All this time Charles chastised me for my behaviour when he'd done so much more.'

'The fallen ones are always the most puritanical.' Mrs Covington sniffed. 'You must stand up to him, my dear, for you will have to stand up to James. He can be very stubborn at times.'

'Good, for if he weren't I might not be so happy.'

'We might not be so happy,' he corrected, kissing the back of her hand. The gentle tickle of his lips raised a shiver of delight along her spine. She saw the wanting in his eyes, felt their heat spreading through her and lowered her head so Mrs Covington wouldn't notice the burning exchange.

The carriage entered Daringford, slowing its mad pace and clattering through the narrow streets to the church situated on the other side. Her heart leapt with the excitement of being so close to home, but it was tempered by a new feeling. Though the familiar stone buildings were comforting, everything now seemed old and small. This place would never be far from her heart, but she couldn't wait to leave it and embark with the captain on the next journey and adventure.

The carriage jostled to a stop in front of the church, the long shadow of the steeple falling over the church-yard. James stepped out, then handed her down. She was not two steps from the carriage when the church's large oak doors flew open and her family rushed to greet them.

'You made it.' Emily threw her arms around Julia. 'We were so worried about you. I brought your dress. You can change in the vestibule.'

'Where are Charles and Paul?'

'Inside, speaking with the vicar.'

'Jim, I brought your other uniform, thought you

might need it,' George said before running his hand over the chaise's high mudguard. 'I recognise this coach.'

'I thought perhaps you might.' Julia laughed.

'Hello, Captain Russell.' Mrs Covington sat forwards at the door, meeting Uncle George with teasing eyes.

'I see you've finally learned her name,' he whispered to Julia.

'You never could keep a secret.'

'Hello, Mrs Covington.' Uncle George held out a steadying hand and she took it, descending from the carriage, her eyes never leaving his. He tucked her hand in the crook of his arm, then led her to Julia's mother, Emily and Annette. 'Everyone, may I introduce Jim's mother, Mrs Covington.'

Emily and Annette stood dumbfounded at the announcement. Only Julia's mother maintained her usual grace and confidence, moving around the others to welcome her.

'It is a pleasure to meet you. We are so delighted you could be here.'

'I wouldn't have missed it. I've waited a long time for this day.'

'We all have.' Her mother winked at George, who tugged on his cravat.

'You made it.' Paul bounded out of the church, washed and cleaned and wearing a fresh uniform. 'The vicar is ready. And who is this?'

He bowed to Annette, who stood away from the group, doing her best not to be seen. A slight blush spread over her cheeks at Paul's sudden attentiveness and Julia stepped forwards to rescue her. 'This is Miss Annette Taylor, Uncle Edward's stepdaughter.'

'I've heard a great deal about you.' Paul motioned

for Annette's hand, which she offered with her usual measure of grace.

'Hopefully not too much.'

Julia noticed Annette's lack of affected London airs, thinking the natural reaction suited her very well. Obviously Paul thought so, too, for he lingered over her hand.

Emily chuckled, breaking the spell. 'Come along, Julia. The vicar will not wait for ever.'

Julia followed Emily and Mother into the church and up the dim side aisle to the vicar's small room behind the nave. The musty smell of cold stone and smoke hung heavy in the air. Charles paced in front of the door, stopping at the sight of her. She cautiously approached, expecting anger but his eyes were soft, almost sheepish.

'I'm glad to see you returned unharmed. We were worried about you.'

'Were you?' Julia ventured, noticing the tender concern in his eyes. She'd only seen it once before, when he'd comforted her after Father's death.

'Of course. I know you believe I think little of you, but I don't. I'm only trying to help and protect you. Perhaps I've been going about it the wrong way. Mother told me about your bargain with the captain. I also spoke to Emily, who gave me quite a tongue-lashing for being so unsympathetic about Paul. I think some of your nature has rubbed off on her for she was quite forceful.'

'She'll need a strong hand to run Knollwood.'

He took her hands. 'You don't have to marry him if you don't want to.'

'I do.'

'Do you?'

Julia nodded.

'Will you be happy with him?'

'I love him and he loves me. Besides, I have a fondness for Navy men.'

He pulled her into a hug. 'Then I'm very happy for you. You couldn't have chosen a better, more deserving man.'

'Thank you.' She rose up and kissed him on the cheek, then slipped into the vicar's room. Her mother helped her exchange the borrowed gown for the London one altered for the wedding. Emily instructed Mary on how to arrange Julia's hair, then they stepped back to admire their work.

'You're beautiful.' Emily smiled and Julia's mother nodded.

'I think the captain will be very pleased.'

Minutes later, Julia stood at the back of the church on Paul's arm. The organist began a hymn, the church doors opened and the guests stood. Some faces she knew well, others were less familiar and she imagined a number of villagers and country folk had come to see for themselves the maid of Knollwood finally married.

Of all the eyes watching, she sought only James's. He stood near the altar with Uncle George, his smile taking her breath away.

'Are you ready?' Paul whispered.

'Yes.'

He escorted her down the aisle, offering her hand to James at the vicar's instruction. The rest of the ceremony passed in a blur and she was conscious of nothing but the vicar's even voice and James standing beside her. She thought of the fountain at Knollwood and her old longings. Standing beside a man who loved her and who she loved with all her heart, those days seemed liked a lifetime ago.

'You may now kiss the bride,' the vicar announced and James leaned over, placing his warm lips on hers. She met his kiss with all the passion in her heart, forgetting the guests and even where they stood.

'Patience,' Uncle George whispered, interrupting them and they broke into happy laughter, hurrying back up the aisle and into the soft evening light.

Outside the church, they received everyone's congratulations, enjoying the festive atmosphere.

Paul approached, twirling her in a large hug. 'I'm so happy for you, Sister. And you, too, Captain Covington. Congratulations.' He held out his hand to the captain, who took it without hesitation.

'Congratulations to you as well.'

'Pardon?'

'I paid a quick visit to Admiral Stuart while we were in London.' The captain reached into his coat pocket and presented Paul with a letter sealed with red wax. 'I rescinded my previous recommendation. Congratulations on your new posting, Lieutenant-Commander Howard.'

For the first time ever, Paul stood at a loss for words. He took the letter and opened it, a wide smile spreading across his face as he devoured the contents.

'My own ship. I can't believe it.'

'It's a sad vessel, barely fit for duty, but if you make something of her, you'll earn a name for yourself.'

'I will. Thank you. You won't regret this.'

'No, I don't believe I will.'

Paul hurried off to show his mother his new orders and Julia threw herself into James's arms.

'Thank you. Though you didn't have to do it.'

'Of course I did. If it hadn't been for Paul, you may never have come to your senses.'

More congratulation accompanied them to the Howard family carriage. Stepping up into it, she noticed, over the heads of the revellers, Uncle George escorting Mrs Covington to his carriage. It seemed she wasn't the only one destined to find love this November.

The carriage set off and with a sigh of relief, Julia settled against the captain's chest, enjoying the feel of his arms around her.

'I have a present for you.' He reached into his coat pocket.

She ran her hand up his thigh, eager for all the wedding events to be over so they could be alone. 'I think you shall have much more before the night is out.'

'Saucy wench.' He pinched her cheek, then held out a slim leather wallet. 'This is for you.'

She took the worn leather and untied the straps. Her heart leapt when she unfolded it and read the old paper. 'The deed for Cable Grange!'

'It is.'

'But how did you manage it? Mrs Wilkins said it was sold to a London gentleman.'

'I told you not to believe her. I had my London solicitor arrange the purchase anonymously. It seems Mr Wilkins owed more to creditors than even his wife knew. He was very eager to part with the estate for the sum I offered. I've since learned their debts were so crushing they fled to France right after the ball. Not even the amount I paid for Cable Grange was enough to save them from ruin.'

'Thank you. Thank you.' She gave him an enthusiastic kiss, teasing his tongue with hers before sitting back. 'But what about Venice and India? You promised to show me the world.'

'So I shall, but we need somewhere to live between

travels,' the captain whispered, nibbling at her neck, his breath heavy. 'Do you still have that book of your brother's, my sweet Artemis?'

'I think I can remember enough of it,' she breathed, pushing his jacket off his shoulders.

He kissed the exposed skin above the bodice of her dress, his tongue making sweet circles on her sensitive breasts. 'Don't you wish to wait?'

'No.' He was hers now without shame or censure and she wanted to feel him deep inside her again.

His jacket fell to the carriage floor and she pulled his shirt from his breeches, then slipped her hands beneath the linen to trace the taut muscles of his stomach. Answering her invitation, he settled her on his lap, his hands firm on her waist, anchoring her body to his. In his strong grip, she felt the security of their future while his tender lips filled her with the excitement of today.

She wrapped her arm around his shoulders, revelling in the feel of him so close to her. With her tongue, she imitated the wet circles on his neck, breathing on the moist skin and smiling when he groaned.

She had little time to delight in her newfound wickedness before his other hand slid beneath her dress, teasing the skin along the line of her calf and thigh. She gasped when he found her centre, unable to think of anything except the pleasure building inside her.

'No,' she protested when he withdrew his hand.

'Yes,' he answered, heavy desire igniting his eyes and making her shiver.

He helped her shift astride him, holding her hips to keep her steady as she worked open the buttons of his breeches. She pulled the material down about his thighs and, taking his desire in her hands, stroked the firm shaft.

'You do remember the book,' he rasped.

'I can't wait to try the positions.'

'First let's begin with just one.'

Pushing up her skirts, he settled her on to the heat of his manhood. She gripped the squabs behind him as he filled her, biting back a cry of delight.

She drew in deep breaths as he moved within her, his fingers digging into the flesh of her thighs. She closed her eyes, bringing her cheek next to his as the rocking carriage made each thrust more fierce. His breath in her ear matched by her own quickened as she tightened around him until they cried out together, clasping each other in quivering excitement.

She laid her head on his shoulder as everything around them came back to her.

'I think we shall have quite an adventure, my beautiful Venus,' he breathed and she looked up, her face close to his.

With one finger, she traced the curve of his smile, feeling his joy deep in her own heart. 'Yes, I think we shall.'

* * * * *

THE CINDERELLA
GOVERNESS

To the authors of The Governess Tales

for all your creativity, collaboration and hard work.

Prologue

August 1811

'Joanna, what are you doing in the library?' Rachel gasped from the doorway.

'I'm wondering if Madame Dubois would notice if I took this book with me.' Joanna Radcliff clutched the thin volume of fairy tales between her hands and threw her friend a mischievous smile. 'In case I have to thump the son of my soon-to-be employer should he make any untoward advances at me.'

Rachel rolled her brown eyes. 'Sir Rodger's sons are still boys and away at school. You won't even be teaching them.'

'Then I'll use it to make his daughters behave.' She laughed and Rachel joined in.

Joanna's cheer faded as she slid the book in the gap on the shelf. This had been her favourite one as a child. It was as difficult to leave behind as her friends, but she couldn't steal it. It would be a poor way to thank Madame Dubois for all her years of kindness.

'Come on, the carriage will be here soon.' Rachel

took her by the hand and pulled her to the door. 'We don't have much time.'

They hurried out of the dark library and into the brightly lit entrance hall. Madame Dubois's School for Young Ladies was a stately house on Cathedral Close facing Salisbury Cathedral. At one time it had been the home of a squire. Echoes of its history remained in the classical cornices above the doorways and the endless lengths of chair rails. The furnishings were less regal, but sturdy to accommodate the many young ladies who'd passed through its rooms over the years. The old rumour whispered to the new students stated it was one of Madame Dubois's lovers who'd deeded her the house. To see the woman in her stern black, her dark hair shot with silver and pulled into a bun as severe as her stance, no one could believe she'd ever been swept away by a passion worthy of property.

At the far end of the entrance hall stood a wide staircase. Rachel pulled Joanna towards it and past a sitting room filled with little girls sitting on benches.

'La plume de ma tante est sur la table,' Madame La Roche said, pacing in front of her pupils.

'La plume de ma tante est sur la table,' the girls repeated in high voices.

It wasn't so very long ago when Joanna, Rachel, Isabel and Grace had sat in the same room repeating those phrases. Their time as students was over. They were at last taking up positions as governesses. Today, Joanna would be the first to leave.

'Hurry.' Rachel rushed up the stairs.

'Any faster and I'll fly.' It wasn't possible, not with the many memories weighing Joanna down. Madame

Dubois's school was the only home she'd ever known. She wasn't ready to leave it, but she must. This was what she'd been trained for by Madame Dubois and the other teachers who'd raised her. It was a parting, but also an opportunity. Perhaps as the governess to the Huntfords, she might finally experience what it was like to be part of a real family.

At the top, Isabel came around the corner, stopping so fast the hem of her skirt fluttered out before falling back over her ankles.

'What's taking so long? I'll die if we can't give Joanna a proper farewell before we're all sent into exile.' Isabel pressed the back of her hand to her head with all the flair of the actress they'd seen performing in the seaside resort of Sandhills last year.

Rachel crossed her arms, not amused. 'It isn't so bad.'

'Says the lady going to the country of Huria and not Hertfordshire.' She waved one hand at Joanna, then pointed at herself. 'Or Sussex. Although I don't intend to stay there for long.'

'What are you plotting, Isabel?' Joanna focused suspicious eyes on her friend.

'Nothing. It doesn't matter. Come along, Grace is waiting.' Isabel tugged Joanna down the hall and Rachel followed.

'You'll be sure to write me when your nothing turns into something,' Joanna insisted, knowing her friend too well to be put off so fast. 'I'd hate to find out about it in the papers.'

'I told you, there's nothing,' Isabel insisted, adjusting a pin in her copper-coloured hair.

'Too bad, I might need some savoury story to enliven my days in the country.'

'Me, too.' Isabel nudged Joanna in the ribs and they laughed together before Rachel placed her hands on their shoulders and pushed them forward.

'Keep going, before we run out of time.'

They hurried to the last room at the end of the hall and stopped at the door to the bedroom they'd shared since they were all nine years old.

'Close your eyes,' Rachel insisted.

'Why?' Joanna didn't like surprises.

'You'll see. Now do it.' Isabel raised Joanna's hands to her eyes.

The two girls giggled as they led Joanna inside. The faint dank of the chilly room warmed by the morning sun combined with the lavender used to freshen the sheets, the sweet smell of Rachel's favourite biscuits, and Grace's Lily of the Valley perfume to surround Joanna. It reminded her of the coming winter, their Christmas together last year and how far away from one another they'd be this December. Sadness dulled the thrill of the surprise.

'All right, open your eyes,' Isabel instructed.

Joanna lowered her hands. Isabel, Rachel and Grace stood around a little table draped with linen. Rachel had baked Joanna's favourite lemon cake and it sat on a small stand surrounded by three wrapped presents.

'Congratulations!' the girls chorused.

'Oh, my goodness,' Joanna exclaimed, amazed at what they'd done and their having kept it a secret. There wasn't much they'd been able to keep from each other over the last nine years.

'Since you're the first to take up your new post, we couldn't let you go with only a goodbye,' Grace insisted with the seriousness which still haunted her after her unfortunate incident. 'We don't know when we'll see each other again.'

Joanna threw her arms around Grace. 'Stop, or you'll make me cry.'

'Don't be silly, you never cry.' Grace hugged her tightly, then released her. 'Let's have our cake.'

They ate their treat while Joanna unwrapped the pen from Rachel, the stationery from Isabel and the ink from Grace.

'It's so you can write to us,' Rachel explained through a mouthful of cake.

'Thank you all, so much.' She clutched the items to her chest, deeply grateful. These three women had been the closest she'd ever had to sisters. She didn't want to lose touch with them, or the deep bonds they'd forged.

Their happy celebration was interrupted by a knock.

Everyone froze as Miss Fanworth stepped inside and closed the door behind her. The short, brown-haired teacher with the soft plumpness of a mother hen tapped her foot in admonition. 'What's this? Food in your bedroom. Madame will have a fit if she finds out.'

'You won't tell her, will you?' Isabel pleaded with more drama than earnestness.

A smile spread across Miss Fanworth's full lips. 'Of course not. Now cut me a slice.'

This wasn't the only secret their favourite teacher had kept for the girls. The other would see Grace ruined and all Madame Dubois's faith in her best teacher and her favourite pupils destroyed.

'I have a present for you, too.' Miss Fanworth exchanged her gift for the slice of cake Joanna held out to her.

Joanna unwrapped it to reveal a small leather pouch half-full of coins.

'It's for the postage, so you can pay for the letters we send you,' Miss Fanworth explained as she tasted her cake. 'I expect to receive a few in return.'

'Of course, how could I not write to everyone?'

Miss Fanworth set aside her plate, then rose. She laid her hands on Joanna's shoulders. Tears made her round eyes glisten. 'You were just a little babe when we first found you on the doorstep with nothing but a blanket and a torn slip of paper with your name on it. Now look at you, all grown up and ready to leave us.'

'I hope I can do you, Madame Dubois and the school proud.'

'As long as you remember everything we've taught you, you will.' She laid one full arm across Joanna's shoulders and turned them both to face the others. 'In fact, you must all remember your lessons, especially those I told you of the gentlemen you might meet. Don't be taken in by their kind words, it never ends well—why, look at poor Madame.'

She tutted in sympathy as she shook her head, making her brown curls dance at the sides of her face.

'What do you mean?' Isabel asked. All of them leaned in, eager for more. This wasn't the first time Joanna or the other girls had heard Miss Fanworth allude to something in Madame's past. Perhaps, with them leaving, Miss Fanworth would at last reveal the headmistress's secret which had teased them since their first day at the school.

Miss Fanworth's full cheeks turned a strange shade of red. She was as horrified by her slip as their interest. Then the clop of horses and the call of the coachman drifted up to them from the street below. Miss Fanworth blew out a long breath, as relieved by the distraction as she was saddened by what it meant. 'Joanna, it's time for you to go. Are you ready?'

No. Joanna laced her hands in front of her, determined to be brave. She'd stay here as a teacher if they'd let her, but Madame Dubois had insisted she seek a position. She hadn't argued. She never did, but always went along, no matter what she wanted. 'I am.'

'I wish I was going with you.' Rachel huffed as she took Joanna's one arm.

Isabel took the other. 'Me, too.'

'I wish we could all go together,' Grace echoed from behind them, at Miss Fanworth's side as they left the room.

'We wouldn't get a stroke of work done if we were in the same house together.' Joanna laughed through the tightness in her throat.

They walked much slower down the stairs than when they'd ascended, all but Joanna sniffling back tears between jokes and shared memories.

Madame Dubois waited beside the front door, watching the girls reach the bottom. Her black bombazine dress without one wrinkle fell regally from her shoulders. The woman was formidable and more than one small girl had burst into tears at the first sight of her, but they soon learned how deeply she regarded each of her charges. She wouldn't hug or cry over them like Miss Fanworth, but it didn't mean she didn't care.

Though she didn't care enough to keep me here. Joanna banished the thought as soon as it reared its head. The school was full of little girls who'd been sent away by their families. She shouldn't expect to be treated any differently by Madame Dubois just because Madame Dubois had helped raise her.

In a flurry of hugs and promises to write, the girls said their goodbyes.

Reluctantly, Joanna left them to approach the headmistress while the others remained with Miss Fanworth. She stood straight and erect before the Frenchwoman. Outside, the coach driver tossed her small trunk containing all she owned up on to the top of the vehicle.

'This is a proud and exciting day for you, Miss Radcliff. You're leaving us at last to become a governess.' Madame Dubois held her arms at angles in front of her, hands crossed, but the softness in her voice and the slight sparkle of moisture at the corners of her grey eyes betrayed her.

She doesn't want to let me go. Joanna swallowed hard, the request to stay sitting like a marble in her throat. She swallowed it down. There was no point asking for something she wouldn't receive. Madame wouldn't give in to her wants any more than she would allow Joanna to give in to hers.

'Yes, Madame.' Joanna wished she could wrap her arms around Madame and hug her like the other girls did their mothers when they bid them goodbye on their first day, but she couldn't. Madame might be as saddened by the parting as Joanna, but there would be no hugging or tears. It wasn't her way.

'You're a bright, intelligent, accomplished young lady who'll aptly represent the quality of pupils at our school in your first position.'

'I will, Madame. You've prepared me well.'

Chapter One

One month later

Madame Dubois didn't prepare me for this!

Joanna clutched the book to her chest as she stood in the dark corner of the Huntford Place library. Frances, the eldest Huntford daughter, and Lieutenant Foreman had burst into the room aware of nothing but each other. Lieutenant Foreman pressed Frances up against the wall and pawed at her breasts and hips through her dress. Instead of fighting off his advances, Frances embraced the lanky Lieutenant, raising one slender and stocking-clad leg to rest against his hip.

Joanna glanced at the door. The sighs and moans of the couple filled the room as she debated how best to slip away without being noticed.

No, I can't. I'm the governess. She couldn't allow Frances to ruin herself, but she didn't have the faintest idea how to separate them. Beyond what Grace had told her, lovemaking was outside her range of experience. Despite understanding the more technical aspects of the act, it was the desire part she failed to grasp, the one which had led to Grace's predicament and was about to ruin Frances, too.

She'd learn more about the physical particulars if she didn't stop this. Lieutenant Foreman's hand was already beneath Frances's dress.

'Ahem…' Joanna cleared her throat, her urgency increasing with their passion when it failed to interrupt the amorous pair. 'Ahem!'

Lieutenant Foreman whirled around to face Joanna while Frances straightened the bodice of her expensive yellow-silk dress behind him. He adjusted his red coat, his sword not the only prominent weapon near his belt. Joanna tried not to notice, but it was difficult for his white breeches obscured very little.

'Excuse me, Miss Radcliff.' He bowed to Joanna, then bolted out of the room, leaving Frances to face her fate alone.

Joanna opened and closed her sweaty fingers over the cover of the book. She hoped this taught Frances something about the man and made her realise her mistake. She was about to say so when Frances, cheeks red with anger instead of shame, fixed on Joanna.

'How dare you barge in on me?'

'I didn't barge, I was already in the room when you and Lieutenant Foreman—'

'Don't you dare speak of it, not to me or anyone, do you understand?' She flew upon Joanna and slapped the book out of her hands. It landed with a thud on the floor between them.

'No, of course not,' Joanna stammered, startled by the command. She was supposed to be the one in charge. She remained silent, afraid to point out this fact and make things worse.

'Good, because if you do, I'll see to it you're dismissed without a reference.' Frances threw back her head of light blonde curls and strode from the room as if it was she and not her father, Sir Rodger, who owned the house. Like all four Huntford girls, Frances was spoiled by her parents. All of them had treated Joanna with nothing but contempt since her arrival.

Joanna found the arm of the chair behind her and gripped it tightly as she sank into the dusty cushions. This wasn't how being a governess was supposed to be. The girls were supposed to look to her for education and guidance, and keeping Frances's secret should've brought her and Frances closer, like it had with her, Rachel, Isabel and Grace. It shouldn't have garnered spite from a young lady clearly in the wrong. She should tell Sir Rodger and Lady Huntford about their daughter's compromising behaviour, but if she did, they might blame her.

I wish Rachel were here. She had a gift for dealing with the young children and even some of the older girls at the school. She'd know what to do, but she wasn't here, none of her friends or Madame Dubois or Miss Fanworth could help her. She was on her own, just as she'd been until she was nine and Grace, Rachel and Isabel had first arrived at the school. She wished she had a copy of the drawing of the four of them Grace had done last Christmas. It would lessen her loneliness to remember how happy they'd been together and make them seem closer instead of hundreds of miles away.

She stood and plucked the book from the floor, refusing to wallow in self-pity. Her friends weren't here and, despite Frances's threats, it was Joanna's duty to guide and chaperon the young lady. She'd have to find a more subtle way to go about it. There was little else she could do.

Luke strode up the steps of the Mayfair town house. The must and damp of the ship which had brought him back from France permeated the wool of his red coat. He rubbed his hand over the stubble on his chin. He should have stopped at the Army Service Club to bathe and shave, but the moment he'd landed in Greenwich, all he'd wanted to do was see Diana Tomalin, his fiancée.

He'd been brought home with instructions to marry and produce an heir for the family. The faster he made things final with Diana, the sooner he might achieve this goal and return to his regiment in Spain. It had hurt like hell to sell his commission four months after he'd risked his life to earn it and he'd be damned if he let it go for good.

Collins, the Tomalin family's butler, pulled open the front door. His small eyes in his soft face widened at the sight of Luke. 'Major Preston.'

'Morning, Collins. Is Miss Tomalin here?' Luke removed his shako and handed it to the man as he strode into the Tomalin family entrance hall.

'She is, sir, but—' He fumbled the army headdress, making the feather in the front waver like his voice.

'Collins, who is it?' Diana called from the sitting room.

'It's me.' Luke strode into the sunlit room and jerked

to a halt. His excitement drifted out of him like smoke out of a cannon.

Diana stood in the middle of the rug, her eyes not meeting his as she ran her hand over her round belly. The gold band on her ring finger clicked over the small buttons along the front of her voluminous morning dress. 'Welcome home, Major Preston.'

The pendulum on the clock beside him swung back and forth with an irritatingly precise click.

'When did you intend to tell me we were no longer engaged?' Luke demanded. 'Or were you hoping Napoleon would solve the matter for you?'

She twisted the wedding band, the large stone set in the gold too big for her delicate fingers. 'Mother said I shouldn't trouble you, not when you had so many other things to worry about. She also said I shouldn't wait any longer for you, that five years was enough, and you might die in battle and then my youth and all my chances to marry would be lost.'

'Yes, your mother was always very practical in the matter of our betrothal.' It's why he'd agreed to keep their engagement a secret until he could return from Spain with a fuller purse and a higher rank. Heaven forbid Mrs Tomalin endure the horror of a lowly lieutenant, an earl's mere second son, for a son-in-law. 'Who's the lucky gentleman?'

'Lord Follett,' she whispered, more ashamed than enamoured by her choice of mate.

'I see.' Like nearly all the women he'd encountered before he'd enlisted, and whenever he'd come home on leave, she'd run after a man with more title and land than him. He watched the pendulum swing back and forth in the clock case, wanting to knock the grand thing over and silence it. 'So it's Lady Follett now. Where is your distinguished husband? In Bath, taking the waters for his rheumatism?'

'With Father's mounting bills and you possibly never coming back, I didn't have a choice but to accept him,' she cried out against his sarcasm. 'So much has changed in England since you've been gone. The cold winters have taken their toll and, with crops failing year after year, Father began to fall into debt like so many others.'

No doubt his gambling habit helped increase it, Luke bit back, holding more sympathy for her than he should have. Her family wasn't the only one facing ruin and struggling to hide it. His father and grandfather had spent years rebuilding Pensum Manor after his feckless great-grandfather had nearly gambled it away. The continued crop failures were threatening to send it spiralling back into insolvency. Like Diana, Luke needed to marry and well. He hated to be so mercenary in his choice of bride, but it was a reality he couldn't ignore. However, it didn't mean he had to wed the first merchant's daughter with five thousand a year who threw herself at him in an effort to be the mother of the next Earl of Ingham. 'Surely you could've chosen someone better suited to you than that old man.'

'My first duty is to my father and my family, not to you, not to even myself.' She settled back into her chair, her brown eyes at last meeting his and filled with a silent plea for understanding. He couldn't withhold it. He'd abandoned his men and his military career to come home and do his duty for his family. He couldn't blame her for doing the same.

'It seems we're both obliged to make sacrifices. You with Lord Follett, me as the heir.'

'But your brother and his wife?'

'After ten years, there's been no child. If things stay as they are—'

'You'll inherit.' She pressed her palm to her forehead, realising what she'd given up by following her parents' demands. However, Luke knew the way of the world. A possible title at some future date was not the same as an old, wealthy baron on a woman's doorstep with a special licence.

Not wanting to torture her further with his presence or his ire, he took the shako from Collins and tucked it under his arm. 'I wish you all the best and future happiness. Good day.'

He left the house and climbed into the hack waiting at the kerb. He knocked Captain Reginald Crowther's feet off the seat where he'd rested them to nap.

His friend jerked upright and tilted his shako off his eyes. He was about to crack a joke when a warning glare from Luke turned him slightly more serious. 'I take it all didn't go well with your fair damsel?'

Luke rapped on the roof to set the vehicle in motion. As it lumbered out of Mayfair towards the Bull in Bishops Street, he told him what had happened inside the Tomalins'. 'This isn't how I imaged this would go.'

'And I can see you're utterly heartbroken over losing her. More like inconvenienced.' Captain Crowther threw his arms up over the back of the squabs. 'You thought you'd marry a tidy little sum, produce an heir with the least amount of bother and be back in Spain with the regiment inside of two years.'

Luke fingered the regimental badge of a curved bugle horn hung from a ribbon affixed to the front of his shako, unsettled by Captain Crowther's frank assessment of his plans and secretly relieved. If he and Diana had entered into marriage negotiations, the Inghams' debts would have been revealed. Diana's family would probably have made her cry off and all England might have learned of his family's financial straits. His rapture for her had faded too much during their time apart for him to go through so much on her behalf. 'Her refusing to marry me before I left and insisting we keep the engagement a secret always did rankle.'

'Now you must give up the hell of battle for the hell of the marriage mart.' His friend chuckled. 'Wish I could be here to see you dancing like some London dandy.'

'When I agreed to come home, I didn't think I'd have to face it.' Or the ugliness he'd glimpsed in Diana's situation. He set the shako on the seat beside him. Worse waited for him in the country. With the future of the earldom hovering over him, all the tittering darlings and their mamas who'd ignored him as a youth because he wouldn't inherit would rush Pensum Manor faster than Napoleon's troops did a battlefield.

'You don't have to do this. Write and tell your brother to pay more attention to his wife and come back to Spain,' Captain Crowther urged.

'I'm sure their lack of a child isn't from a lack of trying and it isn't only an heir they need, but money.' Luke stared out the hackney window at the crowd crossing London Bridge in the distance. He couldn't have refused the request to come home even if he'd wanted to. His father had called on his old friend, Lieutenant Colonel Lord Henry Beckwith, using the connection he'd employed to begin Luke's Army career to end it. Luke might have ignored one or two orders in battle, achieving both victory and forgiveness for his transgressions, but he couldn't dismiss a direct command from Lord Beckwith to return home.

The carriage lumbered to a stop in front of the arch of the bustling Bull Inn. Luke tucked the shako under his arm and stepped out, as did his friend. Behind them the driver unloaded Luke's things while Captain Crowther's stayed fixed on top. After he visited his sister, Reginald was going back to Spain, his mission of delivering dispatches complete.

Luke flicked the dull edge of the bugle-horn badge with his fingernail. He would catch a coach to Pensum Manor, his family's estate in Hertfordshire and take up the position of second in line to the earldom and groom-to-be to some willing, and as of yet unnamed, wife. 'I wish you'd accepted my offer to buy my commission.'

'You know I don't want it, or the debt to secure it. Don't look so glum.' Reginald cuffed Luke on the arm. 'We aren't all meant to be leaders like you. Your intelligence, wit and daring will be missed.'

'But they'll have your ability to charm the locals, especially the gambling men.'

Reginald grinned with self-satisfaction. 'I do have a flair with language.'

Luke snapped off the Forty-Third Regiment of Foot bugle-horn badge affixed to the front of the shako and handed the now-unneeded headpiece to his friend. 'Stay safe.'

Reginald ran his thumb over the bare felt front, a rare seriousness crossing over his face before it passed. 'You're the one who needs to watch yourself. I hear those unmarried ladies can be dangerous.' He tossed the thing inside the coach then took Luke's hand. 'Go on to Hertfordshire, find a wife and give your family their much sought-after heir.'

Reginald climbed back into the carriage and then hung one elbow out the door window.

'Give Napoleon hell,' Luke encouraged, the edge of the badge biting into his palm where he clasped it tight.

'I intend to.' With a rakish salute, Reginald tucked inside as the hack rolled off down the crowded street.

With each turn of the wheels, the most accomplished and contented ten years of Luke's life faded into the past. He opened his palm, the tin against his skin tarnished with Spanish mud and rain. What waited for him in Hertfordshire was everything he'd joined the Army to escape: the oppressive weight of previous generations which hung over Pensum Manor, and his own insignificance to the line as magnified by his brother's importance.

He slipped the badge into his pocket and strode into the inn to arrange for a seat in the next coach to Hertfordshire. He'd do his duty to his family, as fast and efficiently as he could, then he'd return to the Army and a real sense of accomplishment.

Chapter Two

Joanna had never been to a ball before. The Pensum Manor ballroom was decorated with autumn leaves, straw bales, scarecrows and bunches of wheat tied with orange-and-yellow ribbons. The same musicians who played in the church on Sundays now performed on an equally festive stage at the far end. In front of them, young ladies and gentlemen danced in time to the lively music. Everyone in attendance seemed happy and carefree, except Joanna, and, it appeared, Major Preston.

Joanna glanced at the guest of honour again, admiring the dignified arch of his brows, the subtle wave in his dark brown hair where it curled over both ears before touching the smooth skin above his collar. It wasn't only his commanding stature which drew her to him, but the discontent deepening the rich coffee colour of his eyes. He stood beside his brother, Lord Pensum, near the door, nodding tersely at each passing guest while his brother greeted them with a gracious smile and a few words. More than once Joanna saw Major Preston's sturdy chest rise and fall with a weary sigh and she sympathised with him. Like her, he was clearly ill at ease in the midst of all this merriment.

'Watch where you're going,' Frances snapped as she stopped to examine the dancers, forcing Joanna to come up short to keep from bumping into her tiring charge. Then Frances set off again on another circle of the room, no doubt searching for Lieutenant Foreman. Thankfully, they hadn't seen him, but it didn't stop Frances from looking. The girl was stubborn in her desire to ruin herself.

Joanna followed wearily behind her, tugging at the pale-blue secondhand dress Frances had tossed at her last night after Lady Huntford had announced Joanna would attend as Frances's chaperon. It spared the mother the bother of hovering around her headstrong daughter. Joanna played with the small bit of lace along the thankfully modest bodice. It fit her in length, since she and Frances were nearly matched in height, but Joanna had been forced to stay up late to take in the chest. The lack of sleep, combined with Lady Huntford having instructed Joanna to try and manoeuvre Frances to Major Preston, added to her disquiet. The young lady was as co-operative as a donkey. With Frances relentlessly circling the room and refusing to dance, Joanna had been denied the company of the other governesses sitting along the wall and chatting together. She needed some hopefully polite conversation with someone, anyone. She rarely received it at Huntford Place.

To Joanna's luck, Frances's hurried steps brought them closer to Major Preston and Joanna hazarded another glance at him. This time, his eyes met hers and the entire ballroom faded away until only the two of them and the soft melody of the violin remained. There were no wayward charges, laughing country squires or gallant young men to concern her. His gaze slid along the length of her, pausing at her chest which increased with her drawn-in breath.

Instead of stopping him with a chiding glance, she stood up straighter, offering him a better view of her in the prettiest dress she'd ever worn. His silent appraisal of her continued down to her feet and then up again. It kindled the strange fire burning near her centre which spread out to engulf her skin. She touched the curls at the back of her head, returning his attention to her face. With a slow, refined movement she lowered her hand, linking it with the other in front of her, each fingertip aching to trace the angle of his jaw to where it met his stiff cravat. She envied the linen encasing his throat and whatever woman he chose here tonight for his bride. She would experience the thrill of his body against hers, the heat of his wide hands upon her bare skin, the luxury of his height draping her like a heavy coat on a windy day.

'Stop gawking at everything,' Frances hissed, snapping Joanna out of her licentious daydream. 'You're embarrassing me.'

Considering the lady's encounter with Lieutenant Foreman, Frances possessed a strange idea of what might embarrass her. Joanna held her tongue, eager to avoid cultivating any more of Frances's ire.

'Might we not go speak with Major Preston?' Joanna slid a sideways glance at Major Preston. He continued to watch her with an allure which almost made her rush to him, but she didn't move. Instead, she tugged at the back of the dress, wondering what had come over her. She was here to chaperon Frances, not lose her head over a man so far above her the only relationship they could enjoy would risk her livelihood and go against everything Madame Dubois and Miss Fanworth had invested in her. They'd trained her to teach young ladies, not to become a kept tart.

'Why would I want to talk to him?' Frances shifted back and forth on her toes to look over the guests' heads.

'To save your slippers for the delight of dancing,' Joanna joked. Her attempt at humour withered as Frances narrowed her eyes at Joanna. 'And because I've noticed him admiring you.'

It was a lie, but an effective one.

'He has?' Frances's attention whipped around to Major Preston so fast, the blonde curls at the back of her head flew out before they settled back against her neck. Frances thrust out her ample chest and cast Major Preston a none-too-subtle smile.

Frances's interest in him ended his interest in them. He offered Frances a polite nod, then turned to speak to a gentleman Joanna vaguely recognised as someone of local importance. On the dance floor, one dance ended and couples began to form up for the next. Mr Winborn, the son of another local baronet who Catherine, Frances's younger sister, had teased Frances about during their last visit to the village approached them.

'Miss Huntford, may I have this dance?' The lithe gentleman with a head of wild red hair held out his freckled hand to Frances.

'Yes, I suppose I must be seen dancing with someone or people will talk.' Frances placed her hand limply in his.

'We can't have that, now, can we?' Mr Winborn concurred, not offended by her blunt acceptance and just as blasé about taking her to the dance floor as his partner.

Joanna sagged a little in relief. Frances couldn't get into trouble while she danced. Joanna turned, excited to at last be able to join the other chaperons when a mountain of a man stepped between her and them. A badge of a bugle horn hung by a tin ribbon met her before she peered up to the peak to find Major Preston standing over her.

The scent of cedar surrounding him enveloped her and she pressed her heels into the floor to keep from wavering under the pressure of it. His dark coat ran tight along the horizontal plane of his shoulders. Brass buttons with crossed sabres held the wool closed at his navel and emphasised his narrow waist. The dark material stood in stark contrast to the white breeches covering his legs. She didn't dare check to see what kind of buttons held those closed.

'May I have this dance?' He held out his hand to her. His palm was wide, with a faint scar starting at the first finger and crossing down to his wrist. Light red circles of old blisters further marred the plane of it. Here was no soft London gentleman, but one who knew something of hard work and danger. His nearness didn't overwhelm her like the ones of the other titled men and women filling the room. Instead, she admired his confidence and wanted to emulate it.

She raised her hand to accept his, then jerked it back to her side, remembering herself. 'When it comes to reels, I appear more like a horse trotting around a millstone than a lady of poise. It's best for me to avoid them.'

He grinned at her, amused instead of insulted by her refusal. 'Dancing doesn't bring out my natural agility either. Despite lessons, I never developed the talent for it. I mastered riding instead.'

'If only you could do both the way they do with the horses from Vienna I once read about.' She froze, waiting for him to chastise her as Frances had for speaking out of turn. Instead, he rewarded her with a smile as captivating as his height. He was a good head taller than her.

'Not my horse. He's more mule than Lipizzaner and would throw me if I tried to make a dancer out of him.'

'But you'd both be majestic for the moment you stayed in the saddle.'

'It would be a very brief moment.' He smothered a laugh behind his hand, the delight it brought to his eyes as captivating as the pensiveness which had called to her from across the room. 'Do you ride?'

'As poorly as I dance.' Horsemanship was wasted on a governess.

'I imagine you'd be quite elegant in the saddle if you tried.'

'I'm sure I would be, for the brief moment before I was tossed out of it.'

He leaned in, the intensity of his woodsy scent strengthening with his closeness. She noticed a slight scar running along the hairline of his temple, the skin a touch whiter than that of his face. 'I would catch you.'

Joanna stiffened, panic as much as excitement

making her heart race. As a governess, she shouldn't be speaking with him. She should draw this conversation to a close, remember his place and hers, but she couldn't. She hadn't been this at ease since the last time she'd been with her friends. She offered him an impish look from beneath her dark lashes, emboldened by his relaxed manner. 'I'd do the same for you.'

He straightened, his laugh uncontained this time. Thankfully, the music reached a high crescendo, keeping all but those closest to them from hearing him.

'Your catching me would make me a spectacle, more so than I already am.' His laughter died away and his shoulders rose and fell with another weary sigh. 'What I wouldn't give to be riding instead of here.'

'What I wouldn't give to be in a quiet corner reading instead of here.'

'Yet here we are.' He opened his hands to the room as Frances whirled by with her red-headed partner. Mr Winborn said something to her and she rewarded him with a rare and genuine laugh. 'It must be difficult being in Miss Huntford's shadow. You're by far the prettier of the two.'

Joanna studied the square head of a nail in the floor beneath her feet, as stunned as she was flattered by his compliment. Miss Fanworth's warning about young gentlemen came to her and she pinned him with her best disciplining governess look. It worked about as well with him as it did with Frances, which was to say it didn't. 'Thank you, but you really shouldn't.'

'I can't help it. I've been among plain-speaking men for so long it's difficult to not be open and honest with everyone. Imagine if we were all like this with one another.'

'Society would crumble once everyone realised what people really thought of them.'

'They already know but pretend they don't.'

'What about you? Do you pretend?' It was none of her business, but she couldn't help herself.

'Every day.' Sorrow darkened his eyes like clouds over water on a stormy day. 'I pretend to be happy I came home, I pretend to be glad I gave up my Army career for this.'

Luke pressed back his shoulders and clasped his hands behind him, waiting for her to brush away his complaints as his brother Edward, his father and every other young lady he'd spoken with tonight had done. They all expected him to forget his time in the Army, to dismiss it as one might a past Season in London. He couldn't any more than he could forget the faces of all the men he'd lost or the intuition for danger which still kept his senses sharp whenever he rode alone in the woods. All the instincts which had kept him alive in Spain refused to be dulled, but they were useless to him here.

'It can be difficult after so long in one situation to leave it, especially when it means saying goodbye to friends.' She studied him with eyes blue enough to make the Mediterranean jealous, their colour as stunning as her response. They captivated him as much now as when he'd followed her progress around the room as she'd trailed after Miss Huntford. Seeing the sisters together had reminded him of following Edward at school until he'd railed at him for embarrassing him. Luke had caught similar exchanges between the two sisters tonight. The last time he'd seen the Huntford girls had been at a picnic nearly fifteen years ago and they'd proved as vapid as their mother. Whichever Huntford sister this was, and he could only assume she was the second eldest, she'd matured into a beautiful, wise and witty young lady.

'Eventually, you'll settle in again,' she assured him, the light auburn hair framing her round face emphasising her subtle beauty.

'Settling is exactly what I'm worried about. As the second son, there isn't much else for me to do. The estate isn't mine and it may never be.' From an early age, the house, their legacy and their duty to it had been drilled into Luke and his older brother. It had meant something to Edward, the heir. To Luke, it had been nothing but a heavy reminder of his lesser status, the one his family hadn't failed to reinforce. After reluctantly paying to educate Luke alongside Edward, Luke's father had spent as few pounds as possible to purchase Luke's paltry lieutenant's commission. It had been left to Luke to claw his way up the ranks, borrowing from friends to purchase every next higher rank until the day he'd won for himself, through his own daring, the rank of major. Only now, when Luke had become useful to the line, had his father decided to waste an unnecessary fortune to trot Luke out to look over the local eligible ladies. It irritated him as much as having left so much hard work behind in the dirt of Spain. 'I have no desire to inherit, or become lord of the manor.'

Her shock at his honest declaration was obvious in the horrified surprise which widened her stunning eyes as she stared out across the ballroom. The dance had ended and the couples were bowing to one another and making their way back to their chaperons. She seemed to watch them closely, shifting on her feet as if she couldn't wait to flee from him and the heresy of not coveting an earldom. 'It can't be.'

'I assure you, it is.'

'Please excuse me, Major Preston, but I must, uh, see to something, uh, Miss Hartford, very important, at once.' She bolted from him like a horse whose rider had been shot off its back.

His spirits, buoyed by their conversation, sank like a rock. He'd thought her different from the many other ladies he'd met tonight, deeper and more understanding. He was wrong. She was as shallow and covetous as the rest of her family.

'You look as though you need this more than Edward.' Alma, his sister-in-law, offered him one of the two glasses of champagne she carried. She was tall for a woman but willowy with dark hair, light brown eyes and a playful smile Luke hadn't seen much of since coming home.

Luke took the drink and downed a sobering gulp. 'It seems my worth is once again based on the luck of birth and death.'

'I sympathise with you. Providing an heir is the one thing expected of a woman of my rank and I've failed at it.' She focused on the bubbles rising in a steady stream off the bottom of her champagne flute.

'I'm sorry, I didn't mean to add to your distress. I'm being as thoughtless as Edward.'

'Don't be so hard on him. He's struggling to accept our failure and, like you, the changes it means to the family and the line.'

All of their roles and places in life which had once been so secure were being thrown off kilter like a wagon caught in a rut.

'I've seen miracles on the field of battle, men narrowly missed by cannonballs, or those who walked away from explosions with only minor scratches. It isn't too much to hope for another. Don't despair, Alma. I haven't.' He tapped his glass against hers, making the crystal ring. 'You may become a mother yet.'

'We'll see.' Disbelief hung heavy in her response.

He raised his glass to finish it, then paused. Across the room, a man who shouldn't be here slipped out of the opposite door and into the adjoining hallway. 'What the devil is he doing here?'

'Who?' Alma asked, following the line of his look.

'Lieutenant Foreman.' He'd last seen the scoundrel eight years ago riding north from their training grounds in Monmouthshire with his tail between his legs, transferred to another unit at Luke's insistence for compromising a local vicar's daughter.

'There weren't any officers on the guest list.' Alma tipped her flute at the blue-eyed beauty weaving through the guests. 'I believe your conversation partner is following him.'

The young lady paused at the door, taking advantage of Lady Huntford's lack of interest in her to slip into the hallway where Lieutenant Foreman had just disappeared. Apparently, she favoured lower-ranking men more than Luke had realised.

Luke handed his glass to Alma. 'I won't have a

misguided woman ruining herself under our roof, especially not with a man like him. Tell no one about this.'

'I won't say a word.' Thankfully, she understood the need for discretion in this matter.

Luke followed them out of the ballroom, as curious as he was determined to protect his wayward guest.

She travelled the length of the ever-darkening hallway with the agitation of a spy down an alley. Whatever she was doing was wrong and she knew it. Still, she continued on in search of Lieutenant Foreman. Luke was careful not to follow too close. He wanted to make sure he caught them together, but not too much together. Then he'd see to it Lieutenant Foreman never set foot in this part of Hertfordshire again. He detested the man and his lack of honour. He should have done right by the vicar's daughter. At least he hadn't got the young lady with child. Luke would've marched him up the church aisle at bayonet point if he had. He hoped he didn't have to perform the same service for Miss Huntford.

The young lady slipped down another hall, this one poorly lit to disguise the threadbare rug and tired furnishings. The best of the furniture had been moved to the front of the house and the ballroom to keep up the appearance of wealth. No guests were supposed to be in this far-flung and cold wing of the classical-style house.

He stopped at the turn to the hallway and peered around the corner, doing his best to remain undetected. The young lady paused at the door near the far end and took hold of the knob. She turned to survey the emptiness around her. Luke jerked back out of sight and prayed he hadn't been seen. The squeak of the brass and the protest of the old hinges as the door opened told him she hadn't noticed him.

He marched down the hall after her, determined to make his interruption as stunning as possible in order to teach the lady a lesson. He grabbed the knob and threw open the door. 'What are you doing in here?'

He jerked to a halt to keep from colliding with the young lady. She scooted aside as, across the room, Lieutenant Foreman let go of the elder Miss Huntford so fast, she almost fell to the floor.

'Enjoying the pleasures of the country, as you can see,' Lieutenant Foreman sneered, his pointed chin framed by the red coat of his uniform 'And there's nothing you can do about it, *Mr Preston.*'

Luke rushed up on him so fast, he shuffled back into the bookcase behind him. 'I may not have my commission, but I still have my connections, especially with Lieutenant Colonel Lord Beckwith. I won't hesitate to appeal to him to have you drummed out of the ranks for this.'

'No, you can't,' Miss Huntford protested.

He fixed her with a hard look. 'You'd do well to remember your reputation is in grave danger of being compromised.'

Miss Huntford shrunk back, biting her lip like a reprimanded child.

Luke turned to his former comrade, wanting to thrash him for being a scoundrel, but he kept control. His family couldn't afford any broken furniture. 'As for you, Lieutenant Foreman, you'd better think long and hard on your future in the Army because if I ever see you two together again, unmarried, or hear one whiff of scandal regarding you and Miss Huntford, I'll see to it you're shipped to a remote and disease-ridden post. Do I make myself clear?'

Lieutenant Foreman's beady eyes widened. 'Yes.' 'Sir.'

'Yes, sir.' He raised a shaking hand to his forehead in salute.

'Now, get out.'

Lieutenant Foreman slid out from between Luke and the wall, offering not one word of goodbye to his lover as he rushed from the room.

Miss Huntford's embarrassment didn't last long past the exit of her paramour. She fixed hard eyes on her sister, reprimanding her as if Luke wasn't there.

'You brought Major Preston here,' she screeched. 'You're trying to ruin me on purpose. How dare you. I'll see you pay for this.'

She advanced on the poor young lady, who shrank into the corner as if doing her best to become one with the panelling. Luke stepped between the sisters, shielding the lady from Miss Huntford's wrath.

'Your sister didn't bring me here. I followed her. Unlike you, I'm concerned about her reputation and yours.'

'Sister,' Miss Huntford snorted, 'she isn't my sister. She's the governess.'

Luke stepped out from between the ladies and glanced back and forth at them. So much about their previous conversation suddenly became clear, especially her refusal to dance, her insight and her desire to get away. The governess lowered her stunning blue eyes to the carpet, her head bowed like an inferior. It made his blood boil to see her humbled by Miss

Huntford, as it did when he used to see unqualified commanders berate junior officers for daring to display initiative.

Luke turned back to Miss Huntford. With her deep-red dress pressing her generous breasts up against the top of the bodice, she was as well done up as a courtesan searching for a client at the theatre. Her mother shouldn't have allowed her daughter to wear so questionable a dress. Then again, if her mother had shown much interest in her, she might not have been here with Lieutenant Foreman. 'Your governess has more sense than you do.'

Miss Huntford let out a startled squeak at being disciplined for what Luke imagined might be the first time in her life.

'If I hear any word of Miss—what's your name?' he asked the governess.

'Radcliff.' She twisted her hands together in front of her. The vibrant, humorous woman he'd enjoyed in the ballroom was gone, driven away by her spoiled hoyden of a charge.

'If I learn Miss Radcliff has been reprimanded or dismissed for her attempt to aid you, Miss Huntford, I'll ask for an interview with your father and tell him not only what I witnessed, but something of Lieutenant Foreman's background. He won't like it and neither will you. Do I have your word you won't seek revenge against Miss Radcliff?'

Miss Huntford screwed up her full lips in a pout to make a two-year-old proud. He recognised the delay. It was the same reaction he used to receive from soldiers not wanting to answer a direct question. They would hem and shuffle, working to come up with some false reason to justify their poor behaviour. Like his soldiers, Miss Huntford could think of nothing. Her pout eased into a frown and the red drained out of her face. She was beaten and she knew it. 'Yes, you have my word.'

'Good. I'll escort you back to the ballroom and we'll say nothing of this to anyone.' He offered her his elbow.

She wrinkled her nose at it, stubborn as before, but, seeing no choice except to comply, she slapped her hand down over his coat. She flicked Miss Radcliff a fierce look as they all walked into the hallway.

Miss Radcliff followed a few steps behind them as they made for the ballroom. It was she he was worried about, not the lady on his arm. He might have threatened Miss Huntford, but he doubted her ability to honour her word. If she struck at Miss Radcliff, there was nothing he could do to help or protect the poor governess. He couldn't correspond with Miss Radcliff, or visit her at Huntford Place. Despite the pleasure of her presence and conversation, she was one of the few ladies in attendance not available as a potential bride.

The realisation ground on him like a pebble stuck in a boot. The woman behind him possessed more dignity, poise and sense of duty than the daughter of a baronet marching beside him, yet he was forced to overlook her because she wasn't of his class. The indignity of it distracted him so much, he failed to stop on the threshold to the ballroom and allow the ladies to continue in without him. The moment he and Miss Huntford entered the ballroom, all eyes fell upon them and then on her hand on his arm. A few people noted Miss Radcliff behind them, her presence as a chaperon restraining the whispers, but it was clear the pretty baronet's daughter and the potential earl had been outside the room together.

The attention didn't escape Miss Huntford, who snatched her hand off his arm and made for her mother. Miss Radcliff stepped out from behind him to follow her charge.

'Miss Radcliff,' he called to her, not sure why. There was nothing more for them to say. He hoped she'd be all right and wished there was some way he could ensure it, but there wasn't. Meeting his hesitation, she spoke first, aware of those around them watching this strange conversation.

'Thank you for your assistance, Major Preston.' She dipped a proper curtsy, then set off after Miss Huntford, proving she was level-headed in a difficult situation.

It was another reason to admire her and he regretted letting her go, unable to stop watching her until she passed by Alma. His sister-in-law cocked her head in curiosity at Luke, having guessed which lady truly interested him.

He jerked his attention away from them both and strode to a nearby circle of gentlemen discussing pheasant hunting. The topic failed to take his mind off Miss Radcliff's enchanting eyes, or the peace and delight he'd experienced in her presence. She, more than anyone, had understood his frustration at being here and she was the one young lady he was unable to court.

'I bet you're glad to be away from all the nasty business in Spain?' Lord Chilton joked in an attempt to engage Luke. He was one of the many men here with an eligible daughter and money.

'Not when my men are still there dying so we can enjoy balls without Napoleon's boot on our throats.' Luke didn't feel like being pleasant. He hated being forced to parade before all the tittering country women while his men suffered in Spain.

'Yes, bad business, most grateful for their service,' Lord Chilton muttered.

The other gentlemen added a few agreeing harrumphs.

'What will you do with yourself now you're home?' Lord Selton asked. 'I can't imagine country life can hold much charm for a man of your experience.'

No, it didn't. He'd found meaning for his life in the Army, a sense of accomplishment and merit which he'd never had before and now it was gone. 'It does lack excitement, but at least no one is shooting at me.'

It was almost the only benefit to being here.

'I suppose there is that,' Lord Selton agreed before Sir Peter Bell turned their attention back to hunting.

Luke slipped his hand into the inside pocket of his coat and traced the curving line of the bugle-horn badge. He glanced to where Lady Huntford stood beneath the chandelier with her daughter. Miss Radcliff stood behind them, as forgotten as the numerous other chaperons scattered around the edges of the room. Feeling him watching her, she offered him a small, encouraging smile. Then, some sharp remark from Lady Huntford pulled her attention away.

He let go of the badge. There had to be something of merit for him to achieve here besides growing fat while he waited for some inheritance which might never come. He must find it and soon. He wouldn't allow himself to be made to feel as useless as he had as a child. He would find purpose, new things to achieve and accomplish, a reason beyond his ability to sire a child to make himself and his family proud.

Chapter Three

'Luke and Frances Huntford. I wouldn't have guessed it considering the way you used to talk about her when you were young.' Charles Preston, Earl of Ingham laughed across the breakfast table at his younger son before rising to help himself to more eggs from the sideboard. 'Can't say I fancy being related to that brood, but if one of them gives me a grandson, I guess I won't mind. The mother is quite capable of producing children. It bodes well for the daughters.'

Alma paled at the mention of Lady Huntford's fecundity.

'Charles, watch what you say,' Lady Elizabeth Ingham chided as she motioned for the footman to pour her more coffee. 'Especially since we might end up related to them.'

She winked at Luke, then lifted her coffee to her lips, hiding her teasing smile behind the steam.

'I'm not interested in Miss Huntford.' Luke sliced his ham into pieces.

'You'd do well to have an interest in her. Her dowry

could offset our losses from last year's weak crop,' Edward added from across the table.

'I wouldn't get your hopes up,' Luke countered. 'Sir Rodger won't spend so much as a farthing to repair the roof over his head. I doubt he'll give it away with his daughters. But since I'm not interested in her, it is a moot point.'

After the ball, Luke had done everything he could to forget his brief time with Miss Radcliff, but it hadn't worked. Despite a vigorous ride this morning and a round of sparring with the groom, neither her vivid blue eyes, nor her kindness, had faded from his memory. To her, he hadn't been the catch of the year, but simply Major Preston. He wanted to be Major Preston with her again, but he couldn't. Courting a governess was as fanciful as hoping Napoleon would walk away from war.

'If you weren't interested in Miss Huntford, you should've let her return by herself instead of allowing the whole countryside to speculate about the two of you.' His mother sipped her coffee with a sigh of relief, the late night telling in the dark circles beneath her eyes. 'It could prove troublesome, especially while we're guests for their house party.'

Luke and Edward groaned in unison.

'Sir Rodger has the worst staff, especially the butler,' Edward complained. 'He has no grasp of how things are done. He's surly, too.'

'It's because Sir Rodger doesn't pay him enough.' Luke imaged the pittance Miss Radcliff must be earning.

'If the old miser is spending the money on a party, he must be desperate to get rid of Miss Huntford,'

Edward addressed Luke in a rare moment of fraternal solidarity.

After what Luke had witnessed last night, it wouldn't surprise him.

'The only reason we're going is so Luke can look over the other young ladies. Otherwise, we wouldn't bother,' their father offered with uninspiring assurance.

'I haven't said I'll go, but speaking of bother...' Luke sat back from the table and pushed his plate away, determined to discuss the other subject which had kept him up most of the night '...I intend to call on Lord Helmsworth while I'm home. I'd like to arrange for another survey of the disputed boundary land, and, if it's determined to be his, then to arrange a lease of it or the rights to the river. I think it's time we end our feud with him.'

The silence which answered his announcement echoed through the room. Everyone stared down the table at him as if he'd suggested they catch the plague.

Edward's glare was especially sharp. 'You think you'll stroll into Helmsworth Manor and after twenty years he'll deed us the land with the river simply because you asked him to?'

'It's worth a try.' Luke trilled his fingers on the table, struggling to remain calm. He needed more to do in the country than search for a wife. Settling the old land dispute was it. He hadn't thought the idea would receive such a hostile response. 'We need the water to irrigate the west field. Without it, we can't expect to have a profitable enough harvest next year to cover our losses from this one.'

'I'm well aware of what we need, more so than

you.' Edward pointed his knife at him. The conflict between them had returned with Luke from Spain with a vengeance. Except this time it was different. He and his brother were more equal now than in the past and Edward didn't like it any more than Luke did. 'This isn't school. You needn't try and outdo everyone.'

'You were the only one I ever outdid and only because it was so easy.' Luke speared a piece of ham and stuck it in his mouth with a smugness he didn't feel. In the heat of more than one battle, when he thought he wouldn't come home again, he'd longed to end the old rivalry between him and Edward. Now he was here and all he could do was argue with him. It wasn't right, but he seemed powerless to put an end to it.

Alma exchanged a troubled glance with their mother, who flapped a silencing hand at her sons. 'Boys, it's too early for this. If Luke wishes to try to settle the dispute, then he may. After all, it's cheaper to pay a surveyor than a solicitor and if it benefits us, then good. In the meantime, we must make a decision about the Huntford house party. Edward, will you and Alma attend?'

'We will if you want us to.' Alma set her fork aside, her food hardly touched. The circles under her eyes were far darker than they should have been, even after a late night. She rose and made for the door. 'If you'll excuse me.'

'I'd better see to her.' Edward stood, his square chin stiff in the air as he marched to the door. He matched Luke in height, but had their mother's hazel eyes and their father's black hair. 'I wouldn't want anyone accusing me of failing as both a husband and an heir.'

Once he was gone, Luke's mother shook her head. 'Alma tries so hard to be brave and I tell her not to worry. Since we have you, there's no reason to despair.'

Luke resisted groaning at having his value to the line stated so plainly. He rose, the tiff with Edward, as well as the memory of Miss Radcliff and the sleep it had stolen from him, crawling under his skin as much as his change of situation. Luke wasn't likely to ever be the earl, and he didn't want to inherit if it meant his father and Edward's deaths, but he wasn't sure he wished to foist the responsibility for Pensum Manor's future on some unsuspecting son either. He'd seen the demands it had made on his family and the way it had treated him. It wasn't something to envy. 'I'm riding over to visit Lord Helmsworth.'

'Luke, say you'll come to the house party.' His mother reached up and laid a hand on his arm. 'You don't know how much I want to be a grandmother, to have Pensum Manor filled with the giggles of small children as when you and your brother were small.'

He was amazed she could remember the laughter and forget the awful rows he and his brother used to have. Time hadn't made them less intense, only more chilling.

'All right, I'll go.' He'd rather spend time in a French prison than with the Huntford girls, but visiting them would allow him to make sure Miss Radcliff was well and Miss Huntford was upholding her end of the agreement.

He left the dining room and made for the stables.

He shouldn't concern himself with the welfare of a governess, but he hadn't allowed any of the weaker men in his regiment to be bullied by fellow soldiers or even officers. He wouldn't leave a poor governess to suffer under an indifferent, if not hostile employer. Nor would he allow anyone's prejudices to stop him from coming to know her better. He couldn't pursue her, but there was no reason why they couldn't be friends.

'Major Preston is coming here?' Frances wailed from across the breakfast table after her mother made the announcement.

He'll be here. Joanna stared down at the scuff mark on the toe of her half-boot to hide the flush creeping over her cheeks. She unclasped her hands from in front of her and allowed them to dangle by her sides. It shouldn't matter to her if Major Preston was coming or not. His doings were not her concern, but the news made standing still difficult.

She waited behind her three other charges for them to finish their food so their lessons could begin. Since the family ignored her at breakfast, and most of the day, her worry quickly passed. She could drop dead of the pox behind them and they weren't likely to notice.

'All of the Inghams are coming.' Lady Huntford didn't look up from her morning correspondence, taking little note of Frances's distress. Her blonde curls, like her daughter's, were tight beside her full cheeks and small eyes. Bearing six children had made her stout, but not fat, and her lack of interest in anything besides gossip and dresses gave her wide face a perpetually bored appearance. 'I thought you'd be pleased—after all, you were with him for some time last night.'

'I wasn't with him.' Frances all but pounded her thighs in frustration.

This was enough to make Lady Huntford finally put down her letter and look at her daughter. 'Then what were you two doing in the hallway?'

Frances looked to Joanna, who dropped her gaze to the back of the chair in front of her, noticing a chip in the finish. The chit didn't deserve her help. Her silence meant Frances was forced to invent her own excuses for her mother.

'We were talking. Miss Radcliff and I had stepped out for some air and he happened upon us. We discussed, uh, well, it was—what were we discussing, Miss Radcliff?' Frances appealed to the woman she'd declared her enemy for her salvation.

You acting like a harlot with Lieutenant Foreman.

'His return from Spain.' It galled Joanna to use her private conversation with him to defend Frances instead of telling Lady Huntford the truth. She doubted how much good speaking up would do anyway. Lady Huntford would probably blame her favourite daughter's misguided attempt at romance on Joanna.

'Of course, I forgot he was telling us about Spain,' Frances rushed. 'An awful topic.'

'I don't imagine you'll be forced to discuss it much with him since he's resigned his commission.' Lady Huntford sniffed before turning in her seat to face Joanna. 'I noticed you were speaking a great deal with him. What were you thinking dominating so much of his time?'

'He approached me, Lady Huntford, and asked

about Frances.' Joanna hoped she wasn't struck down for lying. 'I answered his many questions about her.'

Lady Huntford's eyes widened. 'What an unexpected surprise. You should have told me about it at once and not kept it a secret. You'll do no such thing in the future, do you understand?'

'Yes, Lady Huntford.' It seemed Frances wasn't the only one to be nearly caught out this morning. Joanna glanced at the young lady who frowned into her plate. The two of them hadn't been alone together since they'd left the ball last night. In fact, Frances had all but avoided Joanna, upholding her end of the bargain with Major Preston. His threat would be more potent while he was here, sleeping in a room below Joanna's, eating at this very table, walking the halls where she might glimpse his confident stance and dominating eyes.

Stop thinking about him!

Lady Huntford fixed on her eldest daughter, her voice snapping Joanna out of her daydream. 'It appears we have even more reason for you to try and impress him.'

'I don't see why. He's only the second son and it could be years before he inherits, if he does at all. A woman might waste her life waiting for nothing.' Frances crossed her arms over her chest in a huff.

Joanna balled her hands into fists at her sides, her nails biting into her palms. After last night, and the quick way Major Preston had defended her, Frances should be grateful. Joanna would give her eye teeth to be able to speak freely with him. All Frances could do was cast him aside and pout over her rake of a lieutenant. Her behaviour disgusted Joanna, but she buried it deep down, afraid it would show in what she did or said. Her one consolation was Major Preston having seen Frances's true personality. She doubted a man as honourable as he would take a genuine interest in a woman like Frances. Though if he didn't, why had he accepted the invitation? Lady Huntford had lamented the lack of a response from the Inghams for days. Joanna wondered what had changed his mind and if it had something to do with her.

Of course not. She was nothing to no one. Not even her mother or father, who'd cast her on the charity of Madame Dubois instead of raising her themselves, had wanted her. It was foolish to think the second son of an earl would defy his parents' and society's expectations to woo her. His concern for her well-being last night had been a fluke, like Catherine completing her French lessons without an argument yesterday. While Major Preston was staying at Huntford Place, he wasn't likely to be kind or attentive to Joanna, but to ignore her like everyone else did. There was no reason for him to behave differently when there'd be so many other eligible ladies here to hold his attention.

Lady Huntford gathered up her correspondence and beckoned her eldest daughter to follow her. 'Come along, we must choose the gowns you'll wear. We can't waste this opportunity.'

'What about me? Can I attend the house party?' Catherine sat up straighter in her chair in eager anticipation.

'Of course not. You're not out yet.'

'Even if you were, he isn't likely to favour you,' Frances sneered at her sister as she trudged after their mother.

Catherine slumped over her breakfast, struggling to hold back tears. Unlike her sister, Catherine had her father's dark hair and long face with thin lips which seemed perpetually fixed in a downtrodden frown. Her one blessing was lacking the petty streak which permanently marred her older sister's personality and beauty. At eighteen, Frances was only two years older than Catherine. Given their closeness in age they should have been friends, but Frances's churlish nature, and Catherine's more retiring one, discouraged it.

The grand clock in the entrance hall began to chime nine times.

'Come, girls, it's time for your French lesson,' Joanna urged, feeling sorry for Catherine and wanting to distract her from her sister's insults with activity.

'I'm too old to be hustled into the schoolroom by a governess.' Catherine's defiance weakened Joanna's pity.

Anne, the blonde seven-year-old, turned around and stuck her tongue out at Joanna. 'We'll tell you when it's time for our lessons.'

Ava, her twin sister, ignored Joanna and continued to eat her half-burned toast.

Joanna stared at the back of their three heads and the bows wound through their curls. The twins were no better behaved or obedient than their eldest sister. She wondered how she would get them to the schoolroom when, to her surprise, it was their father who interceded.

'Girls, get up at once and stop being contrary,' he commanded as he strolled into the room, his large, black hunting dog muddying the carpet as it trotted beside him.

With deep pouts the girls shoved away from the table and stood up to form something of a straight line in front of Joanna.

'That's how you command charges, Miss Radcliff,' Sir Rodger tossed at Joanna as he took his place at the head of the now-empty table. 'One would think you'd have learned such things at that school of yours.'

Joanna's cheeks burned at the insulting rebuke and the sniggering it elicited from the girls. After their father's public reprimand, they'd be even more difficult to deal with once they got back to the schoolroom.

Gruger, the withered old butler, shuffled in and tossed the London newspaper down beside his employer's plate with no attempt at ceremony. Sir Rodger didn't correct the surly man with the pocked and wrinkled face, but picked up the paper and snapped it open in front of his face. Gruger shuffled out, mumbling insults about the cook under his breath.

'Come along.' Joanna led the girls upstairs to another day of fighting to get them to obey her and to do their work. With each step up the curving staircase in need of a polish, past the maids gossiping while the ashes remained in the fireplaces, she wished she could slip off to her room and pour out her heart to Rachel, or Grace or Isabel like she used to do at the school. It wasn't likely anyone would notice her not working since half the staff hid in corners and shirked their duties, but what they did or didn't do wasn't her concern. Her pride in her work and her responsibility for the girls was what mattered and she would see to them, even if it proved as difficult as shooing Farmer Wilson's cow out of Madame Dubois's garden.

The single comfort she found in the long trudge down the halls kept dark to save on candles was the knowledge Major Preston would soon be here. While they crossed the second floor and made for the steep and unadorned third-floor stairs, her excitement faded. He wasn't coming to visit her, and even if he was she had no interest in a dalliance which might result in a child as Grace's had done. After the way he'd assisted her last night, she doubted he'd be anything but well behaved around her. Still, the strange feeling in her chest at the memory of him beside her at the ball made her wary. It wasn't so much his weakness she worried about, but her own. She'd already made one mistake in talking to him at Pensum Manor and allowing his kindness and humour to make her forget herself in a room full of people. She feared what might happen between the two of them during some chance meeting in a darkened hallway.

Nothing will happen. She was too sensible of her place and all Miss Fanworth's old warnings about gentlemen to be corrupted by a man's fine words. She would do her duty and if she found herself alone with him, she'd smile, nod and continue on her way, no matter how much she wanted him to flatter and protect her as he had at the ball.

Chapter Four

'Miss Radcliff.' Sir Rodger waved her over to him with a book as she came downstairs from the school-room. Frances and Catherine were upstairs with their mother discussing the house party while Ava and Anne were with their nurse, giving Joanna a brief rest from her duties.

'Yes, Sir Rodger?' She'd hope to take a walk in the garden. It appeared her plans were about to be way-laid by her employer. She wondered what he wanted of her. He'd barely said two words to her during her time here except to scold her in front of others or question the quality of her education.

'Since it appears you have nothing to occupy you at present, I'd like you to return this book to Vicar Carlson.' He handed her the tome, the blue cuff of his favourite coat sprinkled with food stains. With his wild grey hair frizzed out on either side of his head, he appeared more like some forgotten grandfather than a wealthy baronet. His dog sat beside him, its drool dripping on the stone floor. 'While you walk, think about how you can better manage the girls. I won't pay for a governess who has no control over my daughters. Do I make myself clear?'

Joanna's fingers dug into the leather binding. She wanted to tell him the girls' obstinacy wasn't her fault but his since he rarely reprimanded them. Instead, she summoned up her best prim-and-proper governess stance to answer with all the deference required of her position. 'Yes, Sir Rodger. I'll deliver the book at once and consider what you've said.'

She dipped a curtsy and walked away, indignity making her insides burn as she left the house and headed down the drive. Sir Rodger employed slothful maids, a crotchety butler and a cook who couldn't warm bread, yet he threatened to fire her? She snapped a thin branch off a poorly pruned topiary and swiped it at the air in front of her. It would take nothing short of an exorcism to drive out the wilful streak in the Huntford girls. She'd already employed every trick Madame Dubois and the other teachers had taught her, but nothing had worked. Without the support of their parents, there was little Joanna could do to make them mind. Her failure was almost assured.

She made the sharp turn on to the small path which led into the woods and to the narrow road traversing it. The woods covered the corner of land marking the boundaries between Huntford Place, Pensum Manor and Helmsworth Manor. She and the girls often walked here during their daily outings to study botany and geology. They were no more obedient outside than inside and it was always a chore to bring them home in time for supper, or with the twins not covered in mud.

Why didn't Madame Dubois better vet the Hunt-fords before she sent me here? Or perhaps she'd been so eager to relinquish responsibility for Joanna after nineteen years, she hadn't cared. Her parents hadn't cared when they'd left her on the school's doorstep as an infant without a clue as to who they were, so why should anyone else?

Joanna stumbled over a rock, the old rejection burning in her chest. It was an uncharitable thing to think of Madame Dubois who'd taken her in and been so kind to her, but she couldn't help it. The lone-liness which used to fill her every Christmas when the other girls would go home for the holidays while she remained at the school came over her again. The teachers had done their best to raise and guide her, but with so many students, Joanna had received no special attention, nor had she sought it. The teachers had always praised her for her independence, not re-alising it wasn't independence at all, but resignation. There hadn't been any point asking for something she wouldn't receive.

The teachers might not have cooed over her, but they'd imparted their knowledge to her, preparing her for her present position. Sadly, it was nothing like what she'd been led to believe it would be, or what she'd hoped. When she'd viewed the house from the mail coach on her first day here, she'd been so ex-cited, expecting to at last experience what it was like to be a member of a true family. It had all been a silly dream, like the one she used to have about her mother returning to claim her.

Joanna flung the branch away. It would be a blow to her and the school if she was dismissed and forced to return to Salisbury without a reference. All the many years of effort, time and work Madame Dubois, Miss Fanworth and the other teachers had put into her would be ruined because of her inability to maintain her first position. In the end she might not have a choice but to leave. Sir Rodger had made his unrealistic expectation of her clear and she didn't see how she might meet it.

She reached the small brook cutting across a dip in the road and paused on the sloping and muddy bank. Further away, outside the woods, she could hear the river it came from rushing along its banks. A line of flat stones split the small current which ran clear, showing the smooth pebbles and mud at the bottom of the bed. She wanted to sit down on the bank, drop her head in her hands and watch the water flowing past until nothing else mattered.

No, I can't give up. There had to be a way to succeed, she only needed to find it and soon. She stepped on to the first rock and then the next one. She almost slipped off the third when it tilted beneath her weight. She threw out her arms to regain her balance, then hurried to the far bank. She didn't need wet boots on top of her present troubles.

Reaching the other side, her resolve began to fade. She didn't want to continue with this errand, or her time at Huntford Place. Finding a way to make the girls behave seemed as impossible as finding her mother, but she couldn't give up. She'd write to Miss Fanworth about what to do and ask her not to tell Madame. Perhaps she'd have some suggestions for Joanna.

In a clearing up ahead, the grey-stone vicarage with a tilted chimney releasing a tendril of pine-scented smoke came into view. Over the low roof rose the square spire of the church behind it, squat against the scattered clouds filling the September sky. This wasn't the church she and the family attended on Sunday in town, but a living on Helmsworth Manor which served the Marquis of Helmsworth, his staff and the tenants in the small village a mile off.

She heaved a large sigh as she entered the front garden, too upset to summon her usual steadfast cheerfulness. Let Vicar Carlson see her surly and ill-tempered, she didn't care. A tangle of chrysan-themums, mallow and weeds choked both sides of the slate walk leading to the sturdy door. She knocked lightly on the wood and listened for the answering footsteps of the vicar or a housekeeper from inside. The rustle of the wind through the surrounding trees were the only noises which greeted her.

She leaned off the steps to peer in the front win-dow. Inside was as untidy as the garden with stacks of books piled on every surface. It appeared more like the messy studio of their old art master, Signor Ber-tolli, than the neat and orderly abode of a vicar. Lean-ing away from the window, she caught her pinched expression reflected in the glass.

Taking another deep breath, she forced the crease between her eyes to soften and the impassive look she'd perfected during the last four weeks at Hunt-ford Place to return. No one needed to know anything was wrong with her, especially not a stranger. Even if they did, they wouldn't care. Few people gave a sec-ond thought to a lowly governess.

A few more minutes passed while she waited for someone to return. She tapped the book against her hand. It was clear there was no one here. She could leave the book on the step and be on her way, but she couldn't risk it being damaged. Sir Rodger had given her an errand and she must do it well. She didn't want to fail at every task she'd been set to here in Hertfordshire.

She tucked her skirt under her legs, about to sit down and wait, when the whinny of a horse from behind the house caught her notice. She followed the vicarage around to the back. A horse was tied to a tree in the small graveyard between the house and the church. An older man stood before one of the headstones, staring down at the brown grass surrounding it. He was heavyset but tall, with grey hair slicked back above a proud forehead. Sadness left deep creases in the smooth skin and drew down the lines around his mouth, adding years to his face. He held his hat in one hand as he reached out to trace the etched and weathered headstone in front of him. It was pitched to one side from age, but the small bunch of violets laid on its curving top set it apart from the others.

He hadn't seen her and she didn't want to interrupt his contemplation. She was about to go, but he clenched his fist in his mouth in a stifled sob. She was afraid to approach him, to interrupt his grief, but she couldn't leave him alone any more than she could have the new girls who used to cry during their first night at the school.

She approached him, the dry grass crunching beneath her boots and announcing her presence. 'Are you all right, sir?'

'Yes, just an old man weeping over the past.' He

rubbed the moisture from his eyes with his fingers then dropped his arm and at last looked at her.

Joanna gasped. His eyes were the same colour as hers and just as vivid.

'Jane?' he whispered, dropping his hat. His face went white beneath his grey hair with the same shock Isabel had worn the time she'd come down from the attic claiming to have spied a ghost. In the end it had been nothing more than an old dress dummy covered in dust.

'No, I'm Miss Radcliff, the new governess at Huntford Place.' Joanna was eager to ease his alarm the way she'd eased Isabel's.

He continued to stare at her and she studied his round face and the slender nose set over full lips. Something about him seemed familiar but she'd never seen the gentleman before.

'Of course you are, how silly of me.' The slight ruddiness along his cheeks returned as he plucked his hat off the ground and settled it over his hair. 'You must forgive an old man his foolishness. You reminded me of someone I loved very much.'

Joanna took a cautious step back.

'My daughter,' he clarified. 'You look very much like she did at your age, with the same hair and eyes. The resemblance is remarkable.'

He rubbed his round chin, his previous melancholy threatening to overcome him again.

'I'm so sorry to disturb you, but Sir Rodger asked me to return this book to Vicar Carlson. Do you know when he'll return?' Despite the stranger's kindly manner, she wanted to be done with this errand, to enjoy the solitude of the long walk back to Huntford Place.

She needed the quiet to gather herself before she was thrust back into the pit of she-vipers and their indifferent parents.

'Vicar Carlson? Why, that's me.' He didn't seem too sure but it wasn't her place to question a clergyman.

She handed him the book. 'I won't disturb you any longer. I'll be on my way.'

'No, please stay. You seem troubled.'

She ran her foot over the patch of tall grass in front of her, trying to bite back the worries which had followed her through the forest. At school there'd always been Grace, Rachel or Isabel to commiserate with. She'd written to them, but with each of the girls facing their own trials in their new positions, she'd understated hers. She didn't want to burden them with her problems. She needed to speak to someone, anyone or she'd run mad.

'I'm having difficulty in my new position.' It was all she was willing to hazard with this stranger. 'The girls won't listen and Sir Rodger is threatening to dismiss me if I don't control them, but I can't.'

He winked at her. 'Dealing with the Huntford girls, I'm not surprised. They could use a firm hand and much better parenting. I had the entire brood at a Christmas party once, a long time ago when they were very young. They nearly tore up the music room with their wild behaviour.'

'The twins almost set the curtain in the sitting room on fire yesterday. They're unwieldy heathens.'

Vicar Carlson tossed back his head and let out a laugh as rich as a church bell.

She clapped her hand over her mouth, horrified

by what she'd just said. He might tell Sir Rodger and she'd find herself on the next mail coach to Salisbury. 'I'm sorry. I shouldn't talk about them so, but be grateful to have a position.'

She didn't feel grateful, but exhausted.

'Don't be sorry for speaking the truth. I promise I won't say a thing to Sir Rodger about his precious offspring,' he reassured her with all the authority of a man used to speaking from the pulpit. 'It's the duty of a vicar to help those who are burdened.'

'Burdened doesn't begin to describe it.' She paced back and forth, hands flapping at her sides with her agitation as she explained to him everything about her conversation with Sir Rodger. His willingness to listen unleashed the torrent of words she'd kept inside her for the past month. She even told him of Frances's two instances with Lieutenant Foreman and the impossible position she now found herself in. 'If I'm sent home, the people who cared about me the most will be disappointed.'

'You mean your family?' he prodded.

'I don't have a family, not a real one. My parents, whoever they were, left me for the school to raise when I was a baby,' she nearly whispered the words as she stopped to face him. It was the first time she'd admitted her illegitimacy to a stranger. It wasn't something Madame Dubois or any of the teachers had ever mentioned. A few days before leaving the school, Madame Dubois had cautioned her about revealing it in her new position, though the warning hadn't been necessary. Joanna knew how the world viewed illegitimate children. 'The teachers at the school raised me.'

'And you must be about nineteen?' He scrutinised her with the same curiosity as when they'd first met.

Joanna nodded, wondering what her age had to do with anything, but she didn't care. For the first time since her arrival in Hertfordshire, here was someone besides Major Preston who sympathised with her plight. Unlike the major, who was all but forbidden to speak to her, Vicar Carlson could listen and perhaps help. 'What am I going to do?'

'As someone who's supposed to guide his flock…' he flapped his hand at the church as though he wasn't certain this was his duty '…I'll tell you what you can do. Headstrong girls like to be in charge. Of course they can't be with the governess, but they'll try. The trick is to give them choices, but make sure they're deciding between two things you want.'

'Like studying French or Geography?'

'Exactly. Make them think they're in charge, even when they aren't.'

'I've never heard anything like this.' And if it helped, it might be her last hope of staying on and making Madame Dubois proud.

'I used to do it with my daughter, though it didn't always work.' He looked to the headstone with the violets. Sadness crossed over his expression like a cloud in front of the moon. 'After my wife died, I spoiled Jane. It made her headstrong. The older she grew, the more obstinate she became, like me.'

'I'm very sorry.'

He smiled at her, tender like the fathers used to be with their daughters before they left them at the school. 'Don't be. Her troubles are passed now, but yours aren't and we must focus on those.'

He offered her a few more suggestions on how to deal with the girls.

Then, in the distance, the bells from the village church began to ring. She didn't want to leave the vicar or the tranquillity of this corner of the world, but she must. 'I'm sorry, I have to go. Thank you so much for your help.'

'It was my pleasure. Please, feel free to return whenever you want. I'm often here reading during the day. I like the quiet. And good luck with your students.'

'Thank you and goodbye.'

Joanna hurried down the path towards Huntford Place. The shadows of the trees didn't consume her as they had on the walk here. It was the light coming through the branches she noticed instead. She didn't dread facing the girls, but looked forward to it with a new resolve, eager to try Vicar Carlson's suggestions, confident for the first time in days she might at last settle into her position.

She was well along the path when male voices from somewhere up around the bend caught her notice.

'Why are you trying to stop me from visiting him?'

'Because you don't understand the situation.'

Joanna crept cautiously forward and peeked around a thick oak tree in the bend of the road. Up ahead, two men had dismounted and now stood arguing while their horses grazed nearby. Joanna's fingers tightened on the smooth bark. It was Major Preston and his brother, Lord Pensum.

'If you expect me to linger in your shadow, doing nothing except waiting for providence to make me an earl, you're mistaken,' Major Preston countered.

'Now you know what it's like to be me.' His brother grabbed the reins of his horse from where they dangled below the animal's nose. Lord Pensum stepped into the stirrup and threw one leg over the top of his horse. 'You think I have all the advantage, but I don't. Then again you've never been able to look beyond yourself and all your need for aggrandisement to realise it.'

I shouldn't eavesdrop. Trying not to be seen, Joanna crept through the thick underbrush filling the U-shaped bend, determined to slip past the feuding brothers. She winced with each snapping twig and rustle of leaves, trying not to draw attention to herself, but it was almost impossible. She was just on the other side of the large oak tree, about to step onto the path, when someone grabbed her by the waist and pulled her back. Lord Pensum galloped by on his grey horse, narrowly missing her as she hit the solid chest of the man behind her.

'Are you all right?' Major Preston's chin brushed her temples as he spoke, his voice as tight as her insides.

His firm arm against Joanna's stomach made her heart beat faster than the near collision with the horse. She leaned deeper into him and his fingers twitched against her hip. She reached behind her, ready to grasp his thighs and steady herself like she would against a wall after a shock. Before her fingertips could touch the buckskin of his breeches, she clutched the side of her dress, her breath catching as he shifted against her. She peered up into his dark eyes made more severe by the alternating shadows and sunlight piercing the branches overhead. If she tilted her head, closed her eyes, she might experience his firm lips against hers.

'Miss Radcliff?' Major Preston nudged, easing his hold on her.

'Yes, I'm fine.' She stumbled out of his grasp, mortified at almost losing her head over him. 'Much better, in fact, for not being ground into the forest floor.'

'I'm glad I could keep you from becoming one with the fallen leaves.' He smiled as he bent over to pluck his hat off a bush. His breeches pulled tight over his buttocks when he dipped down then rose, towering over her like the oak above them. 'May I escort you back to Huntford Place?'

Joanna jerked her attention from his thighs to his face. To walk with him would mean the opportunity to listen to his commanding voice and enjoy more of the conversation they'd indulged in last night. It also risked them being seen together. It might be innocent, but people wouldn't regard it as such and her position with the Huntfords was already at risk.

'I can't.' She slipped through the last few brambles to return to the path. 'I must be getting back.'

'I promise to only go as far as the edge of the woods, and then I'll leave you to continue on. I wouldn't want to place your reputation or employment in jeopardy.'

She hesitated. Being alone with him was dangerous, but she wanted companionship and something pleasant before she returned to the annoyance of her work. 'Yes, company would be lovely, especially if any more galloping horses should happen by.'

'Then allow me to fetch mine so we'll be equally matched should we encounter any.' He laughed as he pushed through the brush. The stiff branches raked his long legs before he slipped behind the tree. He soon rounded the turn, leading a large white horse with a patch of brown above his nose.

'A magnificent animal,' she remarked. 'Not at all the mill-horse you painted him to be at the ball.'

'Careful what you say around Duke, I don't want it going to his head. He's already difficult enough to control.' He patted the animal's side and it gave an indignant snort.

'I don't believe a word he says about you.' She reached up to stroke Duke's long nose, making the skin beneath his hair twitch.

'Now you've done it, he won't listen to me for the rest of the day.' He clicked the horse into a walk and the three of them set off towards Huntford Place.

They walked side by side in silence, the twittering birds and the rustle of leaves settling in between them. It wasn't an awkward or uncomfortable quiet, but familiar, as though this wasn't the first time they'd enjoyed the forest alone together. With each of his sure steps, Joanna was keenly aware of the shift of his muscles, the crinkle of his leather gloves as he tightened or loosened his grip on the reins. It wasn't the easy movements of a man at peace, but the constant fidgeting of one with something on his mind. Whatever troubled him, it was none of her business. However, she hadn't been this conscious of another person since the nights at school when she could tell which one of her friends was upset by their constant turning beneath the coverlet, or a sob stifled by a pillow. She couldn't pretend to ignore his difficulties any more than she could have her friends'.

'I didn't mean to intrude on you and your brother,' she offered. 'Is everything well?'

'It is.' Major Preston banged his hat against his thigh to free it of dust and leaves. 'Except we differ on how to resolve a long-standing conflict with Lord Helmsworth.'

'Is it massive enough to divide brothers?'

'It is when it threatens the income of Pensum Manor.' He turned his hat over in his hands, pausing before he settled it down on his hair. 'Miss Radcliff, what I'm about to tell you isn't commonly known and would, like the revealing of Miss Huntford's secret, do a great deal of damage to my family.'

'I won't tell anyone.' She wouldn't do anything to harm him. He'd been too kind to her, and the thrill of being taken into his confidence was as powerful at the grip of his hand on the reins.

He explained to her the dispute about the land as his feet covered the imprints of his brother's horse's hooves in the packed dirt. 'My family isn't as wealthy as we've allowed society to believe. My brother is worried that if we reveal our desperate need for access to the river on the disputed land, Lord Helmsworth might use the information to place pressure on our creditors to strangle us.'

'Is he really so mean?' She'd heard a little about him from Sir Rodger and Lady Huntford. He seemed more eccentric than spiteful, preferring to keep to himself at his estate and never venturing to London.

'Not the gentleman I remember from his Christmas parties when I was a boy. He changed after his daughter's death. It made him irascible and less willing to listen to reason, like Edward.' He plucked a thorn from his breeches and flicked it away. 'My brother thinks I can come home, sit around and watch the seasons change, but I can't. He's been handed everything by right of birth, he doesn't understand what it is to earn achievement or what it gives to a man, and what it's like to leave it all behind.'

'Maybe he does realise it and that's why he fights with you.' They came to a narrow pass in the path between two large yew trees. He stopped to let her go ahead before joining her with Duke. 'Perhaps he wonders if he's worthy of having so much responsibility placed on him because he's the heir and not because he's earned it. Failing to have a child might reinforce his lack of value beyond his place of honour in your family?'

He didn't answer straight away, but it was clear from the slight twist of his lips that he was mulling over what she'd said. It would be nice to think she might make a difference to someone while she was here. The Huntford girls certainly weren't benefiting from her presence.

'I suppose it's possible. I've never considered it from his perspective.' Duke's harness jingled as he tossed up his head before settling back into his steady gait. Luke switched the reins to his other hand and patted the horse's neck.

'Perhaps if you put your grievances against him aside, he might, too. After all, it takes two people to maintain a quarrel.'

He met her eyes, the brown in them appearing lighter with his earnestness. 'What you suggest isn't easy to do, not after so many years.'

'It might be easier if you appreciate how fortunate you are to have him. Not all of us have family to argue with. Sometimes, when Frances and Catherine are sniping at each other, I want to grab them by their scruffs and shake them until they realise how lucky they are to have one another.' She raised her fists before her as if she held the girls. Then she opened her fingers and dropped her arms to her sides. 'All I've ever had were the teachers and my friends.'

'What happened to your parents?'

'They died when I was very young.' She didn't dare tell him she knew nothing about them. She never had. They'd left her on the school's front steps with only the ripped piece of paper with her name on it and a blanket. She'd learned long ago not to ask Madame Dubois about them since there were no details Madame Dubois could give her and nothing she could do to change the truth. 'They entrusted me to the teachers to raise.'

'Then the school has succeeded.' He fixed her with an appreciative smile which made her prouder than when she'd won first prize for French. 'You're a very wise young lady, Miss Radcliff. Miss Huntford doesn't realise how lucky she is to have you.'

'I don't think she viewed my interrupting her liaison, or any of my efforts to influence her, as lucky.'

'It's certainly something to write to your headmistress about.' He laughed, the deep sound silencing the birds.

'Heavens, no.' She didn't want Madame to believe anything was wrong here, or to think Joanna wasn't living up to her expectations. It was better to pretend everything was well and not to complain. There was little anyone could do about it even if she did.

They reached the brook and Major Preston led his horse across, skipping every other stone while Duke splashed through the water beside him. Once on the far side, Major Preston turned the horse in a wide circle to watch her cross. 'Do you need my help?'

'No, I can manage.' Joanna took up the hem of her dress and stepped onto the first stone. She fixed on him as she moved to the next one. The force of his presence drew her across the water more than the need to return to her duties. She envied whatever lady caught his interest at the house party for she'd be very lucky to have him for a husband. Marriage and a family were so far outside Joanna's reach, she didn't dare imagine obtaining it, especially not with a man like Major Preston.

Her foot landed on the loose stone in the middle, pitching her forward. In a flash, Major Preston rushed to her, catching her about the waist before she could hit the jagged rocks sticking up out of the stream bed. Her back arched over his forearm as they stayed linked together above the splashing water. She grasped his arms, bracing herself against the anticipation building deep inside her from the pressure of his fingers against her back. Staring up into his concerned face, the blue sky bright above him, for the first time she understood why Grace had given in to her urges, despite the risks. A moment with a man like Major Preston could make a woman forget the danger of his touch and his flattery.

She didn't move, nor did he try to right her. As they held on to one another, the flowing water indifferent to them, she wondered if what she'd thought impossible a few steps ago might be within her grasp. Even if it was, surrendering to him would mean defying everyone and every responsibility waiting for them outside these woods, and there was no guarantee the passion would last. Duty to his family commanded him, as did her duty to Madame Dubois. They might withstand it for a short while, but eventually it would wear away at them like the water did the mud under the loose stone.

'It seems I'm meant to protect you from a number of dangers today.' His frown eased into a smile. 'Are you all right?'

'Yes.' The forest spun as he righted her. *No.* She wasn't the same Joanna who'd started across the stream.

He held her hand as he led her over the remaining stones to the bank. Leather and cotton gloves separated their skin, but it couldn't smother the heat of his firm grip which drove away the cold which had surrounded her since her first day in Hertfordshire.

On the other side he let go and she straightened her pelisse from where his grasp had twisted it and silently shook herself out of her foolishness. There was no connection between them, there never had been and there never could be.

The bells of the church rang out over the countryside again, marking the quarter-hour, and panic replaced the fading passion, making her stomach flutter.

'I must get back at once.' With half a forest between her and Huntford Place, she wasn't sure how she'd reach the house in time to collect Catherine from the drawing master or the twins from their nurse.

'It'll be quicker if we ride.' He stepped into the saddle and tossed his thick leg over the curving leather.

With his back erect and his feet set firmly in the stirrups, he was the very image of the gallant knights she'd read about in so many stories. Then he held out his hand to her, entreating her to join him.

She hesitated, as shocked by his offer as the muscular curve of his arm beneath his fawn-coloured coat. The young maids in her old books might have won the hearts of princes, but this wasn't a fairy tale. Nothing in her life was. She should run for the house, but her feet wouldn't move. Instead, she slipped her hand in his and raised her foot to cover his in the stirrup. With a powerful tug, he pulled her up so fast she let out a surprised yelp before he settled her across the saddle in front of him.

Their closeness made her dizzier than being up so high. She held on to the edge of the leather saddle as he slipped his arms on either side of her, took up the reins and kicked the horse into a canter. The wind whipped her cheeks, dampening the heat spilling through her from the steady rocking of their bodies together in motion with the stallion beneath them. Each landing of the horse's hooves against the ground made Major Preston's chest press deeper into her shoulders. She'd never experienced something as thrilling as riding this fast, or having Major Preston behind her. His breath caressed her cheek as he stared straight on. His thighs were solid beneath her, every shift of his muscles as he commanded the animal radiating up through her skirt. His arms kept her anchored in front of him, stiff and tight with his control of the reins. The horse turned and she lost her grip on the smooth leather. Without thinking, she clutched his leg to steady herself and felt the low rumble of a groan through his chest. She was too afraid to fall, to snap herself out of this dream to let go, or do anything but sink into him and the steady, rocking gait carrying them through the woods.

The trees were a whirl of green, gold and brown on either side of them as the horse hurried on. Then at last they began to thin and the faint outline of Huntford Place appeared through the naked branches up ahead. The red brick was dulled by years of dirt and weather and covered by ivy turning brown with the coming winter. Joanna sat up straighter in the saddle as Major Preston tugged the horse into a walk, ending the heady exhilaration of their ride.

'I'll leave you here.' He pulled the horse to a halt and leaned into her one last time before dismounting. He reached up and she slid into his outstretched hands, exhaling as he gripped her hard about the waist. As her feet touched the ground, the horse shifted, knocking her into his chest. She clutched his waist to steady herself and his fingers stiffened on her. The pungent scent of leather and cedar clung to him, heightened by the subtle press of his hips against hers. Her insides ached with their closeness and she wished she could climb back up in the saddle with him and be like Grace and ignore all the consequences, but she couldn't. Despite Grace having been so happy during those brief months with her young man, in the end her passion had caused her more heartache than joy. The same thing would happen to Joanna if she forgot herself with Major Preston. Things were difficult enough without her making them worse.

Joanna stepped out of his grasp, recovering her

sense of decorum. 'Thank you, Major Preston, for everything, but I must go.'

'Don't allow Miss Huntford or any of them to push you around, or make you feel low,' he encouraged. 'You're better and smarter than any of them.'

She shrugged. 'And yet they pay my wages.'

'Which, if I know Sir Rodger, are poor.'

She couldn't stop the laugh which sprang out of her. 'Beyond meagre.'

'Then you have little to lose by telling Sir Rodger the truth about what his progeny are up to?'

She sobered at his suggestion. 'You're wrong. I have a great deal to lose by telling him things he doesn't wish to hear.'

'There were many senior officers who didn't want to hear what I had to say and I still told them. It benefited me, and them, more than it hurt me. It could do the same for you.'

'Says a gentleman with family and some station. We aren't all so fortunate.'

Instead of chastising her for rebuking him, he smiled as though he'd won a victory. 'I was worried they'd crush someone as insightful and genuine as you, but I see you have great strength. You'll do well, Miss Radcliff, I have no doubt of it.'

She didn't share his confidence and, with a half-smile of regret, she hurried off to the house. The closer she drew to it, the more the delight of being with Major Preston faded. Despite his faith in her, and Vicar Carlson's suggestions, she wasn't sure all would be well. Major Preston was correct, she should speak up about the girls' behaviour, but she couldn't. Isabel used to speak up and all it ever did was get her in trouble. It wasn't like Joanna to do the same and she wouldn't. Silence had served her well in the past and it would do so again. It would allow her to keep her position and make Madame Dubois proud.

Luke didn't call Miss Radcliff back. In the Army, he'd been governed by the hours of camp life and regulations. He might be done with them now, but Miss Radcliff wasn't free of those commanding her. Luke stepped back into Duke's saddle, but didn't ride for home until Miss Radcliff was out of the woods, across the lawn and inside Huntford Place. Even then he lingered, watching the dark and obscured windows, hoping to catch another glimpse of her. All borrowed traces of the debutante from last night had been scrubbed from her as she'd stood in a sturdy grey pelisse and half-boots, but it hadn't dimmed her natural beauty. It wasn't the wisdom she'd offered him which kept him riveted to the old house, but the impression of her body against his. It left him so agitated it made Duke dance and snort beneath him.

When he'd grabbed her by the waist in the woods, he'd thought of nothing but saving her from being struck by Edward's horse. When she'd pressed back into him, her buttocks shifting against his thighs as she'd peered up at him, her rose-coloured lips parted in surprise and wanting, he'd almost forgotten himself. Once he'd let go of her, he'd dismissed his reaction as the natural response of a man to a beautiful woman after so much time without one. Then she'd tripped on the rock.

He opened and closed his fingers over the reins, the weight of the leather insignificant compared to the memory of Miss Radcliff in his arms. Her near pitch into the water had frightened him the way one of his men rushing headlong into a barrage used to do. He'd wanted to protect her from the sharp rocks as much as he wanted to shield her from the petty meanness of the Huntfords, but he couldn't, nor was it his place to do so.

He jerked Duke round and kicked him into a gallop. The tightness of his thighs against the horse's flanks, his body hunched low over the animal's neck, helped stave off the tension coiling inside him. The weight of Miss Radcliff, the arch of her back over his arm had been as natural as his coat across his shoulders. Her stunning blue eyes had held his, sparkling like the water flowing behind her. It had taken every ounce of strength he'd possessed to set her upright and lead her to the bank instead of claiming her lips, but he'd had no choice. He wasn't Lieutenant Foreman, ready to ruin a young lady of lesser rank to satisfy his desires, nor would he allow emotion to guide him. Even in the heat of battle he'd made every decision based on facts, the lay of the land, the strength of his troops and the French's, not fear or panic. He'd do the same here.

Up ahead, the road forked. Luke pulled Duke to a stop, making the horse rear up at the sudden command before dropping down on to all fours. The path going left led to Lord Helmsworth's. The one pointing right went back to Pensum Manner. His brother's accusations, the desire to show Edward he was wrong and for Luke to achieve something of merit while he was here almost made him turn left. Edward was the one person who could undermine Luke's sense of reason and make him react with his gut instead of his logic. Today it was Luke's command over his emotions as much as Miss Radcliff's advice about family which made Luke tug Duke to the right and head for home. It would sting like hell to endure Edward's glee at Luke not meeting with Lord Helmsworth, but he'd let him rejoice and not say a word. Miss Radcliff was right, it was time to focus on what was important and end the old rivalry. Luke might not have returned home on his terms, but he'd returned. It was more than the many men lying in graves in Spain could say. Besides, there was always tomorrow to approach Lord Helmsworth and perhaps see Miss Radcliff again.

Lord Johan Helmsworth strode through the massive front doors of Helmsworth Manor. The meeting with the young lady in the graveyard had nagged at him during the entire ride home. Her image continued to haunt him beneath the frieze of Apollo in the entrance hall, past the paintings of the former Marquises filling the long main hall. Half of them watched him with the vivid blue eyes so prevalent in the family, Miss Radcliff's eyes.

He clasped his hands behind his back and knocked the single ring he wore on each hand together in time to his steps. In Miss Radcliff's trusting, oval face, he'd caught a glimpse of his past. Memories of carrying Jane high on his shoulders while he'd showed her the horses in the stable rushed back to him as strong as the smell of cut hay in the fields carrying in through the open windows. When he'd sat with Miss Radcliff, giving her advice, it had reminded him of the time he'd sat with his daughter explaining to her how the little spaniel she'd loved was gone, not destined to live as long as her. In the end, she hadn't lived as long as she should have either.

He paused in the hallway and rested one hand on a side table to brace himself. The pain was as fresh today as nineteen years ago when she'd passed. It didn't send him into dark moods like it used to, but it still hadn't eased after all this time.

The shifting of papers in the study up ahead forced him to take hold of himself. Straightening, he took a deep breath and strode inside.

'Lord Helmsworth, you've returned. We need to discuss the issue of the property dispute with the Inghams,' Mr Browning, the bespectacled solicitor, greeted, setting aside a leather satchel filled with the business he intended to discuss with Johan during their regular meeting. 'I received a letter from Major Preston. He'd like to speak with you in regards to the issue of the river land.'

'The young whelp returns home and thinks he can fix twenty years of troubles,' Johan grumbled, in no mood to entertain the Inghams' whining on today of all days.

'This issue has gone on for entirely too long.'

'And it will continue. I won't have one of those Inghams in here thinking he can steal my land from me, no matter how many medals he wears.' He thumped the top of a burled escritoire as he passed it. 'I lost enough to an Army man nineteen years ago. I won't lose more.'

Johan stopped in the centre of the room and stared up at the portrait of his daughter and wife together in front of a view of the columned entrance to Helmsworth Manor. It had been painted the year before his wife had died, when Jane was eight. Beside it was a small portrait of Jane at seventeen, the year she'd come out. She was resplendent in her pink gown, the sash of which curled around her shoulders as if caught in a breeze. She smiled with all the expectation of a young lady poised to find her place in society. It was a far cry from the one who'd stood in here railing at him a mere six months later. They'd argued fiercely after Johan had withheld his permission for Jane to marry. Being under twenty-one, she'd needed it. Unlike her, Johan had seen through Captain Handler's designs on her and her fortune and had cut her off, hoping it would end things. It had only made her more obstinate in her desire for the wretched man and her stubbornness had increased his. All Johan's attempts to make her listen and obey had, in the end, driven her to run away with the Captain. He hadn't wanted to deny her love, but to keep her safe from the heartbreak and ruin she'd ultimately suffered. He'd failed.

The old guilt washed over him, joined by another. He shouldn't have impersonated a man of the cloth, or lied to Miss Radcliff simply to speak with her, but it had been necessary. If he'd revealed his true identity, Miss Radcliff would've dipped curtsies as though he were a king, mumbled her apologies and kept quiet. The young lady had spoken with him like Jane used to do before she'd turned against him in favour of the wicked spendthrift Captain Handler.

'Let's get to our business.' The leather armchair by the fire crinkled beneath Johan's weight as he sank into it. He motioned for Mr Browning to take the less worn one across from him.

The solicitor obliged, setting his satchel on the floor beside him and removing a few papers. 'Lord Faston has vacated the London town house. I'll advertise for a new tenant, unless you intend to go to London soon. I understand Parliament is poised to convene a special session to deal with the Luddite uprisings in the north.'

'I haven't taken my seat in the House of Lords for nearly twenty years. I have no intention of doing so now. Go ahead and let it,' Johan answered with a flick of his hand, unwilling to reside in the London house even for the King. The stately home in Grosvenor Square had been his wife's before she'd married him and he'd retained it partly for the rent, but mostly because he couldn't bear to let it go. He'd intended it as a wedding present for Jane. How he wished his wife had been alive to guide their daughter through the pitfalls of men and balls. Johan hadn't had the talent for it.

'You seem troubled, my lord. Is there anything I may do?' The fortyish Mr Browning had assumed his father's clients when the elder man, who'd been with Johan for years, had at last grown too old to oversee the affairs. The son was sharp and as good a sounding board as his father had been.

'I had a strange encounter today.' Johan pressed his fingertips together in front of his face. 'I met a young woman while I was at the vicarage. The instant I saw her, I thought she was Jane. You would've, too, if you'd seen her. She had Jane's eyes, the Helmsworth eyes.'

The papers went limp in Mr Browning's hands. 'A girl with the Helmsworth eyes?'

'Yes. The resemblance was remarkable.' And unsettling. He'd gone to the graveyard as he always did on Jane's birthday. He hadn't expected to be startled by what he'd first thought was a ghost, nor had he been afraid. For a moment he'd rejoiced, thinking the longed-for reconciliation would finally come to pass. Then the sweet young girl had proven she was as real as him.

'What was her first name?' Mr Browning asked, sliding forward on to the edge of his seat.

'I don't know, she only told me she is Miss Radcliff.'

'How old was she?'

'Nineteen.'

The room grew quiet, filling with the crackle of the fire in the grate. Mr Browning, for the first time in a long time, did not continue with his business or offer Johan advice. Johan regarded the man who sat staring at the flames. He was deep in contemplation, fingers against his chin, and it wasn't over leases or rent.

'What is it, Mr Browning?' Johan prodded.

The solicitor dropped his hand and faced his employer, more serious than Johan had ever seen him before. 'There's something I must tell you, Lord Helmsworth. Afterwards, you may view me, your daughter and everything in a different light.'

The younger man had been friends with Jane in her youth, one of the few gentlemen Johan had trusted around his headstrong daughter once she'd entered society. Mr Browning had been too in love with the woman who'd become his wife for Johan to worry about his falling for Jane. He wondered if he'd been mistaken about the young man. 'Then don't tell me. I'm burdened with enough troubles already.'

'I must, because I can't help but feel it somehow involves what you've told me about the young lady you encountered.'

Johan picked at the nail-head trim on the arm of his chair. 'How so?'

Mr Browning cleared his throat once, then again before at last finding his voice. 'Lord Helmsworth, the day before Jane died, she summoned me on the pretext of preparing her will. During our interview, she told me the truth about her illness. She didn't die of an infectious fever, but childbed fever. A few days before she'd returned to you, she'd given birth to a little girl. It was why she wouldn't allow Dr Scopes to examine her when she fell ill. She was afraid he would notice. She hadn't realised the severity of her illness.'

Johan's fingers dug into the cracked leather as the room around him shook with the man's revelation. Jane had had a child and she hadn't told him. He sank back against the chair, the distance between him and his precious daughter seeming to reopen. 'Why didn't she tell me?'

Mr Browning tapped his knee, pausing before he continued. 'I urged her to, but she refused, afraid you'd reject her again. She thought she would recover and then once you two were properly reconciled, she could reveal the truth to you. Despite your objections to Captain Handler, and your falling out, she never stopped loving you. She even named her baby girl Joanna, after you.'

Johan dropped his head in his hands and closed his eyes, struggling to hold back his anguish. Even in the end when her life had been in peril, she'd still held back from him, afraid he would push her away again. Losing Jane had ripped his heart from him. Having her come home to die a few days later had left the rift between them unsettled for good, until now. He looked up at the younger man. 'What happened to the baby?'

'I don't know. Captain Handler was killed in battle in Europe before he and Jane could marry, leaving her with child and penniless in Austria. She found her way back to England, landing in Portsmouth. She had the child somewhere near Salisbury and entrusted it to an officer's wife who'd helped her in her travails before Jane continued on to here. She'd hoped after reconciling with you to return for the baby, but she never had the chance. It was her dying wish I find the child and see to its future. I did my best, but the officer's wife, Mrs White, had left with her husband to rejoin his regiment in Austria. Her husband died in battle. I don't know what happened to Mrs White, or the child. I'd intended to find the girl and bring her to your attention, but when I was unable to discover anything and you being in such deep mourning, I didn't wish to make matters worse.'

Johan understood and couldn't blame the solicitor for acting the way he had. It had been a year after Jane's death before he'd been able to leave Helmsworth Manor, his grief consuming him until his sister, and many others, feared he might harm himself. To discover there'd been a granddaughter, one he couldn't find, might have pushed him over the edge he'd feared crossing for so long.

He was no longer the same broken and sad father, but an old man in his dotage who could right some of the old wrongs.

'I want you to investigate Miss Radcliff's background and see if there's any connection between her and this Mrs White. If I have a granddaughter, whether she's legitimate or not, I want to know about it.' He'd failed Jane during the last year of her life, driving her away with his anger. He would do right by her child.

Chapter Five

Joanna watched from the third floor schoolroom window as Lady Huntford's house party guests began to arrive. Behind her, the girls sat around the table reading aloud from a French grammar book. A line of carriages stood in the drive, the horses kicking up pebbles and dust. One by one, each vehicle pulled up to the door and discharged its passengers, who greeted Lady Huntford and Frances with smiles, hugs and loud chatter.

Huntford Place was not very large and neither was the house party. Judging by the women in attendance, Lady Huntford had chosen the plainest ladies of Frances's age to give Frances the advantage. A smile crept over Joanna's lips. If Lady Huntford knew how little regard Major Preston held for her daughter, she wouldn't have gone to so much expense or bother, but Joanna wasn't about to tell her. The woman was cutting enough in her censure without Joanna voluntarily risking more.

She rubbed the back of her stiff neck, trying to drive away her exhaustion. All night she'd lain awake in her attic room, staring at the slanted and water-stained ceiling and thinking of Major Preston and his impending arrival. The memory of his firm chest against her back had bothered her more than the lumps in the mattress. She dropped her arm and tried to recollect their conversation and not the more physical aspects of their meeting the other day. He'd considered her opinions as though they'd mattered, despite the difference in their stations, making her feel valued for the first time in a long time. Her desire to experience it again, and the frustration of knowing she couldn't, had kept her awake until the darkness outside her window had begun to lighten.

She'd risen before the sun and set out into the Huntford Place garden for a walk, determined to settle her tumbling thoughts. Any hope of dealing with the girls or continuing to implement Vicar Carlson's ideas had depended on her regaining control over herself, and she had, until the Inghams' carriage rolled into view.

They were the last to arrive and, as their black carriage came to a stop at the front door, the top of it almost brown with road dust, the crowd waiting to greet them swelled. All the eligible young ladies and their mothers clustered around the front entrance while their fathers and brothers remained cloistered in Sir Rodger's study, probably drinking port and listening to him complain about the expense of the weekend party.

Joanna touched the cold glass separating her from the outside and held her breath as the door to the carriage opened. Lady Ingham stepped out first and Joanna near groaned in disappointment. Lady Ingham was followed by Lord Ingham, then Lord and Lady

Pensum, and they all made for their hostess. Major Preston was the last to appear.

He didn't look at the swooning crowd of young ladies on the front steps. With one hand, he shaded his eyes against the late morning sun cresting the roof and gazed up the long front of the Stuart-era house.

He's searching for me.

The voices of the girls reciting their French at the table behind Joanna faded. She stared down at him, not sure if he could see her. She wanted to push open the window and call out to him, or at the very least wave, but she remained still, her fingers stiff on the sill. He was here and she was trapped away like a fairy princess in a tower. Except she wasn't a damsel a man of his rank might fight for, but a servant.

Lady Huntford stepped forward, eager to pull Major Preston into the circle of her influence. She flicked a quick glance up, trying to see what he did. Joanna jumped back from the window before her employer could notice her. It was a warning to Joanna to mind herself while he was here. Major Preston was not for her.

'What's wrong with you?' Catherine asked from the schoolroom table. The commencement of the house party had increased the girl's petulance and made Joanna's job even more difficult today. 'You act as if you've seen a ghost.'

'Perhaps, I did. Mrs Winston tells me there are all sorts of spirits in this house, especially close to your room.' Joanna tapped Catherine playfully on her long nose.

Catherine's eyes widened in horror before she brushed Joanna's hand away. 'That's just the nurse's excuses for not coming up here to make sure the maids have cleaned.'

'I hope you're right. Now finish, it's almost time for our botany lesson in the garden.'

She strode around the table to check the twins' French grammar, doing her best to put Major Preston out of her head. Unless Lady Huntford asked Joanna to be Frances's chaperon during some event, there would be very little interaction between Joanna and any of the guests. As she leaned over to correct Ava's verb conjugation, bringing an irritated wrinkle to the girl's forehead, Joanna prayed she'd be called on to chaperon.

Luke climbed the stairs, following the footmen carrying the portmanteaus for him and the other three bachelors who'd been invited to the weekend party. They were the brothers of the young ladies being trotted out for Luke's inspection. These men were welcome to them. Unless one of the ladies demonstrated more character than they had in the front drive, Luke wasn't likely to find a wife here. The weekend had barely begun and already it felt like a waste, except for the chance to encounter Miss Radcliff.

Despite reaching each corner of Huntford Place and expecting to find her on the other side, he'd convinced himself her presence in the house made no difference to him. He was wrong. She was the entire reason he was here and it was a mistake. His family needed him to marry a woman with money, not be distracted by the governess.

He paused on the stairs to take in the house. The wooden banister beneath his hand was rough from too much use and too few polishes while the sun coming in through the leaded diamond windows along the staircase highlighted the faded carpet beneath his boots. With parts of Pensum Manor in need of refurbishing, Luke couldn't complain too much about the lack of upkeep in Huntford Place. What he could complain about was the lazy footmen commanded by the indifferent butler. The lanky men in their tired livery dumped his and the other gentlemen's things in each room as Gruger with his bent shoulders, pointed nose and sprouting head of grey hair, unceremoniously threw open the four bedroom doors at the end of the hall near the stairs leading to the upper floors.

'I've seen better accommodations in an Army camp,' Luke grumbled aloud at the doorway to his room, his hands on his hips in disapproval of his portmanteau lying on its side in front of the narrow bed.

'Wait until dinner.' A light female voice carried over him. 'I'm sure your camp cooks provided better food, too.'

He turned to find Miss Radcliff standing on the landing behind him in a most proper governess attitude. She held her hands tight in front of her, back straight, shoulders set, ready to rebuke anyone who dared to step out of line. The seriousness of her stance was betrayed by the impish smile softening her face which echoed with the sprightliness he'd enjoyed in the woods. It undermined her stern control as much as the twins behind her tugging at one another in an argument while their elder sister made moon eyes at Mr Chilton.

She turned and let out an exasperated sigh. 'Girls, mind your manners.'

The twins took one last swipe at each other before settling into their line. Even the older girl wandered back to her place, tearing her besotted gaze off Mr Chilton as he closed the door, his grumbling about his room as audible as Luke's.

'Out to the garden, girls,' Miss Radcliff instructed, leading her charges to the stairs like a mother hen does her brood, except the girls were far more wayward than compliant chicks.

'I'm not a girl,' the oldest one complained.

'Stop pulling my bow,' one of the twins whined before hitting her sister hard on the arm.

'Good luck,' Luke called after her, stepping up to the banister and leaning over it.

She peered at him over one shoulder, her eyes highlighted by her dark lashes and white skin. She mouthed 'Thank you' with her pretty lips before she ran out the door after her wild pupils.

Luke thumped the creaking railing, pondering a walk in the garden instead of setting his things to right in his room. He hadn't brought a valet. After seeing to himself in the Army, he didn't see the need to bother or to incur the expense. With the younger Huntford girls present and the excuse of exploring the grounds, Luke might enjoy a few moments of conversation with Miss Radcliff.

Luke turned to fetch his redingote, then stopped. Mr Selton leaned against the door frame to his room with a smirk of congratulations as if he'd surprised Luke in the pantry with a comely maid. Luke's experience with the tall young man with a face as pocked as a church carving was limited, but it was clear he'd noticed the exchange with Miss Radcliff and taken it for more than a friendly greeting. Luke silently dared him to say something about either him or Miss Radcliff. Mr Selton didn't meet the challenge, but pushed away from the wood, strolled into his room and closed the door.

Luke strode into his room and to the one long window on the far side with a view of the barren front drive. His frustration with coming here was beginning to rival that of his coming home. The one woman whose time he wanted the most was the one woman he must avoid. If a brief exchange could capture the attention of Mr Selton, Luke being seen with her in the garden might create a scandal. In the future, he'd have to better mind himself in her presence.

'Why must Frances have all the fun while I'm stuck here?' Catherine flung a stone in the algae-filled gold-fish pond in the centre of the garden.

The twins were busy pulling up long weeds and whacking each other with them. Joanna didn't stop them, hoping they'd wear themselves out and be a little more compliant when they returned to the school-room.

'When you come out next year, you'll be able to enjoy things like house parties.' Joanna glanced again at the French doors leading into the back sitting room, hoping to see Major Preston emerge from the house, but there was no one there. With the twins screaming like banshees, no adult was likely to venture into the garden. She should be glad. No matter how jovial he was, or how handsome he appeared in his dark blue coat, it wasn't her position to speak with him.

'Father isn't likely to spend the money on a Season for me. He's never done anything for me, only for Frances,' Catherine despaired, her head lowered in defeat. 'You don't know what it's like to be ignored. No one will ever love me.'

I know exactly what it's like. But this wasn't about her and her troubles, but those of her charge.

'Keep your chin up,' Joanna encouraged, using her fingers to lift the girl's crestfallen head. She pitied the young woman. Unlike her sister, Catherine's petulance was not from being spoiled, but from a lack of attention. 'Remember, a kind word and a pleasant personality will attract a gentleman as much as beauty.'

'How can you be sure?'

The image of Major Preston at the ball came to her. He'd had so many ladies to choose from for conversation, yet he'd singled her out. It wasn't because of money, or looks, but for a much deeper and more meaningful reason she'd caught in the holding of his breath as he'd cradled her over the stream. 'I've seen it happen more than once. Besides, when Frances finally finds a husband, your mother will have no one to dote on except you.'

'Mother doesn't dote, at least not on me.'

'But she'll help you find a husband. It's a mother's duty to do so.' Joanna smiled, encouraging Catherine to do the same. Deep inside, Joanna wanted to mope as much as the girl. As dismissive as Lady Huntford was to Catherine, she would guide her through a Season, arrange her marriage and show at least the minimal amount of concern. There was no one to do the same for Joanna. Her parents had abandoned her and Madame Dubois had sent her out in the world to make her way the best as she could. Her headmistress might offer advice and suggestions, but it wasn't her place to help Joanna find a worthy gentleman. Hidden away in schoolrooms, Joanna wasn't likely to do it on her own. Over time, her pupils would change, as well as the attic rooms she occupied and she would grow old and withered along with the one dream she'd carried with her since childhood, to have a family of her own. It made her want to complain as much as Catherine, but she couldn't. The young lady needed her comfort and encouragement as much as the new pupils at the school used to. It was her duty to help her and she would.

Luke and the other gentlemen entered the sitting room with the faint scent of tobacco and port still clinging to their coats. The evening meal had been more painful and tedious than a long march. He'd sat between the vapid Miss Carlton and the almost-hostile Miss Huntford, trying to choke down the overcooked venison until Lady Huntford and the other ladies had taken their leave. The male camaraderie after dinner had been a fortifying respite from the sea of hungry sharks which was the ladies, and now it was over.

Every female eye fell on the arriving gentlemen and there was a notable dip in the conversation before the men fanned into the room to revive it. Luke wanted to retreat to his bedroom, but he pressed forward. He was a guest and he must be polite to his host and hostess. It was yet another of the new constraints wrapping around him and trying to choke the life from him.

He approached a group of gentlemen discussing hunting, resigned to another tiresome hour or two before he could retire. Then, a sight as cherished as a breath of fresh air after hours in the hold of a transport ship greeted him. Miss Radcliff stood at the back of the room, almost hidden by the shadows cast from the large plant stand supporting a drooping fern. She remained outside the circle of guests, ignored and quiet, but watching with intelligent eyes which took in everything, including him. The faint flicker of the candles on a nearby table caressed her face, giving her skin a creamy glow. Even in the dim light, she was as beautiful as she'd been beneath the trees. He opened and closed his hand, the weight of her body in his arms as fresh now as when he'd left her. He shifted forward, ready to make for her, then stopped. Showing her favour would draw the ire of the other guests, especially his hostess. He would have to be more subtle in his engagement.

He began to weave his way to her. It took more effort to slide past the mamas in their *bergère* chairs without being waylaid than it did to get his regiment through a steep mountain pass. He was just beyond them when the ladies began their assault.

'Major Preston, would you like to turn my music?' Miss Bell asked from where she sat at the pianoforte as he squeezed between it and a side table.

'My inability to read music would ruin your beautiful playing,' he answered with a bow before continuing on. He was barely two feet away before the voluptuous Miss Selton stepped in front of him.

'Might I draw you? I've saved my sharpest pencil for you.' She leaned close to him and her generous breasts nearly spilled out of the top of her bodice brushing his arm.

'I'm not much of a subject for portraiture,' he answered. 'Mr Chilton has a much more classical profile.'

He motioned to the sturdy gentleman sitting in the chair beside them.

Mr Chilton rose, more interested in Miss Selton's talent than Luke. 'I'd be happy to sit for you.'

Miss Selton wasn't as enthusiastic. She threw Luke a disapproving frown before leading Mr Chilton to the table near the fireplace with better light and her drawing things spread out across the top of it.

Luke left them to dodge Lord Selton and Sir Rodger, stepping over Sir Rodger's large, black hunting dog which snored on the hearthrug in front of the fire.

'Major Preston, what do you think of the Luddite uprisings?' Lord Selton asked.

'We must see these men have other work if they're losing their positions to machines,' he answered before continuing on.

He hadn't done this much manoeuvring since the last time he'd drilled his troops. It seemed like a full half-hour passed before he casually came up beside the fern stand, the plant between him and Miss Radcliff. By then, the husband-hunting ladies had taken to colluding together by the fireplace to devise some amusement for the weekend while their mamas resumed their gossip or sat at the whist table to partake in the play.

Luke perched his elbow on the high wood and surveyed the room as if Miss Radcliff held no interest for him. In fact, he was aware of every shift of her dress, the faint inhale and exhale of her breath, and the clean scent of soap and lavender surrounding her.

'I see they let you out of the garret,' he joked in a low voice.

She shifted on her feet and glanced from Lady Huntford to Frances whose attention was fixed on the red-haired Mr Winborn sitting beside her. 'Lady Huntford would rather speak with her friends than chaperon her daughter. It's why I'm here.'

'A monumental task if I remember.' He didn't face her as he spoke, careful not to draw attention to their conversation.

'Such as you escaping those mamas. They almost had you captured.'

'Like a French patrol once did, but I outflanked them, too.'

Miss Radcliff smothered a smile. This small show of delight intrigued him more than anything else in the room. 'Your battle plans are very impressive.'

'Not so much as the sight of you.' Or his ability to stop offering her the most inappropriate compliments. 'I'm sorry, I spoke out of turn.'

'It must not happen again.' She clasped her hands in front of her as she had on the stairs, the joking young lady replaced by the stern governess.

'It won't,' he promised, though he couldn't bring himself to abandon her enticing humour for any of the droll conversation taking place around them. 'Is Miss Huntford keeping her end of the bargain?'

'Yes.'

'Good, because I've been worried about you.'

She trilled her fingers over her other hand, but didn't soften her stance. 'There's no need to be. I'm perfectly fine.'

He didn't believe her. He'd led enough men from a

number of different backgrounds to recognise when they were settling in with the regiment and when they weren't. 'I want you to know that, should you need any additional assistance, you can call on me, as a friend.'

She unclasped her hands and fingered a feathery leaf of the fern, trying to appear as if it, and not him, held her attention. 'A very kind offer, Major Preston, but you know it's impossible.'

'You think the son of an earl can't have friends outside his station? I consorted with all manner of men in the Army.'

She glanced up at him through her lashes, making his heart stop. 'This isn't the Army and I'm not a man.'

Despite the plain brown dress covering her figure and the equally drab ribbon holding back the richness of her light brown hair, there was no mistaking her for a grimy soldier. He longed to see her in a dress like the one she'd worn at the ball, her eyes sparkling with mirth instead of constantly flicking past him to worry about her employer. Yet, for all his desires, she was correct. If he were still a major, he might come to know her better without raising much scandal, but he wasn't. The divide between them was as deep as one of the gorges in the Pyrenees. When the house party ended, there'd be no chance to approach her or any reason for them to speak. She would go on to lead her life and unless he married Frances Huntford, which was unlikely, their paths wouldn't cross again. 'You're right, it's not fair for me to ask you for something you can't give.'

'Don't think I'm ungrateful for your offer. If I was of your class, I'd most certainly be your friend.' She smiled and his chest stilled at the beauty it brought to her face, then she looked past him. She laced her hands in front of her again and her expression changed from interested delight to the bland deference expected of a woman in her position. 'I believe the other young ladies are about to launch an attack.'

Miss Chilton, Miss Bell and Miss Selton swarmed up to Luke along with Miss Winborn. Only Miss Huntford was absent, remaining by her mother despite Lady Huntford shooing her to join the ladies.

'Major Preston, we've decided to put on a theatrical while we're here, *Hero and Alexandra*. You're perfect for the lead,' Miss Selton gushed to the agreeing tittering of her companions.

Luke tried not to wince. Out of the corner of his eye, he noticed Miss Radcliff sliding away, determined not to be seen by the ladies trying to corner him. He wished he could join her. It wasn't their attention he wanted, but hers.

'I'm a very poor actor, but I understand Mr Winborn is quite talented.' He motioned to the red-haired gentleman as he passed.

Caught off guard, Mr Winborn jerked to a stop, making his port slosh up one side of his glass. 'I wouldn't say talented, but I've shown some flair in my fair share of lead roles.'

He puffed out his slender chest, ignoring the disappointed frowns of the ladies.

'Great, then it's decided.' Luke waited for the group to flutter off, but they proved as stubborn as a bloodstain.

'Major Preston, you must have a part in the play,' Miss Winborn insisted with a most unattractive pout.

'I'll watch and applaud.' He hadn't left the Army to become a house-party peacock.

'He'll be glad to accept a minor role.' Edward dropped a heavy hand on Luke's shoulder and gave it a warning squeeze.

'And so will you.' Luke rolled his shoulder to dislodge Edward. He might be forced to partake in these idiotic distractions, but he wouldn't do it alone.

'Of course,' Edward agreed through clenched teeth. Beside him, Alma did her best not to laugh.

'We'll start rehearsals tomorrow morning.' Miss Selton clapped her hands together in front of her, more he thought to show off her breasts than to celebrate. Then she linked her arm in Mr Winborn's and drew him away, followed by the other ladies.

Luke looked for Miss Radcliff. She stood across the room behind his hostess, as distant as when he'd first entered the room. He shifted on his feet, anger and annoyance mingling like smoke and flame in the fire. She shouldn't be forced to linger in corners while insipid women like Miss Selton commanded the room. Miss Radcliff should be brought into the candlelight to laugh and smile like the others, but it wasn't her lot. Her parents had abandoned her to be all but reviled by young ladies who thought of nothing except laces and landing a husband. It was as unfair as the officers who used to be passed over for commissions because they didn't have the right family or connections. Luke had argued vociferously for those men, sometimes winning, but most times not. The culture of the Army was too entrenched against men of modest backgrounds. So was society. Nothing he could say in Miss Radcliff's favour would change anyone's mind, or help them see her as more than a humble servant. All it would do is cast aspersion on her and create more gossip for the mamas to chew on.

Luke caught his mother's eye and she motioned for him to join her at the whist table. He fingered the bugle badge pinned to the lapel of his coat. Guilt stung him. Soon, his regiment would be enduring the encroaching cold as they settled into their winter quarters while he played cards and performed in theatricals. Already, his time with them and the danger they'd shared was beginning to fade, replaced with frivolities as useless as his place in the family and thoughts of Miss Radcliff. In the last few days, he'd mulled over her precarious situation more than his soldiers'.

Sick to his stomach, Luke marched across the room to join in the game. He'd play along for now, but Edward was correct. At some point, after Luke did his duty, he'd be free to return to his regiment and he would. It was the one thing, beside Miss Radcliff's presence, which kept him from leaving the house party.

Joanna watched Major Preston play cards with the other ladies and envied them. The part of her eager to be special wanted to garner more of his attention. The practical girl who'd learned not to base her life on dreams made sure she kept her head. Tonight wasn't the time to set the room alight with speculation and see herself dismissed.

'You must go play cards with him,' Lady Huntford commanded her daughter from where they sat on the sofa in front of Joanna.

'I don't want to.' Frances pouted. She was the only eligible lady who hadn't thrown herself in Major Preston's path tonight.

'We aren't spending all this money for you to speak with Mr Winborn whom you may see whenever you wish. Now come with me.' Lady Huntford took Frances by the arm and all but pulled her off the sofa. 'Miss Radcliff, you're no longer needed. You may go, but don't tromp through the room like a bull and be discreet about it. I don't want everyone to think I employ an uncouth governess.'

'Yes, Lady Huntford.' Joanna responded, trying not to grit her teeth. No one at Madame Dubois's had ever been this rude to her. She wasn't sure why Lady Huntford felt the need to be or to worry about what others thought of Joanna. The entire time she'd been here, no one had noticed her except Major Preston. She doubted anyone would be conscious of her leaving, except him.

As Lady Huntford dragged a reluctant Frances to the card table, Joanna circled the edge of the room, stepping around Sir Rodger's dog as it chased rabbits in its sleep. She should be glad to be dismissed, to be able to sleep before tomorrow's duties descended on her, but she was reluctant to leave. She passed by the whist table, subtly studying Major Preston. She admired the fine set of his nose, the sharp arch of his eyebrows and the soft wave of his hair brushed back from his strong forehead. She stopped when his eyes rose to meet hers and the two of them remained linked in their silence.

He wants to be my friend. It was a foolish request,

but she appreciated the gesture. *I should have accepted it.*

She needed all the allies she could muster here in Hertfordshire, even if she wasn't sure what one like Major Preston could offer her. Despite her refusal, he'd come to her aid if she asked him, she was certain of it. What else might he grant her if she asked it of him?

Then Lady Huntford made a fuss, insisting Lord Selton rise so Frances could sit beside Major Preston. The shuffling of seats at the table pulled Major Preston back into his world and isolated her once more in hers.

Joanna left the light of the sitting room and headed down the dim hallway to the front stairs. She trudged up the first flight, having to feel her way along the wall to the back stairs at the end. Even with a house full of guests unfamiliar with the rambling layout, Sir Rodger was too miserly to light more candles. Perhaps he, more than Lady Huntford, could see the waste of this weekend and how he wasn't likely to gain more from it than a pile of bills.

It wasn't the dark which concerned her as she climbed the cold and winding flight of stairs to her room, but the subtle change in her situation. Before yesterday, she'd had no friends in Hertfordshire. Now, she had two. Vicar Carlson she trusted. She wasn't sure how to consider Major Preston. The son of an earl shouldn't be concerned about the well-being of a lowly governess, and she shouldn't be flattered by his attention. She'd been warned about overly interested gentleman by Miss Fanworth. It was to her peril if she chose to ignore it. The kindly teacher wasn't here to help her the way she'd helped Grace, if, in a moment of weakness, Joanna forgot herself. Madame Dubois might have taken her in as a foundling, but she wasn't sure she'd welcome Joanna back if she ruined herself. Madame Dubois was understanding about many things, but Joanna doubted the strength of young passion was one of them.

At the top of the stairs, she shivered as she crossed the long, bare hall to her room. This narrow and desolate space was so different from Madame's school, where woven rugs covered the upstairs floor, bright light filled it in the day and the laughter and chatter of girls echoed through it in the evenings. The only sound she heard here was the faint snoring of a maid from behind one of the many doors. When Joanna reached her room Rachael, Grace and Isabel wouldn't be there to greet her with smiles, sympathy and humour. The only thing waiting for her was the peeling plaster walls and loneliness. She would go to sleep in the dark without friends or anyone here who truly cared about her.

Major Preston cares. She breathed into her hands, trying to warm them. Despite the risks in cavorting with Major Preston, his presence offered her something she hadn't experienced in a long time—hope. If a man like him could value her company, perhaps some day another would, too, one of more modest means who'd be free to love her without hesitation and whom she could love openly in return.

She slipped into her room which was no warmer than the hallway. The moonlight falling in through the single window washed out what little colour remained in the thin coverlet draped over the rickety bed. She

wandered past it and to the window. The drive outside was just as bare as her room before the darkness
of the woods enveloped it on either side.

Raising her fingers to the window, she pictured
Major Preston emerging from his coach and searching
for her. If only the man who might some day come to
love her could be him. With a sigh which fogged the
window, she pushed away from the glass and began
to prepare for bed. It was reality she needed to face,
not dreams. Thanks to him, tonight, the reality she
might one day have a family of her own didn't seem
so unobtainable.

Chapter Six

'No, no, no, you're not saying it right. Try again.' Miss Selton raised her hands in exasperation at her brother's poor interpretation of a Greek god.

Luke leaned against the large stone fireplace where a weak flame was limply trying to heat the large room and exchanged an amused look with Miss Radcliff. She sat across the ballroom-turned-theatre near where the mishmash collection of props had been dumped by grumbling servants under Miss Selton's direction. The young lady had even managed to have the lazy staff remove the sheets from the furniture and make a half-hearted attempt to sweep away the dust covering the stage where the musicians, if there had even been a ball at Huntford Place, might play. He was amazed at her accomplishment since Luke could barely get fresh water in his washstand jug. It was the one mark in favour of Miss Selton, along with her having insisted Miss Radcliff stay for the rehearsal. Miss Selton, who'd taken it upon herself to both direct and play the lead, had assigned the younger Huntford girls small parts, necessitating Miss Radcliff's presence.

Miss Radcliff returned to reading the letter which had commanded her attention since she'd sat down to watch the rehearsal. A simple peach-coloured dress flowed over the curve of her knees, stopping just above her feet. The long sleeves covered her arching arms as she held up the missive which appeared to amuse her more than the rehearsal. Her eyes glittered with a mirth which increased each time she glanced up to take in the ridiculous actors. In the midst of the chaos around her, she was calm and serene, but the hint of an imp showed itself in more than one reserved smile.

The glow he'd admired from across the room was the only reason he'd remained here instead of leaving to ride Duke. He'd attempted to avoid the play by lingering in his room this morning, but hunger had got the better of him. Not wanting to starve and unlikely to receive a plate of food from the surly butler, he'd been forced to venture downstairs for breakfast.

I've become soft already. He used to go for days without food in Spain, now he was wrapped up in a play because his stomach had become accustomed to regular meals. He'd hoped a late night of gambling and conversation would have kept people in their rooms this morning. He'd been wrong. The majority of the guests had risen early and he'd been accosted by the ladies the moment he'd entered the dining room. He and the other gentleman had barely had time to finish their eggs before they were ushered off to begin rehearsals.

In the end, it hadn't been so awful. Having the freedom to watch Miss Radcliff read, to enjoy the sparkle of humour softening her face almost made capitulating to his hunger pangs worth it.

Then her smile faded, and a small line settled between her brows as she turned the letter over to read the other side. On stage, Mr Selton stumbled over his lines again, drawing chuckles from the other actors, but Miss Radcliff didn't notice. She was so absorbed in the seriousness of her missive, even the twins sifting through the fake swords and shields searching for treasure had failed to capture her notice. Not even his studying her, wondering what the matter was, was enough to draw her away.

He pushed off the stone mantel ready to go to her before he stopped himself. He'd suffered hunger and not raided storehouses, endured a tongue swollen with thirst but refused filthy water. He would resist the draw of her and the risk of making everyone tut in disapproval at his behaviour as they had Mr Selton's inability to pronounce 'pungent'.

'Major Preston, would you like to share my book and study your lines?' Miss Bell approached him with a little too much eagerness. A number of guests had sent their servants back to their estates to retrieve their copies of the play, but there still weren't enough to go around. The lack of copies provided numerous opportunities for couples to step to one side and talk, especially Miss Huntford and Mr Winborn, who gossiped together at the corner of the stage, the open book in front of them all but forgotten.

'No, I'm quite content to watch the others.'

'I'll study with you,' Mr Chilton offered, but it didn't raise her crestfallen expression as she followed him to a set of chairs near the window.

'At least try and look as if you want to be here.' Edward banged his copy of the play against Luke's chest.

'Is this better?' Luke threw his brother an overly large smile while holding a curt response behind his teeth. It was a wonder he hadn't bitten off his tongue in an effort to not quarrel with Edward as Miss Radcliff had suggested. If his unwillingness to engage Edward had dampened the anger threatening to flare up between them, it was difficult to discern, but he was determined to try.

Edward frowned at Luke. 'You should've accepted Miss Selton's offer to play the lead. It's obvious she has a preference for you.'

'You mean my chances of inheriting a title. You should be glad I'm not encouraging her. She's so determined, she might try and secure my inheritance faster, then you'd have to watch what's in your tea.' He smacked the book against Edward's chest, but held on to it, taking it with him as he crossed the room.

Curse them all and what they thought. It wasn't like him to wait idly by while what he wanted was mere feet away.

'Will you help me practise my lines?' He held out the book to Miss Radcliff.

At last the letter lost its hold over her. She looked up at him, the faint trouble wrinkling her smooth forehead easing as she cocked her head and smiled.

'All three of them?' she teased while she folded the letter and slipped it in her pocket.

'It's a very demanding part. I'm playing the commanding general. Quite against type.'

'It will definitely be a stretch for you.' She took the book from him and her fingers brushed his. They paused at the meeting of their flesh and, for the first time since he'd entered the ballroom, it seemed warm and comfortable. Her eyes, framed by her dark lashes, opened wide with surprise. He lost himself in their brilliant azure and almost forgot all his duty to his family. Thankfully, she kept her head.

'I'm sure your authentic performance will outshine even the lead.' She pulled away with the book and motioned to the stage where Miss Selton indulged in an overly dramatic reading of her lines, her high voice echoing off the rafters.

Luke shook off his momentary and troubling infatuation. In Spain, when he'd gone into brothels to collect his wayward men, even after weeks or months without the tender company of a woman, he hadn't been as carried away or tempted to forget himself in a *señorita's* arms as he was in Miss Radcliff's presence.

'It'll be the talk of the countryside for months. I might even be called to London by the Prince for a command performance.' He sat down in the chair beside hers, kicking aside a bent tin crown to make room for his feet.

'They'll fill newspaper columns with details of your stunning performance.' She shifted a touch on her chair, her back straightening as she tried to place some distance between them, reminding him of their potential audience.

'Will you be able to tolerate me when I'm famous?' he asked as she opened the book to the play and began to flip through the pages. At the turn of each one, she licked her fingers, her tongue flicking out to sweep the delicate tips and send a hard chill racing up his spine.

'I'll remind you of where you got your start.' She ran her finger down the page to the place with his part and he envied the paper. Her fingers were long, ending in small, rounded nails he wished he could feel along the arch of his back.

'Good, I don't want to get a big head.' Part of him was already straining because of her nearness. He shouldn't be here beside her, especially with Alma and Edward watching from across the room. He glanced at the other guests, wondering if they were scrutinising his time with Miss Radcliff, but they were too involved in the rehearsal to notice their surroundings.

'Go ahead and say your first line,' Miss Radcliff urged with a seriousness he imagined she employed in the schoolroom.

'I'm afraid I haven't learned them yet.' Instead of taking the book, he leaned in close to peer at the page, distracted by the curve of her breasts beneath the muslin and the flat fall of her stomach to where it led to thighs perched tight together against the chair seat. The heat from her cheek radiated off his and the scent of soap teased him like a bell sounding through a fog. He jerked back upright, the nearness too dangerous. 'As you can see, I have more than three lines.'

'How very fortunate for you and your admirer.' Miss Radcliff nodded to Miss Selton who approached them with quick, commanding steps.

'Major Preston, your character is on now and we have no one to be the nymph. Miss Radcliff, would you mind playing the part?'

'She's too busy for this,' Miss Huntford scoffed and Luke imagined it was Miss Selton taking over the running of things more than her invitation to Miss Radcliff which tweaked their hostess's nose.

'Nonsense, since your sisters are here we might as well employ her.' Miss Selton brushed off Miss Huntford with a flick of her dark-haired head. 'Miss Radcliff, it's only a few lines, say you'll do it.'

Aware of everyone watching her, especially Miss Huntford, she clutched the open book to her chest and pressed back against her chair. 'I don't think I should.'

'You must, otherwise the play will be ruined.' Luke took Miss Radcliff by the elbow and ushered her up on to the stage before Miss Huntford could open her mouth to protest. Her arm was soft beneath his grip and he slid his thumb over the smooth material to trace the curve of it. Her perfect lips parted with her surprise and he let go of her, just as startled as her by the intimacy passing between them.

'You stand here.' Miss Selton hurried forward to guide Miss Radcliff to her place on the stage.

Luke followed, trying not to notice the sway of Miss Radcliff's hips beneath her dress. What the hell had come over him? If he didn't regain control, he'd embarrass himself, and quite possibly her, in front of everyone.

Miss Selton tilted the book away from Miss Radcliff's chest and pointed to her lines. 'When he approaches, you say this. I know you aren't used to attention, but I'm sure you'll manage.'

She patted Miss Radcliff condescendingly on the arm before retaking her place. Miss Radcliff trilled her fingers on the edge of the book and Luke could almost hear the witty response coming to her lovely lips, but she pressed them closed, refusing to give voice to it. He wished he could hear it. It would be one of the most enjoyable parts of this morning. Instead, he resigned himself to listening to her deliver her lines in a clear, melodious voice before he answered with his.

When they were finished, Miss Huntford and Mr Winborn launched into their very lengthy scene which left Luke and Miss Radcliff alone together upstage waiting for their next cue. Not even Mr Selton took any notice of them as he stood on stage, his lips moving as he silently reviewed his lines.

'You shouldn't have encouraged my participation,' Miss Radcliff whispered, nodding across the room to where the twins were whacking one other with wooden swords in a manner no one would call playful. 'I have other duties to attend to.'

'I'm sure your work is the epitome of excitement and fulfilment.'

'Yes, every day is one of pure rapture and joy,' she offered wryly.

'Who was your letter from?' It was none of his business, but he wanted to know what had upset her.

She flicked the top edge of the book and he thought she wouldn't answer, determined to remain distant from him. At last she did. 'My friend, Rachel.'

'Is all not well with her? You seemed troubled.'

He'd noticed. Everything inside Joanna told her to stop sharing confidences with him. When he'd taken her arm, there'd been no mistaking the slide of his thumb as an innocent slip. The shock it had sent through her was a warning to not allow his kindness to make her forget herself, but she ignored it. Luke's concern melted her reserve and speaking with him was like speaking to Rachel, Isabel or Grace. There was no one else here who wanted to listen and she was tired of being alone.

'All is well with Rachel. She's caring for the children of Sheikh Malik of Huria.' She took the letter from her pocket and opened it. 'Her position appears to be a good one.'

'Unlike yours,' he finished for her, giving voice to a sentiment she feared to utter out loud in this company.

She glanced down at the letter in her hand, her friend's words too brief.

Dearest Joanna,

I never appreciated the rain and abundance of green in England until I arrived in Huria. The endless sea of sand turns everything here different shades of orange. Then the desert ends right where the verdant oasis begins. Sheikh Malik's palace sits in the middle of this paradise surrounded by plants so rich in fragrance they rival one of my recipes.

The people of Huria are accustomed to the harshness of the desert, but I haven't adjusted to it or quite settled in with the Sheikh. While everyone here has welcomed me without reservation, he is more of an enigma than how people can live in this hot and desolate land. His wife's death has left him shaken and his children grieve for their mother. I do my best to help him and to comfort his children. They are the sweetest ones you can imagine.

> *I hope you are finding the same contentment*
> *with the Huntfords.*
> *Your devoted friend,*
> *Rachel*

'Her description of Huria makes Hertfordshire seem dreary by comparison.' And Joanna's employment even more contemptible than before.

'Huntford Place is dreary. The decrepit staff doesn't add to its charm.'

Gruger shuffled by, pretending not to hear Edward asking for some refreshments to be brought to the ballroom. Joanna bit her tongue to keep from laughing out loud. She eyed Frances, wishing she knew the play better and how much more time she had with Major Preston before the scene ended and she must leave him.

'I envy Rachel, especially the warm climate. I've never been further than the seaside in Sandhills in Hampshire.' She raised her head to face Major Preston, refusing to give in to the melancholy threatening to steal over her. 'The sea there was so beautiful, especially how the waves curled over one another. Grace, Isabel and I went there with Rachel's parents. They assured Madame Dubois they'd chaperon us. They had the best intentions, but they were too wrapped up in each other to see much of the world around them, even us. We woke up one morning to discover they'd decided to go on to Brighton since they thought Sandhills was too dull. They left us with a note explaining their departure and a few pounds. We were forced to find our own way home and we did. We purchased outdoor seats on the last carriage to Salisbury and hung on all day, shivering in the rain. It was the grandest adventure I've ever had.'

'So far.' He tilted his head towards her, the question of something between them, friendship or possibly more, heavy in his piercing eyes. This wasn't the licentious interest Mr Selton had thrown at her this morning in the hallway, but something more intense and exhilarating. It reached into the lonely place inside her and pushed it back like a lit candle does the dark. It was everything she'd ever wanted to see in a gentleman's eyes and she couldn't have it because of his rank and hers.

The thrill inside her settled as she shifted away from him, but she kept her head up, refusing to allow sorrow or regret to ruin their time together. 'You're right. I don't know where my duties might take me. It could be Huria, or Austria or even the London stage after this performance.'

'You must invite all your friends to see your first performance, including me. We are friends, aren't we?'

She gripped the book tight. She should stop this flirting and rebuff him, make it clear to him there could be nothing between them, but she couldn't. He'd protected her at the ball, perhaps he could find a way to secure her continued employment if Frances or one of the other girls decided to make trouble for her. It was a great deal to ask of him and she wouldn't, at least not until she needed to. 'Of course we are and you'll be the first to receive an invitation.'

Beyond the stage, the din of the twins' wooden swords hitting the tin shields began to echo through the room.

'Thank you, Miss Radcliff, we no longer need you.' Miss Selton waved her off the stage, wincing with each ringing blow of wood against tin. She wasn't the only one irritated by the girls. Near the windows, Miss Bell pressed her fingertips to her temples at the noise. 'Be sure to memorise your lines.'

Joanna reluctantly handed Major Preston the book, avoiding his touch. Too many people were watching in their eagerness to see her silence the children. She hopped off the stage and crossed the long room, the gulf between her and the rest of the young ladies widening with each step. At Madame Dubois's, she and the other pupils, despite their varied backgrounds, had all been the same, each one preparing for their future duties. Here, the difference between her and the other women was as stark as the line of dust dividing where the maids had cleaned the floor and where they had not. Joanna wasn't like them in any way as they made clear by frowning at her for allowing the children to run wild and interrupt their folly. If they knew she harboured any kind of affinity for Major Preston, and he for her, their disapproving looks would turn into hate of the nastiest kind.

With some difficulty, Joanna wrested the swords from the twins and ushered them to the door, eager to be free of the silent rebukes and the source of her warring feelings. Catherine argued against leaving until a curt insult from Frances sent her all but running away in tears. With an exhausted sigh, Joanna led the twins, who giggled at their elder sister's embarrassment, out of the room, determined to find Catherine and ease her hurt. With the girls demanding her full attention, there was no time to think of herself or what had passed between her and Major Preston. She was glad. She was tired of being reminded of everything she didn't and couldn't have.

Luke stepped off the stage, watching Miss Radcliff as she led her wayward charges out of the room, unable to spare even one last glance at him. He felt more than heard Edward come up beside him.

'You and the governess had a great deal to talk about while you were on stage.'

Luke turned to face his brother, trying to remain civil. 'She helped me in the woods after you nearly ran her down yesterday. I was thanking her for her kindness.'

'I didn't try to run her down. She stepped in front of me, but of course you'd accuse me of being heartless.'

The reminder to not feed their constant conflict showed itself in Edward's stricken expression. It hadn't always been like this. They'd liked one another well enough as boys playing in the woods behind Pensum Manor. Then Edward had gone off to school, the scion of the family, and everything had changed. 'Of course that's not what I meant.'

Edward shifted on his feet, the argument stunned out of him by Luke's near apology. It was the first small victory Luke had enjoyed in his campaign to end the conflict with his brother and even he wasn't sure how to react.

'These came for you,' the butler interrupted, tossing two letters at Luke before shuffling out of the room as quietly as he'd shuffled in.

Luke examined them. One was from Reginald, the

other from Helmsworth Manor. He opened up the one with the Marquis's seal. It was succinct and disheartening. 'Damn.'

'News from the Army?' Edward asked with, if Luke wasn't mistaken, concern. It didn't seem possible and yet it did. His civility with Edward had garnered him the same consideration from his brother. Perhaps the conflict between them could at last be set aside.

'No. Lord Helmsworth. He's denied my request for a meeting.' He stuffed the letters in his pocket. 'I can't discuss the issue with him if he won't even see me.'

'Good, maybe you'll finally stop this fool's errand and take finding a wife seriously.'

Luke levelled a finger at Edward, their truce short-lived. 'I did what you and Father wanted. I gave up all my accomplishments to come home. It doesn't mean I have to strut about like some prized bull every moment I'm here.'

'Bull-headed is more like it. It's hard to find a wife when the only woman you're talking to is the governess. Don't get distracted, Luke, by either a pretty face or Lord Helmsworth.'

Luke stiffened. He detested being reminded of his mission like some new recruit, especially since Edward was right. Miss Radcliff was distracting him like the seized winery with a cellar full of Madeira had once distracted his battalion. If he hadn't rallied them, they would've lost the offensive. If he didn't free himself of this infatuation, he and his family would lose the battle they'd been fighting since his grandfather's time, the one he'd been excluded from when he was younger because he wasn't the heir. 'I won't be made inconsequential again because I'm not you.'

'You think I'm so privileged, but I'm not.' Edward shifted closer and dropped his voice, the tone of it hard. 'Once you find a wife and produce an heir, you'll be free to do whatever you wish. It's an opportunity I've never had.'

Edward marched to where Alma sat looking wan in the deep chair next to the sputtering fire. Edward paced in front of her, railing about Luke.

Luke exited the room, disgusted with Edward, the situation and himself. He'd vowed not to fight with Edward and he'd broken it. He'd also vowed to end the dispute with Lord Helmsworth and by heaven he would. He left the house and followed the long path to the stables. Lord Helmsworth couldn't avoid Luke if Luke appeared on his doorstep.

He reached the stables and called to the groom to prepare his horse. He paced over the packed dirt of the paddock as the groom, as slow as every other Huntford servant, saddled Duke. His determination to ride to Helmsworth Manor faded with each dusty step. Luke's unwelcome appearance would irritate the man further and Luke couldn't hope to speak rationally to him while his insides were twisted like the blown-out end of a cannon. He'd ride instead, and think about the matter, plan and strategise like he used to in Spain instead of rushing in foolhardily and hoping he didn't get hit with a musket ball.

At last the groom finished and Luke stepped into the saddle and kicked Duke into a gallop. He should go home and send a servant back for his things, leave this waste of a party and turn his focus to dealing with

Lord Helmsworth until the London Season saw him back in the middle of the marriage mart. There was no point staying on, there wasn't one woman here worth her salt except Miss Radcliff. The thought of leaving her hit him as squarely in the chest as having given up his commission.

The memory of Miss Radcliff heavy across his thighs, her curving ear close to his lips as they'd raced through the woods, was as stinging as the cold air against his face. Duke's stride was lighter, quicker without her, but Luke wanted her here as much as he wanted to be back in Spain. He bent over Duke's neck and urged him into a run, trying to outrace both desires.

He rode for some time, working to clear his mind until the iron gate marking the road to Pensum Manor came into view. Luke tugged on the reins, slowing Duke into a trot. As they passed beneath the metal arch, fields of wheat spread out on the rolling hills on either side of him. The wind whipped across them, bending each stalk in unison like a contingent of men dropping into firing formation. For all its beauty, the wide swathes of desolate earth along the edges of the harvest and the patches of barren ground where the seeds had refused to grow were evident. This harvest would be no more successful than the last one, compounding their problems, the ones they were looking to Luke to solve.

Pensum Manor and the heavy responsibility of it pressed on him. Growing up, he'd never had to worry about it while it had dominated and dictated the lives of his father, grandfather and his brother. Now, it had ensnared him, commanding who he could and could not speak with or court.

He didn't want to admit it, not even to himself, but Edward was right. If he allowed the single woman he couldn't have to distract him from his duty and hers, his family would suffer and she might, too. He was being reckless in his choices simply to be near her and it was wrong and it must stop. It would help neither of them to continue on.

He turned Duke back towards Huntford Place. He despised allowing the manor, the lineage from which he'd once been excluded, to command him like this, but he couldn't walk away. Like sending men under his command into battle and possibly death to achieve an objective, he must sacrifice his friendship with Miss Radcliff, as well as his own wants for his family. She wasn't here to flirt with him, but to make her school proud and he was stopping her from achieving her goal as much as she was interfering with his. He was a heel to withdraw his friendship after she'd accepted it and it burned to imagine the pain it might cause her, but he must. There could be nothing between them. He would do his duty by his family, marry and produce an heir. Afterwards, he'd be his own man, one way or another.

Joanna pushed open the door to the Huntford Place library and peered inside. She wanted to make sure Frances and Mr Winborn weren't completing what Frances had failed to finish with Lieutenant Foreman. Seeing no one, Joanna crossed the dark room to the bookcase on the far wall to peruse the offerings. The twins were with their nurse and Catherine had joined the other ladies for a lesson with the dancing master, leaving Joanna with a free hour to find a book on Huria.

She frowned as she examined the available selection. There was no rhyme or reason to their placement with geography next to poetry and history. Joanna sighed. It would take her the better part of her free time to find anything in this mess.

She finished examining the books on the bottom shelves and climbed the narrow rail ladder to view those on the higher ones. She was at the top, shaking her head at the jumble of subjects, when the door behind her opened. She tensed, expecting Sir Rodger to appear and claim her free time with another errand. It wasn't him, but Major Preston.

A smile split the tense line of his lips at the sight of her, then it hardened around the corners. 'I'm sorry, I didn't mean to disturb you.'

'Please, come in, I have no special claim to this room.' She climbed down off the ladder, trying her best to be prim and proper, but her weak knees and fluttering stomach made it difficult. All she could imagine was him pushing her up against the panelling, lifting her skirt and doing to her the things Lieutenant Foreman had done to Frances.

Her daydream ended when she faced him. He stood like an officer, aloof and formal in a way she hadn't seen in him before. It reminded her of when Madame had summoned her to her private sitting room to say she'd found Joanna a position. She'd been kind about it, but it had been clear the subtle separating of Joanna from her school life had begun. Perhaps Major Preston had proposed to a lady and he was now going to end their brief friendship. She should be glad, for it removed the threat of his presence to her good sense, but she wasn't.

'I'm trying to find a book on Huria,' she rushed, attempting to chase away her encroaching fear and recapture some of the rapport they'd enjoyed during their previous encounters.

'I'm surprised Sir Rodger allows you in here. When I asked if I could borrow a book, he almost made me give him a deposit in case I should damage one.' The flash of humour eased the lines at the corners of his eyes, heartening her.

'Oh, he was quite adamant I read. He said it would improve upon the limited education I must have received at Madame Dubois's.' She rolled her eyes at the memory of Sir Rodger's insulting directive. 'I should have told him how superior my education truly was, but he wouldn't have believed me any more than he would his role in his daughters' behaviour.'

'He sounds like some of the commanding officers I served under. No matter how much it was to their benefit, they didn't want to hear the truth.'

'Who does?'

'No one. Not even me.' He clasped his hands behind his back and faced her with a seriousness to make her heart race, not with anticipation, but with fear. 'My family has never asked anything of me except one thing, to come home and produce an heir. It seems so simple and yet every day I fight it, especially when I read about the battles in Spain in the papers coming up from London. If I were to be killed over there, my family line would die out and everything they've held dear for centuries would be lost.'

He spoke with the rigidity of a teacher explaining a misunderstood lesson, except regret made his words halting and softened the intensity of his eyes. Madame Dubois had fixed on her the same way the morning when Joanna had turned five and the headmistress had felt she was old enough to understand the circumstances of her arrival at the school. Despite Madame's attempt to make Joanna see how wanted she was by her and the teachers, there'd been no concealing how unwanted she'd been by her parents. Major Preston was about to make it clear to her how far apart they were and how they should remain so. 'I must find a wife, surrender my wants for my family's, which is why…'

'Our friendship is a mistake,' she finished for him, flinching from listening to him say the words aloud. He was being practical and realistic and she must do the same. She brushed a spiderweb from the corner of one ladder step. She didn't want to be practical, but hold on to the hope his friendship had offered, the brief belief someone might come to love her, even while he was pulling it away.

'Not a mistake, only inappropriate.' He cleared his throat as if reluctant to continue. She prayed he would stop and recant his painful declaration, but he didn't. 'You were correct the other night. The difference in our positions makes almost anything, even the most innocent relationship, between us impossible.'

She wrapped one hand around the ladder frame and gripped it tightly. Each of his words pelted her like the rain had during the ride from Sandhills. Except this time there were no friends to brave the onslaught with her or to bolster her flagging confidence in herself and her value to anyone.

'I apologise for pressing you on the matter. I should have known better,' he added. At least he had the decency to recognise and admit his mistake.

She squared her shoulders and faced him with all the calm required of their situation. She might not be a titled woman, but she could conduct herself with all the poise and dignity of a duchess, even while she was crumbling inside. 'We were silly to be so open with one another, but I appreciate your honesty in this and everything else.'

He bowed, then turned and cracked open the door and checked the hall to ensure it was clear. It was and he slipped out, pausing beyond the threshold for one last look at her. It was more than misgiving or apology colouring his eyes, but a longing which called to her from across the quiet room. He didn't want this parting any more than she did and he was waiting for her to summon him back, to fight for him to change his mind. She felt it as keenly as she did his remorse. It would only take a word or two to keep him and whatever had been building between them here. She opened her mouth to speak and he leaned forward, ready to return, but she said nothing. She couldn't. Everything he'd stated was true and nothing could change it, not his wants or hers. He must leave and she must let him go.

With no reply to his silent enquiry, he backed into the hall and drew the door closed behind him. When the latch clicked shut, Joanna sank down to the floor at the foot of the ladder. The cold wood cut through her thin dress, but it was nothing compared to the loneliness swathing her. A short time ago, she'd believed two people here were concerned about her, but she'd been wrong. She appreciated Major Preston's honesty, and his safeguarding her reputation by being cautious when he'd left, but it didn't matter. He could check a thousand hallways and it wouldn't change the reason why he'd walked away and why she'd let him go. She was nobody.

Not to my friends. But they were hundreds of miles away. Feminine laughter echoed through the room from somewhere outside, the joyful kind she, Rachel, Grace and Isabel had shared so many times in the quiet world of Madame Dubois's. Never again would Joanna enjoy the acceptance of people who didn't judge her because of who she was, or, more importantly, who she wasn't thanks to her parents.

The selfish fools. She pressed her fists against her temples as anger filled her. How could they have done it? How could they have given her up? If they hadn't, things between her and Major Preston might be different.

She lowered her hands and took a deep breath, willing herself to calm. It wasn't fair to blame them. She had no idea what situation had driven them to leave her at the school. Maybe her mother had been like Grace, too impetuous for her own good and forced to surrender Joanna to keep them both from being cast into the streets to starve to death or worse. She could no more blame Grace for the choice she'd made in giving up her daughter than she could Major Preston for ending their burgeoning friendship. There was little she could offer him which would ease the burdens and responsibilities he now bore.

Out in the hallway, the large clock rang with the quarter-hour. In a short while, her responsibilities would once again consume her. She should get up and prepare to face them, but she couldn't rise. She wanted to avoid reality for a touch longer.

'You're not enjoying the play?' Miss Selton asked, her thin fichu doing little to hide the too-high curve of her breast. She was beautiful, and rich, but neither were enough for Luke to overlook her lack of character.

'I received a letter with some news about my regiment being involved in an offensive. It's difficult to concentrate on this when I'm worried about them.' And the damage he'd done to Miss Radcliff. She'd been brave in the face of his rejection, struggling to conceal the pain he'd caused, but she hadn't. He'd caught it in her white knuckles as she'd gripped the ladder and in the stiffness of her bearing as she'd faced him.

I had no choice. Everything he'd said about dying in Spain and the end of his family line was true.

'You needn't worry about your men. I'm sure they're fine.' Miss Selton flicked her hand in dismissal as if he'd complained about the overcooked pheasant at last night's dinner. Miss Radcliff wouldn't have been so unfeeling, yet he'd pushed her away because she wasn't the same rank as Miss Selton. He despised himself for what he'd done. He was no better than the commanders who allowed men to die under incapable officers instead of promoting a more worthy and humble candidate. 'Shall we practise your scene together? I can read the part of the nymph since Miss Radcliff isn't here.'

She leaned forward, peering up at him like a simpleton as she batted her eyelashes at him.

'No, I've had enough for today.' He left her, done trying to be anything more than annoyed at this empty-headed chit. Edward rose, hurrying to intercept him, but Luke levelled a halting hand at him. 'Don't.'

He'd allowed Edward to pressure him into giving up his friendship with Miss Radcliff, he wouldn't allow him to force him to stay in this room. He paused in the hallway outside the ballroom, at a loss for what to do and hating this indecision. He'd never been like this in the Army. Everything there had been clear and concise. He'd make his decisions and not second-guess them no matter what the outcome. Here, he was confounded at every turn by duty, family and rank. No wonder some of the seasoned officers turned to drinking and gambling when they came home. At times, it seemed like no other way to relieve the boredom and frustration. Give him a gruelling march any day over this endless irrelevance.

'You've offered him your favours. Why not share them with me?' Mr Selton's low voice slid down the long hallway from near the library.

Luke paused, the hairs on the back of his neck rising the way they used to whenever the forest in Spain grew too still, signalling the enemy was near. Miss Huntford and Mr Selton hadn't been in the ballroom rehearsing. What was the chit up to now? The answering female voice made his blood boil.

'I've given no one my favours and I certainly won't give them to you, now let me pass.'

Miss Radcliff.

Luke marched down the hall and turned the corner. Mr Selton stood with his back to Luke, blocking Miss Radcliff's way.

'Let me by.' She tried to step around him but he shot out his arm and slapped his hand against the wall to stop her from leaving.

'There's no reason for you to be rude to me.'

'If a lady asks you to leave her be, then I suggest you do it,' Luke thundered as he came up hard on the man.

Miss Radcliff sagged against the panelling in relief.

'She's not a lady,' Mr Selton snorted, less enamoured by Luke's appearance. 'And a little fun is what governesses, especially ones as pretty as Miss Radcliff, are practically made for.'

Luke pulled back his arm and slammed his fist into Mr Selton's lecherous face. The man staggered back, hitting the wall before he dropped to his knees.

'You hit me,' Mr Selton wailed, clutching his mouth. 'Over a governess.'

'I hit you because you aren't a gentleman.' Luke stood over him, hands clenched, hoping Mr Selton gave him another reason to strike him. The slime deserved it.

Mr Selton pierced him with a slicing look. 'How dare you! I'm a baron's son, and I'll be a baron some day. You're nothing more than a dirty soldier. Who are you to strike me or tell me what to do?'

Luke's foot twitched with the urge to kick him, but he didn't want to scuff his boots. Mr Selton was everything he hated about the aristocracy, the type of man who'd lorded his supposed superiority over him at Eton while unable to take one prize or win one sporting match against him. He was the worthless officer who'd sneered down his aquiline nose at soldiers as he sent them off to die in a futile offensive meant to impress his commanders.

Luke bent down, hands on his knees, bringing his face so close to Mr Selton's he could see the small veins along the sides of his nose. 'If you're insulted, then call me out, show me how superior you think you are. Remember, I've had a lot of practice shooting at men trying to kill me. I doubt I'll miss your big head.'

Mr Selton's bravado slackened as Luke straightened.

Mr Selton picked himself off the floor, staggering against the wall before he steadied himself on his feet. He wiped his mouth with the back of his hand and winced at the streak of blood left there by his split lip. 'There's no need for it.'

Luke stared down at him, a good head taller than the future Baron. 'Then I suggest you depart at once. I wouldn't want your superior rank and honour impugned by having to explain to everyone how you received your bruise from a dirty soldier so obviously beneath you.'

Mr Selton tugged a handkerchief from his pocket and pressed it to his broken lip. He hesitated and Luke wondered if he'd change his mind and meet Luke's challenge, but he doubted it. The man was a coward and he proved it by rushing off down the hall, calling for Gruger and announcing his immediate departure.

Luke turned to Miss Radcliff. She stood, one hand on her chest, confusion as much as surprise swirling in her eyes. He shifted close to her, aching to take her in his arms and run his hand along the arch of her back to smooth her shock. 'Are you all right?'

'Yes.' The whispered word brushed his neck above his cravat. He opened and closed his fingers, wanting to draw her into his arms and let her quick breaths subside against his chest as she leaned against him in comfort. Neither of them closed the small distance separating them. 'Once again you've saved me. Soon I'll owe you so much for your help, I'll have to single-handedly extinguish a house fire to return the favour.'

Her limp smile punctuated her attempt at humour and Luke felt less like a hero and more like a heel.

'About our discussion earlier,' he stammered, warring with the urge to hold her close and the one to push her away. He could almost hear Captain Crowther's advice to forget everyone and do what he damn well pleased.

She laid a silencing finger on his lips and he almost groaned as her warm skin met his. It hurt to hold back from taking her hand and pressing his lips to her palm, but her gentle touch was a warning, not an invitation. 'There's no need to explain. I understand.'

'You don't.' He shifted closer, his fingertips brushing her skirt as she withdrew her hand.

She stared up at him, head back, lips parted, her desire as strong as his. The conflict ripping at him tore at her, too. It was in the hitch in her breathing, the stiffness of her shoulders and the delicate craving for him in her eyes. If there wasn't so much standing between them, he would claim her lips, and her, but he wouldn't cross the line he'd just pulled Mr Selton away from. 'If things were different…'

'But they aren't.' She darted around him, her skirt whispering against her legs as she fled down the hall, back to her life, leaving him to his.

The faint scent of dust and damp quickly overcame the fresh lavender scent of her. Luke leaned against the wall and tilted his head against the unpolished panelling. This wasn't the first time he'd stepped in to protect a woman from a man's unwanted advances, but it was the most personal. Miss Radcliff was alone in the world, made more so by his rejection of her friendship. It made her vulnerable to men like Mr Selton. Luke might have been here to protect her this time, but he wouldn't be in the future. She wasn't his to protect and she couldn't be. Neither his father nor his brother would sanction a match with a penniless girl of questionable birth. It didn't mean he had to like it. For the first time ever he cursed his honour and sense of duty. It was strangling him, but he wouldn't set it aside. Without the accomplishment of his Army career, honour and duty were all he had left.

Chapter Seven

The yapping and howling of the hunting dogs and the calls of the trainers outside on the drive filled the schoolroom. The guests were gathered downstairs in the entrance hall to escape the misty day, drinking brandy and preparing to ride out. The ladies would accompany them, enjoying the fresh autumn air as they galloped with the men over the rolling hills of the Huntford estate.

Joanna hadn't been downstairs since the incident in the hallway yesterday afternoon. It wasn't Mr Selton she feared. He'd departed soon after leaving them, causing his sister to bitterly complain about it ruining her play. It was Major Preston Joanna didn't want to see.

When she'd laid her finger on his lips, the passion which had sparked between them had stolen the air from the hallway and nearly carried off her resolve to keep her distance. She shouldn't have touched him, but she didn't want to hear his words, not when they contradicted everything in his eyes. She craved him as much as he did her and she could have rested her hands on his shoulders, risen up on her toes and kissed him, but she'd held back. His words in the library had been too fresh, the truth of his situation and hers too raw to allow either of them to weaken. His family's hopes for a future rested on him and she wouldn't be the one to wreck their expectations. If she did, they'd accuse her of ruining him in a quest to raise herself and their criticism would drive a wedge between him and them. He'd been willing to put aside their friendship for his family. He would deny his heart for them, too, and it was to her peril to ignore this.

'I don't want to study French. I want to go downstairs and see the guests getting ready for the hunt,' Catherine whined. The twins joined in the chorus of complaints about being kept upstairs while everyone gathered below.

Joanna was about to change the subject, when she remembered Vicar Carlson's words. If the girls wanted a reward, then she'd make sure they got it, but only if they did their work. 'If you complete your lessons, we might have time to sneak down to the landing and watch the riders before they leave.'

Instead of fighting her as they usually did, they set to work. Joanna might not want to venture down from the third floor, but it wasn't fair to keep the girls locked up here because of her fears. Besides, with so many people about, she and Major Preston weren't likely to be alone together. She'd make sure they weren't.

In a few minutes, the girls' work was complete and they followed Joanna down the stairs to the first-floor landing overlooking the entrance hall. Joanna held tight to the banister as she watched the women in their dark riding habits stand with the men in their breeches and coats. They didn't interest her as much as the possibility of seeing Major Preston, but he wasn't here. Perhaps he hadn't come down yet. Every sense became aware of the hallway behind her as she wondered if he would appear there before continuing down. She hoped he didn't. She couldn't trust herself to be so close to him.

With a surly sneer, Gruger oversaw the footmen moving among the mingling guests carrying silver trays of hot brandy to fortify the riders against the bracing weather. Sir Rodger's black hunting dog sat beside his master, who chatted with the men in their tweeds and boots. The ladies in their long habits were spattered among the men, their voices filled with their anticipation for the coming ride. The clouds which had hung over Huntford Place all morning began to clear and thick shafts of sunlight dropped in through the windows over the front doors, much to everyone's delight.

'I want to go all the way down,' Catherine whispered, shifting from foot to foot at the excitement just out of her reach.

'Your father said you're not allowed to, but if you're good here, I'll talk to your mother about joining in charades after dinner.' She hoped she refused the request. It would keep Joanna out of the sitting room and away from Major Preston.

Catherine considered the choice and decided going along was better than fighting Joanna and risking her father's reprimand. Even the twins were behaving as they knelt at the balustrade to watch the guests. Whether or not their new obedience would last, or be enough to secure Joanna's position here, she wasn't certain, but she was happy for the change, no matter how small. It restored the confidence shaken out of her by Sir Rodger's warning and Major Preston's rejection.

Minutes passed and Major Preston still didn't appear among the guests. His family wasn't present either and she wondered if the incident with Mr Selton had driven them from the house. If it had, it was for the best. She wouldn't be at ease until he was gone, then he would fade in potency like the overly spiced biscuits Rachel had once baked.

The tinny notes of the hunter's horn filled the entrance hall. Guests filed out of the house, the barks of Sir Rodger's dog mixing with the yipping of the hunters made louder by a footman holding open the front door. The excited chatter of the guests hurrying to their mounts joined the eagerness of the hounds for the hunt. Joanna wished she could share in the thrill of riding out. It would give her something more to look forward to than the dreary passing of one same day into the next.

As the entrance hall grew quiet, the footmen began to collect the drink glasses. More than one of them finished the contents before they carried them out on their trays. Gruger trailed behind them, mumbling his usual abuses. Behind her, the girls rushed to the landing window overlooking the front drive to watch the riders preparing to set off.

Not seeing Major Preston, and not wanting to keep torturing herself with what she couldn't have, Joanna moved to gather up the girls. Then Major Preston's voice caught her notice and made her halt.

'It amazes me how much you want me to stay now that I'm of some use to you. You were all too eager to pack me off when you purchased my commission,' Major Preston accused, following his father who stormed out of the sitting room. 'I'm surprised you spent what you did to make me a lieutenant.'

Lord Ingham whirled on his son, ready to snap back before he seemed to think better of it. He settled his shoulders, his words measured and calm. 'I didn't buy you a posting as a lieutenant to get rid of you! I did it because I wanted you to make something of yourself and you did. I'm proud of you for doing it.'

The tightness along Major Preston's jaw eased at his father's response, but it didn't settle the tension in each of his arms as he dug his fists into his hips. 'Then you asked me to give it all up.'

'I asked no more of you than my father asked of me when my elder brother died.' His father laid a steadying hand on his son's shoulder. 'I realise the sacrifices you've made on behalf of the family.'

Major Preston glanced past his father, up the stairs to where Joanna stood. 'I'm not sure you do.'

She held her breath, afraid to move and make Lord Ingham aware of her. Like every other guest except Major Preston, he'd failed to notice her.

'I do because I made the same one when I became the heir and had to sell my commission. Trust me, a year from now when you're settled with a wife and, God willing, a son, you'll feel very differently than you do now. However, I can see it won't happen with any of the ladies here, which is fine.' Lord Ingham let go of his son and tugged on his gloves. 'There are more lucrative women in London anyway.'

Lord Ingham strolled out the door, unaware of his son's lingering frustration as he stood in the centre of the entrance hall staring at Joanna. The conflict hardening the lines at the corners of his eyes matched the one in her heart. He lowered his hands to his sides and she dropped down a stair, ready to go to him and ease the pain torturing them both. Despite having silenced him yesterday, if he summoned her to him now, she would answer it. The sound of the barking dogs and chatting guests from outside faded as they continued to regard one another. She shouldn't want this, but she did. In the smoothing of his face as he viewed her, she knew he did, too.

Then, with a small frown, he nodded and strode out the door to join the others.

Joanna grasped the rough handrail, bracing herself against the weakness and relief filling her. Thank goodness he hadn't motioned to her and she hadn't been foolish enough to fly down to him and throw everything away on the promise of a mere conversation. It wasn't her place to be his confidante, especially not with the girls chatting at the window behind her. Anna and Ava would've run through the house yelling about Joanna and Luke at the top of their lungs if Joanna had been so rash.

'Miss Radcliff.' Mrs Winston, the nurse, came up behind Joanna and the girls. The nurse's crisp voice brought Joanna back to her duties and responsibilities. They did not lie with Major Preston. 'It's time for the twins' walk.'

'Of course, and, Miss Catherine, you have lessons with the drawing master,' Joanna reminded her.

'I hate drawing lessons,' Catherine mumbled as she tromped off down the stairs.

'Miss Radcliff, I almost forgot, this arrived for you.' Mrs Winston removed a letter from her apron and handed it to her.

Joanna took it, thrilled to recognise Isabel's small, neat handwriting decorating the front. Mrs Winston took the twins by the hands and led them to the nursery to collect their coats and sturdy shoes. With the girls occupied, Joanna had two hours to herself.

She ran upstairs to fetch her pelisse from her room, then made for the back garden. She hurried across the weedy gravel path and up the back rise to the Greek temple perched on top. After seeing so many people gathered together, laughing and talking, she needed some words from her friend to remind her she wasn't so alone and to stop her from thinking about Major Preston.

Luke tugged on Duke's reins, forcing the animal to fall behind as the other riders surged forward, fast on the heels of the hounds. This wasn't so much a fox hunt as it was a husband hunt, with the most eligible young ladies circling him like a regiment of Hessians. More than one skilled female rider had tried to isolate him from the herd. He'd outwitted them all, having dodged too many enemy soldiers in battle to let a few Amazons in search of a mate outflank him. After an hour of evasive manoeuvres, he craved the peace of a solitary ride and time to ponder the conversation with his father, and his silent encounter with Miss Radcliff.

He turned Duke around and guided him into the woods to keep from being noticed by any eagle-eyed ladies. The sun warming the moist earth and the tart smell of old leaves and moss reminded him of his time with Miss Radcliff here the other day. When he'd seen her at the top of the stairs this morning, his vow to remain on course and not be distracted by the arch of her hips, the alluring brush of her curls against her ears had almost deserted him. He'd wanted to go to her and not give a damn about anything or anyone else, but his father's words had grounded him, even while he'd struggled to accept them.

He slowed Duke to an amble and the fall of the horse's hooves was muffled by the soft forest ground. His father suggesting he'd adjust to being home was like telling a prisoner he would come to love gaol, yet his father had said something similar the day he'd seen him off to the Army. He'd been right then, as he'd been right about Luke working his way up the ranks. For the first time, Luke wasn't mad at his father for being stingy with money to purchase his commission. He'd had a reason for it, not to foist Luke off on the world with the least amount of expense, but to give him a chance to make something of himself. And he had. The bitter sense of rejection Luke had carried since the day he'd been told of the commission faded. His father had been proud of his accomplishments. He would make him proud again.

If only it didn't mean turning away from Miss Radcliff.

Luke guided Duke out of the forest and back across the field towards the peaked gables of Huntford Place. The sight of Miss Radcliff this morning had added to the disquiet making every small annoyance from the lack of coal in his bedroom fireplace to the tittering of the ladies grate on him. In the hallway yesterday, with Miss Radcliff's finger on his lips, her pulse flickering faintly against his skin, he'd almost taken back everything he'd told her and every promise he'd made to himself and his family. He couldn't disappoint them or lead Miss Radcliff in a merry dance. She didn't deserve to be trifled with.

He manoeuvred the horses around the house to the stables. In the paddock, he dismounted and left Duke with the groom, who was as slow in coming to fetch him as he was leading him inside. Luke considered going to the sitting room and composing another letter to Lord Helmsworth, or even Reginald, and then changed his mind. He couldn't sit still inside with Miss Radcliff somewhere about. He needed peace, not the constant distraction of listening for her voice.

He followed the winding path leading from the stables through the garden too wild to be considered fashionably unkempt. Heavy ivy covered stone statues and the topiaries had escaped their confines to obscure the original animals. The plants here were a great contrast to those in Spain. They'd been tougher there and more woody, their leaves sparser but green against the dry grass and brown earth of the fields. The air had been warmer, too, except in the mountains in winter.

He started up the small hill at the far end of the garden and the Grecian temple set atop it, all the while imagining returning to Spain when the war was over. He longed to see the country through eyes not looking for an enemy or a tactical advantage. In his musings, he wondered what Miss Radcliff would think of the land of Isabelle and Ferdinand with its mix of Catholic and Moorish influence. He didn't doubt she'd embrace the bright colours and varied flavours of Spain. He would show them to her if he could, help her to break out of the bleak existence trapping her as his duties trapped him, except it wasn't his place to do so.

Luke admired the Grecian temple as he approached it. The stone building with the columned veranda and domed roof appeared out of place so close to a Stuart-era house. In the shadow of the dome, statues filled tall niches set at even intervals. As he grew closer, one of the statues on the far right stepped out of the shadows, revealing itself to be Miss Radcliff.

Instead of waiting for him, she slipped around the back of the building and out of sight.

'Miss Radcliff, wait.' He hurried after her, ignoring the instinct telling him to walk away. He climbed the stairs and rounded the grey stone to see her standing at the far edge, her back to him and a letter dangling in one gloved hand. 'Is everything all right?'

'Yes, I'm quite well.' It was clear the moment she turned that she wasn't. Her pretty lips were drawn thin and her eyes were hard with her troubles. 'I often come here to think when the girls are taking other lessons or with their nurse.'

'But that's not why you're here today, is it?' He dragged his fingers over the rough wall as he approached her, noting how her distress intensified the blue of her eyes.

'Not today.'

'Bad news?' He motioned to the paper.

'No, not at all.' She raised the letter and it fluttered in the breeze. 'It's from my friend, Isabel. She's married Viscount Langford's son.'

Apparently, Luke wasn't the only son of a titled gentleman enamoured with a governess. 'You don't approve of him?'

'I don't even know him. She barely knows him.' She paced back and forth across the unpolished stone. The plain, brown pelisse hanging shapeless over her curves fluttered with each stiff step. 'There's almost nothing in her letter saying why she married him, except that she had to and he hasn't turned out to be the husband she imagined, but she doesn't say how. What if he's a monster?'

'Or better than she expected.' Given what Luke knew of William Balfour and his reputation, Miss Radcliff's worries weren't unfounded, but he said nothing. He didn't want to add to her distress. If Mr Balfour was at last settling down, then maybe he'd changed. He wouldn't be the first wild rake tamed by a gentle hand. He leaned against a pillar, far more philosophical than usual. 'That's the thing about chances, you never know how they'll turn out until you take one.'

She crossed her arms beneath her breasts, pulling the pelisse tight to trace the curve of their fullness. 'Don't tell me you're a romantic.'

'Not at all, but I've taken a chance or two in my time.' He dug the regimental badge from his pocket and held it out to her. She opened her palm and he dropped it on the soft cotton of her glove. 'Back in May, at Fuentes de Oñoro, there was a break in the line. My men, alongside the Light Division, were sent to reinforce the right flank. During the fighting, some distance away, I noticed a squad trapped by heavy fire and on the verge of being overrun. I could've wasted time telling my commanding officer, leaving it to him to order men to their aid. Instead, I took a chance and led my squad to cover them. We were outnumbered, but we held the French off until the men and their wounded could retreat, then we crushed the French, helping to secure the line. It earned me a promotion to major.'

She fingered the badge, then handed it back to him. 'Chance seems a very unpredictable way to plan a life.'

'It's a mistake to think you can plan it.' He slipped the badge back in his coat pocket. 'I'd intended to enjoy my major rank for longer than four months. You came here to mould young ladies. I'd say neither of our plans unfolded as we'd expected.'

'No, they didn't.' Her words trailed off with the same disappointment which racked him every time he thought he might never return to his regiment. He raised his hand to take hers, then rested it on a column instead. He couldn't allow his misguided sense of chivalry to make him cross the boundaries which separated them.

'All will be well with your friend.' He hoped so for Miss Radcliff's sake and her friend's.

She folded the letter and shoved it into the pocket of her drab pelisse. 'Isabel is taking a chance and I should wish her the best, and I do, but...'

'You envy her.' They shouldn't be sharing confidences, but he couldn't walk away. She'd helped him in the woods with Edward. It was only right for him to do the same for her.

She nodded, her pale round cheeks colouring with her shame. 'She's going to have everything I've ever wanted, a real family and children. You must think I'm awful for being so petty.'

'No, I don't.' Together, they stood at the edge of the temple and looked out over the woods at the leaves turning brown and orange and red. Her nearness awed him as much as the stunning breadth of the land and the sky above it. He understood the conflict making her sigh with frustration because it was his, too. 'Yesterday, I received a letter from my friend, Captain Crowther, telling me of their victory in a skirmish. I should've written at once to congratulate him, but I didn't. I'm jealous because he's there and I'm not. We wouldn't be human if we weren't petty sometimes.'

'Maybe it's not even her I'm jealous of, but her position. It gave her opportunity.' A flock of crows took off out of the trees. The wind supporting their flight whipped past Joanna and Luke, making the bonnet ribbons beneath her pert chin flutter over her neck and chest. The satin slid across her fine skin as he longed to do with his fingers while his lips smoothed the small furrow between her brows. 'Here, there isn't even a chance for me to take in order to change things.'

'There will be.'

'When?' She turned to him, the demand for an answer sharp in the cool depths of her eyes.

Chance. It was here in front of him, eclipsing everything he might lose with what he stood to gain. He should walk away, stay true to his vow to resist the allure of her rich curls beneath her plain bonnet and dismiss the faint scent of lavender distracting him. He should ignore her wit and intelligence and the craving for her understanding that tugged at him, but he

couldn't. She held something more precious and necessary to him than money, status or even security. It
was peace. 'Now.'

He took her in his arms and pressed his lips to hers.

Joanna fell into his comforting embrace and the
temptation in his kiss. Her heart pounded with the
risk and the thrill of his body as solid as the temple
against hers. She rested her hands on his chest and
his strong pulse beneath her fingertips reminded her
she was young and alive and all her dreams might still
come true. A shiver coursed through her as he traced
her lips with his tongue, his breath one with hers as
he held her close. He tasted like the drink of strong
port she'd sneaked once at a soirée for the school
patrons, rich, sharp and forbidden. She savoured him
as she had the liquor, each illicit taste making her
crave more.

She slid her hands up over the sturdy curve of his
chest, past the white cravat and collar surrounding his
neck. With small circles she traced the smoothness of
the skin before raising her fingers to slide them into
his hair. His grip tightened around her and his arms
crossed behind her back as he rested his hands on her
hips and enveloped her in his embrace. In the circle
of his arms was a belonging she'd never experienced
before, not even at Madame Dubois's. Despite being
hidden away and ignored, he'd seen her for who she
was and he wanted her. It almost made every risk she
was taking with him worth it.

A faint darkness crept in beneath her bliss, like a
mist along the ground at dusk. He had little to lose
with this liaison while she might sacrifice everything

for a fleeting bit of happiness. She clung to it like she did his biceps, his muscles hard beneath her grip, trying to forget reality, duty and consequences. Beyond the strength of his kiss, the tightness of his fingers against her back, nothing else had changed, not his situation or hers.

She withdrew her fingers from his hair and broke from his lips, but not his embrace. He eased his arms from around her waist, but left his hands to linger on the narrowness of it. Every argument against their being together nearly died on her tongue as she held his fierce gaze. The dreams of being with him that she'd entertained in the middle of the night felt more real than anything she'd experienced at Huntford Place. Her heart urged her to embrace whatever was happening between them and perhaps gain everything she'd ever desired.

'Miss Radcliff, are you out here?' Mrs Winston's voice carried over the temple, piercing Joanna's bliss. 'I need your help.'

The twins yelled like devils as they tore through the garden, silencing the birds twittering overhead.

Joanna stared up at Luke, reluctant to let him go and step back into the awfulness of her life, but she had to. She wasn't ready to lose what little she had over a single kiss no matter how marvellous.

'Miss Radcliff?' Mrs Winston's voice grew closer and needier.

Major Preston opened his arms. Joanna slowly backed away and eased around the curve of the temple, reluctant to look away from him until she was forced to turn and face the house. Mrs Winston waddled up the rise, through the high grass, her round face red with the exertion of her walk and having to deal with the Ava and Anne.

'Here I am.' Joanna rushed down the stone steps to meet her.

'Oh, thank heavens.' Mrs Winston sighed, laying a hand on her generous bosom. 'I can't control the twins and you have such a way with them.'

Joanna struggled not to roll her eyes at the unconvincing flattery. The nurse was as useless as the rest of the Huntford servants and Joanna was sure Mrs Winston wanted to gossip with the other maids instead of minding the hellish imps, but she held her tongue. She was afraid to speak too much and reveal in her wavering words the fear settling over her. She'd nearly been caught in an intimate situation with Major Preston and her secret was still in danger of being discovered.

Joanna glanced back at the temple as she wrested a stick from Anne before she could pummel Ava. There was no sign of Luke and she was confident he would remain hidden until it was safe for him to leave. It didn't meant she should dawdle here and risk the twins racing up to the temple and finding him. She took Mrs Winston by the arm and led her back towards the house while urging the twins to come along. Thankfully, the promise of a sweet if they listened resulted in the girls following her and the nurse like obedient ducklings.

With the shadows of Huntford Place coming over her, she was more confused now than when she'd left it to read Isabel's letter. It wasn't her friend's rashness which stunned and concerned her, but her own. She'd taken a chance. Time would tell what it would gain her.

* * *

Luke stayed at the temple until the sun touched the top of the trees. He watched it drop behind the forest and listened as the songs of the birds gave way to quiet. In the distance, the windows of Huntford Place lit up, but still he didn't return. Inside, ladies who considered the house party the highlight of autumn would be wondering where he was. They would sit down to supper, puzzled the prized catch hadn't joined them. He couldn't, because Miss Radcliff wouldn't be with them and he could no longer pretend it didn't matter.

An owl screeched, and a chill wind whipped across the stone. Luke drew his coat tighter about his neck as he rose at last and left the circle of the temple dome. If he stayed out here much longer, Gruger might be roused to arrange a search party and Luke didn't want the whole house out looking for him. If he found a way to pursue Miss Radcliff, it would cause enough of a stir, especially among his family.

He rounded the curve and descended the steps, thinking of Miss Radcliff as he parted the long grass with each stride. To have her at last in his arms, her curves easy and sweet against his hard planes, proved more tempting than seizing a poorly guarded outpost. Yet the tenderness of her lips, the eagerness with which she'd folded in to him, didn't erase the obstacles facing them.

Luke crossed the garden and entered the house through the music room at the back. He slipped past the sitting room unnoticed, the draw of charades distracting everyone. Inside, Mr Chilton danced around like an Italian opera performer as he tried to mimic who knew what. Luke should announce his presence, but he couldn't, not to these empty-headed twits.

He climbed the stairs to the first floor and instead of making for the bachelor rooms, he turned left and went to his mother's room. Light flickered beneath her door and he knocked. 'It's Luke.'

Her apple-cheeked lady's maid pulled open the door and his mother heaved a sigh of relief from where she sat by the fire. 'Oh, thank heavens. Miss Chilton said she saw you ride back to the house and the groom said Duke was in the stable, but it's been hours. Where have you been?'

'Out walking.' He hugged his mother, wondering how she'd react if he told here where and with whom he'd really been. 'I'm sorry I worried you.'

'Don't do it again.' She swatted his arm, then motioned for the maid to leave them. 'I know your father has given up on you finding a wife here, but I had a chance to speak with Miss Winborn at dinner. She's a very charming lady with a three-thousand-pound dowry, and is quite overlooked by everyone. It must be the red hair, such an unfortunate family trait. I believe she's worth another look.'

He ground his teeth at the frank mention of the lady's true value. 'What if I choose a lady of greater character than Miss Winborn, but with no money?'

His mother fingered the tassels at the end of her shawl. 'Luke, you know the situation we're in and how much a wife with a healthy dowry will help us.'

'And what about my happiness? Does it mean nothing to you?'

'Of course, but marriage is difficult enough without the added burden of bills.' She jerked the shawl across her shoulders, making it clear there were indeed limits for her to his happiness.

'If I resolve the issue with Lord Helmsworth, I wouldn't need a wife with a dowry.'

'It's a very uncertain outcome to base all our futures on.' She laid one finger on her chin. 'Who are you considering? Is it Miss Bell? I understand her family's means are as strained as ours. Imagine Edward's reaction if you chose her. That alone should put you off her.'

'I have no interest in Miss Bell.'

'Then who are you speaking of?'

'No one. It's simply a hypothetical question.'

He wasn't about to reveal the truth because he had yet to determine exactly what it was. Joanna cared for him as much as he did for her, but nothing was settled between them. Until it was, and they could stand proudly together before everyone, there was no point in risking her reputation—no matter how much he wanted to be with her.

Chapter Eight

Joanna hurried down the path in the woods. In the distance, through a break in the trees, she noticed the large grey clouds gathering on the horizon. The faint scent of rain hung in the air. For the moment, the afternoon was warm and the echoes of guns sounded over the trees as the men took advantage of the fine weather to hunt. The ladies were once again rehearsing the play, while the twins were with their nurse and Catherine with her music teacher. It gave Joanna time to visit Vicar Carlson, to escape the house and the agitation of being confined with every possibility of encountering Major Preston.

After yesterday, and a restless night of trying not to think about him, she wasn't ready to face him or the lingering questions left by his kiss. If Rachel, Grace or Isabel were here, she could chat endlessly about Major Preston the way Grace used to gush about her young man, until the enthusiasm had died and her real troubles had begun. Joanna didn't need Grace's kind of problems.

She stopped on the bank of the brook and opened

and closed her hands. The press of his fingers against hers was as immediate as the water flowing by. He wanted her, not in Mr Selton's licentious way, but as something more, but what she couldn't say. Caring for him meant defying everyone, including Madame's expectations, and it wasn't like her to flaunt convention for a fling.

But is it more than a fling? She didn't know, and with only one way to find out she wasn't about to try. He was distracting her from her duties enough already. All morning, she'd barely been able to concentrate and her lax supervision had made her charges even more wild than usual. If she didn't focus on her position, and not on a fantasy, she'd soon find herself returned to Salisbury and separated from Major Preston for good. Would he follow her if she left? She wasn't sure and the uncertainty troubled her as much as the memory of his kiss.

She reached the brook and, holding out her arms to better balance herself, hopped across the rocks. She stepped over the loose one, for there was no Major Preston here to catch her if she stumbled, then finished her crossing and walked up the opposite bank. Isabel might rush headlong into a relationship and Grace might lose her head on a whim, but not Joanna. She was too sensible and practical, or so she'd believed until yesterday afternoon.

At last the vicarage came into view and she hurried towards it. She needed someone to talk to who could distract her, even if the one subject she most wanted to discuss couldn't be broached. Vicar Carlson might understand her situation at Huntford Place, but she imagined he wouldn't approve of a governess dallying with a gentlemen. Few people did.

The gate at the end of the walk hung open and she slowed as she passed it. The tangy scent of chimney smoke didn't greet her, nor did the gentle neigh of the vicar's horse. Her excitement waned at the sight of the front door standing slightly ajar. She pushed it open and her heart dropped. There was nothing in the room except a suite of old furniture in front of a cold fireplace and a few papers scattered across the dusty floor.

'Vicar Carlson,' Joanna called out as she stepped inside, hoping the absence of clutter was he or his maid having cleaned. She moved deeper into the house, past the faded chintz of the armchair and a matching *chaise* to where the bookshelf stood empty except for the dust outlining where the books used to be. She clasped her arms across her chest and rubbed them to warm herself. 'Where did he go?'

'To London.' A male voice sounded from behind her. 'He received a more lucrative living there.'

Joanna whirled around to find Major Preston in the doorway. He wore his tweed hunting clothes and the faint acrid scent of gunpowder clung to him. During every moment when the twins had focused on their work and allowed her to dream, she'd pictured him in the Greek temple, the low afternoon light softening the angle of his chin and the slight scar along his hairline. The memories of his curved and strong lips beneath a regally arching nose were nothing compared to him in person. She glanced at a round water stain on the table beside the chair, already missing the kind old man, especially with Luke standing mere feet away. If he were here, she wouldn't be so worried about being weak with Major Preston. 'He said nothing to me about leaving when he invited me to come see him.'

'You must have made quite an impression on him. He wasn't an inviting vicar. Must be why the Marquis liked him so much.' Major Preston laughed and the low sound moved through her like the tide in Sandhills had. He stepped deeper into the room and set his hat on the bench beside the door.

'I seem to have made an impression on a number of gentlemen here, wouldn't you say, Major Preston?' She didn't have time to be coy or the stomach for sneaking around. She needed to know where they stood, what he hoped might come of yesterday, assuming it was anything at all.

'Yes, you have,' he admitted without hesitation, driving more pressing questions from her mind. 'And, please, call me Luke.'

She should resist this informality, especially after their prior breech of etiquette, but she couldn't. Even without the books and personal items, with Luke here the vicarage was more inviting than the cosiest room in Huntford Place. 'And you may call me Joanna, in private of course.'

'Of course.'

'What are you doing here?' she asked, eager to pull back from the craving for intimacy drawing her deeper into this forbidden friendship.

'I was on my way to Helmsworth Manor when I saw you come in here.'

He followed me.

All night she'd imagined him taking her in his

arms and claiming her once again. In the sunlight, the dream faded and reality took its place. Major Preston came here to find a rich wife with a nobler lineage than hers. If she didn't end things between them, they might do something they'd regret. Joanna already mourned the many things she wouldn't have in life. She didn't want to make it worse by losing her heart to a man she couldn't have.

'You shouldn't have followed me. It isn't right for us to be alone together.'

She tried to pass him but he caught her hand.

'Don't leave. Not yet.'

She whirled to face him, and didn't pull away as his fingers tightened around hers.

'I can no longer ignore my feelings or my concern for you. I admire you, and care for you more deeply than I should.'

Her heart began to race with both fear and excitement as he made small circles on the back of her hand with his thumb. She knew she should go, but the tenderness in his eyes was making her insides burn and it wouldn't allow her to leave. Instead, she shifted closer and tilted her face up to his, craving what he offered despite the risks. It went against every rational thought she'd ever possessed about right and wrong, possible and impossible, but his chest against hers and his heavy arms drawing her close were the only things that mattered.

Then their lips met and the fluttering rising in the pit of her stomach filled her entire being. She could think of nothing but his mouth on hers, his hand on the small of her back. She rose up on her toes, eager for his hand to slide lower as she pressed further into his kiss. Against her stomach she felt the intensity of his need and it made her wobble on her toes before his firm embrace steadied her. His breathing matched hers as he at last gripped her buttocks and bent her deeper into the curve of his body. The gentle flick of his tongue against her lips drew hers out to caress his and the salty taste of him made her forget all of her misgivings.

The bliss was broken by the distant peal of the village church bells. They rang out over the forest while the church beside the vicarage remained silent. The sound ended the kiss which had held them together for so many glorious moments. There was no wresting apart, but a slow coming down as she settled onto her heels. She ran her fingers along his temples and across the planes of his cheeks to rest on his shoulders.

Then the clop of a horse's hooves and the low 'whoa' from a rider outside made her stiffen in his arms.

'Who's here?' an angry voice called out from the front gate.

'It's Lord Helmsworth.' Luke pulled her to an open door of a large, empty cupboard and waited for her to climb inside. 'Stay here. He can't see you.'

He closed the door. Light fell through a crack in the top, but there was no way for her to see through the wood. The stomp of boots on the vicarage floor announced Lord Helmsworth's ill-timed arrival. She cringed away from the door and struggled to keep her breathing even and quiet, afraid of being detected and ruined.

'Major Preston, what are you doing here?' Lord

Helmsworth demanded. She'd never met the man, but his voice sounded familiar.

'I came to see Vicar Carlson,' Luke answered as if giving him the time. She envied his steady nerves. Hers were running wild.

'Liar. You knew he was leaving, everyone did. You're here with a woman. Where is she?' Lord Helmsworth stomped past the cupboard and Joanna froze as she heard the door to another room creak open on its hinges. 'I thought I saw someone with you through the window.'

'There's no one here but the two of us.' Luke's voice revealed nothing while Joanna swallowed hard against a dry throat.

'Typical military man. This isn't a place for your secret trysts.'

Lord Helmsworth thundered past the cupboard, making the door rattle before another door creaked open, this one too close to where Joanna hid. One more door and he'd find her. Her laughter with Luke and their easy conversation seemed so much more perilous than before. Even with her heart pounding in her ears, she didn't regret it. He was no Lieutenant Foreman, escaping from a woman in order to save himself the moment they were discovered. He'd find a way to keep her safe, just as he had the night of the ball. He wouldn't abandon her.

'I didn't come here for a tryst,' Luke answered, still polite and calm. 'Given your friendship with Vicar Carlson, I'd hoped he could help us to resolve the land dispute.'

Lord Helmsworth finally gave up his frenzied search. 'There is no dispute. The last land survey—'

'The one you paid to have conducted and then re-fused to allow my family to observe?' Luke challenged.

'It doesn't matter who paid. The surveyor took the measurements and he said the land along with the river is mine—and it will remain so.'

Luke wasn't so easily dissuaded. Lord Helmsworth's arrival was both annoying and fortuitous. An agreement with him would smooth the way to a more pleasurable one with Joanna. 'Then allow us to lease it from you, or to negotiate the use of the river for our fields. We don't need to own the land to have access to it.'

'You won't trick me into parting with it or anything on it.' Lord Helmsworth crossed his arms as if to say the discussion was over. With his blue eyes narrowed, their colour strikingly similar to Joanna's, it was clear there'd be no rational conversation. 'A captain cost me my daughter, I won't let a puffed-up major cost me my land.'

Luke opened and closed his fist by his side, determined to keep hold of his temper. He'd seen what Lord Helmsworth's grief for his only child had done to the laughing gentleman he remembered from the Christmas party and he pitied him.

'Were it in my power to punish the man who ruined your daughter I would, but I can't. Nor can I answer for his crimes as they aren't mine,' Luke replied with more ease than he normally would have granted a man disparaging him and his hard work for his country.

The anger in Lord Helmsworth's eyes settled down to a more subtle roar. Luke waited, wondering if a touch of sympathy was enough to bring the man around to seeing reason. It wasn't.

'Get out of here and don't bother me again.' He stormed past him and out of the vicarage.

Luke watched him through the window, disappointed but not deterred as the Marquis mounted his horse and rode off. Given the stubbornness of all parties involved, it was no wonder the boundary dispute had continued for so long. It would end with Luke, one way or another. Until then, there was another, more vexing matter dominating him.

He tugged open the cupboard door and guilt racked him as the sunlight illuminated Joanna's wide, nervous eyes. He'd never compromised a woman before, yet he'd almost done so today.

'He's gone.'

She stepped out and peered around, as though still in danger. 'What if he comes back?'

'He won't. Not given the speed with which he left. I'm sorry for jeopardising your reputation. It was wrong of me to do so.'

'And it was wrong for me to go along. I must return to the house.'

She rushed out the door and down the path.

He stared through the half-open door at the dead and sagging heads of the flowers in the garden beyond. He could follow her, mount Duke and ride to catch up with her, pull her into the saddle and savour the sweet curve of her buttocks rocking against him with each pounding thud of Duke's hooves, but he didn't move.

He'd followed her to the vicarage to tease out more of her true feelings for him. In the softness of her lips and the way she'd clung to him, he had. It hadn't clarified anything, but had only made everything much more complicated.

He snatched up his hat and settled it over his hair. Instead of strengthening the growing connection between them, their indiscretion had almost ruined her and had probably driven her away. He shouldn't have been so foolhardy, but when they were alone together his desire for her was stronger than the need for caution. That was dangerous, especially for Joanna.

He strode outside to where Duke stood tied to a tree. He grabbed the edge of the saddle, ready to mount, when the pounding of hooves echoing off the trees made him pause. Down the road, Edward rode fast up on him. His brother pulled the reins of his horse to a stop, his face grave as he stared down at Luke.

'You must return to the house at once.'

'Found another excuse to keep me from visiting Lord Helmsworth, have you?' Luke hauled himself into the saddle. He shouldn't be curt with Edward and risk another fight, but the setbacks in the vicarage had shortened his patience. 'You needn't bother, I've already spoke to him.'

'This has nothing to do with him. Lord Beckwith has arrived to speak with you.'

Luke's heels halted over Duke's flanks. There was no reason for anyone from the Army to come all this way to see him, except one.

Chapter Nine

Joanna stood against the wall across the sitting room, watching Luke speak with the newest addition to the house party. Lord Beckwith had created quite a stir with his unexpected arrival, throwing both Gruger and Lady Huntford into a tizzy. Thankfully, Mr Selton's departure had freed a bedroom, settling the matter of Lord Beckwith's accommodations but not his reason for needing it. If either he or Luke had enlightened anyone as to why he was here, it hadn't reached Joanna. Lady Selton and Lady Chilton hadn't heard the reason either judging from their conversation on the sofa in front of her.

She was as curious as they were, but prudent enough not to approach Luke in search of an answer. Without one, her mind created plenty and none of them were good. The faint darkness beneath his eyes, the hard set of his features as he stood in deep conversation with Lord Beckwith told her something bad had happened since she'd left him. She wished she could cross the room to him and speak as freely with him as she did during their time alone together, but she couldn't. She'd already caught Lady Pensum examining her and Luke on more than one occasion, as though she suspected something between them. Whether she disapproved or not Joanna couldn't discern, but her mere suspicion made Joanna's skin clammy.

It wasn't Lady Pensum eyeing her now, but Lady Huntford. Joanna dropped her focus to the woven swirls in the green rug beneath her feet. If the woman realised her efforts to land Luke for her daughter were being threatened by a mere governess, she'd throw Joanna out of the house tonight. After a short while, she dared to look up, relieved to find Lady Huntford distracted by Frances telling her something before quitting the room, but not Luke. He examined her, his need for her evident in his dark eyes. It tore at her to deny him comfort, but she must, especially with Lady Huntford approaching her in a flutter of purple and red.

'Frances doesn't feel well and is retiring for the evening. You may go to bed.' Lady Huntford barely paused on her way to the game table to deliver the news.

Joanna walked slowly along the edge of the room towards the door, aware of Luke watching her, but she didn't return his questioning glance. Whatever was troubling him, there was no chance of finding out about it tonight. She meandered down the dimly lit hallway, unwilling to rush. She needed the activity to calm her agitation.

As she reached the stairs, the quick fall of boots on the stone floor behind her made her turn. Luke was hurrying to catch up to her.

'What are you doing?' The question was barely out of her mouth before he caught her by the arm and pulled her into the shadows on the far side of the stairs.

'I need to speak with you. It's important.'

'We can't. What if somebody sees us?' It was one thing to dally with him at the vicarage. It was entirely different in the main hall of Huntford Place. She tried to peer around him, but the staircase jutting out from the wall above kept them in the shadows. They were out of view of guests leaving the sitting room, but in plain sight of anyone coming down from the first floor. She wouldn't put it past the twins, or Catherine, to be up there right now trying to catch a glimpse of what was happening downstairs. If they saw anything it would be the end of her time here. She must think of her employment and her future.

'No one followed me. I told them I didn't feel well and was going to bed.'

'Then you'd better go to your room and allow me to go to mine.' She tried to step around him, but he slid in front of her, blocking the way. It didn't send a chill of fear through her as it had with Mr Selton. Luke's determination to be near her and the bracing scent of his cologne overwhelmed her. She wanted to fall into his arms, press her lips to his and enjoy the weight of his hands on her back. It was a powerful and dangerous urge.

'Please, we must speak,' he implored.

He should be turning to his family or someone else, not her, but the anguish in his voice pierced her and she couldn't leave him to suffer. 'Meet me at the vicarage in an hour.'

'Thank you.' He laid a lingering kiss on her forehead and she sighed, wanting to be with him now, to not even wait until they were safe. Let Catherine or Frances see them, it would be a relief to stop this sneaking around and admit to everyone how much she wanted him.

Then he fled from the shadows and up the stairs.

Joanna leaned back against the wall and pressed her fingertips against the smooth panelling. What was she thinking to suggest a private meeting? To do so meant risking being caught sneaking in and out of the house, or not in bed should some emergency arise with the girls. Lady Pensum's earlier scrutiny in the sitting room had been a warning, and if Joanna was wise, she'd put an end to this little affair. She couldn't, not before she found out what was wrong with Luke. If Lord Beckwith was here, it must have something to do with Luke's commission. Perhaps he was going back to the Spain. If she didn't meet him tonight, she might never see him again, unless he decided to take her with him. In Spain, they could escape the demands of his family and society, but she doubted it. He was too honourable to leave his parents to deal with their troubles, or to run away from duty. He needed her and she would go to him, but it didn't mean she'd be foolish enough to compound her mistakes with the greatest one an unmarried woman could make. She was too sensible to forget herself, or so she hoped.

Joanna followed the path through the woods to the vicarage. Overhead, thick clouds filled the sky. The gaps between them allowed the moonlight and a few stars to peek through, but with the stiff wind pushing them together, the faint light would soon be gone. The smell of rain which had punctuated the air all evening was heavier now and seemed to dampen the forest sounds. Joanna pulled her pelisse tighter around her neck as the vicarage came into sight. She hoped the rain held off until this meeting with Luke was over. It would be difficult enough to sneak back into Huntford Place and up to her room without leaving a trail of wet footprints behind her.

The first flash of lightning lit up the darkness as she slipped inside the vicarage and closed the door. Luke knelt in front of the fireplace, blowing the embers beneath a log to life. The curve of his back as he bent over the fire entranced her. She gripped the smooth door handle tight. Alone with him, it was only her own determination keeping them apart and it was already wavering.

'Aren't you afraid someone will see the smoke?' she asked, worried, keeping the danger in mind despite her eagerness to warm her frigid hands.

'No.' He stood to face her as the rising flame sent its light out into the room to illuminate the chairs, the walls and him. His face was ashen, and his mouth tightly drawn.

'What's wrong?' Joanna hurried to him, stopping before she reached him. She was here to listen and comfort him, not to tempt him with her touch.

'Captain Crowther and the rest of my squad are missing. They were surprised by the French in a narrow pass. There was no escape.'

'Are they alive?'

'I don't know.' He raked his hand through his hair, causing a few strands to fall over his forehead. 'The commander hasn't received a request to exchange prisoners or officers.'

'Then they might have survived.'

'Or no one has found their bodies yet.' He paced the small room, his heels striking the floor. 'I've seen it happen before, men slaughtered and left for the birds to pick at until another regiment finds them.'

'You can't give up hope until you hear more,' she encouraged. His losing his friend would be like her losing Isabel, Grace and Rachel and she could imagine his despair.

'I should've been with them. I know those passes and the local men, informants and sympathisers, all of them. I might have learned of the ambush, or found another way out of the pass before it was too late.' He stared out the window into the darkness. Rain began to plink against the roof, lightly at first before falling hard and steady. 'I could've helped them.'

She slipped up behind him and stroked his back. In the face of his pain, she couldn't remain aloof. 'Or been captured or killed. Think what your death would do to your parents.' *To me.* Her heart almost stopped at the thought.

'Yes, they'd have been crushed along with all their hope for their precious heir.' His muscles tightened beneath her palm. 'I shouldn't have left my men.'

Joanna wrapped her arms around Luke and laid her cheek on his back, hoping to soothe the bitterness marring his words. She shouldn't touch him like this, it was too intimate and enticing, but he was hurting and he needed her comfort. 'Don't give up on them. They may still be alive.'

'And if they aren't?' He turned in her embrace and

rested his chin on her head, his chest rising and falling beneath her cheek. She closed her eyes and inhaled his scent of smoke mixed with the faint heat of his skin. He held her as if she alone could provide the strength to hope for his friends. She would give it to him, as he'd given it to her.

'Then make sure they, and the families who need them, aren't forgotten. Speak with Lord Beckwith, the War Office, anyone who can make a difference to your men and their loved ones.'

He leaned back to look down at her, the wild grief in his eyes settling. 'It seems a paltry reason to be spared from sharing their fate.'

'Not to those they left behind.'

He brushed a strand of hair off her face before his hand came to rest on the nape of her neck, heavy against the faint exposed skin. 'What if it isn't enough?'

She didn't want him to doubt himself, but to be the determined man she'd come to adore, the one who'd stand beside her the way he did his men. It was the real reason she was here, risking everything to be near him. She wanted him, despite all her efforts to convince herself and him otherwise. In his embrace, so many things she'd yearned for at last seemed possible. 'You won't give up. It isn't who you are. You'll keep fighting until it is enough and then you'll do more.'

He rubbed his thumb against the fluttering pulse on her neck. Hesitation marred the smoothness of his touch and it made her breath catch in her throat. Like her he was wavering between holding back and pressing forward. Then, the frustration and desperation which had filled his eyes was gone and she knew he'd made his decision, and so had she.

'I used to think duty and honour were the only things worth coming home for, the only things keeping me here, even at Huntford Place.' He lowered his face so close to hers each word whispered across her cheeks. 'I was wrong. It's you.'

The roar of the rain on the roof overhead faded as he claimed her mouth, his need for her deeper than lust. She didn't dare call it love. It couldn't exist in so short an amount of time no matter what the old fairy tales said. This was a bond between the two of them which eased her aching loneliness. It might not last beyond the sunrise, but she didn't care. Only Luke and the thrill of being in his arms mattered. She hadn't wanted to be a governess any more than he'd wanted to leave the Army, but she'd done what was expected of her. Tomorrow she would do the same, but tonight was for her, and him.

Lightning flashed as he lowered her onto the *chaise* behind them, covering her body with his. The weight of him on top of her, his lips teasing and tickling her neck, were exquisite. Fire swept through her as he raised the hem of her skirt and traced the smooth skin of her calves, his hand hot against the cool air of the house. The faint voice of reason urged her to end this, but she ignored it as she sank deeper into the desire pulling them together.

As he stroked the line of her thigh, she freed his cravat from the confines of the knot holding it closed. She drew it out from around his neck and dropped it to the floor. With hesitant flicks of her tongue, she tasted the sweet flesh of his neck, as curious as she was tempted by the play of his fingers over her hips. In this moment, she wasn't the governess, prim, proper, mute and ignored, but shameless and free with a man who'd made her glow like one of the embers.

Luke drank in Joanna as she lay beneath him. He shouldn't compromise her or surrender to this fervour, but he couldn't pull himself away. He'd never been carried off by emotions like he was with her and tonight he didn't fight it. He wanted her in his life, to make her happy and no consequences or anyone's opinions could separate them.

Rising up, he slid his hands along her slender waist and over her flat stomach to undo the small buttons holding together the front of her pelisse. Her eyes were alight with her desire as she watched him remove the layers of clothing separating her flesh from his. The cold of the room faded as he slipped the chemise off her shoulders and past the curve of her hips. She was gorgeous in the soft firelight, her unpinned hair falling over her full breasts which rose with each breath. He sat up on his heels and took off his coat, waistcoat and shirt, making himself as vulnerable and open to her as she was to him.

She shivered, her breasts drawing tight with the chill. He knelt before her and raised one of her curving legs. Her calf was supple against his palm as he removed the plain stocking covering her skin. He dropped the simple garments still warm with her heat onto the floor, then lowered her foot to the *chaise*. He guided her down against the rumpled pillows and lowered himself to cover her. She didn't question him, but followed his lead, believing in him as his men had done. He wouldn't betray her any more than he had them, but lead them on to a victory neither of them could've imagined before they'd entered this cottage.

He stood and removed his breeches, revealing his full need. Far from shrinking away, she embraced him as he continued to explore her body. Her soft moans when he found her centre were more precious to him than even the cries of triumph over a battlefield. She was not an enemy to conquer or to avoid like the other ladies in the house, but a joy to savour and celebrate and he would.

He slipped between her legs and claimed her mouth as he sought entrance. She granted it, drawing him into her body as she had her heart. As they moved together, he lost himself in her. He didn't want it to end, but as her breath quickened in his ear and her moans gave ways to cries of pleasure, a wave of release carried them both beyond everything except each other.

The fire crackled in the grate while the storm outside continued to rage. Joanna lay entwined with Luke on the *chaise*, more at ease than she'd ever been before. Sweat glistened on their bodies and the cold nipped at her back as they hugged one another close. A gust of wind drove the rain against the window and another bolt of lightning lit up the room. Regret seemed as far away as Huntford Place while she lay in his arms, this peace worth every chance she'd taken tonight to be with him.

'I'll be right back.' Luke made for the bedroom down the short hall past the cupboard where she'd hidden the other day. The firelight caressed the curve of his buttocks as he walked, emphasising every taut ripple of his muscles. Joanna bit her lip at the temptation in his stride as he returned with a blanket and nothing else.

'Quite the devilish smile.' He grinned as he flicked the blanket over her.

'You bring out the hellion in me.' She threw her leg over his hips as he joined her beneath the thick quilt.

'I like this wanton Joanna, it's quite a surprise.' His heavy arm pressed against her back, keeping her close beside him.

'You'll have her all night. I won't be able to cross the stream, not in this rain.' It was as if Mother Nature was granting them this special time together.

'Good, because even if you could, I wouldn't let you go.' He pressed her against the *chaise*, claiming her once more. She surrendered, eager to be one with him. In a few hours, the sun would rise and she'd be forced to face the consequences of her decision, but not now. Despite everything trying to keep them apart, tonight they were together and she would accept him for however long this lasted.

Chapter Ten

The sun, tempered by the fading storm clouds, poured in through the vicarage window. The fire had burned down to a smouldering red glow, leaving a stern chill in the room. Joanna snuggled deeper under the heavy quilt and against Luke, craving his heat and the languid pleasure of him. She closed her eyes, about to fall back asleep when the distant church bells rang across the forest.

Joanna jerked upright, all the peace of last night shattered by the stark morning light. Their time together was over and with it the fantasy of an illegitimate governess being with the second son of an earl. Despite what she'd done with him, she hadn't been raised to be a mistress, nor would she become one and bring shame on Madame Dubois, the school or herself.

'Good morning.' Luke ran his wide hand down the curve of her exposed back.

She twisted around to see him propped against the faded chintz pillows, one arm behind his head, the quilt draped across his hips to conceal the tempting part of him. He smiled at her and she wanted to press her bare chest to his, bring their mouths together and forget all the reality waiting for them at the edge of the forest. She tugged her side of the quilt up to cover her breasts. 'We should be getting back. If they discover we're both gone, they'll think the worst.'

'Let them. They'll dismiss you anyway once they learn we're to be wed.' He slipped his hand in her hair and drew her into a kiss of promise.

She allowed the quilt to fall away, her breasts taught against his bare chest, the desire which had consumed her last night flaring once again. He craved more than her body, but her life and future. It was everything she'd ever wanted and all impossible. His family wouldn't accept her and she'd always be an outcast, despised for stealing their son and their one chance at a much-needed dowry. She wouldn't be hated in the very family he wanted to make her a part of, it would be like spending the rest of her life in the employment of the Huntfords.

She pressed her hands against his bare chest and pushed herself away from him. 'We can't. It's impossible.'

It hurt to utter the words.

His chest stilled beneath her palms. 'I've been outnumbered in battle more than once and seized victory. Don't tell me our wedding isn't possible.'

His determination made her sit back. Here was a man who always strove to achieve what he wanted and it was clear he wanted her. Despite the answering challenge in her heart, she remained steadfast against it and him.

'Yes, you've faced down armies, but you know as

well as I do how difficult it is to face down society.' She rose, gathered up her discarded clothes and began to dress. 'The Huntfords have treated me poorly because they think I'm below them. Imagine the scorn they and their friends will heap on me for marrying before Frances and above my station?'

'I've faced too many real perils to be intimidated by imaginary ones.' The languid brown of his eyes hardened.

'Is your family an imaginary one? I'm illegitimate, Luke. What will happen when your parents or your brother learn of it? I've heard the things he's said to you, I doubt he'll shrink from voicing his disapproval of me.' She slipped her chemise over her head and took up her discarded stays.

'You'd rather remain in drudgery than take a chance on defying others to claim your own life?' He flung back the coverlet and stood. Joanna did her best not to stare at everything he revealed, afraid it would pull her back into the sweet memories of last night and distract her from being reasonable and realistic.

'Of course not, but I'm not foolish enough to believe in fairy tales.' She tugged tight the laces of her stays, then snatched up her dress. Everything seemed clearer in the bright morning light, including the mistake they'd made in forgetting themselves last night. 'You've been wrestling with your responsibilities ever since you've come home, not happy about the requests your family has made of you, or the sacrifices you've made for them. A relationship with me, a nameless governess, is a way of granting their wishes while also showing your rebellion.'

He snatched his breeches off the floor. 'You think my concern for you so slight?'

'No, but I won't have you break your pledge to help your family, to compromise your honour because of me.' She was convinced he cared, very much, but she knew it wasn't enough. Perhaps her mother had loved her, but it hadn't stopped her from giving Joanna up. Madame Dubois had been like a mother to her, but it hadn't prevented her from sending her to the Huntfords. Luke might prize her company this morning, but it didn't mean he could defy everyone to be with her, no matter what he said. 'But constant criticism and rebukes will erode your regard for me, and even if you can win your family to our cause, what about Lord Beckwith? What will he think of this arrangement?'

'It doesn't matter. I allowed him to pressure me to leave the Army. I won't let him decide who should be my wife. He no longer commands me.'

'But he commands those who can help your men and those influential men have wives who'll gossip and turn their husbands against you. You won't be able to help your soldiers if you become an outcast because of me and I won't allow people to suffer so that I can be happy.'

He pulled up his breeches then halted, his bare chest rising and falling as he breathed. 'Aren't you tired of others dictating your life? Of not fighting for what you want?'

She pulled on her pelisse and with shaking fingers fumbled to button it. 'It's easy for you to say when you have choices for earning a living. Not all of us are so fortunate.'

'I say it because I've done it, not because it's easy. I clawed my way up from lowly lieutenant to a major in command of men. I didn't do it by making the best of things, but by exceeding all expectations, taking risks, challenging people and proving my mettle and my worth to my commanders and myself.' He strode up to her and cupped her face with his hands, his words powerful despite the softness of his voice. 'You're a brave woman, Joanna. Don't allow your fears to make you throw away everything you've ever wanted.'

His tender hands on her face made her hesitate and consider sharing in his conviction, but everyone would despise her if she did. Eventually he would too. She stepped out of his grip, struggling to reclaim the calm and steady countenance which had served her so well for so many years. It warred with the part of her which wanted to believe in his confidence.

'I don't have the same freedoms you do, so don't demand the same things of me.'

She made for the door before his single question stopped her.

'And if there's a child?'

She fingered the cold, brass doorknob. If there was a child, she couldn't do to it what her mother had done to her by denying it a place in society, or the knowledge of its father, but she wouldn't allow the phantom of it to guide her now. She looked over her shoulder at him, her heart aching. 'We'll deal with it if the issue arises.'

She fled out the door, her boots sending up splashes of rainwater from the wet ground as she rushed through the woods. The rising sun cut through the trees and she knew, no matter what she did or said once she arrived back at Huntford Place there'd be no hiding her absence. She struggled through the emotions torturing her to come up with some excuse for her tardiness or a legitimate reason for why she'd been out of the house the morning after a storm, but she could think of nothing except Luke and leaving him behind.

When the roof of Huntford Place at last came into view, a new failing began to trail her. In her selfish desire to be special, to forget everyone and everything for one night, she'd betrayed Madame Dubois and the people who'd raised her. Perhaps she shouldn't have walked away from Luke, but marry him the way Isabel intended to marry Mr Balfour. Luke had offered her the protection of a union, but not even his name or a ceremony could stop people from condemning or insulting her and it was a long way between here and the banns.

Poor Madame La Roche, the French teacher, had once fallen in love with the son of a Salisbury magistrate, a man of title and property. His family had objected so strongly, in the end the young man had cried off a mere week before the wedding. Madame La Roche had returned to the school embarrassed and alone. How much castigation she'd received for her ill-advised engagement, Joanna wasn't sure, but shortly after her return she'd resumed her teaching duties. Joanna hoped Madame Dubois proved as generous with her as she'd been with Madame La Roche if she was forced to return to the school. There was nowhere else for Joanna to go. In the end, even if she went home in disgrace, it was better to leave. It would place distance between her and Luke, make him fade from memory, even as his touch still burned on her skin.

Joanna skirted the front drive, then followed the house around to the back. She tried the library doors, but they were locked. Cursing her luck, she tugged at the music-room door, relieved when it swung open. She slipped into the dark room and stood quietly in the semi-darkness beside the pianoforte and struggled to compose herself. She picked a few leaves off her skirt and swiped at a bead of water clinging to her bodice, unsure how she'd face her charges or her employer.

Lady Huntford's muffled voice, and those of some other ladies, carried in from the adjacent sitting room. It plucked at Joanna's already tense nerves. Joanna couldn't reach the stairs, or anywhere else in the house without moving past it. Unable to stand here all day, or hide behind the pianoforte until everyone dispersed to their chosen amusements, she screwed up her courage and hurried down the hall. She moved on the balls of her feet, trying to slip unnoticed past the sitting room. She was nearly away when Frances cried out, 'There she is!'

Joanna froze, wincing at her failure.

'Miss Radcliff, come in here at once,' Lady Huntford ordered.

With heavy steps Joanna entered the room. From the looks of it, the entire house had been roused in a search for the wayward governess, or, more likely, they'd been gathered to participate in Joanna's total and utter downfall. Everyone sat in silence except for Miss Winborn and Miss Chilton, who whispered together near the back of the room.

Luke's parents stood among the guests, more mortified than amused, while his brother stared at her with the same look of disgust as Lady Huntford. Lady Pensum sat beside him, not looking well and perhaps the one person least interested in the drama playing out before her.

Lady Huntford rose out of her chair and advanced on Joanna, her puce dress fluttering ominously around her legs. Joanna braced herself, hoping this reprimand would involve nothing more than a scolding for disregarding her morning duties with the girls, but the hard line of Lady Huntford's lips, and Frances's smug look of revenge from where she sat beside her father and his dog told Joanna otherwise.

'Where have you been?' Lady Huntford peered at her with eyes made narrower by her overly full cheeks.

'I'm sorry I was late for my duties, but I took a walk…'

'Don't lie to me. We all know where you've really been and who you've been with.'

'Come, Lady Huntford, we don't know for certain if she was indeed with Luke,' Lady Ingham interjected with an edge of exasperation.

'Yes, I'm sure it's only a coincidence he and the governess were both missing this morning,' Lord Pensum huffed. 'Especially since they've been noticed conversing so much.'

Miss Chilton and Miss Winborn gasped at the not-too-subtle accusation. Lady Ingham pressed the heel of her hand to her forehead and Lord Ingham rolled his eyes at Lord Pensum having aired his suspicions about his brother in mixed company. Whatever the

Inghams thought of her and Luke's behaviour, it was clear they didn't appreciate his misstep being announced for all to hear. No one seemed concerned with discussing Joanna's failings aloud.

'I was not with Major Preston.' Joanna stared down her accusers, determined to be convincing in an effort to save something of her reputation. It wasn't like her to lie, and guilt over this as much as her rash behaviour last night with Luke needled her, but she was forced to ignore it. With Lord Pensum and Lady Huntford all but accusing her of acting like a tart in front of so many titled people, it wouldn't be long before they wrote to their London friends about it. Joanna's reputation as an employable woman would be destroyed, assuming an illegitimate child didn't wreck it for her. Her one chance at salvation was to convince everyone she was innocent. It was a Herculean feat and one she hated trying to achieve with deceit.

'Don't you dare lie to me, you whoring little wench,' Lady Huntford screeched and her hand twitched at her side as though she wanted to slap Joanna. She probably would have if there hadn't been so many people present. 'You're dismissed. Pack your things at once and go back to that awful school of yours. If this is the kind of governess they're educating, I want nothing more to do with it and will tell all of my friends to avoid it, too.'

Joanna willed her shoulders not to slump in defeat. In her one act of defiance, she'd ruined her whole life and quite possibly the prospects of many other girls at Madame Dubois's school. For the first time, she understood why her mother had given her away. She'd probably stood in a similar position once, with all chance of a respectable life gone and no ability to bring up her child.

Her dignity and reputation in tatters, Joanna moved to curtsy and take her leave when Gruger shuffled into the sitting room.

'Lord Helmsworth has arrived to see you, Lady Huntford,' he mumbled as though inconvenienced.

Vicar Carlson entered as the butler finished his announcement.

'It's an honour to have you grace us with your presence this morning. What can we do for you?' Lady Huntford all but grovelled in front of the distinguished man before rising out of her curtsy and hissing at Joanna, 'Show the proper respect, girl.'

'My apologies, Vicar Carlson.' Joanna curtsied, confused by the stillness which had enveloped the room.

'Vicar Carlson? He's the Marquis of Helmsworth!' Frances spat out with contempt hot enough to boil wine. Her mother glared her into silence.

Joanna stumbled a bit as she rose, her head spinning at this latest revelation. She'd poured out her heart to a marquis and given her body to a major. The morning was turning out to be more stunning than last night.

'Miss Radcliff needn't kowtow to me.' Lord Helmsworth smiled at her. 'The two of us are already friends.'

Lady Huntford looked as confused as Joanna.

'You said you were the vicar. Why did you lie to me?' Joanna asked, struggling to reconcile his real identity with his false one and the contrast between the kind man in front of her and the one who'd raged against Luke in the vicarage.

'You wouldn't have talked to me so openly if I'd told you who I really was.' He took her hand and patted it. It was warm and soft, not like Luke's, but in the way she imagined a father's might be. 'Since you now know who I really am, I must tell you who you really are.'

'I'm a governess.' In reality she was no longer even this, but she didn't want to see the kindness in his eyes replaced with the same disgust which the Huntfords and their guests had flung at her. It would follow soon enough when Lord Pensum, Frances or Lady Huntford decided to blurt out their very correct assumptions about what she'd been up to last night.

'You're much more than a governess. You're the granddaughter of a marquis.' He laid his hand over his heart, examining her as if she'd brought him the greatest treasure. 'You're my granddaughter.'

The gasp from everyone in the room almost extinguished the fire.

'No, you're mistaken. I'm nobody's granddaughter. I don't even know who my parents are.' This elicited another small squeak of surprise from Lady Huntford as she realised she'd been employing not just a governess with questionable morals, but an illegitimate one.

'Your mother was my dear daughter Jane.' He explained to her about her mother and father, their illicit love, his death, her mother's confinement and leaving Joanna with Mrs White who'd brought her to Madame Dubois. All the guests leaned in to catch every word of the story. Joanna guessed it would be included in their letters to London within the hour. Her mind reeled as she worked to comprehend everything Lord Helmsworth said. The family she'd always wanted, the lineage she'd often wondered about, was being revealed to her at last. It far surpassed even her most childish dreams and the plot of any of the fairy tales she'd ever read. It couldn't be real. 'How can you be sure I'm the child?'

'After my solicitor located Mrs White she told us about the school. She was amazed you knew nothing of your background. She said that she'd not had time to stay and explain, but that she'd pinned a note to your blanket with your name and who you belonged to when she'd left you before departing for Austria. When my solicitor visited Madame Dubois to discuss with her my suspicions about you, she confirmed having found you on her doorstep, but said there'd been nothing but a torn piece of paper with your first name on it. If there'd been more, she would have contacted me at once.'

'Of course.' Madame Dubois was too caring to have left her an orphan if she could have prevented it.

'I had this miniature of your mother made on her sixteenth birthday.' He held out a gold locket on a chain and opened it. Inside was a painting of a young lady with Joanna and Lord Helmsworth's blue eyes and slender nose.

Joanna took the locket and cradled it in her hands. For years she'd wondered what her mother had looked like, now she knew. Seeing her mother's face was like seeing her own and Lord Helmsworth must have noticed the resemblance at once. It explained his reaction to her when they'd met at the graveyard.

'Jane meant to return for you, but she didn't have the chance.' Sadness deepened the lines at the corners of his eyes. 'Had I known of your existence, I would have claimed you at once.'

Joanna closed the locket and curled her fingers around it, the gold warming beneath her skin. 'What does this mean?'

'You have a good heart, Miss Radcliff. I recognised it the day I met you. You were kind to me when I was hurting and I appreciated it. Not everyone is so understanding of my grief.' He slid an accusatory look at Lord Ingham before focusing back on her.

'You're the one who listened to me,' Joanna countered with a humble smile. 'Your advice made a great deal of difference.'

'I want to make even more of a difference in your life.' He reached out to touch her cheek, then pulled back his hand, as awkward as Joanna about where they stood. 'Will you come with me, allow me to make up for the years of my absence and do for you all I wished I could have done for Jane?'

He was offering her the truth about who she was and where she'd come from. She was the granddaughter of a marquis who wasn't afraid to publicly claim her. It should be the happiest day of her life, but worry tainted her excitement. Lord Helmsworth disliked the Inghams. When Lord Pensum's suspicions about her time with Luke reached Lord Helmsworth's ears, would he still be proud to call her his granddaughter, or would he cast her back where he'd found her?

Luke's words about giving in to her fears echoed through her mind. She'd allowed fear to dictate her actions with Luke and surrendered a chance to marry an honourable man. She wouldn't allow them to stop her from seizing the opportunity to claim a real family and a place in the world. Whatever happened between her and Lord Helmsworth, whatever stories he heard or judgements he made because of them, she would face them and do her best to overcome them. She laid her hand on her grandfather's arm. 'Yes, I will.'

Luke emerged from the woods and stepped onto the main drive. Between him and the front door to Huntford Place stood Lord Helmsworth's carriage with its gold crest on the green-lacquered sides. Luke groaned. Of all the days for their paths to cross, this had to be the worst. Between the news of Captain Crowther and his men, and Joanna's sound rejection of him after a pleasurable night together, he was in no mood to face Lord Helmsworth's vitriol.

He considered going to the stable, fetching Duke and riding home. He was finished with this party and his visit here, but he didn't. Too many times he'd entered a battle mourning friends or dealing with a myriad of other troubles. Today, like then, he wouldn't allow his personal feelings to dissuade him from doing what needed to be done. He'd resolve this lingering issue between Lord Helmsworth and the Inghams by meeting the Marquis's anger with kindness.

To his astonishment, the front door of Huntford Place opened and the Marquis himself appeared with Joanna at his side. Lord Helmsworth escorted her outside, beaming as if he'd just been made a duke. Joanna glowed as much as he did, her joy a far cry from the parting despair she'd left him with at the vicarage.

Luke gaped at them. There was only one reason Lord Helmsworth could be leaving with Joanna, and for them to appear so ecstatic together. She must have been entertaining him as well as Luke, and Lord Helmsworth intended to make the governess his wife. It didn't seem possible, and went against everything Luke had come to believe about her, but he couldn't deny the evidence.

Her happiness dimmed at the sight of him watching them from the middle of the gravel drive. Lord Helmsworth scowled at him like a badger. As they passed, Joanna paused to say something, but Lord Helmsworth didn't break his stride, drawing her along.

'Come, my dear, we must hurry.' Lord Helmsworth patted her hand in a way which made Luke want to pull her away from him, but he didn't. He was too furious.

Once again he'd been tossed over by a lady in search of a husband with a loftier title and more money. No wonder she'd been so eager to get away from him this morning and so fast to come to him last night after all her prior protestations. She'd probably wanted a taste of a virile man before binding herself to one with more lineage than stamina.

Luke stormed up to the house without sparing the happy couple a second glance. It turned his stomach to think of Lord Helmsworth's gnarled hands on Joanna and her willingness to endure his touch. He ground the bottom of his boots against the iron scraper outside the door, not caring if he tore up the leather. Despite everything he'd done for her, it hadn't been enough to trump his lack of position or wealth. Nothing ever was.

Leaving a small pile of mud beside the door, he marched inside and jerked to a halt in the entrance hall. Everyone stood there and their conversation ceased at the sight of him.

What the hell happened while I was gone?

'Lord Helmsworth's granddaughter.' Luke groaned. His family had waited until they were alone in his mother's room to tell Luke the news. The one consolation was he hadn't been thrown over for the old man, at least not in the disgusting way he'd imagined. It still didn't ease the sting of Joanna having run from his proposal. When he'd held her last night, he thought he'd won her. He'd been wrong.

'And all you could do was treat her like your whore,' Edward fumed, shaking off Alma's restraining hand. 'Do you know how embarrassing it was to have your peccadilloes announced to everyone by a hysterical Lady Huntford, or was that your intent all along? To court a governess to spite us?'

'Contrary to what you believe, not everything I do, or each decision I make, is done with you in mind,' Luke hissed, struggling to control his temper. 'I pursued Miss Radcliff because she has more intelligence, common sense and regard for me than any other lady I've met.'

'Apparently not enough to avoid bedding you.'

Luke grabbed his brother by the lapels and slammed him against the wall.

'Boys!' their mother shouted, advancing on them as she used to when they fought as children. Luke let go of Edward, his anger checked but not cooled.

'Enough of this. What's done is done.' She scowled in motherly disapproval at them. 'Miss Radcliff has gone with Lord Helmsworth to lead her life with him and we must go on dealing with the challenges of ours.'

'One thing about Miss Radcliff being Lord Helmsworth's granddaughter is she'll probably receive a grand dowry now,' his father mused, as practical as ever. 'If she and Luke have an interest in each other, I see no reason why they shouldn't continue to pursue it.'

'Except Miss Radcliff has already refused my offer of marriage,' Luke clarified for everyone, his pride smarting.'

'That's a pity.' His father shook his head, his optimism fading. 'Perhaps she can still help us resolve the land dispute?'

'Not once Lord Helmsworth hears of her little tryst with Luke—and he will,' Edward spat out. 'Lady Huntford will probably attach a note about it to Miss Radcliff's things when she sends them over. Lord Helmsworth hated us before. Imagine how he'll react once he learns Luke has had his way with his long-lost granddaughter.'

Luke winced at the truth. In his desire to be with Joanna he'd inadvertently driven them apart. If he'd shown more restraint last night, then this morning and perhaps even the future might have unfolded differently. But he hadn't.

He reached into his pocket and clutched the bugle badge. His mistake was as sharp as the thin edge of the metal. Between her having already rejected him and Lord Helmsworth's animosity there was little Luke could do to overcome the consequences of their intimacy. However, if she asked him to, he'd find a way to stand with her against the mounting rumours, and even against her new grandfather's disapproval.

He let go of the badge. Even as he thought it he doubted it would happen. Joanna hadn't been willing to fight with him for their future when their ranks had been so different. As the newly minted granddaughter of a wealthy marquis, she wasn't likely to want anything to do with him now, not after he'd humiliated her in front of the entire countryside.

The idea of giving up pricked at him, but he couldn't chase after a woman who didn't want to be won. He must focus on his lost men and ignore the upsetting of all his plans and the severe blow to his heart.

Chapter Eleven

Joanna shifted in her seat and the silk of her dress rustled as she tried to concentrate on the play. The new blue gown was tasteful and flattered her eyes, or so the expensive French modiste had insisted during her fitting. Or perhaps it was her grandfather, or Mrs Petit, her lady's maid and sometimes chaperon who'd said it. After the whirlwind of the last month, it was difficult to remember.

Joanna adjusted the thick strand of pearls around her neck, their weight too heavy against her exposed décolletage. The Drury Lane theatre was far more dazzling than the one she'd been to in Sandhills, and its production of *Romeo and Juliet* opulent.

Thousands of candles in wide chandeliers illuminated the players and the numerous guests filling the seats. Lord Helmsworth sat beside her in the private box he'd hired for the evening. He'd insisted they come to London, thinking the small Season the perfect time to introduce her to society. She wasn't so certain. While he watched the young lovers, Joanna tried to overlook all the people watching her, as she searched among the curious faces for one. With the House of Lords in session, Lord Ingham might be here and possibly Luke. After all, there was no better place than London for Luke to search for a rich wife.

The realisation that it would not be her made her sides ache more than her new stays. She'd spied Lord and Lady Pensum in a box across the way, but Luke wasn't with them. She hadn't seen Luke or heard anything from him since the morning she'd refused his proposal. She flicked one stick of her fan with her finger. For all his confessed determination to be with her, he hadn't even tried to seek her out, or concocted some reason to come to Helmsworth Manor while she'd been there.

It's for the best, she reminded herself for the hundredth time since leaving him. The spectre of her indiscretion with Luke had haunted her until her courses had arrived. Not being with child had given her some peace, but it hadn't quietened the rumours racing through the countryside or the fear that her grandfather would cast her aside once they reached him. To her amazement, he either hadn't heard the stories or had chosen to ignore them, and Luke had stayed away. She was both disappointed and glad. His presence might have forced her grandfather to face the truth about Joanna's lapse in judgement, and possibly tainted her in his eyes.

Joanna tapped her fan against her palm. *If only Lord Helmsworth had found me sooner, then there might never have been rumours.*

She and Luke could have become properly acquainted at country events and behaved together like a respectable courting couple instead of being so secretive. She let out a long sigh, making the lace along the edge of her bodice quiver. Even if Lord Helmsworth had found her months ago, his prejudice against Army men and the Inghams would have prevented him from considering Luke as Joanna's suitor. It seemed that, no matter what the situation, they weren't meant to be together.

'You're not enjoying the play, my dear?' her grandfather asked.

'I'm distracted by everyone staring at me.' It was a half-truth. She'd long ago wished to be the centre of attention for one night. This wasn't exactly what she'd had in mind. By now the tales from Huntford Place must have reached London and she could imagine what everyone was saying about her.

'They're merely curious. In time it'll pass,' he assured her, seemingly oblivious to the scrutiny. Her grandfather raised his hand in greeting to someone across the theatre then rose. 'If you'll excuse me, Lord Jarsdel, an old friend of mine, is here and I must see him. I'll return shortly.'

He left, and a few moments later she saw him enter a box across the way to speak with a gentleman she didn't recognise. His absence left her to face the audience alone. She stroked the warm pearls and watched Romeo climb the wall into the Capulet orchard, but then a tingle of awareness made her turn. Her fingers froze on one of the smooth orbs as across the theatre her eyes met Luke's. He stood at the back of the box below where her grandfather was, his black coat austere compared to Lord Beckwith and the other high-ranking officers with their medals, ribbons and blue Horse Guards uniforms. She pulled the long strand through her closed fist to click against her new rings, still able to feel his chest beneath her fingertips, the ecstasy in his arms and the pain of having walked away.

One of the officers said something to Luke, forcing his attention back to them. Then a moment later, Luke made his excuses and left the box. His leaving should have been a relief. She'd already been made enough of a spectacle without him being here in London to make it worse. However, the first sight of him after so long proved as precious as her new family. In spite of everything, she still cared for him but doubted he even thought of her.

She settled against her seat, trying to lose herself in the drama and the way the tale of forbidden love pulled at her heart. She shouldn't ruminate on her troubles but enjoy her advantages. She was very lucky to be here, as all the letters from Rachel, Grace, Isabel and even Madame Dubois and Miss Fanworth had told her. She didn't feel lucky, but alone. This wasn't her world and it was difficult settling in.

She shivered as a light draught played along the back of her neck, followed by the flutter of the curtain behind her.

'Good evening, Joanna.' Luke's voice slid over her, making her heart still in her chest.

She hazarded a look at him, cautious not to turn too far and alert everyone, especially her grandfather, to his presence. Despite her change in status, they were as unable to converse openly here as in Hertfordshire. He stood in the shadow of the doorway, around the slight bend blocking him from view of the audience. Each of his steady breaths plucked at her like a harp and she clasped the side of the chair. He shouldn't be here and they shouldn't speak but she didn't have the will to send him away.

'Good evening, Luke.'

The strain that had marked him at the Ingham's ball hardened his expression and spread out to envelope her.

She turned back to the stage, mourning the loss of their easy rapport and what it had meant to her. The spicy scent of his cologne filled the box like incense. She closed her eyes and inhaled, silently willing him to defy everyone to reclaim the intimacy they'd experienced in the country. She longed to feel his heavy hands on her bare shoulders and she listened over the noise of the play for the fall of his boots behind her, but there was nothing. She opened her eyes and the theatre seemed less magical and even more lonely and isolating than before.

'I'm sorry if my coming here troubles you,' he offered.

'Why did you come?' she asked over her shoulder.

'I wanted to make sure all is well with you.'

The intent of his question was clear and she swallowed hard, ashamed of herself. He'd been considering the consequences of their night together as much as she had. No wonder he'd crossed the theatre to speak to her. She shouldn't have left him wondering. 'There was no child.'

He didn't sigh with relief, and a shared sense of disappointment passed between them. A baby might have forced them together when people and expectations had driven them apart. However, force was a terrible way to enter a marriage.

'How are you adjusting to London?' he asked, his concern as genuine tonight as when he'd protected her from Frances.

It made her heart catch with a spark of hope before she could smother it. His concern was part of who he was, not an indication he still held any regard for her. She could give him a glib answer, ease his worries and be done with this meeting, but she wouldn't. She had trusted him with the truth many times before. There was no reason to lie to him tonight.

'It hasn't been easy dealing with so much in such a short amount of time. I haven't said anything to anyone because I don't want to appear ungrateful. Grandfather has given me so much, not just clothes or jewellery, but stories about my mother and my family, and a place in it. It's everything I've ever wanted.' Almost.

'You aren't ungrateful. A wise young lady once told me, it can be difficult after so long in a situation to leave it. Eventually, you'll settle in.' The intimacy they'd shared during their stolen moments at Huntford Place whispered between them once more. He shifted on his feet before settling himself. 'I should go.'

'No, wait.' She turned to face him, loath to snip the faint bond between them.

His eyebrows rose a touch before the façade of a disciplined officer settled over him again.

'Is there any news about Captain Crowther and your men?'

'No.' He cut the word with his teeth and she crossed her ankles beneath her gown to keep from rushing to soothe him as she had at the vicarage. 'There were rumours they were being held in Ciudad Rodrigo, but nothing solid. I'm doing all I can to make sure the Army continues to search for them and provides for their families until we learn of their fate. Returning to London has made speaking with Lord Beckwith and other influential men in Whitehall much easier.'

'I'm sure your efforts won't be in vain.'

'We'll see.' He looked past her to the stage. 'None of the other goals I've set for myself these last two months have been achieved.'

Her cheeks burned under his none-too-subtle reminder of their last few moments together.

'I'm sorry. I shouldn't chide you for your decision in Hertfordshire.' His low voice was nearly drowned out when Mercutio laughed on stage. 'At the time I didn't agree with your reasons, but I came to see they were sound.'

'No, they weren't.' She opened and closed the fan over her skirt. 'They were made from fear of having to fight your parents had we told them we were engaged.'

'It wasn't fear, but the truth. You should've heard Edward rail at me. You being the granddaughter of a marquis didn't silence him, although my father hasn't given up on us maintaining something of an acquaintance.'

'Have you?' she asked, her heart racing with her daring.

She shouldn't crave any connection with him, either slight or deep, but with her memories of their time together and what it had meant to her as potent as his presence, she couldn't help it.

He didn't answer right away and she held her breath, waiting to see if anything between them could be salvaged. Then he laced his hands behind his back and stood, as he had in the library when he'd tried to end their friendship.

'I don't think Lord Helmsworth would approve.'

'No, he wouldn't.' Her heart dropped, especially when she glanced across the theatre. 'Grandfather has left his friend's box and will return soon.'

He didn't challenge her silent request to go, but bowed, his eyes never leaving hers as he backed away, allowing the curtain to fall closed between them.

'Where have you been?' Edward asked when Luke entered the box they'd engaged for the evening.

'Speaking with Lord Beckwith.' Edward didn't need to know Luke hadn't been in the Horse Guards box this entire time. His brother had been less irascible since they'd come to London, but it didn't mean there wasn't a fight in him waiting to be unleashed.

Luke took the chair on Alma's other side, as tense as he usually was before a battle. He looked up at Joanna. She sat like an unobtainable princess in the box above the stage, radiant in her silk. The blue brightened her eyes and emphasised the faint blush of her skin. She watched the play while her fingers worried at the creamy pearls caressing the tops of her full breasts. He hadn't expected to see her in London, not with Lord Helmsworth's well-known distaste for town. Her presence brought back everything he'd worked hard to forget in the country: her sweet smile, her wit and the moment she'd spurned him.

In this regard his expectations hadn't been disappointed. She'd gone off with a titled man and forgotten about Luke, not even bothering to write and calm his concerns about her being with child or the impact of the rumours surrounding her. With silence she'd conveyed her wish to have nothing more to do with him.

Then why was she so reluctant to see me leave her box?

The about-turn baffled him, but he knew better than to give it much credence. The request had probably been an attempt to ease the cut of her rejection, but it had failed.

She glanced at him and he looked away, trying to focus on the play. He had no patience for tragic love stories tonight.

He was about to rise and leave when Lord Helmsworth and an older gentleman Luke didn't recognise entered Joanna's box. Luke settled back against his chair and watched as Lord Helmsworth introduced his companion, who bowed over Joanna's hand with a solicitousness to make Luke bristle. Then the man sat down beside her to say whatever he needed to say to a woman half his age. Joanna didn't shift away but smiled and chatted, appearing quite charmed by her new acquaintance. Lord Helmsworth hovered behind them like an eager mother and Luke crossed his arms over his chest at the spectacle. It was more gripping than the one on stage.

'Who's the gentleman speaking with Miss Radcliff?' Luke asked Alma. He shouldn't begrudge Joanna her new life but something about the exchange bothered him.

Alma tuned her spyglass from the stage to the Helmsworth box. 'Lord Jarsdel, a widower with a sizeable estate outside Bath. He has two grown sons, so the woman he marries this time won't be the one to give him an heir.' The mention of a child brought a slight smile to her lips instead of her usual frown.

'She'll be married to a man nearly in his dotage.' Regrettably, Luke couldn't call him old or gouty. Lord Jarsdel was slender and fit, with a full head of dark hair greying at the temples, making him more distinguished than handsome.

'His next wife will be a countess and quite wealthy. It could be Miss Radcliff, unless a more suitable candidate offers for her first.' She lowered her glasses and threw him a wry smile, her humour matched by the new fullness in her cheeks. The return to society had been good for her, adding a little weight to her lithe frame and removing the strained expression she'd worn in the country.

Luke didn't share her amusement 'There isn't much an alternate suitor can offer when a young lady has a marquis for a grandfather and an earl for an admirer.'

'There's a great deal a man can offer a lady which has nothing to do with titles or money.' She reached out and took Edward's hand and raised it to her lips. He smiled at her and squeezed her hand before lowering it to rest on his thigh. She didn't let go of her husband as she faced Luke again.

'And without either, most of it is debt and worries.' Edward might not have given Alma wealth, but he had land and a title. It was more than Luke possessed.

'I remember you once telling me not to despair because you'd seen miracles. It sounds as though you need to start believing in them again. I have.' Her eyes twinkled with the reminder as she turned back to the play.

Around them the theatre quietened while Romeo

crept beneath the balcony to listen to Juliet. As the scene played out Luke studied Joanna. She seemed oblivious to him as she watched Romeo embrace Juliet with a tender kiss. Then her attention darted to him, and this time he didn't look away. In her eyes was the same mournful longing which had pulled him away from the Horse Guards box and nearly had him stepping over the audience to reach her now, but he didn't move. She was surrounded by the trappings of her new life and he didn't want to intrude on it. Regardless of the change in her situation, with the softness of her voice and her concern for his men she'd shown she was still the woman he'd fallen for—the one he would have fought to keep if she'd wanted it.

Lord Helmsworth leaned close to say something to her and she turned to him.

Luke rose and left the box. She'd made her choice and it hadn't been him.

'What did you think of Lord Jarsdel,' her grandfather asked from across the dark carriage carrying them home from the theatre.

'He was very nice.' She'd given little thought to the earl since he'd left them. His company had been pleasant enough, but it had been Luke who'd dominated her attention. Before he'd left her, he'd made it clear that there was nothing more between them. His distant gaze from across the theatre had told her something different. It was as if he still wanted her. It didn't seem possible.

'Your future is my greatest priority. I very much want to see you settled, to have a home and a family of your own in case something happens to me,' her grandfather continued with enough concern to make her stop musing and listen. 'It would mean a great deal to me if you'd consider Lord Jarsdel as a suitor. He's a very kind man and I think the two of you would do well.'

She gaped at him, his announcement as shocking as seeing Luke tonight. 'You wish me to become a countess?'

'You're the granddaughter of a marquis. Why shouldn't you become a countess?' He puffed out his chest with a pride she didn't share.

She could think of a number of good reasons, including her illegitimacy. He might ignore it, or pretend it didn't matter, but no one else would, especially if she gained so lofty a title. 'I barely know him.'

'You needn't decide anything tonight. I simply ask you to become better acquainted with him and see what happens.'

'All right, I will.' Something in this exchange reminded her of the day she'd agreed to Madame Dubois's suggestion to accept the offer of employment at Huntford Place. It had been a disguised demand, one which had determined the course of her life, just like her grandfather's might. She picked at the edge of the leather seat with her finger, irked by the way others kept deciding things for her while she went along. She was growing as tired of it as her turmoil over Luke.

She twisted the pearls around her finger as she leaned back against the squabs. In the country and tonight he'd been willing to let her go, yet in the midst of the play he'd watched her as if in need of her solace. While her eyes had held his there'd been a moment when she'd thought he might climb the box to reach her, as Romeo had done to Juliet, and show everyone his admiration of her until no one—not even her grandfather—could keep them apart.

She'd held her breath, waiting to see if he would.

But instead of coming to her he had left.

She let go of the pearls and they clacked together as they dropped over her chest. But the disappointment of the night didn't overwhelm her. In the silent exchange, before he'd stormed out of his box, she'd sensed she could have called him back to her. She wondered if she still could, and if she had the conviction to stand with him if she did? She wasn't sure, and there hadn't been a chance for her to find out. There probably never would be. Even if a future gathering brought them together, she doubted he'd speak with her.

There was little left for them to say.

Chapter Twelve

Luke stepped into Hookham's Lending Library and stopped short. Joanna stood browsing through the selection in one of the aisles. It had been three days since he'd left her at the theatre, but the sight of her struck him like the recoil of a cannon. Besides battling the Army Pay Board on behalf of his men he'd thought of little else except her—much to his chagrin. He didn't want to pine for a woman who didn't want him.

She stood on her tiptoes, the hem of her dark green walking dress rising to reveal slim ankles covered in fine silk stockings tinged cream by the skin beneath. He touched his fingertips to his palm, the memory of cupping her calf at the vicarage teasing him. She must be wearing silk now and he imagined the softness of the material and the suppleness of her skin against his. Then she raised one lithe arm to reach for a book. It emphasised the swell of her breasts beneath the spencer covering them and made his cravat tight against his throat.

Luke might not like the Marquis, but he couldn't

deny the change he'd wrought in Joanna. She'd been beautiful in her plain clothes in the country. In fine muslin, tailored to suit every curve, she was stunning.

She failed to notice him as she stretched towards a book on the top shelf. Luke cast a quick glance around the library. He didn't see Lord Helmsworth, but he knew that either the Marquis or a chaperon must be lurking nearby. He'd be wise to slip off and leave her to the tranquillity of her new life while he tried to recapture his, but her struggle to grasp the book drew him to her.

'Do you need help?'

She dropped down on her heels and faced him, her mouth forming an O of surprise. 'Y-yes. I can't reach that book on Huria.'

He plucked the book off the shelf and handed it to her, avoiding touching her fingers, which were covered by new kidskin gloves. In the narrow aisle, with his back to the library, he blocked her from the view of the other patrons, giving them a touch of privacy.

'Thank you.'

She rewarded his assistance with a smile, but there was no mistaking the tension marring the corners of it. He wondered if she wanted him to go. He should— but he couldn't. Instead, he watched her flip open the tome to a coloured plate of a palace decorated in rich red and gold and a garden filled with exotic birds and plants. A slight crease furrowed her brow, as it had the day in the Huntford Place ballroom when she'd read her friend's letter.

'It's not what you're looking for?' Luke asked, her dismay troubling him.

'It is, but it reminds me of how much I miss Rachel and how far away she is.'

'Since your fortune has changed, surely you could visit her?'

'I suppose I could, if Grandfather allows it.'

He hooked his thumbs in his waistcoat pockets, his indignation rising at the mention of the Marquis. 'He shouldn't object to you leading your life.'

She snapped the book closed and hugged it against her chest, something of the governess coming over her. 'He's very protective of me and I'm grateful for it.'

'Good, you deserve to be cherished.' He shifted closer to her and inhaled her new scent. The simple aroma of soap and lavender which had flavoured her skin in the country had been replaced by the richer fragrance of cherry blossoms and cinnamon. Like the cloth of her walking dress and the fine bonnet covering her luminous hair, the more fashionable attire didn't diminish the simplicity of her beauty or turn it garish, but adorned it like a fine sculpture did a well-tended garden. 'But don't let gratitude make you surrender who you are, or what you want. I know the torment of sacrificing even the most cherished things for family duty.'

Her eyebrows rose in surprise as though he'd discovered a secret. The image of her and Lord Jarsdel together rushed to him but it was blotted out by her unsettling frown. 'At the theatre, you didn't think we could maintain an acquaintance. Now you're concerned with how I conduct my life?'

'I've always been concerned about you. I still am.

It's your concern for *me* I question,' he challenged. 'You couldn't even spare me a word in the country.'

'I wanted to, but I feared if I encouraged you it would create problems between me and Grandfather.'

She bit her bottom lip, as nervous as when he'd approached her near the fern stand at Huntford Place. Luke stared at her, stunned out of his ire. She hadn't ignored him because she'd coveted wealth but because she thought she'd had no choice.

Then her spirit flashed, and it was her turn to accuse him. 'Besides, you made no effort to come and see me.'

'I didn't think you wanted me to.'

Their honesty with each other dissolved the tension between them.

'While we were apart it seems we were mistaken about each other's intentions,' he said.

For all the many times he'd been the one to search her out, she was the one approaching him now. In her eyes was the same hesitant anticipation which had been there when he'd first kissed her in Hertfordshire.

'I think we still are.'

Her fingers, clasping the book in front of her, were close to his. If he reached out, he could touch her, but he didn't move.

'Are we?'

'Yes.'

She curled one finger around his and his pessimism about her place in his life faded, along with every reason he'd concocted for trying to forget her. It was as impossible as leaving his men's families to starve. She'd been a tranquil retreat in the midst of the chaos of his worries and family concerns, a unique woman among the many he'd met since returning home. He should have fought against her excuses, remained stubbornly beside her and told anyone who challenged them to go to Hades.

He could do that now. And it was clear in her azure eyes that she wanted him to.

He opened his mouth, ready to speak to all the questions and uncertainties passing between them, when a man's voice shattered the moment.

'Joanna, is this man bothering you?' Lord Helmsworth bore down on them like a constable did a pickpocket while Lord Jarsdel remained politely at the opening to the aisle.

'No, not at all.' Despite his ominous approach, Joanna didn't shrink away or stutter in her response as she held up the book. 'Major Preston retrieved this book about Huria for me. He was quite helpful on the matter in Hertfordshire.'

'Yes, I'm sure he was.' Lord Helmsworth eyed Luke with enough suspicion to tell him he'd heard something about the dust-up concerning Luke and Joanna and the storm.

Joanna noted it, too, for she lowered the tome, more reserve coming over her than at his hasty approach, but she didn't cower in silence. 'He's campaigning on behalf of soldiers now, trying to ensure their families are provided for while their men are missing in Spain.'

'Are you?' Lord Helmsworth eyed Luke as if he was about to snatch his watch and dart out the door.

'I'm working to secure their pay for their families if they're still alive and their pensions if they're not.' Luke paused, refusing to imagine them lying forgotten in some field. He had to believe they'd survived.

'The treatment of our veterans who've given so much for their country is deplorable.'

'I agree, and something should be done to help them.' Her grandfather rubbed his chin. Luke and Joanna exchanged surprised glances at his having agreed with Luke. 'I'm glad someone is fighting for their due, even if it is you.'

Luke kept his expression passive. The man was stubborn in his dislike, except this time Luke was to blame. Luke's behaviour in Hertfordshire had convinced the Marquis that he wasn't worthy of honourable company, or Joanna.

'Lord Jarsdel, would you please escort Miss Radcliff to the carriage?' her grandfather asked.

'It would be my pleasure.'

Luke's irritation flared as the earl offered Joanna his elbow. He eyed her, silently challenging her to stand with him and refuse, but she didn't.

'Good day, Major Preston.' She walked with Lord Jarsdel to the door, but when the earl stepped forward to open it, she turned and threw Luke one last look. He caught it, and the conflict between wanting to stay with Luke and obedience to her grandfather. Lord Helmsworth noticed it, too, before she hurried outside.

'You might fool an innocent girl, but you won't fool a man of my experience,' Lord Helmsworth warned in a low voice. 'I've dealt with a poor military man in search of an easy life with a rich wife before.'

'I'm not trying to fool anyone.' If Lord Helmsworth were a younger man, Luke would strike him for the insult and call him out, but he'd been raised to respect his elders, even when they didn't extend him the same courtesy. 'I have a great regard for your granddaughter, one I developed long before her situation changed.'

'And how convenient for you it has. Now you can hold your head up when you try to seduce her instead of sneaking around.' He slapped Luke on the chest with the back of his hand. 'Chase after all the heiresses in London if you want, but you will not wed Joanna.'

Lord Helmsworth strolled past Luke and out the door, twirling his walking stick as he went.

Luke watched through the large front windows as the Marquis climbed into the curricle where Joanna and Lord Jarsdel sat together. Lord Helmsworth smiled too widely at the couple as the driver took up the reins and snapped the horses into motion.

Determination rose up in Luke as the vehicle melted into the London traffic. Alma was right. There was more to affection than money or titles, and no obstacle Luke couldn't overcome. In the faint sweep of Joanna's finger against his, and in her potent look from across the library, she'd made it clear she still wanted him as much as he did her.

He wouldn't secure her hand at the expense of her relationship with the only family she had. Winning her and her grandfather's approval would take more tact and subtle manoeuvring than he was accustomed to. But Luke possessed the strength for battle. Hopefully Joanna did, too.

Joanna sat in the window seat of her grandfather's Grosvenor Square town house, the book on Huria resting on her lap. She tried to read about its history, but she couldn't picture the palaces and villages it described. She could only see Luke, standing in front of her in Hookham's. She could feel his finger intertwined with hers and hear his words echoing in the quiet.

I've always been concerned about you. I still am.

She'd spent the last month resigned to letting him go, but their brief time together today had changed everything. She'd invited him back to her, and with his firm touch he'd answered her call. This—his explanation for staying away and the softness of his touch—had rekindled the possibility of her being with him once more.

Unease undermined her elation and she struggled to sit still on the bench. Luke's warning not to surrender what she wanted to others had resonated deep inside her. However, speaking up had never been her strength, not at school, in Hertfordshire or here. She hadn't even been able to tell Luke of her agreement to entertain Lord Jarsdel's interest. It would have meant admitting he had been right about her inability to govern her own life.

There was also her grandfather to consider. With everything still so new between them she was hesitant to begin demanding her way. After all, her small attempt to make her grandfather see Luke in a different light by telling him about Luke's good works hadn't accomplished anything. She could well imagine how her insisting he see Luke as a rival to Lord Jarsdel would only further harden him against Luke, and possibly her.

'Jane loved to read, it's why there are so many novels in the library, though I'm afraid they're a little out of fashion,' her grandfather announced as he strolled into the room.

'It doesn't matter, they're all new to me.' She slipped the ribbon in the book on Huria and set it beside her. It was a potent reminder of Luke and everything she stood to lose if she didn't learn to ask for what she wanted, but so was her grandfather smiling down at her.

'This house was going to be hers when she married. It belonged to her mother's family and came with her when we wed.' His gaze slid to the portrait of her mother as a young girl cradling a small, black-and-white spaniel. It hung near the door across the room, opposite the painting of Joanna's grandmother in her wide hoops and powdered hair. A winsome look dulled his expression before he turned back to her. 'It'll be yours when you marry.'

'No. You've already been so good to me, I can't take more.'

He settled down on the window seat beside her, wrinkling the brocade pillows propped against the wall. 'I want you to have it and everything that isn't entitled to the estate to make sure you're secure, no matter what happens to me.'

'I don't know what to say.' She'd worried so much about her future at Huntford Place. Now, she'd never have to worry about it again, except where Luke's place in it was concerned.

Her grandfather sat back, serious in his regard of her. 'My gift makes you quite the wealthy heiress and a very eligible young lady. It means you must be on guard. You don't want to fall prey to a fortune hunter like your mother did.'

Joanna clasped the locket and ran it back and forth along its gold chain, sensing where the conversation was leading. 'I'll be cautious.'

'I'm sure you will be and I'll do my best to guide you through this Season, as I should have done with your mother. I could ask my sister, but a spirited girl like you doesn't want some old bat hovering around and she was too careless with your mother for me to trust her again.' He sneered in displeasure before he settled himself. 'It also means you must not speak with Major Preston again. Army men know how to wheedle their way into a lady's affection.'

Her heart thundered in her chest. She appreciated his looking after her, but not his dictating with whom she could and couldn't consort. If she intended to stand up for what she wanted, then now was the time to begin.

Taking a deep breath, she steeled herself against her fears and with a trembling voice she spoke. 'You've asked a great many things of me and I've happily done them all, but I can't do this. Whatever you may think of Major Preston, he's my friend. He was kind to me at Huntford Place and protected me when my employers would have done me ill.'

He cocked his head, the gesture as close as he'd ever come to chastising her. 'I understand he was a touch too kind to you.'

Joanna's hand stilled the locket on its chain. He had heard the stories of her and Luke and suspected the worst. Fear made her shiver, despite the blazing fire in the grate, and all desire to challenge her grandfather vanished. 'I'm sorry.'

'There's nothing to be sorry about. You aren't

experienced enough with gentlemen to realise the lengths they'll go to in order to get what they want. I'm sure Major Preston promised to defy his family and society in order to win your trust, all the while keeping things between you a secret. Then, when it became known, where was he? Not beside you defending you against the Huntfords, but protecting himself.'

'I was the one who left him at the vicarage after I refused his offer of marriage,' she whispered, admitting two sins at once.

'At least he had enough honour to make an offer,' he grudgingly conceded. 'But if he really loved you, he would've followed you and refused to take no for an answer. Instead, he stayed where he was and left you to your fate.'

'It wasn't like that at all.'

'Are you sure?' her grandfather pressed.

No, she wasn't. At the vicarage, Luke had been adamant he could overcome any obstacles to them marrying, but as soon as she'd refused him, he'd dismissed her as fast as Lieutenant Foreman had left Frances. He hadn't tried to visit her at Helmsworth Manor or contrived any other meeting between them. He'd said it was because he thought she didn't want him, and she'd believed him until this moment.

'I imagine you're far more appealing to him now that your situation has changed,' her grandfather pointed out, further increasing her doubts.

My situation. She rubbed the locket with her thumb. Luke had spoken of his family seeing the advantage in her new position. Perhaps they were the ones who'd changed Luke's mind and that was why he'd been so friendly in the library. Maybe they were encouraging him to use his connection with her to press their case about the river land. Luke was dedicated to his family and he'd do almost anything to help them, including woo her.

No, Luke wouldn't be so deceitful.

Joanna pinched the bridge of her nose, trying to sort out her warring feelings. Everything she'd heard today from Luke and her grandfather swirled in her mind until she couldn't decipher what was the truth and what wasn't. Her exchange with Luke in Hookham's spoke to her heart. What her grandfather said added to all the warnings from Miss Fanworth and the other teachers about gentlemen and minding herself in their presence. She hadn't minded herself today.

'I'm sorry if I upset you.' Her grandfather patted her hands, as loving now as he'd been through the last month. She turned her hand over in his and clasped it tight, grateful for his unfailing faith in the face of her weakness. It soothed her worries of being separated from him, but it didn't settle her confusion about Luke. 'What happened between you and Major Preston no longer matters and, as long as you don't see him again, we'll never speak of it.'

She didn't agree to his demand, but she didn't reject it either. Her grandfather had proved patient with her and she didn't wish to test the limits of his acceptance, especially with so much between her and Luke still unsure. As much as she cringed at having everything dictated by her grandfather or anyone else, she balked at leaving it to Luke's changing whims or her own. She'd be practical and realistic and decide nothing today. Instead, she'd wait for their next meeting and press him enough to discover the truth of his heart and hers.

'Can't you see the importance of making sure my men's families aren't left to suffer?' Luke paced in front of Lord Beckwith's desk, exasperated by this continued foot dragging. He'd spoken to half the superior officers in the Horse Guards and quite a number in the War Office. Each one had promised to help him, then foisted him off on another who'd done the same. Luke had got nowhere in securing funds for Reginald's sister, or his men's families. Despite the government's stalling, he wasn't about to give up.

'I can, but it isn't up to me.' Lord Beckwith twirled his pen between his fingers. He'd been sympathetic and helpful in his assistance, but all too willing to stop when he faced any resistance. 'Regulations state the soldiers must be dead before their families can receive a pension.'

'Then make sure they receive their pay.'

He tossed his pen on the desk. 'They can't be paid if they're missing and not confirmed dead'

Luke dug his fists into his hips and stared down at Lord Beckwith, fighting to remain calm. It seemed it wasn't just Edward who could rouse his emotion, but the dithering of the Army Pay Board. 'This isn't acceptable and it has to change.'

'Lieutenant General Calvert is already working to implement many changes, including treatment of our wounded.'

'It isn't enough.'

'The government is a monolith which cannot be

easily moved, if at all.' Lord Beckwith leaned back in his chair and laced his fingers over his wide torso. He was sturdy like an ox, with a square chin with a divot set in the centre and the first hints of fat creeping in beneath the line of it. He'd been out of the field and in Whitehall too long. 'What we need are more men like you.'

'To do what? Rail at the lords who refuse to take action?' It wouldn't win him any allies any more than railing against Lord Helmsworth would win him over. He hadn't seen Joanna since Hookham's two days ago. He'd visited Lord Helmsworth's twice, but had been told both times they were not at home, and his few notes to the Marquis and her had gone unanswered. More than likely, Lord Helmsworth had stopped them from reaching her and no society events had brought them together, further frustrating Luke's attempts to see her. He was trying to be patient and smart in his pursuit but if it didn't produce results soon, he'd change his tactics.

'They'll listen to you before they do other soldiers.' Luke levelled a disbelieving look at Lord Beckwith who held up his hand, motioning for him to hear him out. 'You may not be the earl, but you come from their class, you speak their language, as well as the enlisted man's. We need someone like you who can attest to what conditions are really like and why they must be changed. I could find a commission for you and a position within the Army here in London.'

Luke stared at the sword lying across the top of the mahogany desk, Lord Beckwith's gold regimental insignia engraved on the lancet. Luke hated the wrangling of politics as much as he did the rules of society, but Lord Beckwith's suggestion intrigued him. This was the first time anyone had suggested Luke use his status as an earl's son for more than securing a loan to purchase a higher rank. He'd have to do it again to obtain enough money to pay for a commission. If he did, he could make a difference while he was stuck here in England, but it would take months or years and his soldiers' families needed help now.

'I'll think about it, but at the moment I have the more pressing matter of my men's pay. Who else can I speak with?'

'Lord Craven didn't return for the little Season and Lord Farley is too entrenched in his ways to see reason.' Lord Beckwith held up five fingers and lowered them as he ticked off men until one remained. 'You haven't spoken to Lord Jarsdel yet. If you can make progress with anyone, it's him. He's the most reasonable of the lot and very sympathetic to the plight of enlisted men. He's well acquainted with the Duke of York, too. Appealing directly to the Duke through him could be your best chance of getting what you want.'

Luke bit back a groan of frustration. Lord Jarsdel was the last man Luke wanted to speak with, but the answers he'd received to his enquiries into his men's families, especially Reginald's sister, weren't good. They were struggling. If it was in Luke's power to give them money, he would, but with the funds he'd secured by selling his major's commission tied up in Pensum Manor, there was little to be spared. Time was also working against him. When the special session of Parliament ended, the lords would exit town as fast as they'd returned, making it difficult to rouse them to do anything before the next session opened in the spring. He wasn't sure Miss Crowther or the other families could make it through the winter without assistance. Luke must swallow down his reluctance and speak with Lord Jarsdel.

Chapter Thirteen

Luke entered the hallowed entrance hall of White's, still amazed Lord Jarsdel had agreed to this meeting. After Lord Helmsworth's numerous refusals to see him, Luke was beginning to think the only titled men he might ever speak to were Lord Beckwith and his father.

The butler led him down the hall, past a room where young bucks stood drinking, talking and laughing. They paid no attention to Luke as he passed. He'd come here once before with Edward and found it as tedious as a night watch on an outpost.

The butler stopped at the last door on the left and pushed it open. He announced Luke to Lord Jarsdel and then ushered him inside. It was a small sitting room with dark panelling covered with paintings of terriers and cavaliers in gilded frames hung three high on every wall.

Lord Jarsdel rose to greet Luke.

'Major Preston, it's an honour to meet you. I'm well acquainted with your exploits in Spain.' Lord Jarsdel sat in a chair beside the fire and waved Luke into the matching one across from him. Luke perched on the edge of the fine leather, noting the faint scent of polish mixing with tobacco and coal. 'Miss Radcliff told me about your work on behalf of your men at tea yesterday. Lord Helmsworth mentioned it, too.'

Luke wondered what else Lord Helmsworth had told him and hoped it hadn't damage his cause. It was also galling to hear Lord Jarsdel had seen more of Joanna in the last three days than Luke had, but he wasn't here to press his suit with her, but his soldiers' cause.

'My men have faithfully served the Crown. I ask the Crown to show them the same respect until we discover what's happened to them. Their families need their pay or the pensions to survive.'

Luke described their plight with hunger and housing while they grieved and worried for their missing fathers and brothers. Lord Jarsdel listened, nodding sympathetically every now and again, instead of yawning and fidgeting as Lord Stuart or Lord Hadden had done when Luke had approached them.

'I can't guarantee anything, some of my fellow board members are quite stubborn about rules and regulations, but I assure you I'll do my best to convince the pension board to grant them money. If the Duke of York is at Vauxhall Gardens tonight when I accompany Miss Radcliff and Lord Helmsworth there, I'll speak to him on your behalf. If not, I'll arrange to visit him tomorrow,' Lord Jarsdel offered when Luke finished.

As much as Luke wanted to despise Lord Jarsdel for his interest in Joanna, his willingness to consider the case for Luke's men impressed him. 'I greatly appreciate anything you can do.'

Luke rose to bow and take his leave, but Lord Jarsdel waved him back into his seat. 'A moment more of your time, if you don't mind?'

'Not at all.' Luke sat down, wondering what the man wanted.

'I understand from Lord Helmsworth you're well acquainted with Miss Radcliff from your time in the country.'

'I am.' Luke regarded the languid earl, wondered if he was going to take him to task for the rumours swirling about the two of them.

'She's a rare lady among many in London, quick witted, sensible and caring. She reminds me of my late wife when she was young.' He took up a drink from the table beside him and swirled it over the edge of the chair arm as he spoke. 'Do you know my wife and I were married over the anvil at Gretna Green?'

'I didn't.' He knew very little about Lord Jarsdel except what Alma and Lord Beckwith had told him.

'My family didn't approve of her. She was a baronet's daughter with a modest dowry, too humble for a man destined to be an earl, and I was one year away from my majority.'

'So you defied your family.' His admiration for the man was growing even while he anxiously waited for him to make his point. Luke was certain he wasn't going to like it.

'Not until the night she told me if I didn't claim her she would marry another.' His eyes wandered to the ceiling and a smile of delight made the years fade from his face. Then he turned serious as he studied

Luke. 'I had a decision to make, Major Preston, and I suspect you do, too. If you fail to offer for Miss Radcliff, I will. My wife may still hold my heart, but it doesn't mean I can't care for another or wish to remain alone for the remainder of my years.'

It wasn't a threat, but a polite warning. 'I intend to propose to Miss Radcliff once certain impediments are removed.'

'And if they can't be removed?' Apparently, Lord Helmsworth had offered Lord Jarsdel his opinion of Luke.

'I don't court defeat.' *Not from the Army Pay Board or a stubborn marquis.*

'Nor should you.' Lord Jarsdel rose and extended his hand to Luke. 'Good day to you, Major Preston.'

As Luke took his leave Lord Jarsdel's warning added a new urgency to his pursuit of Joanna. The very things Luke admired about Joanna—her understanding of hard work and sacrifice, her desire to place duty and responsibility to family above her own whims and wants—might now be the very things which would end any chance of them being together. If Lord Jarsdel proposed before Luke could secure Lord Helmsworth's approval the Marquis might pressure her into accepting the Earl and he'd lose her.

No, he would not. If Joanna was going to be at Vauxhall tonight, then he would be, too. It was time to stop being patient and become more aggressive in his campaign.

Fireworks exploded above the lake, sending sparkling tendrils of red to cascade down over Vauxhall

Gardens. Joanna clapped along with the other guests filling the private box.

'Quite a spectacle,' Lord Jarsdel commented to Joanna as another burst lit up the sky.

'It's amazing.' Almost as much as her sitting here. Every one of her grandfather's friends who'd joined them tonight for a light supper and the opening of the garden had been kind to her. It was the various people passing outside the box who hadn't been as considerate. They'd stare at her, then duck behind their fans to whisper together, less curious than contemptuous of her sudden rise in prominence. Like her grandfather and Lord Jarsdel, she did her best to ignore them, but it was difficult, especially when Lady Huntford, Frances and Catherine came strolling by.

'Lord Helmsworth, what a pleasure to see you return to London at last,' Lady Huntford sang out. She approached the edge of the box from the path, staring down her nose at Joanna even as she all but grovelled before her grandfather. Frances trailed behind her, as peevish as ever while Catherine gawked at everything as Joanna had done when she'd first entered the pleasure garden.

'I didn't have a good reason until now.' He motioned to Joanna, making it clear his neighbour must acknowledge her.

Tugging her wrap up higher on her shoulders, Lady Huntford dipped a grudging curtsy. 'Miss Radcliff.'

Frances wasn't as polite, staring everywhere but at Joanna, determined to cut her until Lady Huntford snatched her daughter by the arm and pulled her up to the box. 'Frances, you must greet Miss Radcliff.'

'It's a pleasure to see you again.' The sarcastic

sneer already dampening her natural good looks became more pronounced as she curtsied, then rose and called out in a loud voice to her sister, 'Catherine, come greet your former governess.'

The conversation in the box quietened at the not-too-polite reference to Joanna's previous position. Joanna wondered if the chit would climb the Chinese pavilion to announce it to the entire garden. Joanna shouldn't be ashamed of her background, and her grandfather's title staved off a great deal of open criticism about it, but it was clear by the whispers behind her not everyone wanted to be reminded of her humble origins.

'Good evening, Miss Radcliff,' Catherine greeted, with a genuine smile. She wore a new gown of yellow muslin trimmed in blue, but it didn't match her sister's elegant attire.

'I see your father allowed you to come out at last,' Joanna remarked, encouraged by Catherine's pleasant attitude. It appeared Catherine had taken Joanna's advice to be kind and it heartened Joanna to think she'd made something of a difference to the girl.

'Yes, he thought the small Season the perfect opportunity for it, especially now Frances is engaged to Mr Winborn.'

Joanna was as amazed by the announcement as the thought of a gentleman willingly yoking himself to Frances, but it was far from her place to question the better sort, even if she was now, strangely, one of them.

'He only did it to spare the expense,' Frances scoffed and Catherine's shoulders slumped.

Joanna caught her eyes and raised her chin, reminding the young lady to do the same.

Catherine, bolstered by the silent encouragement, set back her shoulders and Joanna winked at her in approval of her confidence. With any luck, the girl would find a husband and a life of her own where she could blossom away from the cruel remarks and painful indifference of her family.

'Come along, girls, we're expected at our box,' Lady Huntford announced, drawing away her daughters with unnecessary alacrity. She was probably eager to escape from Joanna and any taint she might visit on their family.

'Don't allow them to trouble you,' Lord Jarsdel encouraged from beside her.

'I'm worried they're saying what a number of people are already thinking.' She didn't belong here and it was true.

'People in society will always find a reason to judge everyone else. It's something you must harden yourself against.'

'I hope I don't become so hard I turn to stone, as or sharp with my tongue as Miss Huntford.' Or as alone as Madame Dubois and without a husband or children. She'd never thought of Madame Dubois as lonely, but one time she'd seen her from an upstairs window in the garden reading an old letter with a melancholy expression to make Joanna's heart hurt. Whatever Madame's regrets, and she'd never shared them with Joanna, Joanna didn't wish to carry any of her own into her maturity, although it seemed unavoidable. Already she was burdened with too many about Luke. It had been three days since Hookham's and she'd had no word from him, nor had she seen him, leaving her to be tortured by her doubts about him.

'A woman as generous in spirit as you could never be so petty,' Lord Jarsdel complimented, but it didn't reach into her heart the way Luke's did. Lord Jarsdel was kind and caring, but with him there was no passion or eagerness to defy everything to be near him. Perhaps she should be glad. She'd seen what passion had done to Grace, what it had nearly done to Frances, and how it had ruined her mother. It was something to be avoided.

'Let's take a walk. I'm tired of cold ham and I want to see the bonfires down by the lake,' her grandfather called out to the delight of his guests.

Soon they were making their way along the wide, winding walk leading to the lake. Overhead, the fireworks continued hissing, whining and popping as they launched, then exploded. Lord Jarsdel strolled beside Joanna, explaining to her his work with the Army Pay Board. She could barely concentrate on what he said as she studied every passing male face in the flickering light of the torches, hoping to see Luke.

Surely he'd take advantage of this opportunity to try and see her? However, he hadn't done so at any of the art showings or fashionable hours in Rotten Row over the past few days. Maybe her grandfather was correct and he didn't really want her. No, that couldn't be right.

Then why isn't Luke here? A moment with him might settle everything.

Then, in the white burst of a firework, she spied him standing near the water's edge with his parents and Lord and Lady Pensum. While the others oohed over the bright explosions, Joanna stared at Luke. She wanted to hurry down to him, slip her hand around his arm and breathe in his cedar scent. Her grandfather's warning to be cautious and avoid him kept her at Lord Jarsdel's side. She couldn't risk her already fragile reputation, or reward her grandfather's kindness and patience by spitting in his eye in front of everyone. It was a good thing she chose to be prudent.

Luke hailed a young woman who stood nearby with a few older people. The strange young lady was petite with dark hair and round eyes. She left her party to meet Luke, admiring him as though he were as bright as one of the sparklers on the floating pavilion. He was generous with his smiles as he spoke to her and overly friendly with her in a way which made Joanna's heart drop.

Grandfather was right. Her desire to be loved had kept her from seeing the truth. Joanna had been good enough for Luke in dark corners and isolated houses, but not in front of others.

As if sensing someone watching him, Luke turned and noticed her as the white light faded overhead. She clasped her locket to steady herself against the pain eating at her, refusing to allow him to see her hurt. His glance flicked to Lord Jarsdel and he pressed his lips together in disapproval, then turned back to his companion, making it clear he was finished with her.

'Lord Jarsdel, come and explain how they make fireworks,' one lady implored, drawing him away from Joanna's side and closer to the front of the group.

Joanna fell behind the others, the distance between them widening as they approached the lake. If she could slip off back to the carriage and home, she would. The sparkle of the garden had lost its appeal.

The quick fall of boots on the path behind her made her step out of the way of whoever was coming. She was stunned when a hand took her by the arm and pulled her into the shadow of a large oak tree beside the path.

She whirled around, ready to strike her attacker when she came face to face with Luke. He stood over her, his chest so close to hers she could see the flourishes on the buttons of his coat in the faint lantern light. 'What are you doing?'

'This.' He leaned down to kiss her but she pushed against his chest and twisted to one side, avoiding his lips.

The hardness of his body beneath her palms shocked her as much as all the questions and anxieties surrounding them. Her stiff elbows weakened under the urge to revel in his embrace, but she remained strong. She was a sensible, controlled woman, not some senseless flirt. 'No. I won't sneak around with you any longer, not when you're courting another woman in plain sight.'

He kept his arms tight around her. The pressure of them weakened her resolve as much as the earnestness in his eyes. 'I'm courting no one except you.'

'Because I'm rich now and I can convince my grandfather to give you and your family the river land?' She winced at the harshness in her voice and the way it made him pull back in disbelief, but he still didn't let go of her.

'You think so little of me?'

'My grandfather does and I don't know what to

think.' In his embrace it was easy to believe in his affection for her, but difficult to calm her fears and concerns. 'First you want me, then you don't, then you do again but in secret while you cavort in the open with another woman down by the lake.'

'The woman by the lake is Captain Crowther's sister and recently betrothed to a vicar in Hampstead Heath,' he answered gently, not flinging the truth at her in the same harsh manner she'd delivered her accusation. 'It's why she and her friends are here tonight. She needs a bit of joy since her brother has gone missing.'

Joanna stumbled in her anger, but not her determination to continue on until she had the truth, all of it. 'And my ability to help you and your family?'

'It has nothing to do with my desire for you. Despite your relationship to Lord Helmsworth, you're still the woman I came to adore in the country, the one who cares about me and others, who understands duty and honour and loyalty to those you love.' He brushed a strand of hair off her forehead and tucked it behind her ear. His hand lingered near her cheek as the shimmering light of another rocket lit up his face. 'I still want you for my wife, I would even if you weren't a marquis's granddaughter.'

She held tight to his arms and stared into his eyes, made brighter by the intensity of his regard for her. He admired her as much tonight as he had the day she'd stumbled in the stream and he'd caught her, when he'd protected her from Mr Selton and when he'd asked her to marry him in the vicarage.

He pulled her closer and she didn't resist, but fell against him, clinging to him as she had the night they'd been intimate. Beneath her fingertips, she felt his heart beat with the same power as the exploding fireworks. 'I love you, Joanna.'

She clutched his lapels, steadying herself as the truth of what he said and what it meant struck her. Not even Madame Dubois or Miss Fanworth had ever uttered the sentiment. In their own way, they'd given her love, but the words had never reached her ears until this moment. Beneath the flickering torches, with the fireworks flashing, all the chances she'd taken with him, the risk and losses, insults and censures no longer mattered.

'Tell me you love me,' he urged, bringing his face close to hers.

'I do.' She raised her lips to his, all fear of rejection and her grandfather's demands disappearing in his passionate kiss. Despite the difficulties separating them, he'd remained true to her, never giving up and neither would she. She wanted to be his wife and she would struggle with him to achieve it.

'Joanna?' her grandfather's worried voice carried over the topiaries. 'Where are you?'

She broke from Luke's kiss to peer through the bushes. Her grandfather stood in the centre of the walk, searching for her. 'What about him? I can't break his heart the way my mother did.'

He clasped her shoulders and turned her to face him, his eyes piercing hers. 'I promise I'll never make you choose between duty to your grandfather and your heart. We'll find a way to win him to our cause.'

She rested her hands on his trim waist, elated by his promise. He would fight for her as he did his men and their families and love her as she'd always longed to be loved.

'Now go, before he worries.' He swept Joanna's lips with a parting kiss, then nudged her back towards the walk.

She stumbled out from behind the tree, struggling to settle herself as her grandfather rushed up to her.

'My dear, where have you been?'

'I'm sorry, I didn't mean to wander off, but the garden is so confusing.' She prayed the dim paper lanterns hanging overhead hid her moist lips and her too-red cheeks from his notice. It was difficult to tell from his expression if they did.

'Don't do it again or you'll be mistaken for a woman of easy virtue.'

He'd raised his voice, saying it more in the direction of the tree where Luke hid than to her. Joanna fingered the gold chain and locket, now heavy on her skin. He'd guessed where she'd been and with whom.

'Come, the others are waiting.'

She followed him back to their party and Lord Jarsdel's side. Thankfully, a dazzling display of sparklers and candles from a pavilion situated in the centre of the lake kept everyone focused on it and not her. She couldn't see how this mess would end, but Luke loved her and she loved him and somehow all would be well.

Luke watched from the shadows as Lord Helmsworth guided Joanna back to the party and directly to Lord Jarsdel. The earl was as solicitous in his attention to Joanna as a besotted suitor. Luke wanted to march down the walk, take her in his arms and make it clear to everyone she was his, but he didn't move. Making a scene wouldn't help them. Instead, he returned to where his family stood a short distance away by the lake, ignoring the hard stares being flung at them by the Marquis.

Miss Crowther approached him before he reached his parents.

'I want to thank you again, Major Preston, before my party and I leave, for all you're doing on Reginald's behalf and mine.' She had her brother's dark hair and pale brown eyes, but she was much shorter and more slender in build. Luke suspected it had more to do with meagre meals than natural inclination. 'He always said you were too honourable for your own good and his.'

'I did my best to influence him, but he always resisted, especially where frequenting tavern gaming rooms was concerned. At least he has a knack for winning.'

'He's probably gambling with French soldiers right now, assuming he survived.' Her smile faded at the very real possibility they might never see Reginald again.

'He'll come back. He's too charming to perish,' Luke encouraged for her sake and his.

'You're right. We must continue to have faith. Goodnight, Major Preston.'

She left him to rejoin her party, her steps a little slower than before.

'Luke, come here quickly.' His father waved him over. 'Your brother has the most exciting news.'

Edward stood beside Alma, the hard planes of his face softer than Luke had seen them at any time since coming home. Even Alma seemed different. The glow which had surrounded her in London was brighter and Luke wondered what had brought such a change over them.

'Well, go on, tell them,' his father insisted, nearly hopping back and forth on his feet in excitement. Edward took Alma's hand and opened his mouth to speak when their father cut him off. 'Alma is expecting a child in the new year.'

A rocket exploded overhead, making Edward and Alma's smiles dazzle beneath its silvery light. Luke's mother's burst into tears. She rushed to Alma and embraced her, blubbing out words of congratulations. Luke's father shook Edward's hand, his eyes red with his tears of excitement.

Luke stared at them, amazed. A child. He looked to Alma, who winked at him over his mother's shoulder. So this was what she'd meant by still believing in miracles and it was one. Alma and Edward would be parents at last and he would be an uncle, and with luck a husband soon, too. It was an exhilarating night.

Their father let go of Edward and Luke stepped forward to clasp his brother's hand and give it a hearty shake. 'Well done.'

'Alma said you believed it would happen and helped her to do the same.' Edward pulled him off to one side, away from their parents, who were gushing over Alma. A rare humility came over him as he let go of Luke. 'Thank you for not giving up on us and your willingness to make sacrifices. I'm sorry if I haven't been kind to you. It's been difficult these last few years. You were right, I was jealous of your accomplishments because I'd failed in the one most expected of me. I shouldn't have taken out my frustrations on you. Siring a child might not seem like much to a man of your achievements, but for me it means not seeing all of my hard work and Father's come to an end. We've fought so long for Pensum Manor. To have someone to pass it on to and to give a child the security we've always lacked, means a great deal to me.'

The strain between them evaporated like a horse's breath in the cold. Joanna had been right about his brother and, for the first time, he saw how alike he and Edward were. Like Luke, Edward had been struggling with his failures, but in the end he'd triumphed. Luke hoped to emulate him in this regard. 'I admire what you've done for Pensum Manor and the line. I haven't always given you enough credit for it. You're a good man, Edward, and you deserve your success and all the happiness of a family of your own. I can't wait to welcome the new Ingham.'

He grabbed his brother and gave him a hearty embrace before stepping back.

'If all goes well, you could return to the Army,' Edward said, sobering Luke.

'I could.' He looked to where Joanna stood with her group at the lake's edge. The joy he'd longed to see in her face in Hertfordshire decorated it now, filling him with as much happiness as her. The rush to return to Spain, which had once been so powerful, had lost its grip. Lord Beckwith said he could serve his men in a new way. It wasn't the same as standing beside them in a hail of musket fire, but it would make a difference and he could do it here in England near Joanna. Once they were married, she could help him. For the first time since coming home, he had a purpose, more than one, and both important enough to make him stay.

The carriage wheels against the cobblestone mimicked the steady rhythm of Joanna's heart as the vehicle carried her and her grandfather home. Outside, the streets were still and dark except for the swinging lanterns of the young boys lighting groups of men home. Their breath rose about their heads in the autumn chill. Inside the carriage it was as warm as Luke's lips had been against hers.

He loves me.

His words were as precious to her as his commitment to see them together. After years of everyone letting her go, her mother, Madame Dubois, here was someone at last striving to keep her close. She pressed her lips together, savouring the taste of Luke lingering there. He wanted her, not out of guilt for seducing her or to help his family, but as his wife and nothing could ruin her elation.

'I have a surprise for you. I've arranged to hold a ball in your honour next week.' her grandfather announced.

Except this.

'Why didn't you discuss it with me before you decided?' She sat up, rocking to one side as the carriage made a turn, trying not to be scolding. She should thank him and be grateful. This was something any young lady might wish for, but she was as annoyed by the news as the constant squeak of the carriage wheel behind her seat. She didn't want to be the centre of so much attention, most of it unpleasant as Lady Huntford had made clear tonight.

'I'm sorry, but I've wanted to do this since the moment we met.' He shifted across the carriage to sit beside her. 'I have something to show you.'

He produced a letter from inside his coat pocket and handed it to her. The paper, despite the fine quality, was yellow with age and the edges were wrinkled. She turned it over to reveal the one line indicating who it was meant for.

To My Daughter

'What is this?' Joanna asked.

'A letter to you, from Jane. She wrote it the day before she died and gave it to Mr Browning in the hopes he'd find you. He gave it to me once you were found. I'd thought of showing it to you sooner, but I decided to wait until you were more settled.'

Joanna swallowed hard, afraid to hold the paper too tight for fear it would crumble and she'd lose the only words she'd ever had from her mother.

'Go ahead, open it,' her grandfather urged.

Joanna turned the letter over and gently unfolded it to reveal her mother's cramped and shaky handwriting.

My dearest daughter,
There is so much I wish to say to you, but in my weakness I struggle to write the words. Last year I followed my heart and it has brought me both great joy and crushing sorrow. Your

*father is gone, died in battle, and I fear I will
leave you, too.*

*I wish I could be there when you take your
first steps, to teach you to ride like my father
taught me. Perhaps some day your grandfather can give you the coming-out ball I used
to dream of when I was carrying you. I cry to
think I will not be there to see it.*

*There isn't enough time for me to tell you
everything you will ever need to deal with the
world, so I'll write the most important. I loved
you from the first moment I felt you move inside me, and I love you still. Never doubt this,
or how much you were wanted, and never be
afraid to follow your heart, but do it wisely. It
is a lesson I fear I learned too late.*
Your loving mother

Joanna's chest tightened, but there were no tears.
There was too much regret for everything she and
her mother had lost for her to cry. The childhood she
might have had if her mother had lived teased her in
the darkness, but she refused to entertain the sense
of loss for too long. Joanna rested her head on her
grandfather's shoulder and he put his arm around her.
She was grateful for the gift of the letter. For so many
years she thought she hadn't been wanted by her parents, but she'd been wrong.

'Do you see now why I arranged the ball?' her
grandfather asked, his voice thick with tears.

'I do.' She stared down at the yellowed edges of
the parchment resting on her lap and read the last line
over and over.

Follow your heart, but do it wisely.

Her mother hadn't regretted her time with her father, but the damage it had wrought. This, more than her desire for a coming-out ball, spoke to Joanna. In her mother's words was the permission to pursue a life with Luke and how she might accomplish it. If she was smart in her choices, less impetuous in her decisions, and more willing to work to earn the approval of her grandfather than her mother had been, she might succeed in love where her mother had failed.

'I think the ball will be lovely, but there is one thing I'd like to request.' She sat back from her grandfather. Her fingers shook as she folded the letter and guilt gnawed at her over the stipulation she was about to place on her concession, but she must do it. If Luke was willing to fight for her, she must do the same for him instead of being afraid to act because of her worries. She would follow her heart, but in a way her mother had failed to do. 'I should like you to invite the Inghams.'

Her grandfather started in surprise, and then his eyes began to narrow with his old hate. 'I won't have them here.'

Joanna braced herself and continued on. 'You speak of making things right for your daughter and me. Now there's one more thing that must be righted. This disagreement between the two families must end.'

'I asked you not to see that man,' he reprimanded, but she didn't allow it to stop her this time.

'I know.' She took his hand and squeezed it gently. 'But you've been so kind and generous to me over this past month and I want everyone, including the

Inghams, to see what a loving and wonderful man you are.'

Her grandfather didn't answer, but stared for a long moment at their intertwined fingers. In the silence, punctuated by the clack of the carriage over the cobblestones, she struggled to beat back her worry. She'd asserted herself and it remained to be seen how he would react.

At last he raised his face to hers. There was something stiff about his expression, a reluctance of sorts, but it clashed with his words, giving her hope. 'You sound like your mother tonight. She used to be the peacemaker in the family when her mother was alive, until nothing could bring peace between us. You're right, this feud has gone on too long. I will invite the Inghams and do what I can to put this rift behind us.'

'Thank you, Grandfather.' She kissed him on the forehead, her heart filled with a love and confidence she hadn't experienced in a long time. She'd spoken up and the world hadn't come crashing down on her. Instead, her courage had brought her grandfather and the Inghams closer to reconciling and opened the way for her happiness with Luke.

Chapter Fourteen

'Lord Helmsworth to see Major Preston,' the Inghams' butler announced.

Everyone set down their silverware and forgot the roast as they turned down the dinner table to stare at Luke.

'It looks like you've finally succeeded with the old man. Well done,' his father congratulated, lifting his wine goblet to Luke. 'This is turning out to be quite a week.'

'I wouldn't be so quick to celebrate.' Luke pushed back his chair and rose, wondering what had brought Lord Helmsworth here. Perhaps Joanna had worked her subtle charm on the old man, but he doubted it. Like a too-quiet morning before a battle, this unannounced guest made Luke wary.

'Major Preston, what a pleasure it is to see you this morning,' Lord Helmsworth offered with an overly wide smile as Luke entered the sitting room.

'To what do I owe the pleasure of your visit?'

'I wish to speak with you about Miss Radcliff.'

The two of them remained standing, eyeing each

other like a couple of cocks in a pit. Lord Helmsworth had lost some of the wildness of his appearance from the country. It was as if the Savile Row tailors had finally had a crack at him instead of the local ones from the village. It wasn't so much his fine suit which made Luke pause, but the cat-who-ate-the-canary gleam in his eyes. 'You see, I'm holding a ball in her honour in a few days and I'd be delighted if you and your family could attend.'

'Delighted?' He didn't believe it.

'Very much so because I think it's time we finally put our differences aside. I'm prepared to deed to your family the disputed land on one condition.'

'Which is?'

'You must never see Joanna again after the ball.'

His offer nearly knocked Luke across the room with the same force as the cannonball that had once exploded too close to him. 'You think my regard for her so slight I can be bought off?'

'I know it was you she was dallying with at Vauxhall. You weren't content to ruin her in the country, but wanted to compromise her here so that no man will have her. I'll not have it and I will see to it she doesn't make the same mistake her mother did.'

'The only mistake she'll make is walking away from what she wants because of someone else's demands. I won't let her do it, not for land or money or anything else you wish to throw at me.'

'Then let me to appeal to your sense of honour and responsibility. If you continue in your pursuit of Joanna, I will not only withdraw the very generous dowry and inheritance I've settled on her, but my protection. I will return her to the school where she was raised and leave her to make her way in the world without me.'

Luke levelled a hard look at Lord Helmsworth. 'How can you be so heartless?'

'Because I had my heart ripped out once before and lost my only child and nineteen years with my granddaughter because of a scheming man like you. I can't bear it again,' he shouted, his eyes wild with hurt and his hands shaking at his sides.

His pain pierced Luke's fury and he took a deep breath. He'd seen so many men wounded without scars or physical injuries, their ability to endure hardship and horrors weakened by their experiences. The same suffering drove Lord Helmsworth to make this awful proposal and he pitied him. Luke addressed him as he would one of his soldiers afflicted by the mental anguish of war. 'Joanna has a very generous heart with enough love for both of us. There's no need to make her choose.'

Lord Helmsworth's frenzied grief eased with Luke's reassurance, and a long minute passed, filled by the laugh of a servant from somewhere in the house. It was clear the Marquis loved Joanna, but the past was blinding him so much he could no longer discern between events from twenty years ago and now. Luke hoped his compassion could convince the good man he remembered from the long-ago Christmas party to assert himself over the wounded one standing before him.

Then Lord Helmsworth jerked at his lapels, the stony façade of the titled man he'd always worn with Luke descending over him again. His pain had won in the struggle against his goodness. 'I will if you force me to and it might not end the way you wish. She may choose me over you and then where will you be? Without the river. I know about your family's debts. A few more bad harvests and they'll overwhelm you until you're forced to sell Pensum Manor. If that happens, it'll be your fault.' Lord Helmsworth removed a paper from his pocket and held it out to Luke. 'Here's the deed to the land. If you promise to walk away from her, I'll give it to you today so your family may do with it as they please.'

Luke stared at the deed folded in on itself and tied with a slender red ribbon, struggling to find some way out of this ultimatum, but he couldn't. He didn't doubt Lord Helmsworth's resolve to make good on his threat and place Joanna in a heartrending situation. Luke couldn't be the means of her suffering or see the glow which had surrounded her at Vauxhall Gardens extinguished because of him. With Lord Helmsworth, she would have a comfortable life, all worries of money and a home vanquished. As a second son, Luke could offer her little except debts, or the hard life of an officer's wife. Instead of managing a grand estate, she'd be trudging through the mud behind troops, exposed to disease or advancing armies, always worried he might not come back from the front and then she'd be left destitute, or reliant on the charity of his family who could barely afford to keep Pensum Manor. He couldn't see Joanna in peril because of his own selfish wants. He'd regret what he was about to do, but he had no choice. He'd sworn to not make Joanna choose between him and her grandfather. He must keep his promise.

'I will end our relationship, but not for the deed or

for you, but for her. I love her enough to give her up to ensure that she has a better life than I can give her. The kind of life she deserves.'

To his credit, Lord Helmsworth appeared more surprised than gloating at Luke's announcement, as if at a loss for what to do because he hadn't expected his plan to work. Then he tugged at his waistcoat and recovered his usual crotchety stance. 'Good. You'll come to the ball and tell her yourself that there can be nothing further between the two of you.'

Luke nodded, his own heart clenching at the thought of having to break hers.

'And, since you've proved yourself a man of honour, you may have the land.'

'I don't want it.'

'Take it anyway. After today I want nothing more to do with you or your family.' Lord Helmsworth flung down the deed on the table beside him, then turned and strode out of the room, head held high in triumph.

Luke watched him go and for the second time since coming home cursed his honour. It had cost him his heart.

Joanna stood in the receiving line in the ballroom of her grandfather's London house, trying not to shift and fuss like the little girls at school used to do before they became accustomed to Madame Dubois's discipline. The last two hours had been an endless round of people, titles and introductions. Everyone had been too eager to openly scrutinise the new granddaughter of the Marquis of Helmsworth to avoid the receiving line, except for Luke. He had yet to arrive.

She'd nearly skipped with delight when, during a walk in Rotten Row a few days ago, her grandfather had told her he'd sent the invitation to the Inghams and they'd accepted. He said he'd paid them a visit, too, and settled the dispute between the two families, although he hadn't told her how. It didn't seem possible and it had made all her preparations for tonight more thrilling.

'I think we've had enough standing about. Anyone else who wants to greet us can find us in the crush,' her grandfather announced to the hoarse butler.

He escorted Joanna to the dance floor. Mrs Petit, Joanna's chaperon, followed close behind, less awed by their surroundings than Joanna had been at the Pensum Manor ball. Luke had been the brightest point of that night as he would be again tonight.

If he arrived. *No, he'll come, he must.*

They passed beneath the evergreen garlands hanging between the pillars of the room. The finest musicians played on a raised platform at the far end while disciplined and liveried footmen offered the best wine to an overflowing room of guests. Joanna searched the crowd for Luke, at last understanding Frances's obsession with finding her lieutenant. Nothing else mattered except seeing him, not her new dress, the dancers, the guests, or even the strange looks she received from more than one matron. Luke's acceptance of the invitation, the fact her grandfather had sent it at all, created possibilities she hadn't allowed herself to imagine a few days ago. It made his having not arrived yet even more troubling.

They reached the edge of the dance floor and worry continued to undermine her excitement. Luke wasn't among the many gentlemen who came forward to claim a dance. She had no choice but to accept one short young man's hand, the son of a peer whose name she couldn't recall. A month ago, men like him wouldn't have acknowledged her, tonight they clamoured to dance with her, a possible connection to a marquis and a fine dowry enough to make them overlook her less-than-sterling past. It amused her to turn their heads, but not enough to make her forget Luke, or to stop fretting about why he wasn't here.

Then the dance began and she was forced to concentrate on the steps the dancing master had taught her over the last few days. The other young ladies surrounding her moved with effortless elegance while she focused on not stumbling. Her partner was patient when she missed more than one turn, but it was clear a few women lined up along the side of the floor weren't so charitable. Her inability to dance properly reinforced their view of her unsuitability to be in society. She wasn't sure she disagreed with them, but accepting her grandfather meant accepting her place with him. She must learn to adjust to this as she had to being at the Huntfords'.

She held her head high and moved with her partner through the promenade. That cold lonely life seemed like so long ago, never to return again. There were people here hoping she'd fail and she wouldn't allow them to lower her as Lady Huntford and Frances had tried to do at Vauxhall Gardens. This was who she was and she would at last embrace it instead of shying away. It would be a greater triumph if Luke were at her side.

Her partner stopped and raised her hand as she circled him. Awareness rippled across her bare shoulders and slid beneath the gold chain holding her mother's locket encircling her neck. She glanced at the crowd. Luke stood at the edge of the dance floor, ignoring the ladies on either side of him turning to and fro in an effort to catch his eye and secure a partner. His black coat increased the sharpness of his chin and the dark brown of his hair. She opened her fingers, ready to rush to him before she remembered herself. Instead, she rewarded his arrival with a coy smile.

His only response was a slight twitch in a muscle along his hard jaw. Her joy dropped to the floor to be trod on by the other dancers. Something was wrong, terribly so. She made a turn, getting another look at him. He appeared as he had the night he'd told her of his men's disappearance, his expression dark with trouble. She trussed up her resolve, refusing to allow his stern appearance to drag her down. He was here, and whatever was bothering him, they would make it right together as they had every other challenge they'd endured since the night they'd first met.

At last the dance ended, and Joanna forced herself to walk slowly next to her companion as he escorted her back to her grandfather. Tonight, Lord Helmsworth played the role of chaperon more than Mrs Petit. He was about to offer her to another partner when Luke shifted forward, blocking the man.

'May I?'

She glanced at her grandfather, expecting him to object since the next dance was a waltz, but he waved Luke forward to Joanna. A strange smile split her grandfather's pale lips, not of irritation or amusement, but something more unnerving. Whatever it was, her concern vanished the moment Luke's fingers curled over hers.

While they walked side by side to the dance floor, the memory of him covering her in the vicarage and the sense of peace she'd experienced in his arms teased her. The peace wasn't here. There was no amusement in his stride, no interest when he rested his hand on the small of her back, then took her other one to bring her into the circles of his arms and prepare for the dance. All around them people whispered and practically pointed, their presence together reinforcing all the rumours they must have heard. Joanna ignored them, too concerned with Luke and what was wrong to worry about what others said or thought.

'You're so late I thought maybe you'd changed your mind.' Joanna eyed him from beneath her lashes, prodding as much as tempting him. She'd dared to doubt him before Vauxhall Gardens and been proven wrong. She wanted him to counter her qualms again.

'How could I stay away?' It might as well have been Mr Selton saying it for all the feeling in his words.

Her stomach rolled as the music began and it grew tighter with each turn as her feet moved in rote steps to match of his. They danced with as much passion as the wooden figures on her grandfather's German cuckoo clock.

'What's wrong?' Joanna demanded, unable to keep the note of panic out of her voice.

Luke stared over her head as if it hurt him to acknowledge her. 'I must speak with you alone at some point this evening.'

'Tell me what you need to now, I don't want to wait.'

'Not here in front of your guests.'

Her hand stiffened in his, his need for secrecy as potent as Grace's when she'd first told Joanna she was expecting a baby. 'Then escort me off the dance floor.'

'People will talk.'

'Then tell them I'm ill.' She was sick with worry.

He stopped them in their whirling, making more than one couple break stride to stare before better sense swept them back into the dance. Luke escorted her away from her grandfather who was too deep in conversation with Lord Jarsdel to notice. The watching crowd parted to let them through, casting a parcel of whispers at them as they left the dance floor. What should have been the dance of the evening, the one she'd looked forward to for days, became a long, painful march.

In a moment, Mrs Petit was behind them, giving their spectacle a modicum of respect.

They passed through a door at the far end and cut through the empty and silent music room separating the ballroom from the rest of the house.

'Miss Radcliff, where are we going?' Mrs Petit asked, her slippers fluttering over the wood floor in time to Joanna and Luke's decided stride.

'Major Preston and I have something to discuss.'

'Alone? You can't.' She rushed to place herself between Joanna and the door to the sitting room on the far side of the music room. There was no one in this part of the house, the ball having been relegated to the more spacious rooms at the front.

'I must, now stay out here,' she snapped, as irritable as Frances had been. Shame engulfed her and she reached out to rest one hand on the thin woman's arm. 'I'm sorry, I don't mean to be cross, but I must be alone with Major Preston for a few short minutes.'

'But, Miss Radcliff…' she began to protest.

'Please,' Joanna begged. 'It's important.'

Mrs Petit glanced between her and Luke. He stood with arms stiff at his side and back straight. It was clear whatever she and Luke were about to discuss didn't involve lovemaking.

At last Mrs Petit relented. 'All right, you may be alone, but only for a bit and I'll be right here outside this door.'

'I wouldn't expect you to be anywhere else.' She gave Mrs Petit's arm an appreciative squeeze, then pushed open the sitting room door and led Luke inside.

'You haven't come to propose, have you?' she demanded before the door was even closed. The silent portraits of her mother and grandmother watched them as they faced one another.

'No, I've come to end things.'

Joanna grasped the back of a chair as the entire house shifted around her. She stared at him, trying to convince herself she'd heard him wrong, but it was clear in the set of his jaw she hadn't. All the eagerness to see him, the expectation they might be free to be with each other shattered, leaving nothing but a hollow sensation in the centre of her chest. He'd chased her through Hertfordshire and then London, slowly undermining her refusals and protestations while capturing her heart. After all his effort, his words, the risks they'd taken, her grandfather had been right. He didn't love her. No, it wasn't possible. This wasn't the

Luke she'd come to know, the one who struggled and fought against any difficulty in his determination to succeed. 'Why?'

'In the last week, I've realised the obstacles between us are too great to overcome.'

'You're giving up? I don't believe it.' There must be some reason why he'd suddenly changed his mind. Over his shoulder, the portrait of her mother stood out against the green-papered wall. At once, she knew what had happened. 'My grandfather made you break with me in return for the land, didn't he?'

Luke silently cursed Lord Helmsworth and his wicked demand. He couldn't tell her the truth. It would make her hate her grandfather and he'd vowed not to come between the two of them, no matter how much it pained both him and Joanna. She wanted a family and she would have one, but not with him. 'No.'

'Then what's going on? Please, tell me the truth.' Her sweet fragrance embraced him as she came forward. He wanted to kiss away the pain clipping her words, but he couldn't. He could only stand and retain a measure of dignity while he tore himself down in her eyes. 'You said you loved me.'

She might as well have shot him for the hole it left in his gut.

'I do and I always will, but it was wrong of me to court you, especially since it was always my plan to return to Spain. I can now since my brother's wife is with child.'

'You mean it was wrong of you to finally admit in front of everyone there was a connection between an earl's son and an illegitimate governess whose reputation you ruined.' Hate turned her sapphire eyes stormy and she balled her hands at her sides. He braced himself, ready to feel her blows on his chest but she stood still. 'Grandfather was right. You got what you wanted from me in the country, in secret, but when it came time to make it known you were too ashamed to be seen with me. No wonder you arrived late. I'm surprised you came at all or had the courage to dance with me since it might compromise your ability to find a woman with a purer past and lineage than me.'

He ground his teeth at the insult, but he let it stand. If hate eased her pain she could hate him for ever. 'You're wrong about yourself. You're worth more than any other woman in the ballroom and you deserve a man who can give you everything you've ever dreamed of. I'm not him. It was never possible for me to be him and I'm sorry.'

'You're only sorry your lies have at last been exposed. Get out.' She jabbed one slender finger towards the door, her stiff arm shaking with rage. 'I'm through with you.'

He nodded, and placing one foot behind him, turned as if taking leave of an officer. Outside in the music room, the chaperon grasped her fan in worry as Luke passed. He said nothing as he forced himself across the marble floor, away from Joanna and everything he'd fought in his attempt to win her.

The doors to the ballroom opened and the music washed over him along with a hundred curious stares. He only saw Lord Helmsworth observing him from his place beside Lord Jarsdel. Luke stopped and, from across the room, bowed to the Marquis in surrender. If he'd had his sword he would have broken it across his knee and chucked it at the man's feet. He straightened and strode out of the entrance, leaving the candlelit room. Each step hurt as much as if he'd marched a hundred miles barefoot, but he kept going. His reputation and honour were all he'd possessed when he'd returned to England. It was all he had now. He'd left his heart behind with Joanna.

Joanna paced until the muscles of her legs protested and still she continued on, eyes dry, too furious to cry. The grating of metal against metal met the fall of each of her feet as she tugged the locket back and forth on its chain. It wasn't Luke's rejection feeding her fury, but her gullible stupidity. She'd been so desperate to be loved, she'd believed in his lies and continued to entertain his secret advances even in the face of her grandfather's evidence.

'How could I have been such a fool?' If she'd kept away from Luke as her grandfather had warned her to, guarded her heart instead of throwing it at him, she'd be dancing and having a wonderful time in the ballroom, not hiding here in humiliation.

She stopped and stared out the window at the carriages filling the street outside. The drivers stood together laughing at jokes Joanna couldn't hear. She envied their good humour, hers was at an end.

The door squeaked open behind her, but Joanna didn't turn to see who it was.

'Miss Radcliff, are you all right?' Mrs Petit asked.

'Yes, I need some time alone. I'll be out soon.'

The door clicked shut and Joanna sighed. She

couldn't stay in here all night. She'd have to return to the ball soon and smile and pretend everything was all right. She wasn't sure she could. Raising her hand, she touched the cold window, tempted to throw the sash up, slip outside and command one of the drivers to carry her away. Except there was nowhere for her to go. The school was no longer her home, this was. Even if she could go back to Salisbury and Madame, it would mean running from her troubles instead of facing them with the comportment and dignity Madame had instilled in her. She wanted to prove to her headmistress she was the strong, capable woman she'd raised her to be, not a senseless goose, despite having acted like one with Luke.

Joanna turned and caught the silent eyes of her mother watching her from the portrait. Regret as powerful as that over never having met her mother smothered her. She let go of the locket, wondering if she'd avoided sharing a similar fate with her. If she'd continued with Luke, they might have met again in a dark room in defiance of everyone and she could have found herself with child. She'd wanted to make a decision about her life, but Luke had proven she wasn't capable of doing so, or trusting her own heart. When he'd held her in Vauxhall Gardens, she'd been as convinced of his love as of Grace's, Rachel's and Isabel's friendships. When he'd told her he still loved her tonight, she'd wanted to believe him, despite the anger driving her to deny it. It was difficult, even now, to accept she'd been so misled, but she had been. She'd craved him and had imagined their future. In the end, he'd disappointed her and her expectations as much as the position with the Huntfords' had.

'I wish you were here,' she said to her mother, craving another letter, and more words to help her deal with the pain crushing her heart. She would have understood Joanna's torment and wouldn't have judged her for her mistakes, but she wasn't here. No one was. There was nothing except silence. Once again Joanna was left to forge ahead alone.

The door opened. This time it wasn't Mrs Petit, but Lord Jarsdel who entered.

'Is everything all right, Miss Radcliff? You've been gone from the ballroom for a long time.'

'Yes, only I haven't had a moment to myself all night.' Despite his kindness, she couldn't admit her mistake with Luke and have him think less of her than she already thought of herself.

'I saw Major Preston leave. Is everything all right between the two of you?'

'There's nothing between us any more.' Her voice cracked and she closed her mouth, afraid to say too much for fear the dam inside her would break. Once she began to cry, for herself, her mother and everything she'd lost and would never have, she feared it wouldn't stop.

Lord Jarsdel nodded sagely, not gloating over his rival's departure. Her anger lost some of its edge under his calming presence. He didn't press her to speak, or ask her awkward questions, but remained with her so she wasn't alone. She appreciated the gesture. She needed friends now. Grace, Rachel and Isabel were too far away.

The clock on the mantel chimed eleven times.

'We should be getting back.' She wasn't sure how she would maintain her composure in a room full of strangers determined to stare at her. In the past they'd ignored her, she wished they would again, but they wouldn't. It would be like facing down Lady Huntford the day after she and Luke had made love. She must endure it, like everything else in her life, and not speak out or complain. Frustration chipped at her as hard as disappointment. She'd spoken up about Luke and it had won her nothing except a broken heart.

'Before we go, I'd like to ask you something,' Lord Jarsdel began, his usual steadfastness ruffling around the edges.

Joanna clasped her hands in front of her, having an inkling of what he might say. She would have stopped him a few hours ago but so much had changed since then. 'Yes?'

'I'm sure you're aware, your grandfather is very interested in us marrying.'

She remained silent and the part of her which had come alive under Luke's touch settled back to sleep. She let it. It was no longer of any use to her.

Lord Jarsdel approached, his confidence tempered by humility. 'I may not be as dashing or young as Major Preston, but I'll be a kind and respectful husband. With me you'll have a home of your own and children. We can be happy together. Miss Radcliff, will you marry me?'

He held out his hand, silently urging her to take it.

She studied the lines of his white glove crossing his palm. Here was an earl willing to raise a former governess to a countess, to openly share his life and wealth with her despite the rumours. It spoke to his good character, yet all she could think was, *he's not Luke*. In the end, Luke had abandoned her, too

ashamed of her to resist whatever influence her grandfather had exercised over him. Lord Jarsdel wanted
her for better or worse. She didn't have to accept him.
She could take her grandfather's money and remain
single, but it seemed a very lonely life.

She glanced past him to the silent portrait of her
mother. Her mother hadn't found lasting contentment
with the man she'd loved and neither had Joanna, but
it didn't mean Joanna must remain alone. In Lord
Jarsdel's offer was the chance to be a wife and to
give future children security and a place in society.
It wasn't a grand passion, but the safe and sensible
arrangement her grandfather wanted for her. Joanna
had followed her mother's advice, and her heart, and
it had resulted in rejection and sorrow. It was time to
follow her head and sensible guidance.

She laid her hand in his, unable to meet his eyes
as she answered, 'Yes. I will marry you.'

Chapter Fifteen

'Let's raise another glass to Major Preston. In two weeks he'll be back kicking Napoleon across Spain.' Captain Arnold toasted and the gathered officers lifted their tankards and shouted.

'Huzzah!'

Their cheers echoed through the walls of the Army Service Club in St James's Street, a rollicking London refuge for officers on leave between campaigns or on half-pay. The white-plastered walls were lined with portraits of battles, rearing horses and solemn officers in full dress.

Luke raised his tankard, too, but set it aside while his mates drained theirs. The red coat felt heavy on his shoulders and the tinkling of his medals as he moved irritated him today. He'd borrowed a tidy sum to buy back his major's epaulets, to get away from London and Joanna. Even with the money already spent, he wondered if he'd made a mistake.

Lord Beckwith, who stood out in the sea of red uniforms in his Horse Guard blues, slapped Luke on the back. 'Not having a change of heart, are you?'

'No.' Although he should.

His parents had tried to talk him out of re-enlisting, for the first time allowing their anguish over his safety to show. In it he'd seen that it wasn't the family line they feared dying, but their son. Luke had no intention of getting himself killed, even if, at the moment, a bullet through the chest seemed preferable to the ache lodged there since his last meeting with Joanna.

'Too bad. I still believe you'd better serve the military here than risking becoming cannon fodder in Spain.' Lord Beckwith took a sip of his port, preferring the genteel and more potent spirit to the common one being consumed *en masse* around them. 'I can still find you a place at Whitehall. It isn't too late.'

Yes, it is. He'd read the announcement in the papers about Joanna's engagement to Lord Jarsdel and their wedding date. Remaining in London where he would see the new Lady Jarsdel at every social event of the Season wasn't his idea of a good time. 'No, I'm going back to Spain.'

Another cheer went up from the gathered men, this one louder and more enthusiastic than before. Officers crowded around someone Luke couldn't see near the door. They'd already saluted Wellington's health, the ladies of Drury Lane and Luke. There wasn't much left to give them a reason to drink, although they hardly needed one. They'd toast any old sod for a sip.

'Captain Mercer must have smuggled in a few actresses again?' Lord Beckwith mumbled. Women without reputations were the only ones who could enter a club in St James's without being ruined and even they had a difficult go of it.

Luke tried to peer through the mass of drunk and celebrating men, but it was difficult to tell one red coat from another. 'I don't think they're cheering for a woman.'

Then the group parted and Luke almost dropped his tankard.

'Having a party without me, are you?' Reginald threw open his arms as he approached Luke. He was leaner, his hair longer and touching the dirty collar of his coat. The circles beneath his eyes were thicker, too, but his smile was as wide as ever.

'You're alive.' Luke shoved the tankard at Lord Beckwith and rushed to grab his friend in a hearty embrace.

'I've been gone for ages and you don't even offer me a drink.' Reginald laughed as Luke stepped back.

'I'll buy you a whole bottle.' The heavy mood which had crushed Luke for the last two weeks began to lift as he sat down with Reginald. A bottle was procured and with it cold meat and cheese. Reginald ate and drank while regaling everyone with the harrowing account of how he and the squad had barely escaped being caught in a narrow pass and had ended up trapped behind enemy lines. They'd avoided capture for weeks by dodging patrols, collecting intelligence and being sheltered by sympathetic Spaniards.

'One Spanish family hid us in their barn for a week. Seeing them made me realise I'd like one of my own and a more settled life.' Reginald threw his worn boots up on the table. After rounds and rounds of good cheer, the two of them had been left alone near the corner to speak. 'I'm grateful for the help you gave my sister. All the men were thankful to come home and find their families not starving.'

'It was the least I could do.'

'Now, let me help you. How come, at your hail and farewell, you look like a man about to be hanged? What's been going on since I left you at the Bull?' Reginald took an ivory toothpick out of his coat pocket and slipped it between his lips.

Luke rapped his knuckles against the top of the table. 'The woman I love is at the church today, about to marry another man.'

The bells rang, one after another, their deep toll reverberating through the old church. Joanna sat in the still of the vestry room, waiting for her grandfather to collect her for the service. The white-silk wedding dress covering her was soft against her skin and she worried a small section of lace on the cuff between her thumb and forefinger. The last two weeks had been a flurry of activity to prepare for today. The dress had been rushed to be sewn, the special licence secured, the wedding breakfast arranged and a bevy of invitations sorted and sent. She'd been thankful for the activity. During the day it had kept her distracted, but at night, when it was quiet, her conscience tortured her. It still did.

I shouldn't marry Lord Jarsdel, I don't love him. She rose and crossed the marble floor, her veil whispering against her dress with each step. He didn't love her, but his caring way was reminiscent of Miss Fanworth's. There were worse men she could wed, someone like Lieutenant Foreman who might abandon a lady when she needed him most, or someone like Luke who'd never cared at all.

I should have listened to Grandfather.

She made a turn, flipping the veil behind her so as not to step on it. Her grandfather had tried to guide her with Luke but she'd resisted. Yet she'd followed his counsel in this instance, and instead of being a radiant bride she was fretting.

She crossed the room again, her feet falling faster and faster on the stone. She wished Grace, Isabel and Rachel were here to make her see how marrying Lord Jarsdel, like Isabel marrying Mr Balfour, was the best decision she could make. Despite Joanna sending them invitations, none of them had been able to come for the hastily arranged affair, not even Madame Dubois. She and Miss Fanworth had pleaded the expense for sending their regrets. It meant all the guests in the pews were friends of her grandfather or her fiancé and there were few in the church for her. She was almost as alone as the day in Hertfordshire when she'd stumbled upon her grandfather in the graveyard. It made what was supposed to be a happy day even more dreary.

The church bells ceased their ringing and the deep tones of the organ began to fill the room. Joanna stopped in panic to listen. The time for the ceremony was quickly approaching.

'My dear, you look gorgeous.' Her grandfather entered, regal in his new dark green coat and gold waistcoat. He'd been near fluttering with elation for the last three days. 'I have a surprise for you.'

'What is it?' She tried to meet his announcement with the appropriate pleasure and gratitude. It was growing more difficult with each organ note to stand still, much less appear excited.

He pulled open the door and waved to someone outside. 'I couldn't let the day pass without doing this for you.'

Madame Dubois stepped into the room. She was in her Sunday best, a dark blue velvet dress with a high collar rimmed in white lace. Her hair was done up in her usual tight twist, but the smile gracing her lips and lighting her grey eyes softened the severity of her appearance. She appeared to Joanna as she imagined a mother would on the day of her daughter's wedding, proud, thrilled and with the mist of tears in her eyes.

Instead of squealing in delight at her arrival, Joanna burst into tears.

For the first time ever, Madame Dubois came to her and enveloped her in a tender hug. Joanna held her tight while sobs shook her entire body.

'Perhaps you should leave us alone for a while,' Madame suggested to her grandfather, who stared at them, stunned by Joanna's response.

'I think you're right.' He backed out of the room, drawing the door closed behind him.

Madame held Joanna tight until the sobs began to subside.

'What's wrong, Miss Radcliff?' Her pointed question, delivered with the same authority as when she used to speak at the school, snapped Joanna out of her crying.

Joanna rubbed her wet cheeks with the back of her hands. 'I don't want to marry Lord Jarsdel.'

'Sit down, we must talk.' She guided Joanna to the sofa beneath the window, then laced her hands together in front of her and raised one sharp eyebrow. 'Tell me why, despite standing in your wedding dress, you don't want to marry him.'

The words began to pour out of Joanna while they sat in the warm sunlight falling through the window. Joanna told Madame everything about her relationship with Luke, their meeting at the ball, in the woods, even their night at the vicarage and his saying he loved her. She described his having left her, and how it had led to her accepting Lord Jarsdel.

'You must think I'm foolish to not want to marry an earl.' Joanna sniffed, too wrung out to fear Madame's disappointment in her being so misguided about so many things. 'Or for being so weak with Major Preston.'

'You're not foolish for having followed your heart. I wish I had.'

'You?' This silenced Joanna's sniffles.

Madame rested her hands on her lap and a remorse Joanna had only seen the time she'd spied her in the garden with the letter came over her. 'When I was young, I fell in love with the oldest son of a titled man. It wasn't a girlish passion or a backstairs liaison, but real and true love. He wanted to marry me, but I was in no position to claim a place as his wife. Not wanting to stop him from fulfilling his role as the heir, I refused him. He married a woman he didn't love because of it and I lost him. I've regretted it every day of my life since.'

'Oh, Madame.' Joanna grasped her hands in sympathy. 'I didn't realise.'

'Because I never told you.' Madame covered Joanna's hand with her other one, clasping it in her tender grip. 'I haven't always been the most mothering of guardians to you, but I believed if I didn't coddle you, you'd grow up strong and prepared to face the difficulties and challenges of life. I was right. Already you've dealt with so much and so well. You've made me as proud as any mother can be of her daughter.'

Joanna's heart stilled and tears threatened to overcome her again. She'd been so wrong about Madame and everything. 'All my life I prayed for a real family, but I shouldn't have, not when I already had one in you and Miss Fanworth and my friends. Instead of appreciating them, I kept looking for something else. I shouldn't have.'

'We're all capable of not seeing what's in front of us while reaching for something else. It takes great courage to admit it and to reject other people's plans in favour of your own.' She settled back and looked down at Joanna just as she used to whenever she wished to impart something important to her. 'It is time for you to be courageous, Miss Radcliff, and to tell everyone exactly what you want.'

'Yes, you're right.'

A knock at the door interrupted them.

'Is everything well in there?' Her grandfather's anxious voice followed.

Madame Dubois rose with her usual elegance and crossed the room to open the door.

'Lord Helmsworth, Miss Radcliff has something she wishes to discuss with you.'

She didn't remain, but slipped outside, leaving Joanna and her grandfather alone. He rushed up to her, concern clouding his aged blue eyes.

'What's the matter?'

Joanna took a bracing breath. Once the words were out there'd be no taking them back, but she must be brave and trust in his love. 'I can't go through with the wedding.'

She explained to him everything she and Madame Dubois had discussed. Her grandfather stared at the floor beneath her feet while she spoke, rubbing his chin in contemplation. She wasn't sure what he thought, but she kept speaking, revealing everything in her heart, especially his place in it.

'I appreciate all you've done for me. It's the whole reason I agreed to this marriage.'

His hands stilled on his chin and at last he looked up at her, not angry or disappointed but accepting. 'I suspected as much. Many times over the last two weeks I have thought I was imagining your distress. I told myself that once you married Lord Jarsdel everything would be well. I was mistaken. You were suffering in an effort to make me happy. I was wrong to allow it to continue and to do what I did with Major Preston.'

Shock rippled through Joanna. 'What do you mean?'

Her grandfather took in a deep breath before he continued. 'I offered him the river land in exchange for his promise to end things with you.'

'And he accepted it?'

'No.' He took her hands, more serious than he had been when he'd warned her not to speak with Luke. 'But I deeded it to him anyway, because when I asked him not to take you away from me he behaved more honourably than I did.'

She stared at her grandfather, an elation she hadn't experienced since Vauxhall rising inside her. 'Then he wasn't lying or ashamed of me. He really did love me.'

'Enough to leave you because he thought you would have a better life without him rather than with him.'

'Not at all.'

'I see that now.' Tears filled his eyes and his hands trembled in hers. 'Please don't hate me for what I did. I'm not cruel. I simply wanted to protect you.'

'I know.' She threw her arms around him, unable to withhold her forgiveness. His confession had raised her hopes. It was more than she'd allowed herself to believe in the country, or during these last two weeks. Luke loved her and she loved him, and there was still a chance that they could at last be together.

He hugged her tight with relief and then held her at arm's length. 'All these years I've been bitter and angry over what I had lost. Then, when I gained you, instead of letting it go, I allowed it to guide me. You aren't Jane and Major Preston isn't Captain Handler, I see that now, and I want grandchildren, little ones to liven up Helmsworth Manor and that draughty London house.' He winked at her, the caring humorous man with her once more.

Joanna smiled sheepishly at him. 'I'm sorry I didn't say something sooner, before all this expense and effort. I should have told you how much Luke meant to me instead of allowing things to go on for so long.'

'And I should have listened instead of trying to make you do things my way. Don't worry about the expense, I can afford it.' He chuckled before turning serious. 'But you have no time to waste if you want to claim your young man.'

'What do you mean?'

'Lord Jarsdel told me Major Preston purchased a commission and is leaving to rejoin his regiment tomorrow.'

'Then I must see him, at once.' She didn't know if she could win him back, or if he still wanted her. With her grandfather's blessing secured, she had to try before he was beyond her reach.

'Take the carriage and go to his parents' house in Kensington. They can summon him from the Army Service Club to speak with you.'

Assuming he would. No, she had to believe she'd succeed. She gathered up the veil, about to rush to the door, then stopped. 'What about Lord Jarsdel, shouldn't I tell him?'

'I'll talk to him and don't worry too much about it. He's a man with a great deal of experience who can deal with a little disappointment. If nothing else, his sons will be relieved to not have to share their inheritance with any new half siblings.' He laid a tender kiss on her forehead, then examined her with the same pride Madame Dubois had shown. 'For all my pig-headedness in regards to Major Preston, I do believe he will make you happy. You haven't glowed this much in all the time you've been with me.'

'Thank you, Grandfather.' Joanna grabbed the hem of her dress and rushed out of the church. She hurried down the steps and into her grandfather's open-topped landau. The driver turned around, stunned.

'Shouldn't you be inside, Miss Radcliff?'

'No, drive on at once.'

'Where to?'

Joanna considered his question. If they went to Kensington it would waste valuable time. Luke might leave for Greenwich or Portsmouth and she would miss him. There was only one place she could go. 'The Army Service Club on St James's Street.'

The driver shook his head. 'No respectable woman can be seen riding alone there, much less going into a gentlemen's club. What would Lord Helmsworth say?'

'He's the one sending me there.' It was a white lie, but a necessary one. She wouldn't be stopped by a coachman. 'Now hurry, we must reach Major Preston before he leaves. It's urgent.'

'If Lord Helmsworth wants it.' The driver shrugged, then took up the reins and flicked them over the backs of the horses, setting them off in the direction of St James's.

Joanna unpinned the long veil from her hair and laid it on the seat beside her. She'd walked away from one suitor and was about to toss aside her already questionable reputation for another. If Luke refused to see her, she'd never recover from the scandal. It didn't matter, she had to try. She loved him and it was time to fight for his heart.

* * *

'Sir, there's a young lady here insisting to see you.' Tibbs, the club butler, announced to Luke. 'She's in her wedding dress.'

Silence settled over the party which seconds before had been quite rowdy.

'A lady in her wedding dress?' Luke questioned. He hadn't drunk enough to have his brain so fuddled he couldn't understand the butler. 'What's her name?'

'Miss Radcliff. I tried to tell her women aren't allowed in here, but she won't listen.'

'It seems your lady has had a change of heart and at the altar of all places.' Reginald threw back his head and laughed.

Luke could only stare at his friend, stunned. Joanna hadn't married Lord Jarsdel. She'd walked away from him and come here of all places. Excitement as much as curiosity pulled Luke out of his chair. He should stay where he was and not debase himself any further with her, but he couldn't.

'Show her in, Tibbs, I'm dying to meet the woman who's captured Luke's heart,' Reginald ordered before Luke could answer.

'No, I'll go to her.' Luke pushed past the butler and into the hallway.

He elbowed his way through the huddle of soldiers gawking at Joanna from along the balustrade at the top of the entrance-hall stairs. Luke jerked to a stop at the sight of her. She stood beneath the high ceiling of the columned room, a feminine contrast to the arms and weapons, men and battlefield paintings surrounding her. Her smooth skin was radiant against the white silk of her dress. Her light hair was done up in little ringlets woven with small, white flowers which shivered each time she took a breath. The sight of her was more glorious and beautiful than the first sunrise after the close cannonball blast had knocked him unconscious. He'd awakened that morning thankful to be alive, like he was at this moment in the presence of her beauty.

The confidence of her arrival was betrayed by the twisting of her gloved hands in front of her and the nervous dart of her eyes to the sniggering men staring at her. Luke couldn't leave her to suffer their curiosity and marched down the stairs towards her.

'Luke,' she exclaimed at the sight of him, her smile increasing her radiance. The intensity of it almost made him halt, but he continued on, taking her by the arm and drawing her into a small room off the entrance hall. There was no door here and nothing to stop the officers from shuffling by as they gathered outside, not too close, but close enough to hear, as curious as a bunch of cats.

'What are you doing here?' Luke demanded, aware of each subtle move of her lovely arm beneath his fingers. He let go, not wanting to be so affected by her presence, or her cherry blossom-scented skin. He'd left her to protect her relationship with her grandfather. He didn't want his weakness or hers to make him renege on his promise. 'You're supposed to be at the church getting married.'

'I'm not going to marry Lord Jarsdel. I love you too much to pledge myself to him.'

It was as if Luke had been concussed by the cannonball all over again. For two weeks he'd thought her lost to him, now she was proclaiming her love to him and everyone listening outside the door.

'Please, don't tell me it's too late.' Her eyes shone like the ocean at sunset as she studied him. 'Grandfather isn't against us any more. He told me about the promise he extracted from you and he won't hold you to it.'

Luke didn't believe what he was hearing and he forced himself not to march back to the sitting room and drain his tankard. Luke had been relieved from his obligation to his family. Now he'd been released from his promise to Lord Helmsworth and Joanna was here before him, as free to be with him as he'd dreamed of in the country. It was everything he'd wanted since the ball at Pensum Manor and yet he still couldn't have her. 'I leave for Spain tomorrow to rejoin the regiment.'

'Then take me with you.'

'I can't.' He traced her cheek with the back of his fingers, her smooth skin increasing the ache of desire building inside him. He couldn't place her in danger, no matter how much he wanted her by his side. 'There are very real threats to the wives of Army officers— the enemy, hunger, disease. If you were to die, think of what it would do to your grandfather, how he would blame me for your loss. I'd blame myself if anything happened to you.'

She laid her gloved hand over his and pressed her cheek into his palm. 'Then don't go. Stay here with me.'

'I can't turn my back on my commission now I've pledged myself to it.' His honour wouldn't allow it.

'Then it's over, isn't it, us and our future?' Her hope dimmed, as did his.

He glanced past her and out the arched doorway to where Lord Beckwith and Reginald leaned against a high table, trying to pretend they weren't watching, and it came to him. He didn't have to leave and he didn't have to surrender his commission. 'No, it isn't over.'

He took her by the hand and pulled her with him out of the room.

'Lord Beckwith,' Luke called out to the Lieutenant Colonel.

'Yes, Major Preston.' He and Reginald jerked up, looking at everything but Joanna and Luke in an effort to pretend they hadn't been listening. Let them eavesdrop, it made no difference now.

'You said if I wanted it, there was a position for me at Whitehall, a way to work here in England towards Army reform.'

Lord Beckwith's mouth dropped open before he pulled it shut. 'Yes, of course. You have only to ask for it.'

'Then I want it. You're right, I can make a difference to the soldiers in Europe.'

Lord Beckwith extended his hand to Luke. 'I'm glad to hear it. I'll tell Whitehall at once.'

'And Captain Crowther, he must have a place, too,' Luke insisted before facing his friend. 'What do you say? Do you want to fight a different battle with me here?'

'If it means seeing you accompany this beautiful woman down the aisle, then I do.'

Luke turned to Joanna. 'We'll visit the vicar at once and prepare the banns.'

'Banns nothing, you'll have a special licence,' Reginald proposed. 'What do you say, Lord Beckwith, do you think it can be arranged?'

'Him being the son of an earl, and with my connections to the Archbishop's office, I'm sure it can be done.'

'I can't pay for it,' Luke protested. He was in debt enough for his commission and refused to become a husband on the verge of penury.

'You won't have to.' Reginald snatched a shako from the line of them on the bench beside the front door. He turned it over and hustled to the gathered officers snorting and chortling at the spectacle. 'Pass the hat, men, Major Preston is getting married and needs a licence.'

While they dug in their pockets for coins, Luke turned to Joanna. 'What do you say? Are you ready to be my wife?'

With a bright laugh, she waved her hand over her dress. 'Were I any more prepared we'd already be in a church.'

'We soon will be and together for good.'

He took her by the waist and pulled her to him, the silk and her curves soft beneath his grip. He ignored the whistles and hoots from the men in the hall as he lost himself in her cobalt eyes.

'Imagine what society will say when they hear about this?' A grin drew up one side of her mouth, her question more amused speculation than worry.

'They'll say I caught the most beautiful woman in London.'

He pressed his lips to hers, the taste of her the sweetest victory he'd ever known.

* * * * *